MISSING AT CHRISTMAS

K.D. RICHARDS

COLTON 911: TEMPTATION UNDERCOVER

JENNIFER MOREY

MILLS & BOON

www.harpercollins.co.uk

HarperCollins*Publishers*
1st Floor, Watermarque Building,
Ringsend Road, Dublin 4, Ireland

Special thanks and acknowledgement are given to Jennifer Morey for her contribution to the *Colton 911: Chicago* series.

ISBN: 978-0-263-28350-1

0821

MIX
Paper from responsible sources
FSC™ C007454
FSC www.fsc.org

This book is produced from independently certified FSC™ paper to ensure responsible forest management.

For more information visit: www.harpercollins.co.uk/green

Printed and bound in Spain
by CPI, Barcelona

MISSING AT CHRISTMAS

K.D. RICHARDS

To Bryson and Miles.

Chapter One

Adelaide "Addy" Williams's feet ached, and a headache throbbed behind her temples as she pulled the restaurant door open. The bells above the door jangled, drawing the attention of the middle-aged man behind the host podium. The smell of fried onions and beef slapped her in the face as she stepped toward the man.

He gave a tight smile, probably annoyed to have a customer come in less than an hour from closing time. "Dining in or taking out?"

"Neither." Addy pulled the photograph of her sister from the oversize purse she carried. The bottom edges were creased from having been taken in and out of the purse all day, but Cassie's effervescent smile remained unblemished. "I'm looking for my sister." Addy thrust the photo at the man. "Have you seen her?"

The man flicked a glance at the photo then back to Addy. "No."

Addy fought back the annoyance swelling in her chest. She'd gotten the same reaction from at least half the people she'd shown Cassie's picture to over the last two days. Indifference or outright irritation was the most common reaction from people when she explained her nineteen-year-old sister was missing. She couldn't help but wonder if she'd have gotten the same reaction if Cassie had blue eyes and blond hair instead of caramel skin and coarse coils.

"Please, look again," she said, thrusting Cassie's photo closer to the man.

He sighed, but pulled a pair of glasses from the pocket of his suit jacket and slipped them on before taking the photo from Addy. A lock of dark brown hair fell over his forehead as his studied the picture. After a moment he said, "I'm sorry. I've never seen her."

"Are you sure?" Addy pressed, taking the photo back. She'd been in the restaurant earlier that day and had gotten the same response from the young woman behind the podium at the time, but she'd hoped she might have better luck with the evening staff.

The man sighed. "Yes, I'm sure. Now, I'm sorry about your sister, but if you aren't going to order something, I have to ask you to leave."

As if on cue, Addy's stomach rumbled.

The man's dark eyebrows rose, making it clear he'd heard her body's protestations. She'd forgotten to stop for lunch, propelled by the ticking clock metaphorically hanging over her head. Addy knew the statistics. The longer a young woman was missing, the less likely it was that she'd be found alive.

"Kitchen is closing in five minutes, but the dining area is open until nine."

Addy glanced at her watch—8:25 p.m. Living in Manhattan, it was nearly impossible to imagine a restaurant closing up shop so early. But Bentham, New York, was no Manhattan.

"Miss?" the man said.

"I want to order. I'll take it to go."

The man grabbed a plastic-clad menu from the top of the stack on the podium and thrust it into her hands. It listed traditional Mexican fare. She ordered a chicken burrito.

"Have a seat." The man waved vaguely toward the nearest cluster of tables. "Your order will be out momentarily." He dropped the menu back on top of the stack and turned.

"Do you mind showing this photo to the kitchen staff? Please?" Addy added at his frown. "She's my sister." She fought to get the last words out around the sob lodged in her throat. Showing vulnerability in front of a complete stranger was not something a tough-as-nails corporate attorney from Manhattan did. But if she had to beg this man to help her, she would. She couldn't leave any stone unturned.

The man's eyes finally softened. He took the photo from her hand. "I'll see what I can do."

Addy watched him disappear through swinging doors she assumed led to the kitchen, then fell into one of the chairs at the nearest table to wait for her dinner.

Cassie taking a day or two to return a call hadn't alarmed Addy at first. Cassie was nineteen, adventurous and far more impulsive than Addy had ever been. After the first few missed calls and texts, Addy had expected a call from Cassie recounting a fun-filled last-minute trip to the mountains or someone's vacation house in the Hamptons.

But that call had never come, and Cassie hadn't answered any of Addy's subsequent calls or texts. By the fourth day of silence, Addy had become concerned enough to reach out to Cassie's roommate, Suri. Worry transformed to fear when Suri said Cassie had packed her things and moved out. Addy had resisted the impulse to call Cassie's boss, not wanting to embarrass her sister at her first real job, but at that point, there was no other choice. Over the phone, Ms. Webb, the head of human resources and Cassie's boss, informed Addy that Cassie had resigned from her internship with the company almost a week earlier with no notice.

Cassie had been over the moon to land the internship with Spectrum Industries, a leading computer chip manufacturer in the area. For Cassie, who was headed to MIT to study computer science after finishing this gap year between graduating high school and college, the internship was a dream come true. There was no way Cassie would have quit.

Something was very wrong, yet Addy felt in her bones that Cassie was out there somewhere. Alive.

She'd hoped to be heading back to New York, having found some clue to where Cassie was or at least having convinced the sheriff of the urgency of the situation, but she'd accomplished neither. Which meant she'd have to do the one thing she was hoping to avoid.

Addy pulled out her phone and scrolled through her contacts. She tapped Jarod Cunningham's name and hoped he wouldn't answer.

Her boss picked up on the third ring.

"Addy? Didn't expect to hear from you this evening. Is everything okay with the merger?"

That was Jarod. All business. She had no idea where Jarod currently was, since she'd called him on his cell phone, but it wasn't hard to imagine him in his twenty-second-floor corner office even after eight on a Sunday night.

"Everything is fine with the merger, Jarod. It's Cassie,

my sister. You know she's gone missing and I spent the weekend in Bentham looking for her. I'm still here, actually, and I'm going to need to stay a few more days."

She'd avoided requesting time off initially by driving up on Friday after work. Asking the head of the corporate law practice at Covington and Baker for time off was always a fraught endeavor. Despite the firm marketing itself as a place where work-life balance was valued, when it came down to it Covington and Baker, just like every other big New York law firm, expected the balance to come down on the side of work, not life. She had just been assigned to one of the biggest mergers the firm had ever landed, a deal that would make her upcoming partnership vote a given as long as everything went perfectly.

And asking for time off just days before they were scheduled to meet the client wasn't the way she'd envisioned starting things off.

It wasn't what Jarod had envisioned, either.

"You can't be serious," Jarod bellowed. "Now is really not a good time to take a vacation. We need you here."

"It's not a vacation, Jarod. My sister is missing." Addy let out an angry breath. She'd worked hard to prove her value to Jarod, and she resented the insinuation that she was blowing off a major deal to sip mai tais on the beach.

Although Jarod brought in a lot of the merger business, as his right-hand woman, Addy did most of the work. It was a position she was content, if not happy, to be in. It wasn't easy to be a Black woman in a large law firm. She was the only Black associate in the corporate practice, one of three Black female senior associates or partners in the whole of the two-hundred-person New York office.

"Of course, of course, and we all feel for you," Jarod

said, his voice lower now but still lacking all hint of sympathy. “But really, isn’t this a job for the police?”

She didn’t disagree, but the authorities didn’t seem to be taking the situation seriously. “The sheriff thinks Cassie will turn up on her own in a few days.” He hadn’t even wanted to take a missing person report. Luckily, seven years as a corporate attorney had given her a lot of experience convincing obstinate men to listen to her.

“If you can just wait two, maybe three weeks,” Jarod continued. “The Browning–Tuffs merger will be done by then. I bet your sister will have turned up by that point as well, and the two of you can take a nice long vacation.”

“My sister is the only family I have. I’m not just going to sit around doing nothing while she’s missing.” She didn’t try to hide the iciness in her tone.

“You wouldn’t be doing nothing, Addy. You’d be doing your job.”

She bit back her reflexive response. He was a talented attorney, but like a lot of powerful men, he was also a major jerk. For maybe the millionth time in the seven years since she’d started working at Covington and Baker, she considered quitting. And like each time before, she pushed the thought away, reminding herself how close she was to finally making partner and getting out from under Jarod’s thumb and how many medical bills were still left to pay from her father’s illness.

She took a deep breath and let it out slowly. “We don’t meet with the client until Thursday. I’m ready for the meeting, and I have my laptop with me, so I can do any last-minute changes from here.”

“I don’t like it,” Jarod said, but his hesitation gave her hope.

"Jarod, you know me. You know I can handle it. And I'll be back no later than Thursday."

Several silent seconds passed.

"Fine." Jarod sighed loudly on the other end of the line. "But nothing can go wrong with this meeting, Addy. This deal is just as important for you as it is for me." He disconnected from the call.

Jarod was not known for his subtlety, but he also wasn't wrong. She knew the stakes.

She had three days to find Cassie.

The doors to the kitchen swung outward, and the man reappeared, a white plastic bag in one hand and Cassie's picture in the other.

Addy slid her phone back into her purse and rose. The pity she saw in the man's face as he drew nearer dashed the hope that had swelled in her chest.

"I showed your sister's picture to everyone who's still here, and no one recognized her. I'm sorry."

Two solid days of showing Cassie's picture everywhere she could think of in Bentham and nothing. No one remembered seeing her.

"Thanks, anyway." She didn't bother trying to muster a smile of thanks. She reached in her purse for her wallet.

"No charge," he said, thrusting her food and Cassie's picture at her. "You take care of yourself."

Addy looked up into the man's now compassion-filled eyes and wiped away the single tear she couldn't stop from falling. "Thank you," she croaked out before turning and fleeing the restaurant before the dam of tears broke.

Silver garlands hung from the streetlamps along with fluttering signs ordering the denizens of Bentham to have a happy holiday. The lamps themselves were spaced too far apart for the weak yellow light they cast off to beat back the dark December night. Five blocks west, cars coasted along one of Bentham's main thoroughfares, but the street in front of Addy was clear and quiet, the surrounding businesses having long since closed for the night.

She'd left the metallic-blue Mustang she'd rented for the two-hour drive from Manhattan to Bentham in the hotel's parking lot. It was easier to canvass the neighborhood on foot. All she had to show for her effort were sore feet.

A footstep sounded as she pocketed her phone. Shooting a glance over her shoulder, she squinted into the darkness but saw no one.

You're just not used to so much quiet, she thought, walking on.

She'd lived in New York City since she was twelve but spent summers on her grandfather's ranch in Texas. She'd loved the ranch almost as much as she loved the city, but New York wasn't called the city that never slept for nothing. There was always something to do and see, and she was used to being surrounded by thousands of people, even though she'd been very much alone since Cassie moved to Bentham.

A scraping sound came from close behind her, followed by the unmistakable sound of fast-moving footsteps.

She turned, intending to move to the side, when a hand clamped around her ponytail, jerking her backward against a hard chest.

It took a moment for her brain to catch up with what was happening, and by the time it did, her assailant had taken his beefy hand from her hair and clamped it over her mouth.

Addy fought her rising panic. Like any savvy city girl, she'd taken self-defense classes, but it had been a while since she'd brushed up. She'd never thought she'd actually have to use any of those techniques.

She tried to pull away, but the man's arm was like a vise around her neck.

"Don't fight, and I won't hurt you," the man growled.

She didn't believe that for a minute. She'd left the small gun she carried for protection locked in her car's glove compartment, a decision she regretted now. Who'd have thought the streets of Bentham were more dangerous than Manhattan?

Well, she had no intention of going down without a fight, gun or no gun. She sent up a quick prayer and fisted her hands at the same time a yell came from somewhere in the night.

SHAWN WEST STOPPED at an intersection not far from the offices of the company he'd been sent to investigate.

Half a block away, on the opposite side of the street, a Black woman strolled toward him.

She was too far away to see her clearly, but the tailored slacks, black wool peacoat and dark gray loafers marked her as a professional, probably on her way home from work. A feeling of familiarity washed over him, but he quickly dismissed it. Despite its proximity to Manhattan, he'd never been to or met anyone from Bentham before.

A figure clad in black, a man based on the figure's height and size, peeled away from a darkened doorway as the woman approached the far street corner. The man grabbed the woman by the hair and wrapped his arm around her neck.

Shawn sprang from the Yukon.

He raced toward the man and woman, yelling as he did. "Hey!"

The man looked up, surprise on his face. The darkness, combined with the baseball cap the man wore, didn't allow Shawn a good look at the man's face. His arm stayed around the woman's neck, but his grip loosed enough that the woman's feet touched the ground again.

She took advantage of her assailant's distraction. Bracing herself, she bent her right leg and drove her heel back into the man's knee.

Her courage impressed him even as he put on a burst of speed, knowing that her fighting back had the potential to further aggravate her attacker. Shawn kept his eyes on the struggling pair.

The man's arms fell from around her, and he let out a torrent of curses Shawn could hear clearly from a block away.

"Help!" the woman's scream echoed off the empty buildings.

The man reached for the woman again.

"Hey!" Shawn yelled again. "Leave her alone!"

The man seemed to finally realize that Shawn wasn't just going to mind his own business and walk away.

He backed up, flinging the woman to the ground with another curse and fleeing.

Shawn slowed as he approached the woman. She lay on the pavement facing away from him on her side, coughing in an attempt to catch her breath. He scanned her body, looking for injuries. She didn't appear to be seriously hurt, but he still couldn't see her face.

Shawn glanced around the corner where the man had disappeared. The darkened doorways and parked vehicles along the street made for several good places to hide. He saw no one.

His heart pounding from exertion and adrenaline, Shawn turned back to the woman's side.

The feeling of familiarity struck him again, and when she pushed up to a sitting position, he understood why.

"Addy?"

Now she turned her gorgeous brown eyes on him, shock shining in them.

Her shoulders relaxed when he stepped out of the circle of light that engulfed her. "Shawn? What…what are you doing here?"

He and Addy Williams had spent an incredible weekend together six months earlier at Ryan's destination wedding. He'd tried to see her again after they'd returned to New York, but she hadn't answered any of his calls.

"Are you okay?" Shawn asked, ignoring her question for one he deemed more important at the moment.

He squatted next to her.

"Yes." Addy's voice cracked, and she stopped, clearing her throat before speaking again. "He didn't hurt me."

Fury that she could have been hurt rose in him, but he tamped it down. She looked shaken but otherwise okay.

"We should call the cops." Shawn reached into the pocket of his leather jacket before remembering he'd left his phone in his car.

Addy pushed to her feet and pulled the sides of her coat closed around her. "No. No cops. I'm fine."

He stood, wondering whether she'd hit her head in the fall. They had to report the assault. "We should call. That guy could attack someone else."

She chewed her plump bottom lip, and a spark of attraction shot through him despite the frown that marked her pretty face.

Several seconds passed before she nodded in assent.

"I left my phone in the car," Shawn said, tilting his head toward the Yukon idling at the stop sign, the driver's door still wide-open.

He wanted to get her into the truck to wait, just in case her assailant came back.

"You can use mine," she said, unlocking the phone with her thumb before handing it to him.

They walked together toward his car. Shawn assessed the woman beside him as he dialed.

Why didn't Addy want to call the police? Why was she in Bentham?

And why didn't she want to call the police?

Chapter Two

It took less than ten minutes for two deputies to arrive. After getting the description of her attacker, the first deputy left to patrol the area in an attempt to find the attacker. The second requested Addy and Shawn return with him to the sheriff's department to give formal statements. Addy elected to ride with the deputy, needing a moment to process the shock of finding herself staring into the mesmerizing eyes of Shawn West. For a second, she'd thought she must be hallucinating. It had been a few months since the incredible weekend they'd spent at her friend Nadia's wedding to Shawn's brother Ryan in St. Bart.

She'd met Shawn at the rehearsal dinner, and they'd clicked immediately. They'd chatted throughout dinner, then taken a moonlit stroll on the beach. Dancing at the reception under the stars, Shawn holding her close, she'd forgotten all about her vow to forgo romance in favor of her career. She'd invited Shawn back to her room, where they'd spent the entire night and most of the following day in bed.

And then she'd gone back to her real life in New York and completely ghosted him.

Addy wasn't sure whom she dreaded facing more: Sheriff Roger Donovan or Shawn West.

She pressed her palms against her forehead and groaned.

"Are you okay, ma'am?" The deputy glanced over at her.

"Yes. Sorry." Addy smiled weakly. "It's just been a day."

The deputy returned her smile with one of his own. He pulled the cruiser into a parking lot adjacent to a utilitarian brown building. Stone signage on the small grassy patch in front of the building proclaimed it the Bentham County Sheriff's Department.

SHAWN MET ADDY and the deputy at the front door. The three of them entered, and the deputy led them to a reception desk.

Addy stole a sly glance at Shawn as he signed in.

Six foot three and broad shouldered, he was a man who got noticed by men and women alike when he entered a room. Despite the cold temperatures, he wore a black leather jacket that looked as if it was molded to fit his powerful arms. Underneath the jacket, a gray shirt accentuated well-defined pecs and tailored slacks hugged a tight bottom. A thin dusting of stubble covered the rich brown skin along his jaw.

A fleeting memory of dotting kisses along that jaw brought a surge of heat to her cheeks. She quickly pushed the memory from her mind.

After they signed in, the deputy had them take a seat before he disappeared behind a thick gray door. A row of green folding chairs comprised the waiting area in the small lobby. The chairs faced a long metal desk topped with clear Plexiglas, no doubt bulletproof.

She took a seat next to Shawn, struggling to come up with something to say. He saved her by speaking first.

"You sure you're okay?" Shawn looked at her with concern in his eyes.

"Yes, thank you for helping me back there." Remembering that he'd never answered her question from earlier, she asked again. "What are you doing in Bentham?"

"You're welcome. I'm here on business," he responded without giving any further details.

The deputy's return stopped her from probing more.

"Ms. Williams. Mr. West. The sheriff is ready for you now."

Shawn stood and waited for Addy to move ahead of him. They followed the deputy down a long hallway, past a large room where other officers sat staring at computers or talking on the phone. She'd spoken with Sheriff Roger Donovan earlier that day and was surprised when the deputy stopped several doors short of the sheriff's office.

Addy felt her shoulders stiffen, but she followed the deputy into an interrogation room, Shawn at her heels. She'd never been in an interrogation room before, but it looked like the ones she'd seen on television. Soft padding, ripped in several places, covered the lower section of the wall. A rectangular table took up most of the small space, its faux-wood top chipped at one corner.

She settled herself next to Shawn again, tension coiled in her body.

If Shawn felt anxious at all, he didn't show it. He sat, legs spread, his hands on his thighs, a slight smile on his lips. Cool, calm and collected. And incredibly sexy.

The deputy excused himself, and less than a moment later a man in his late fifties with a full beard gone mostly gray entered the room.

Sheriff Donovan dropped a yellow legal pad and pen on the table. "Ms. Williams, I'm sorry to see you under those circumstances. I take it you weren't hurt?"

"Thank you, Sheriff. I'm fine," Addy answered stiffly.

"Good to hear." Sheriff Donovan nodded. "I have to say, I was surprised to learn you were still in town." The sheriff watched her with raised eyebrows.

She hadn't told the sheriff she planned to stay in town and look for Cassie on her own since he'd made it clear he would be of little help. She needed to find irrefutable evidence that Cassie hadn't just taken off, then she could force the sheriff to take action.

Sheriff Donovan's stare hadn't wavered. An intimidation tactic—one she was familiar with from negotiating her fair share of corporate mergers.

She held the sheriff's gaze, saying nothing.

Several seconds ticked by before the sheriff blinked and turned to Shawn. "And you must be the gentleman who saved Ms. Williams?"

Shawn's lips turned up into a cocky smile that matched his body language. "She saved herself. I just called your guys."

Sheriff Donovan scratched his jaw, his gaze shooting back to Addy, a look of disbelief on his face. "So how 'bout you folks tell me about the trouble you had tonight."

"I was walking back to my hotel after stopping for dinner when a man attacked me."

"And what hotel would that be?"

"The Madison Hotel downtown."

One of the sheriff's eyebrows rose. "That's a bit of a walk."

Addy shrugged. "I don't mind the cold, and I needed the time to clear my head."

Which wasn't totally untrue. She didn't mind the cold, but she'd been canvassing the area around Cassie's job and apartment, hoping someone had information that would help find her.

"Go on." Sheriff Donovan motioned with the pen in his hand.

"I'd just left the restaurant, headed back to my hotel. A man grabbed me from behind. He put his hand over my mouth and told me not to struggle."

The yellow legal pad sat in front of the sheriff untouched.

"Is that when Mr. West came along?"

She nodded. "Yes."

Sheriff Donovan turned to Shawn. "And I take it you intervened?"

"I was a half block away, about to turn onto the street when I saw Addy being attacked," Shawn answered.

Sheriff Donovan's brows drew together over his nose. "Would have been wiser to dial 911." His gaze moved from Addy to Shawn and back. "You could have gotten both of you killed."

"I'm a PI. I know how to handle myself."

"A private eye?" Sheriff Donovan scowled.

Shawn nodded.

"Well, Mr. Private Eye, in my town the sheriff's office handles crime and private investigators chase cheating spouses."

Shawn glared.

The conversation was quickly devolving into a competition between the two men, but Addy had better things to do with her time.

"Getting back to tonight," Addy said pointedly, "Shawn

yelled loud enough to catch the guy's attention and give me the opportunity to land a kick to his shin."

Addy recounted the rest of the details, thankful that the sheriff's focus no longer seemed to be on her acquaintance with Shawn. She wasn't comfortable explaining their relationship to a stranger. She wasn't even sure she could explain it to herself at this point.

"Did you get a look at him?" Sheriff Donovan asked, finally picking up his pen.

Addy shook her head. "No. He grabbed me from behind. I never saw his face."

"And what about you?" The sheriff turned to Shawn. "Did you get a look at this guy?"

"Only a glimpse. I doubt I could reliably identify him." Shawn's expression turned dark. "He took off when he saw me."

Sheriff Donovan turned his attention back to Addy. "Did he reach for your purse? Take anything of value before he ran off?"

"No." Addy tilted her head, thinking.

Why would a mugger attack her and not take her purse or wallet? He might have seen her leaving the restaurant and figured she had to have money or a credit card on her, but she'd been some blocks away from the restaurant when he attacked. A darker thought jumped into the forefront of her mind.

Addy knew the sheriff didn't think there was anything nefarious behind Cassie's disappearance, but Addy couldn't ignore the possibility that tonight's attack could be related.

Sheriff Donovan set his pen down. "I have to tell you, you haven't given me much to go on here."

The tone of the sheriff's voice piqued Addy's ire. "Does that mean you won't investigate?"

Sheriff Donovan's face turned hard. "The department will investigate as it does any complaint we receive."

"Sheriff, I don't think this guy was trying to rob me. I don't know why, but I think he was after me. Have you made any progress at all on locating my sister?"

"Ms. Williams, I assure you I am doing everything I can." Sheriff Donovan paused for a beat, looking at her over the tops of his rimless spectacles. "But your sister isn't a local."

Already frustrated by the sheriff's lack of urgency about Cassie's disappearance, she had to fight back the fury that rose inside at his comment. Beside her, Shawn tensed.

"I don't know why that should matter. Cassie has lived in Bentham for six months now. Does not having lived here longer make her disappearance less of a priority for you?"

Sheriff Donovan's gaze hardened. "I didn't say that," he ground out. "Small towns aren't for everyone. Someone like your sister, someone who's used to a big city like New York," he added quickly, "might find it hard to adapt. If your sister didn't go back to New York, maybe she tried another big city like Boston or Philly."

She knew what the sheriff was getting at. He'd talked to Cassie's roommate and boss.

Addy narrowed her gaze on the sheriff. "I don't believe my sister would just up and move without telling me."

"All her things were gone," the sheriff said, his arms spread wide as if the missing items proved his point.

Addy knew differently. Cassie hadn't mentioned a thing about moving back to New York or anywhere else for that matter in any of the phone calls or texts the sisters had shared over the last few weeks.

Addy shook her head, trying once again to get through the lawman's thick skull. "If Cassie moved back to New York, why hasn't she returned any of my calls? And where is she now? It's not as if she has anywhere to live in New York other than with me."

"Maybe she's staying with friends." She shook her head, and the sheriff sighed. "Tell me again why your sister moved to Bentham in the first place," he said, ignoring her question.

Once again she pushed back her frustration with the sheriff. Getting on his bad side wouldn't help her find Cassie, and that was all that was important to her at the moment. Gritting her teeth, she said, "Cassie wanted to take some time off before starting college in the fall. Experience the real world."

Sheriff Donovan nodded his head, taking notes, although she'd already told him all this when she'd called last week to make the missing person report and again when she'd spoken to him earlier that day.

"Bentham was close enough to New York that she could come home to visit whenever she wanted but far enough that she felt like she was out on her own."

"Didn't you tell me before that your father passed away recently?" The sheriff flipped through the pages in his notebook, presumably looking for the notes he'd taken during their last meeting.

"Yes, this past February, a few months before Cassie moved to town."

Their father had passed away seven months ago, but that didn't stop a fresh wave of grief from swelling in her chest. Shawn's hand moved to cover hers on the table, and the compassion she saw in his eyes nearly broke her.

Ryan and Nadia's wedding had taken place a month after her father's death and a year after her divorce. Addy didn't need to be a therapist to see the connection between these events and her one and only one-night stand. That was one of the reasons she hadn't returned his calls when she'd gotten back to New York. That and the butterflies that fluttered in her stomach whenever she thought about having him in her life beyond that single weekend.

She quickly directed her gaze back to the sheriff.

Sheriff Donovan set his pen on top of his pad and folded his hands in front of him.

"Sometimes people do weird things after a loss." His gaze flicked to Shawn's hand, which still covered hers on the table. "Did your sister ever mention hurting herself?"

Addy pressed her lips together, afraid of what she might say if she spoke at the moment. She knew grief made people act out of character. But there was no way Cassie would ever do anything to hurt herself or anyone else.

"No." Addy shook her head vehemently.

Like Addy, Cassie grieved their father's death. She'd insisted on taking the internship with Spectrum to get real-world work experience before college. But Addy suspected that the move was as much about Cassie needing some space to process her grief and get away from all the memories of their father that still lingered in New York.

Addy didn't think of herself as a pessimist, but she was more of a realist than her father and sister. Although their father had tried to remain upbeat and hopeful while he fought the cancer, she'd been aware not too long after their father's diagnosis that the prognosis was bleak.

Cassie had a much tougher time dealing with the death of their father from cancer, months before her high school graduation. She'd held fast to hope that her father could beat the cancer right up until the end. A miracle that had never come.

With one month left in her senior year, Cassie had become depressed and nearly despondent. Her grades had taken a precipitous dive, although luckily, her GPA was strong enough to withstand the hit, and she'd already gotten her acceptance to MIT for the fall. When Cassie announced she'd deferred her college start date and wanted to move out of the city, Addy had thought it was a good idea, hopeful that the change would give her sister some much-needed time to grieve and heal before starting the next phase of her life.

Now she wondered if she'd live to regret supporting Cassie's decision to come to Bentham.

Sheriff Donovan used both hands to remove his glasses, laying them on his open notebook.

"Look, why don't you go on back to New York? Most likely your sister will turn up there a few days from now. I'll call you if I have anything to report."

The sheriff sent her a tight smile that Addy interpreted to mean he was done with both the Williams sisters and their problems.

Addy leaned forward, pressing her palms into the table and enunciating each word so the sheriff didn't miss a syllable.

"My sister did not just leave this town of her own volition. She's in trouble, and I'm not going anywhere until I've found her."

Chapter Three

It was nearly midnight by the time Shawn had settled into his room at the Madison Hotel. He would have to pay a fee since he'd canceled his original reservation at a nearby hotel so late, but instinct urged him to stick close to Addy. Something in his gut told him the attack on her tonight hadn't been a run-of-the-mill mugging.

Not that Addy's life was any of his business. She'd made that pretty clear by not returning any of the phone calls or texts he'd sent after their night together.

So why had he gotten a room at her hotel?

His phone rang before he could work out a satisfactory answer to that question. He didn't need to see the screen to know the call came from his older brother Ryan.

"'Ello," Shawn answered.

"Why haven't you been answering your phone? Are you there yet?" Ryan asked without preamble.

"I'm great, thanks. The drive was lovely," Shawn deadpanned, attempting to cut through some of the tension coming from Ryan's end of the call.

The loud, exaggerated sigh on the other end of the line was an increasingly familiar, and annoying, sound.

Ryan was indisputably the most serious of his brothers, which made him well suited to the position of president of West Investigations, but Ryan was also the most dramatic of the four West brothers.

Their father, James West Sr., had founded West Investigations, although he was semiretired and only saw a select few clients now. James Sr. liked to joke he'd reached the age where he could earn his money on the golf course, and Shawn and Ryan didn't disagree. They'd taken over the reins at West since their two older brothers' interests lay elsewhere.

Maybe it was the added pressure of being newly married with a baby on the way, but Ryan had been riding everyone at West harder than usual, Shawn in particular.

"Shawn, this is serious. Intellus Communications is one of our largest clients, and they will be in major legal and financial trouble if they don't find out who's counterfeiting their computer chips."

Shawn rolled his eyes even though his brother couldn't see it.

"Relax, Ry. I'm here and everything is under control."

He'd been scoping out the headquarters of Spectrum Industries, one of the businesses West had identified as possibly being involved in the corporate espionage against Intellus, when he'd seen Addy being attacked. Spectrum had two other business addresses, warehouses where they made their computer chips, that he still needed to check out.

"Good. Whoever's behind this has to have knowledge of and regular access to the manufacturing side of things as well as the management side. That suggests someone fairly high up in the company if Spectrum is behind this."

Shawn didn't bother responding. They'd gone over all this before he left for Bentham.

Zelig Ernst, CEO of Intellus and longtime client of

West Security, had called Shawn from Intellus's headquarters in Silicon Valley this morning in a panic. Counterfeit computer chips with Intellus's logo had popped up all over the country. Ernst had ordered an investigation into their factory's production that had determined that the chips weren't coming from Intellus. Based upon the geographic location where most of the chips appeared to have entered the sales stream, Intellus had narrowed the possible source to two competitors in the market, one of which was Spectrum.

Intellus had hired West to investigate the two suspect companies and obtain proof of the guilty party. Ernst wanted to go to the police and the public with evidence that Intellus was a victim and had nothing to do with the fraud. So far Intellus's clients that had received fraudulent chips were willing to give the company the benefit of the doubt and a little bit of time to figure things out. Ernst wasn't sure that would hold if another batch of counterfeits made it into the market.

Shawn hesitated for a moment, considering whether to tell Ryan about the earlier incident with Addy. Before he could make up his mind, Ryan began speaking again.

"We don't have a lot of time. There's likely to be another batch of counterfeits in the market in a few days." The counterfeits appeared to flow into the market like clockwork every six weeks for the last three months, which only gave Intellus three days before the next batch of chips were scheduled to show up if the counterfeiters stayed on schedule.

Shawn bit back his irritation. He'd be the first to admit that Ryan shouldered more of the administrative weight of running the company. But Shawn knew he was a damn good private investigator and had brought several new clients into the firm, including Intellus, in the four years since James Sr.'s retirement.

"I know that, Ry. I was on the call with Ernst just like you were. I'm on it. Gideon is checking out the other possible source, and I'm already in Bentham. If either of these companies is the source of the counterfeits, we'll nail them."

Ryan blew out a breath. "Good. When we find these guys, every company in the city will look to us for corporate cybersecurity."

Shawn worked his jaw, trying to lessen the tension there. "I know. I got this. You know I care about the company as much as you do."

"You need to be laser focused on this case."

"I got it, Ry," Shawn bit out. "It's late. I'm turning in for the night." He ended the call without saying goodbye.

They were long overdue for a discussion about Shawn's role within the company, but it would have to wait. He'd handle his job, hopefully finding out quickly if Spectrum was involved in the fraud.

And he'd keep an eye out for Addy while he was in Bentham, because something told him she was going to need it.

CRISP EARLY-MORNING AIR swept over Shawn's face as he walked back to the hotel from the café where he'd picked up breakfast. He strolled through the lobby without drawing so much as a glance from the desk clerk, having made a mental note of the room number Addy gave Donovan at the police station the evening before.

The sheriff had received an emergency call right after Addy had declared she wasn't leaving Bentham without Cassie, and Shawn had given her a lift back to the hotel.

She'd remained stoic, her fury at Donovan still hot on the drive to the hotel. Not that he blamed her. Donovan certainly didn't appear to be taking Cassie Williams's disappearance too seriously. Still, Shawn had figured it wasn't the best time to explain his impromptu fib or to convince Addy to continue playing along with it.

After getting over the shock of seeing Addy again, he'd realized his plan for keeping a low profile while in Bentham was blown. He'd had no choice but to reveal his occupation when Donovan collected his personal information for the formal statement. Although he'd declined to give specifics regarding his stay in Bentham, New York City private investigators didn't just turn up in small-town Bentham for no reason.

Shawn's concern now wasn't just with finding the source of Intellus's fraudulent chips, but also helping Addy find her missing sister and keep her out of danger. After all, he wasn't about to leave Addy to investigate on her own, even though she was clearly able to handle herself. He'd been surprised and impressed with how she'd taken on her attacker. There was nothing sexier than a beautiful woman who could take care of herself.

Shawn gave himself a mental slap. He wasn't going to go there. Addy clearly wasn't interested in him, and he wasn't about to put himself out there a second time and have her dance all over his heart. She needed help finding her sister, and quite possibly protection. Those were jobs he knew how to do, so he'd offer his help, but that was all.

He balanced the coffee holder and a bag of food in one hand and rapped on Addy's door with his free hand. A full minute passed without any sound from within the room. He knocked again, harder this time, worry furrowing his brow. It was early, not quite eight, but he'd wanted to make sure he caught her. Maybe she'd gone down to the hotel restaurant for breakfast.

After a moment more, he turned away from the room, heading for the restaurant, when the locks clicked open. The door swung inward, and Addy peered around the side of the door at him.

"What are you doing here?" Addy asked in a voice still heavy with sleep.

His blood heated at her sultry rasp.

Ignoring the spark of attraction, he flashed a smile. "Just being a good neighbor. My room is down the hall. I bought breakfast," he said, holding up the coffees and the bag.

"What time is it?" She swung the door open, and he just about stopped breathing.

Her New York Knicks T-shirt stopped at midthigh, revealing what seemed like miles of smooth brown skin ending in fiery-red toenails. She crossed her arms, pulling her shirt tight across her chest and revealing curves that had his mouth feeling like it had been stuffed with cotton.

He swallowed hard and cleared his throat. "Ah, it's almost eight."

Addy's eyes widened. "I never sleep this late."

"Can I come in?"

Her eyes narrowed, and he shifted so he wouldn't get hit if she slammed the door in his face.

He thrust one of the coffees at her, hoping the offering would tip her calculus in his favor. He was rewarded.

She grabbed the coffee, closing her eyes and inhaling deeply before taking a long sip.

"Okay." Addy's dark brown eyes fluttered open, sending an electric charge through him. "You can come in."

She turned away from the door and strode to the round table pushed into a corner of the room.

He blew out a ragged breath and followed.

Unlike the suite he'd reserved three floors above, Addy's room needed renovations, but it was clean and had all the expected amenities—two queen beds; a square side table between them; a flat-screen television atop a wide, six-drawer dresser; Wi-Fi and USB hookups. One of the two beds had a laptop at its center with a handful of papers scattered around it. Rumpled bedsheets covered the other mattress.

Addy set her coffee on the table. "I need a minute," she said, grabbing her travel bag and carrying it to the bathroom.

He caught a glimpse of a large rectangular mirror over a white countertop before the bathroom door closed.

Shawn sat at the table and reached in the bag for one of the two breakfast sandwiches he'd picked up on the way to the hotel. The small stack of papers perched on the edge of the table fluttered to the floor.

He picked them up, glancing at the sheet on top. A copy of the missing person report for Cassie Williams, dated five days earlier.

Shawn's eye traveled down the page, drawn to the name of Cassie's employer.

Spectrum Industries.

From the bathroom, he heard the sound of the toilet flushing and the sink faucet turning on. Addy would be back any second.

He righted the stack of papers, searching his memory for whether Addy had mentioned her sister worked at Spectrum during their chat with the sheriff last evening. He recalled her saying Cassie had moved to Bentham for an internship, but not where. Cassie's disappearance could be unconnected to his case, but he didn't believe in coincidence.

The bathroom door opened, leaving him no more time to ponder the information he'd just learned.

Addy walked back across the room to the table, and Shawn couldn't help being disappointed that she'd pulled a pair of yoga pants over her shapely legs.

"Thanks for the coffee," she said, sitting in the chair across from him and pulling her legs up under her.

"I bought breakfast, too." He pushed the second sandwich across the table.

She unwrapped it and frowned. "What is this?"

"Egg whites and spinach on a whole-grain English muffin."

She shot a steely look across the table and slid the sandwich back toward him. "You can go now."

Shawn rolled his eyes. "Just try it," he said, pushing the sandwich at her again.

Addy's cell phone rang, and she went to the bedside table where it lay charging. She frowned, pressing her finger to the phone's screen and carrying it back to the table. It buzzed in her hand as she reclaimed her seat. She glanced at the phone again, her frown deepening.

"Everything okay?"

She smiled tightly. "Fine. You never answered my question. What are you really doing here?" She ignored the sandwich and reached for her coffee cup.

He wasn't ready to answer that question just yet, so he replied with his own. "How long has your sister been missing?"

She took another sip of coffee before responding. "I

haven't heard from Cassie in more than a week. The sheriff seemed content to believe she's just picked up and moved, but I know Cassie wouldn't do that without telling me."

"How old is Cassie?" Shawn asked, unwrapping his sandwich.

"Nineteen. She's taking a gap year before starting MIT in the fall."

"And she chose to spend it in Bentham?" He failed to keep the skepticism from his voice.

Addy chuckled. "It's not exactly Paris, but I think she just needed a little space."

"You mentioned your father died recently."

She swallowed hard. "Yes. Cassie insisted her move from New York was about experiencing the real world before college, but I think she needed some space from all the memories of our father in the city."

"Could she have decided Bentham wasn't far enough away?"

Her hands curled into fists on top of the table. "If she was going to go somewhere, she would have told me or one of her friends. I reached out to all of them, and none have heard from her. Cassie would call to ask if I thought she should have vanilla bean ice cream or rocky road for dessert. Then eat both." She chuckled, and the smile that lit her dark brown eyes sent his heart stuttering. "She ran everything by me or one of her other friends. No way she'd move without mentioning it to anyone." She hit the table with her fist, punctuating the statement.

He had no doubt she believed what she said, but everyone kept secrets, even from those they were closest to. Addy could be right about her sister, or she could be too close to the situation to see it clearly. The fact that Cassie worked for Spectrum and someone there might be engaged in major fraudulent activity added a layer of intrigue to the situation.

A pang of guilt shot through him, but he swept it away. West had promised Intellus they'd keep the fraud on a need-to-know basis for the time being, so telling Addy the truth about why he was in Bentham was out of the question. He couldn't be sure she'd let him stick close if she knew he thought Cassie could be involved in fraud. And he had every intention of sticking to her like glue, because if Cassie was involved, Addy could be in danger.

"So what do you think happened? Where do you think Cassie is?" Shawn asked.

Anguish flooded her face, and he had the sudden urge to wrap her in his arms. "I don't know." Her voice faltered, and she took a moment to steady herself before going on. "But Sheriff Donovan doesn't seem to care to find out, so I'm going to have to do it myself."

Definitely a strong woman.

"When you last heard from Cassie, did she sound worried or upset?"

"No." Addy picked at the English muffin, popping a small piece into her mouth. "Why are you so interested?"

"Questions are an occupational hazard in my line of work."

"Yes, but you aren't my PI. I haven't hired you."

He raised an eyebrow. "I've been known to do some pro bono work."

Addy tilted her head, her eyes narrowed. "You're good at avoiding my questions. Eat your breakfast." She eyed her own English muffin before taking a bite. "How can you eat this? It tastes like sand mixed with seaweed."

He swallowed. "It's healthy. Did Cassie have a boyfriend?"

"You get to ask questions, but I don't?"

"You can ask. I just may not answer." He smiled to soften his words.

She took another small bite of her sandwich, then tossed the rest in the trash. "Why should I answer your questions if you don't answer mine?"

"Because I have experience finding missing people. I can help you if you let me." He tapped her to-do list for emphasis.

She studied him like the sharp negotiator he knew she was. He'd googled her after Ryan's wedding and learned she was an up-and-coming legal superstar. She'd been at the helm of a number of big mergers and acquisitions. According to the intel he'd been able to glean from his brother Brandon, Addy was on the fast track to partnership at her firm.

Seemingly having made up her mind to let him help, Addy finally answered. "Cassie was dating a guy named Ben. They worked together at Spectrum here in Bentham."

"What did she do at Spectrum?"

"I'm not sure, exactly. I know she thought the internship would help her careerwise. Cassie plans to get her degree in computer science."

His Spidey senses were tingling. There were way too many events converging around Spectrum—Addy's sister's disappearance and evidence that Spectrum was behind the fraudulent chips—to be mere coincidences.

He could use Cassie's disappearance as his in at Spectrum. Cassie's coworkers were more likely to talk to him if they thought he was helping her to find Cassie. It was a decent plan, though not perfect.

He slid a look across the table. Addy had twisted her shoulder-length brown hair into a bun and applied some shimmery powder to her cheeks. She looked fresh-faced and gorgeous.

"I have a proposal for you. I am in town doing a job for a client, but the client has demanded I keep the reason for my presence confidential."

Her eyes lit with understanding. "And you think I can help you do that."

Shawn grinned.

"I had planned to keep a low profile while in town, but that's out the window now. I need a reason to be in town."

"And you want me to be that reason? Even though you won't tell me what you are working on?" The corners of her mouth turned down.

"I can't tell you. But I can help you look into your sister's disappearance."

She chewed her bottom lip, studying the tabletop. "I don't know."

Shawn leaned back in the chair. In his experience, the best way to convince someone to do what he wanted them to do was to provide a sober recitation of the advantages. In this case, his main advantage was that Addy didn't have the skill or expertise to conduct a missing-person investigation. "I've handled several missing-person cases, and West Security is one of the best investigative firms in New York. You'll have all our resources at your disposal. Free of charge."

He waited while she thought it over, confident she'd

accept the offer. Addy was a smart cookie, and more importantly, she was motivated to find her sister.

"Okay," she answered after a moment of hesitation. "But you have to get out now. I need to shower."

She stood, and he did the same.

He accepted the win and contemplated how he'd convince Ryan to devote West resources to their new pro bono case. It shouldn't be too hard. Ryan still owed him one from a year earlier when West had become involved in helping Nadia's brother get out from under the mob. It was time he collected on that IOU.

"Great. Thank you for doing this." He headed for the door. "If you pack your stuff, I'll move it to my room when you're ready and you can check out of this room."

Addy's eyes went wide. "Hang on. I didn't agree to share a room with you."

"Relax," he said, retreating to the door. "I have a suite." A one-room suite, but he'd sleep on the pullout couch in the living room. Addy's expression remained skeptical. "You'll have your own room, but Cassie is missing and you've already been attacked once. I think it's safer for you if we stay in the same room."

Her nose wrinkled as if she'd smelled something foul, but she nodded finally. "I'll be ready when you get back."

He called Ryan as soon as he got back to the suite.

"You got anything yet?" Ryan answered without preamble.

"There may be something bigger than fraudulent computer chips going on here."

Shawn explained the situation with Addy, the attack on her last night and Cassie working for Spectrum and going missing.

"And you think all that is connected to our investigation."

"It would be one hell of a coincidence if it wasn't," Shawn answered, tossing his meager belongings back into his duffel bag and moving them out of the bedroom. The suite had a tiny powder room near the door that he could use for everything except showers.

Ryan swore under his breath. "You got a plan?"

Shawn explained his cover as a PI working with Addy to help her look for her sister.

"I don't mind using West resources to help her out, but don't forget why you're there. Intellus's job has to come first," Ryan clipped out.

"I got it." Shawn's voice came out sharper than he'd intended. Ryan treating him as if he didn't know how to do his job grated. As soon as this case was over, they were going to talk.

He gave Ryan Addy's and Cassie's full names and asked for background checks on both before hanging up.

The look of anguish on Addy's face when he'd asked what she thought happened to Cassie flittered through his memory. He hadn't mentioned the likelihood of finding Cassie alive diminished exponentially every day, but he wasn't surprised that she seemed to be aware of that fact. Cassie had already been missing for nine days; that didn't bode well for finding her alive. But finding Cassie, dead or alive, would give Addy some closure; he could already tell she wasn't the type who'd be able to move on with her own life without knowing what had happened to her sister. Intellus's job would come first, but he'd also do everything in his power to find Cassie Williams.

Chapter Four

After Shawn left, Addy took a shower and packed before dialing a number that was becoming increasingly familiar to her. As with the last two times she'd called, Suri Bedingfield's phone rang until the voice mail kicked in. Biting back frustration, Addy left a third message for Cassie's roommate, then called up to Shawn's suite and checked out of her room.

She wasn't sure whether sharing a suite with Shawn was wise given their history and the attraction she still felt for him. In the end, the balance in her bank account and the bills waiting for her back home tipped the scales. That and the fact that she felt safe with him. The more she thought about the mugging, the more convinced she became that she hadn't been just a convenient victim. The attacker had targeted her specifically.

After helping her move her things to his suite, Shawn agreed that they should go see Cassie's boss. On the short drive from the hotel to Spectrum, Addy relayed what little she knew about Caroline Webb, Cassie's boss, and Ben Konstam, Cassie's coworker and boyfriend. She'd purposely chosen a hotel not far from the center of downtown Bentham so she'd be close to Cassie's office and the duplex where she rented an apartment.

Located in a midcentury limestone building, Spectrum's headquarters spanned a half block. Shawn parked in a nearby surface parking lot, and they took the elevator to Spectrum's seventh-floor offices. Since most of what she knew about tech companies came from the movies and television, she'd expected Spectrum's offices to be a bright space with lots of chrome and glass and hipster employees sipping lattes in their open-floor-plan offices.

The elevator doors opened into a typically dull office space with harsh overhead lighting and industrial-gray carpeting leading through a maze of corridors.

A middle-aged, red-haired woman in a tan sweater and cardigan sat behind the reception desk. "Welcome to Spectrum. How may I help you today?" she said with a practiced smile.

The receptionist gave Shawn the once-over, a reaction Addy found irritating even though the woman was at least two decades older than Shawn and her.

Shawn offered a smile but didn't speak. They'd discussed how they planned to approach Ms. Webb on the drive over. Since Addy had spoken with Caroline Webb over the phone the previous week, they'd decided she would take the lead. It would also be harder for Cassie's boss to refuse to speak to the sister of a missing employee.

"My name is Addy Williams. My sister, Cassie Williams, is an intern here. I'd like to speak to her boss, Caroline Webb, please?"

The woman tapped the keyboard a few times in front of her before her gaze shifted back to Addy. "Do you have an appointment?"

Addy smiled tightly. "I don't, but I'm hoping Ms. Webb has a bit of time to see me. You may be aware that my sister is missing, and I'm sure everyone here at Spectrum wants to do what they can to help locate her."

She had no compunction about using a little manipulation to get around Spectrum's gatekeeper.

"One moment, please."

The receptionist dialed a number, and after several seconds announced that "an Addy Williams and a gentleman" were there to see the person at the other end of the line. Moments later the receptionist replaced the phone's receiver and directed them to take the second right at the end of the hallway.

Addy and Shawn passed several smartly dressed employees in designer dresses and tailored suits, reminding Addy of the corridors of Covington and Baker and the stable of suits in her closet back in New York. Like at Covington and Baker, Spectrum's corridors were a labyrinth of passageways seemingly designed to be as confusing as possible.

Cassie's direct boss was the human resources director, Caroline Webb. She and Shawn finally found her office nestled in a far corner of the floor, between the men's room and what appeared to be the company break room.

A balding Caucasian man in an impeccably tailored blue suit and a white woman in a boxy gray dress greeted them.

The man, in his early seventies and round everywhere, held his hand out to Addy. "Ms. Williams, I'm Martin Raupp, CEO of Spectrum Industries."

Addy shook his hand.

Martin Raupp held himself with the self-assurance of a man with power. "Caroline called to tell me you were here. Everyone at Spectrum is just distressed to hear that

Cassie is missing, and we'll do whatever we can to help the police locate her safe and sound."

Martin Raupp's voice rang with sincerity. Addy was touched that he'd made a point to see her when he'd heard she was in the building.

"Thank you, Mr. Raupp. This is my friend Shawn West. He's a private investigator, and he's helping me to find Cassie."

Caroline Webb pressed her lips together. Heat rose in Addy's cheeks, but she didn't take her hand from Shawn's.

Mr. Raupp clapped his hands together in front of him. "Well, I'll leave you in Ms. Webb's capable hands. Please know that my wife, Madeline, and I are praying for Cassie's safe return."

He flashed one more smile their way and exited the office.

Caroline motioned them to sit. Addy lowered herself into the chair next to Shawn and opposite her desk. A full-figured woman in her mid to late fifties, Caroline had pulled her gray-brown hair up into a tight bun at the crown of her head.

"Ms. Webb, thank you for seeing me without an appointment. I'm sorry to barge in on you like this," Addy offered, not feeling a bit sorry but hoping to smooth any ruffled feathers.

Caroline pursed her lips again, although Addy couldn't tell if it was in annoyance or merely a habit. "Not a problem. I'm sorry to hear that Cassie is missing. I shall do anything I can to help."

Caroline Webb had a pronounced British accent. She shot a glance at Shawn, although Addy noted it wasn't more benign than the receptionist's assessment had been.

"I'm hoping you can help me fill in some of Cassie's movements in the days before she went missing. Sheriff Donovan said that Cassie had resigned her internship, but Cassie never spoke of it to me."

Caroline nodded. "Yes, I was quite surprised, to be honest with you. Cassie seemed happy, and she was well-liked."

"What exactly did she do as an intern?" Shawn asked, rubbing his thumb against the back of Addy's hand and sending little shivers down her spine. She stole a glance at him, wondering if he knew what his touch did to her. His gaze stayed focused on Caroline Webb.

Get a grip. You need to focus here.

"Cassie did whatever we needed her to do. Mostly filing and other paperwork. But because she was so interested in computer science, I made it a point that she should be allowed to shadow the engineers over at the factory twice a week." Caroline folded her hands atop her desk primly.

Shawn's grip on Addy's hand tightened ever so slightly. She looked over at him again and saw that his body had also tensed, although for the life of her she couldn't figure out why. It made perfect sense that Cassie would jump at the chance to hang out with computer engineers, since that was what she'd be studying once she got to MIT.

"Has she had any trouble at work lately?" Shawn asked, their agreement that Addy would take the lead apparently forgotten.

Ms. Webb shook her head. "No. As I said, Cassie was very well-liked around here. A hard worker. Always to work on time and willing to stay late to meet deadlines if necessary."

That sounded just like Cassie and proved she hadn't simply quit without notice, as far as Addy was concerned.

"My sister was dating a Spectrum employee who worked in Spectrum's factory. Ben Konstam," Addy said, making sure not to let how she felt about Cassie's choice in boyfriend show on her face.

Addy had had reservations about her sister dating a co-worker. She'd warned Cassie against starting a workplace romance, but Cassie was Cassie. Stubborn. Bullheaded. Determined to live life on her terms and make her own mistakes. Cassie had accused Addy of not wanting her to date Ben because he wasn't white-collar enough. Addy had denied it, hurt that Cassie would suggest such a thing, although when she dug down deep inside, she couldn't deny that the education and potential income disparity likely had something to do with it. Addy's divorce had devastated her, especially when she'd realized the only reason her ex-husband, Phillip, had married her was for her law firm salary. She didn't want Cassie to end up in the same situation.

Caroline's mouth turned down in a frown. "I am aware." She didn't speak for a moment, then added, "Mr. Konstam no longer works in the factory. He's been promoted to management."

"He works in this building?" Addy asked, surprised. Cassie hadn't mentioned Ben getting a promotion.

She glanced at Shawn but found his expression unreadable.

"Down the corridor." Caroline Webb inclined her head toward the hall beyond her office. "You passed his office on the way here."

That was perfect. They could kill two birds with one visit.

"What did Cassie say when she quit?" Addy asked, directing the conversation back to the days right before Cassie disappeared. "I mean, did she give you a reason why she was leaving the internship almost eight months early?"

"Well, I didn't speak to Cassie. I found her letter of resignation, effective immediately, on my desk one morning." Caroline scowled, no doubt aggrieved at the unprofessional way Cassie had supposedly resigned.

To Addy, it was only further evidence that something was very wrong. Their father had instilled a strong work ethic in both of his daughters. There's no way Cassie would quit a job without notice and without talking to her boss in person.

Addy's heartbeat ticked up with an increase in the fear she felt for her sister. "Did you try calling her?"

Caroline's back stiffened. "I did," Ms. Webb answered, a haughty undertone creeping into her voice.

Shawn squeezed Addy's hand. "I don't think Addy was implying you did anything wrong." Shawn flashed a boyish smile. "We're just trying to get a clear picture of things. Were you ever able to speak with Cassie?"

Caroline's shoulders relaxed, but she didn't return Shawn's smile. "Miss Williams never returned my calls. It wasn't like her as far as I knew her, but young people these days are so self-involved." She shook her head, unhappiness with the youth of the day chiseled in her expression. "I simply filed the paperwork to terminate her employment. Now, I truly am sorry, but I must get on with my workday."

"One more question. Could I have a look at Cassie's resignation letter?" Addy said.

Caroline shook her head. "I'm sorry. That wouldn't be appropriate, as it's part of an employee's personnel file."

Addy scooted forward in her chair.

"You wouldn't have any way of knowing if Cassie's signature was genuine. I'd know if it was a forgery."

Caroline's head continued its side-to-side motion.

"The sheriff could get a warrant," Shawn said, as if the idea had just occurred to him. "There is an active missing-person case open. But that would mean formally engaging the company in a legal process, and you know how cops can be. If they start asking for one thing, they'll ask for a dozen extra things."

Caroline bit her bottom lip, her expression thoughtful.

The woman seemed to be fond of Cassie, but Addy could tell she was at war with herself over breaking the rules. A rule follower herself, Addy understood the struggle, but if breaking the rules helped locate Cassie, she would break them all and induce whoever she needed to do the same.

"Please?" Addy pleaded. "Just a glance at the signature, that's all. You said yourself that resigning this way wasn't something you'd have expected from Cassie. What if she didn't really sign that letter?" Addy pleaded.

Caroline nodded and turned to the computer at the edge of her desk and hit several keys. The printer behind her whirred to life.

She reached behind her and snatched the paper the printer spit out.

"We don't keep much paper around these days." Aside from a small stack of files on her desk, there was no paper in the office, not even file cabinets that might have held paper files. "Everything is scanned to the system, then sent off-site."

Caroline handed the paper from the printer across the desk to Addy.

A copy of Cassie's resignation letter.

Addy skipped over the text of the letter, going straight to the signature. She evaluated every loop, line and dotted *i* for any sign that the name at the bottom of the letter hadn't been penned by her sister.

After a minute of inspection, her heart sank.

She recognized the signature as Cassie's.

Chapter Five

Shawn could tell by the look on Addy's face when she read the letter that it was Cassie's signature. Caroline didn't have any more information to give them, so they said their goodbyes.

They retraced their steps back toward the exit, agreeing without words to drop in on Ben while they were in the building. Shawn scanned the office doors on the left side of the hallway while Addy did the same for the doors on the right. As he did, he thought about what Caroline had said about Cassie and her role at Spectrum. He hadn't been able to control the involuntary twitch of his hand when he'd heard Cassie worked on both the management and production sides of the company. And he knew Addy had noticed.

Cassie fit the profile for a Spectrum employee involved in the fraud. Based on what he knew about her, Cassie seemed to have the knowledge of computer hardware and the process of chip making necessary as well as the access to carry out the fraud. Not that he thought for a minute she could carry out a fraud like this on her own. But with a boyfriend that had contacts within Spectrum spanning years? It would also explain why a nineteen-year-old from New York, on her way to one of the premier universities in the country, would put it all on hold to take an internship in a small town.

He and Addy finally found the door with Ben's name on it. Shawn knocked on the open door, drawing the attention of the broad-shouldered white man sitting behind the desk. He looked younger than Shawn had expected, although he knew from what Addy had told him on the way over that Ben was twenty-six. He could tell the age difference between Cassie and Ben bothered her.

Ben's light brown hair curled around the back of his neck to skim the top of his ill-fitting suit. He looked like a teenage kid who'd borrowed his dad's suit for a job interview.

Addy stepped around Shawn into the office. "Ben Konstam? My name is Addy Williams. I'm Cassie's sister. Do you have a moment?"

"Of course," Ben said, rising but remaining behind his desk. "Have you heard anything from Cassie?"

Ben's words had been right, but there'd been no emotion behind them. A glance at the frown marring Addy's pretty face had Shawn thinking she felt the same way.

"No. That's why we're here," Addy answered. She quickly introduced Shawn before turning to the reason they were there. "I'm hoping you can shed some light on the situation."

Ben spread his hands in front of him. "Anything I can do, I will. I care for Cassie very much." He motioned for them to have a seat in the square-backed chairs positioned across from his desk.

Shawn sank into the chair, watching Ben closely.

"How did you and Cassie meet?" Shawn started the questioning off, taking Ben's measure. He wanted to see if Ben's description of his relationship with Cassie matched up with what Addy had said.

"I was working on the loading docks when Cassie first started with Spectrum. There was a mix-up in some paperwork for one of the shipments. Cassie brought the correct invoices over." Ben's voice remained emotionless.

For a man with a missing girlfriend, he was uncharacteristically nonplussed.

"This building has loading docks?" Shawn pressed.

Ben gave a half smile. "Not here. This is the corporate office of Spectrum. There's another building where the sausage is made, so to speak." Ben chuckled at his joke.

"And where is that building?"

Ben tilted his head to the side, his forehead scrunching. "Oh, not far, just about three miles outside town. It's impossible to get a large enough space for a reasonable rent downtown."

"Of course. It's too bad. I tinker with computers myself, and I'd hoped to get a chance to see how the sausage is made," Shawn said, hoping to allay any wariness.

A smug smile swelled across Ben's face and his chest puffed out. "Anytime you want to take a tour of the facility, just give me a call, and I'll set it up. I have an in with the guys in the warehouse since I used to be one of them. Just because I'm in the corporate suite doesn't mean I'll be forgetting my roots."

Shawn slid a glance at Addy, catching the suspicion in her eyes. Ben had just confirmed the lease that West's property search had turned up was in fact held on the factory, which was helpful to his case but did little to find Cassie.

"So you worked on the loading docks nine months

ago. What did you do?" Shawn said, getting them back on track.

"I loaded the trucks and then delivered the chips to customers up and down the East Coast."

Ben picked up a pen and began tapping it against the top of the desk.

"From delivery driver to assistant shipping manager. That's a hell of a success story," Addy said.

"I got an associate's degree in business management," Ben said defensively, jerking his head toward the framed diploma in the wall. "Spectrum is all about moving employees that prove themselves up through the ranks. Employee retention and all that."

"When was the last time you saw Cassie?" Addy questioned.

"It's been a few weeks now." Ben tilted his head back, looking up at the ceiling as if searching for the date up there. Or avoiding making eye contact. "Yeah, more like a month ago."

Shawn's eyebrow rose. "Was it normal for you two to go that long without seeing each other?"

Ben's eyes darted around the room. "Normal? I mean, we weren't married, man. I don't know what she told you," Ben said, looking at Addy, "but things with us were casual-like."

Addy opened her mouth to speak, but Shawn sensed that whatever she was going to say wouldn't further the conversation.

"Did Cassie seem worried?" Shawn spoke up before Addy. "Maybe preoccupied when you saw her last?"

Ben closed one eye, squinting in thought. "No, not that I remember."

"Suri, Cassie's roommate, said Cassie told her she was moving back home to New York. Did Cassie mention a move to you?" Shawn pressed on.

"Yeah. I told the sheriff all this." Ben tapped the pen faster. "Cassie was ready to go home."

"Why didn't she tell me if she was coming back to New York?" Addy spat.

Ben shrugged. "Maybe she wanted to surprise you. Maybe she…she wanted to be in New York but didn't want to deal with family yet. I don't know, but I know she said she was going home."

Silence ensued as Ben looked down at his desk, avoiding Addy's disbelieving glare.

He was hiding something.

"What did Cassie do for Spectrum?" Shawn asked, hoping a different approach would yield more answers.

Ben tore his attention from the desktop.

"Filing. Answering the phone. Taking notes in meetings. She pretty much did whatever needed to be done." His answer matched what Caroline had said.

"Did she have problems with anyone at work bothering her? Argue with anyone?" Shawn asked.

"No. Let's be honest, Cassie wasn't in a position to argue with anyone around here," Ben snapped. "It's not like she gave orders or was a supervisor. Look, I need to get back to work." Ben stood, indicating the end of the conversation.

Addy and Shawn followed suit, leaving Ben's office and heading down the corridor toward the elevators.

"He's not telling the truth," Addy said as soon as they were out of hearing distance of Ben's office. "Cassie would not have moved without talking to me."

"He definitely wasn't telling us everything, but that doesn't mean he had anything to do with Cassie's disappearance."

Addy shot him a murderous look. He was sure she was prepared to argue the point, but a petite woman stepped out of an office to their right before she could get started.

"Excuse me. You're Cassie's sister, right?" the woman asked.

"Yes. Addy Williams. This is Shawn West."

"I'm Claudia." The woman's gaze darted down the hall. She took a step back into her office, though not far enough to allow Shawn and Addy to enter.

"I debated saying anything, but if it was my sister—" Claudia wrung her hands.

Addy took a step forward. "Please, if you know anything that could help me find Cassie—"

"I overheard a conversation between Cassie and Ben. An argument, really. The day before Cassie went missing."

Shawn assessed the woman in front of him. She twisted her hands nervously in front of her.

"What were they arguing about?" Addy asked.

"Well, I don't want to get anyone in trouble." Claudia reached for her office door.

Addy slid forward, placing herself so the door could not be closed. "Please. It might help us find Cassie."

Claudia sighed. "I didn't hear much. Ben asked if they could talk about 'it,' and Cassie said no, they'd already talked and she had nothing more to say to him about it or them. She said they were through and she was going to do the right thing."

Claudia shook her head and wrung her hands more.

"And neither one of them mentioned what the 'it' they were talking about was?"

"Sorry, no. I didn't hear anything else. Cassie walked away from Ben then."

"Did Ben follow her?" Shawn asked.

The skin on Claudia's forehead creased. "I don't know. Neither of them walked directly past me, but I could hear Cassie's heels. That's how I knew she walked away. It's possible Ben followed her or he could have gone down the other hall there." She pointed to where the hall jutted off to the left.

"Did you tell Sheriff Donovan about the argument?"

"Oh, well, no. Like I said, I don't want to get anybody in trouble." Claudia edged back into her office.

Shawn had met too many people who didn't want to "get involved." If Claudia had told Donovan what she'd seen and heard, he might have taken Cassie's disappearance more seriously from the beginning. Shawn bit back his annoyance with the skittish woman.

"Telling the sheriff what you heard would be helpful."

"I'll think about it." This time Claudia did push the door until Addy had no choice but to move or be hit by it. The door clicked closed in their faces.

Shawn wouldn't be placing any bets on Claudia going to Donovan, but he made a mental note to pass on the information himself. Hopefully, Donovan would follow up.

"You think that's what Ben was holding back? That he and Cassie argued right before she disappeared?" Addy said.

"It's possible. It might explain his obvious nervousness and reluctance to talk to us. As the boyfriend, he's already under the microscope. If it's known that he and

Cassie weren't getting along, that makes him even more of a suspect."

"Let's go back and see what he has to say about it."

Ben's office was empty and dark when they returned.

"We need to go see Sheriff Donovan. Ben knows more than he's saying about Cassie's disappearance." Addy marched down the corridor and out of Spectrum's offices.

"Slow down," he said, following her. "We've got no evidence that Ben had anything to do with Cassie's disappearance."

She punched the elevator down button before whirling on him. "What are you talking about? He wouldn't have run out of here right after we talked to him if he had nothing to hide."

"We don't know why he left. He could have a lunch meeting." He raised his hands to stop the onslaught he felt coming. "I'm not saying I believe that, but we can come back later and question Ben again. Hopefully, we'll have more information then and we'll be able to confront him with some facts."

The elevator doors opened.

"Okay, how are we going to get this information?"

Shawn frowned, afraid she wasn't going to like his answer. "I don't know."

Chapter Six

Addy stayed silent until they'd stepped onto the sidewalk in front of the building. "Ben is lying."

Her skin felt as if thousands of needles were pricking it. What little control she had over her emotions was rapidly fraying. She didn't know why everyone was so quick to believe that Cassie had moved back to New York, but she knew that hadn't been her sister's plan. "Maybe Cassie broke up with him and he kidnapped her. It happens. We need to get Sheriff Donovan to search Ben's house."

Shawn's hand landed on her shoulder, holding her in place. "Hold on a minute."

"We don't have a minute." Addy shook his hand off her shoulder. "I know Cassie is still alive. I can sense it, but it feels like I'm running out of time to find her."

"Chasing after Ben isn't going to make him tell you what he knows about Cassie's disappearance. If he knows anything."

"What do you mean, if he knows anything? Did you see how nervous and jittery Ben was?"

"I saw, but he could have been nervous about anything. Or a general nervousness could be his usual state of being."

She gaped at Shawn for a moment before turning and stalking away down the sidewalk. He was no better than the sheriff.

Tears pricked at the backs of her eyes, blurring her vision. “Agreeing to let you help me was a mistake.”

She missed the dip in the sidewalk and stumbled. Strong arms latched on to her waist from behind, righting her before she fell.

“Are you okay?”

Addy twisted, looking up into Shawn’s dark eyes. Desire sizzled between them. “Yes, I’m fine. I’m just hungry. I didn’t have much breakfast.” She shot him a look.

Shawn smiled wryly. “Look, let me buy you something to eat, and we can talk about our next steps.”

She was anxious to find Ben and question him further. But a wave of light-headedness swept over her at the mention of food, making her glad his hands were still clasped around her waist. A couple of bites of whatever Shawn had brought to her hotel room this morning had not cut it.

“Okay, but I pick where we eat,” she said, stepping out of his arms. As she did, a wave of regret swept through her.

Shawn West had the potential to uproot all her carefully laid plans. But would that be so bad?

Addy pushed the question from her mind and focused on her growling stomach.

She’d noticed a diner adjacent to the lot where they’d parked. She led Shawn back toward the parking lot now, stopping just before they reached it at double glass front doors with The Golden Spoon etched on them in gold.

Addy cocked an eyebrow, waiting to see if he’d complain. He looked at the door warily but kept silent.

Addy reached for the door at the same time he did. Their hands touched, and another sizzle of electricity shot through her.

The sound of a clearing throat broke their reverie. Addy stepped into the diner, aware of the man's cheeky smile even as she avoided making eye contact with him. "Rockin' Around the Christmas Tree" played from the diner's overhead speakers, and the smells of bacon and fresh coffee rushed at them as they entered. Addy's stomach growled again at the sight of pancakes and fresh strawberries on a nearby table.

A waitress, with the name Becky stitched on her uniform, quickly seated them.

Addy wasted no time turning the conversation back to Ben once they were alone with the menus.

"What do *you* think of Ben?"

"I think you're right. But we need leverage if we want to get him to tell us what he's hiding."

She felt the beginnings of a headache coming on. "What kind of leverage?"

"Something that would prove he's lying or at least strongly suggest it."

"That makes sense." Addy looked at him inquisitively. "How would you get that kind of evidence?"

Shawn smiled devilishly. "There are many ways, but in this case, I'd start with talking to Cassie's roommate, Suri."

"Suri? Why?"

"Both Ben and Suri told the sheriff that Cassie had moved. That suggests that they either believed that or they coordinated their stories."

Addy nodded slowly, digesting what he'd said.

Becky returned with a pot of coffee and two cups. She set the cups on the table and poured.

"When I didn't hear from Cassie for three days, I called Suri. She didn't know much, and she hasn't responded to any of my subsequent calls," Addy said, breathing in the coffee smell.

"If you're talking about Suri Bedingfield, she moved out of town about a week ago."

"You know her?" Addy turned her surprised eyes on the waitress.

"There may be a bunch of Suris in Hollywood, but not in Bentham. Suri waited tables for me. Left a message on the restaurant's voice mail last Tuesday saying she'd found a job in Garwin and she quit. Worked here for three years. I would have never thought she'd leave me in the lurch like that."

Suri's abrupt departure sounded suspiciously like Cassie's.

Addy and Shawn exchanged a knowing look. "Did Suri say anything else?"

Becky looked at Shawn as if he'd suddenly grown two heads. "What else is there to say after 'I quit'?"

A fair point.

"You ready to order?" Becky set the coffeepot on the table and pulled a pen and pad from her apron pocket.

Addy ordered the Americana breakfast—four pancakes, eggs, toast, bacon and sausage. She ignored Shawn's wince when she asked Becky for a side order of home fries.

"I'll just have a fruit cup," Shawn said.

Addy grinned as the waitress walked away from the table.

Shawn quirked an eyebrow. "What? You're laughing at me when you ordered enough food to feed a small army."

"I spent the first twelve years of my life on a ranch. I guess the hearty meals stuck with me," Addy said, adding cream and sugar to her coffee and noting that Shawn took his black.

Shawn sipped his coffee. "A ranch, huh?"

"Yeah. My mom's parents owned a small ranch in Texas." Addy smiled as memories of her grandparents, horseback riding and cloudless starry skies flitted through her head. "My parents met when my dad was doing his residency at a hospital in town. He'd grown up in Brooklyn and had every intention of returning as soon as his residency ended."

"Meeting your mom changed his plans, I assume."

"You assume right. My mom couldn't imagine leaving her family or Texas. Dad used to say if Mom had wanted to live on Mars, he would have rented a rocket to get them there. They were madly in love."

"They sound great," Shawn said.

The chatter in the diner ebbed and flowed around them, mixing with the clink of silverware against porcelain cups and plates.

"They were. And I loved growing up in Texas. A year after Cassie was born, Mom was diagnosed with cancer. She was gone a few months later. My dad and grandparents were devastated. My grandmother passed three months after my mother from a broken heart."

Shawn reached across the table for her hand. "I'm so sorry, Addy."

"It was a long time ago. When my grandfather passed a year later, Dad sold the ranch and moved us back to New York so we'd be near his family."

"Making you half city girl, half country girl and totally fascinating," Shawn said, lacing his fingers through hers and looking into her eyes.

She held his gaze, her heart doing a fluttery stutter.

An image of holding Shawn's hand as they strolled the Mall in Central Park or took in the view from Belvedere Castle ran through her mind.

Dangerous thoughts for a woman who had sworn off relationships.

She pulled her hand from his and cleared her throat. "Maybe we should talk about our next steps for finding Cassie."

Shawn frowned but leaned back against the booth and went with the change in subject. "Do you have any ideas?"

"We need to talk to Suri, but she won't answer my calls. We need to figure out how we're going to get her to speak to us," Addy said.

"We'll have to track her down. I'll get someone at West started on that now. What's Suri's last name?"

"Bedingfield," Addy said just as something else popped into her mind. "Hey, why were you so interested in Ben working on the loading docks?"

An expression she couldn't name passed over his face, but before he could answer her, his phone rang.

He looked at the screen. "It's my brother. What's up, Ry?"

Addy turned toward the window and tried not to eavesdrop on Shawn's conversation, an impossible task given there were only a few feet between them.

The familiarity in Shawn's tone coupled with the undercurrent of irritation and a hint of idolization marked the sibling interaction. She wondered if that was what people heard when she and Cassie spoke. And whether she would ever speak to her sister again.

Shawn kept the call brief, but he asked Ryan to locate contact information for Suri Bedingfield.

"Your brother?"

"Yeah." Shawn shifted to put his phone back in his pocket. "He's been a little overbearing."

"About the case you're really in town for?" Addy said with open curiosity.

Shawn made sure no one was near enough to hear them before answering. They were hours after the typical breakfast rush and ahead of the lunch crush. The only other people in the diner were a pair of teenaged girls occupying a table at the other side of the diner. Becky had seated the customers she did have well away from each other. "Yeah. We have a time crunch, and getting a favorable outcome for our client would mean a big boost for our business."

"Yet you offered to help me."

A look she couldn't name crossed Shawn's face for a fleeting moment before disappearing.

The smile that replaced the look was cocky. "I can handle both. I'm that good."

Addy rolled her eyes. She read the cockiness for what it was—a deflection to keep her from asking more questions—but let it go for now.

Becky stopped at their table, plates balanced on her arm. She set Addy's pancakes and eggs in front of her and slid a second plate with toast to a stop. She turned to the waitress that stood behind her and took the plate with a small mountain of bacon and a small bowl from the girl's hands and placed them on the table in front of Addy and Shawn.

"Anything else I can get you, folks?"

Addy had already forked a generously sized bite of pancake in her mouth, so Shawn answered.

"We're good, thanks," he said, humor dancing in his eyes as he watched her eat.

Becky moved away from the table.

"Excuse me," Shawn called out. "Do you know who Suri Bedingfield's new job is with?"

Becky's nose scrunched in thought. "She didn't say a company name or anything in her message, but I just assumed she'd found a better-paying waitressing job over there in Garwin. They got fancier restaurants than we do here, which means bigger tips."

Addy hadn't realized how hungry she was. She finished her food quickly, then rested against the back of the booth.

"Feeling better?" Shawn asked with a raised eyebrow.

"Actually, I am." She looked at his empty bowl. "How can a man your size survive on a wheatgrass muffin and a bowl of fruit?"

"It was a whole-wheat muffin, and egg whites and spinach are packed with protein. Eating healthy gives me energy."

Addy shook her head, smiling. "I'd rather have bacon." She bit into the piece of bacon in her hand.

Shawn's eyes locked on Addy's. "Well, it doesn't seem to be hurting you any."

A sexy grin turned his lips upward. Her entire body flushed and her heart beat triple time. "I don't recall you being so big a flirt."

He cocked an eyebrow. "I'm stepping up my game since my meager charms didn't hold your attention the last time."

Embarrassment brought heat to her cheeks. "I owe you an apology for ignoring your calls after Ryan's wedding. That weekend was a mistake." She flinched at the hurt expression that crossed his face. "I didn't mean—"

Shawn held up a hand, stopping her. "No, I shouldn't have called you out like that. It was one weekend."

"It was one *incredible* weekend." She pushed her empty plate aside. "It's just, I don't date."

Now both his eyebrows shot up, forming an upside down V over his nose. "Never?"

She shrugged, then rolled her shoulders to relieve some of the tension there. "I have a few friends—just friends," she emphasized, though she wasn't sure why she was explaining all this to him, "I call if I need an escort to a work function or something like that, but since my divorce…" She let her voice trail off.

"I can't imagine what kind of man would let you go." He shifted his gaze to the ceiling as if in thought. "I'm envisioning the world's biggest half-wit. No, half-wit is too many wits. A quarter wit?" He looked at her with a smile tickling his lips. "Or maybe a two-tenths wit."

Addy laughed, as she knew he'd intended.

"No, no. I'm going to go with he's a one-fifth wit," Shawn declared with exaggerated finality.

"Two-tenths is the same as one-fifth," she said with a smile.

"I've never been good at math." Shawn grinned. "But he's definitely short on wits."

"You won't hear me contradicting you, although I'm more than a little biased as I'm the one who got dumped. Or cheated on, to be precise." Addy swallowed the last drops of her now-cold coffee, all traces of humor gone from her voice. "Although to hear Phillip tell it, I drove him to cheat."

Shawn shook his head. "Not possible. You know that, Addy."

She nodded. "I do, but that doesn't mean hearing it from the man you'd planned to spend your life with doesn't affect you."

The muscle on the side of Shawn's jaw jumped and his eyes darkened, but he watched her silently.

For some inexplicable reason, she wanted to tell him about her ex. "Phillip never liked the long hours I worked. I guess when it came down to it, he couldn't stand being the man waiting for his wife to come home."

Shawn shook his head again. "That's a cop-out. I'd consider myself the luckiest man on earth to find myself waiting for you to come home to me."

The surrounding air crackled with unspoken desire.

"Is he why you never returned my calls after our night together?"

"It wasn't about you. You were my first and only one-night stand. I've sworn off relationships."

Whatever response Shawn might have given was forestalled by their waitress's reappearance.

She slapped their check on the table, oblivious to the sexual tension. "Can I get you anything else?"

Addy pushed herself out of the booth. "Excuse me for a minute. I want to, uh, wash my hands."

She wove through the tables to the dimly lit hallway separating the kitchen from the dining area at the rear of the diner and into the ladies' room. She braced her palms against the sink's edge, taking a minute to collect herself after the charged moment with Shawn. She had no idea why she'd told him about her failed marriage, except that some innate instinct told her she could—should—trust him.

Cassie's disappearance had thrown her off-center. She was blowing off work and trusting a man she barely knew. That wasn't exactly true. She knew some parts of him very well.

Addy looked at her reflection in the mirror over the sink. Focus on finding Cassie. And she would, although she didn't think she'd be able to stop her feelings for Shawn deepening with each passing moment they spent together.

She washed her hands and exited the restroom, nearly colliding with a man standing outside the ladies' room door.

A four-inch scar ran along the side of the man's face, combining with sunken eyes and angular cheekbones to give him a menacing, skeletal look.

A shiver ran down Addy's spine. She averted her gaze. "Excuse me." She put as much room as possible between them as she attempted to move past the man.

"You ought to take those fancy manners and go back to New York City," Scarface hissed. "You won't find what you're looking for here."

A wave of fear rolled through her, but she straightened to her full five-foot-eight height and met the man's ugly glare. "Back off."

"It's you who better back off if you know what's good for you." Scarface took a threatening step forward, and Addy moved two steps back.

"Who are you?"

"Wouldn't want you to disappear, too, now, would we?"

Fear turned to fury in an instant. *Too.* Did that mean Scarface knew where Cassie was?

The man took another step forward, filling the space between them.

In the next instant, Scarface spun away from Addy, his back slamming against the wall on the opposite side of the corridor. Shawn put his large frame between Addy and the man.

"Was that a threat against the lady?" Shawn wasn't touching the other man now, but his hands were fisted in front of him, his body taut and ready to strike.

"Not a threat. Just an observation." A scowl twisted the man's face, making it even more grotesque.

"Well, since you seem to be in a sharing mood, why don't you tell us what you know about Cassie Williams's disappearance," Shawn said.

"I ain't telling you nothing." The man pushed off the wall, ready to strike.

"What's going on back here? Half my customers are standing in this hallway." Becky stopped at the mouth of the corridor. Her eyes fell on the man, and her expression turned to one of disdain. "Teddy Arbury. Why am I not surprised? I warned you about coming in here with your trouble." Becky's fist landed on her hip.

"I ain't the one making trouble, Becky. I'm just trying to use the facilities."

Becky's expression screamed disbelief. "Well, go on, then. Get out of here," she said, her chin jutting toward the men's room.

Teddy shot Shawn a dark look. Teddy slid by, purposely walking closer to Addy than was necessary. Shawn growled a warning as Teddy pushed through the door into the men's room.

"Are you okay?" Shawn asked. He put his arm around

Addy's shoulders, pulling her close and leading her toward the diner's doors.

"I'm fine. He didn't touch me. Just caught me off guard," Addy said, soaking in the warmth from his body. "We need to pay."

"I settled the bill already."

"You didn't have to do that. I ate twice as much as you did."

The corners of Shawn's mouth turned up ever so slightly. "More like four times as much."

She reached into her purse for her wallet, but he waved her off. "Don't worry about it. Let's hurry. I want to see where Teddy goes when he leaves."

Chapter Seven

Addy went over the encounter with Teddy in her head as she and Shawn crossed the street to the public surface lot where he'd parked the Yukon. They'd just closed the doors when Teddy lumbered out the diner doors. He turned in the opposite direction from the parking lot where they sat and headed down the sidewalk.

Shawn put the car in gear and followed.

Teddy made a left at the corner and mounted a black motorcycle. He tore off down the street.

"Make sure your seat belt is fastened tight. I'm not sure how long I'll be able to follow him without him realizing it. Yukons aren't exactly commonplace around here."

She'd seen lots of SUVs, but more of the soccer mom variety, with lots of space for kids, dogs and gear. There were very few of the massive SUVs of the kind Shawn drove.

He wasn't wrong about Teddy catching on to the tail. They'd gone about five blocks when the motorcycle made a sudden hard left, crossing over two lanes of traffic and nearly sideswiping a parked car. Shawn couldn't follow.

"Damn." Shawn hit the steering wheel with the palm of his hand.

"We have to go back and find him. I think he knows where Cassie is."

"He'll be long gone before I can turn around in this traffic."

Shawn continued to drive with the flow of traffic. She felt like crying out in frustration. Her phone rang from inside her purse.

Addy accepted the call without looking at the screen, expecting to hear Jarod's irate twang. At last check he'd sent her half a dozen emails, mostly to remind her of things she'd already taken care of.

Instead, the voice on the other end of the line was much more familiar and welcome.

"Addy?" Cassie's tear-streaked voice came from the other end of the phone.

Addy's heart raced at the sound of Cassie's thready voice. "Cassie? Oh my God, Cassie, are you okay?"

Shawn cut across a lane of traffic, drawing an angry honk from a red sedan, and threw the car into Park at the side of the road. He motioned for Addy to put the call on speaker.

She pressed the microphone icon on her screen and held the phone between her and Shawn. Static crackled from the phone.

"My shoulder…okay, though, I think." The line dropped in and out as Cassie spoke.

"Cassie, where are you?" Addy's heart pounded loudly in her ears. The only response was the sound of static. "Are you there? Cassie?"

"Here… Woods…" Cassie's voice came in a ragged burst between static. It almost sounded as if she were running as she spoke.

Shawn leaned in close and spoke into the phone.

"Cassie, my name is Shawn West. I'm helping your sister find you. Can you see anything around you?"

"Not sure..."

The line went silent, Cassie's voice and the static both gone, followed by the telltale beeping that showed the call had dropped.

"Cassie!" Addy cried, the panic in her voice sucking the air from the interior of the car.

She pressed the speaker icon and brought the phone to her ear, hoping that the move might somehow bring her sister back.

Shawn took the phone from her hand, navigating to the recent calls list and hitting redial.

They listened to it ring for thirty seconds before the line went dead again without being picked up or rolling over to voice mail.

Addy gripped Shawn's arm. "We need to go to the sheriff, right now. Maybe he can trace the call or something."

Shawn nodded, putting the Yukon in gear and getting them to the sheriff's office fifteen minutes later. She and Shawn showed the deputy at the desk their IDs and explained that they didn't have an appointment with the sheriff but that they needed to see him. The deputy hesitated but lifted the receiver of the phone on his desk after several seconds and punched four buttons.

He spoke too softly for Addy to hear what he said through the Plexiglas and over the chatter coming from the people sitting behind her in the waiting area.

The aftershocks of emotion from Cassie's call still vibrated through her.

If Shawn was as impatient to speak with the sheriff, he was better at hiding it. Still, his shoulders were taut.

And the assessing sweep of his eyes over the lobby and the officers behind the Plexiglas screen screamed that he was on guard.

The deputy put down the phone, pushing a sign-in sheet and pen through the slit in the glass. They signed in, and less than a minute later the locks on the door to their right clicked and another uniformed deputy waved them through.

Sheriff Donovan looked up from the file he was reading as they entered.

"Ms. Williams. Mr. West. To what do I owe this pleasure?" Donovan's tone conveyed the opposite of his words; he found no pleasure in their reappearance in his office.

Since she was in no way happy to be in his office and the sheriff's cavalier attitude toward Cassie's disappearance may have put her sister in danger, Addy didn't hesitate to engage.

"I just got a call from Cassie. She's being held by someone, possibly in a wooded area." She'd marched from the door to his desk while she spoke, stopping on the visitor's side of the desk and staring down at the sheriff, her hands balled into fists at her side.

"Hold on a minute." Sheriff Donovan pushed back from the desk, raising his hands. "Why don't you have a seat and tell me about this call?"

Shawn stepped up next to her but seemed to understand that this was a fight she wanted to wage by herself. He kept quiet. "I don't want to have a seat, and I just told you about the call. What are you going to do to find out where my sister is being held?"

Sheriff Donovan stood, forcing her to crane her head up to look at his face. "Have a seat, Ms. Williams." The sheriff gestured to the chairs behind her, his voice and eyes hard.

Neither she nor Sheriff Donovan moved.

Somewhere in the back of her mind, she understood this wasn't a test of wills she could win. She needed the sheriff more than he needed her if she had a hope of finding Cassie. Sheriff Donovan had made it clear that it would suit him just fine if she went back to New York City and let him handle Cassie's disappearance the way he saw fit. If she wanted him to do more than wait and see if Cassie turned up, she might have to try to win him over with honey rather than vinegar.

Possibly thinking along the same lines, Shawn said softly, "Addy, you should sit."

After several seconds, she relented. Shawn took the second chair, while Sheriff Donovan also sat.

"Now tell me about this call." Sheriff Donovan eyed her from across the desk.

Addy recounted the call in detail. It wasn't difficult. Every word of the short conversation was burned into her memory.

"With your permission, I can try to see if the phone company can attach a name or location to the number your sister called from," the sheriff said, digging through a pile of papers on his desk and handing a sheet across to Addy.

A consent form allowing the department to request her records from the telephone company.

"That's it?" Addy asked, looking up from the form in her hand.

"I know you don't want to hear this, but there's nothing more I can do. Not without a location, and it doesn't sound like your sister gave you one."

Addy slid to the edge of her seat. Shawn reached out, taking her hand as if he feared she might launch herself at the sheriff. Frenetic energy coursed through Addy, making launching herself at the sheriff possible, although she held herself in check. She couldn't seem to make the sheriff understand the danger she knew Cassie was in.

"Maybe she couldn't tell us, but the call proves she's being held against her will."

Sheriff Donovan shook his head, sending a thick strand of gray hair onto his forehead. "Maybe."

Addy felt her ire rise to near boiling, but she checked it for Cassie's sake. "What do you mean, maybe?"

"Kidnappers don't usually let their victims make phone calls to family, despite what you see on television. You said the call was choppy. And that your sister said she was okay when you asked how she was. Maybe you just had a bad connection."

"Sheriff—" Addy started, but Sheriff Donovan held up a hand.

"Look, I understand your concern. I do. But there isn't much we can do right now. If your sister called once, she'll probably call again. You may have a better connection next time." Sheriff Donovan stood, crossing his arms over his chest.

Shawn also rose, still holding Addy's hand and pulling her up with him.

"That she called is a good sign, Ms. Williams." The sheriff's gaze cut to Shawn and held some silent communication Addy didn't understand.

Addy started to ask about it when Shawn spoke.

"Let's go, Addy." He moved his hand to her back and guided her out of the sheriff's office.

Addy signed the consent form to allow the sheriff

to have her phone records and left it with the deputy at the front desk on the way out. She and Shawn crossed the small parking lot behind the sheriff's office. A light snow fell, and people hustled past the sheriff's department laden with shopping bags. A Salvation Army volunteer stood on the corner across the street, his rhythmic bell enticing passersby to drop change in his red kettle.

Addy hoisted herself into the Yukon, closed the door and turned so she faced Shawn across the middle console. "What was that back there between you and Sheriff Donovan at the end? What did he mean that Cassie's calling was a good sign?"

Shawn took her hand, looking at her with compassion. "It's a good sign because it means Cassie is still alive."

They made their way out of the parking lot, but the words Shawn hadn't said hung thick in the air. Cassie was alive.

But for how much longer?

Chapter Eight

Addy sank into the Yukon's heated leather seats and let her eyes drift closed. She and Shawn had spoken to two of the three people on her list, but it felt like they were no closer to finding Cassie. The call from Cassie had left Addy feeling even more fearful that they were running out of time.

Shawn hadn't yet started the car's engine. She felt him shift in the driver's seat and opened her eyes.

He pulled a bottle of aspirin from the console between them and offered it to her.

"Thanks." The smile she gave him was genuine, albeit weak.

She swallowed two capsules dry. Her mild headache had turned into a raging inferno somewhere between the confrontation with Teddy and their chat with Sheriff Donovan.

Shawn gave her hand a comforting squeeze before hitting a button on the steering wheel.

"Call Ryan."

The sound of a phone ringing came through the car radio's speakers.

"Shawn." The gruff tenor floated through the car.

Shawn turned his gaze on Addy, taking her hand in his again. "You're on speaker, Ry. Addy's in the car with me."

"I'm sorry your sister is missing." The gruff voice on the other end of the phone softened. "West Security will do our best to locate her."

"Thank you. And please call me Addy."

"Addy got a call from Cassie about forty minutes ago. It was short, and the connection was bad," Shawn said.

Ryan asked for her phone and which carrier she used. "I'll see what I can do, but it will take some time."

"There's something else. Before Cassie's phone call, a guy named Teddy Arbury threatened Addy." Shawn quickly recapped the scene at the diner and following Teddy's motorcycle. "I tried to follow him, but he got away from me," Shawn said, his jaw clenching.

"Given how you drive, I'd love to know how that happened," Ryan grumbled.

They could hear Ryan already typing furiously.

Shawn ignored the brotherly dig. "Arbury was riding a black Fireblade."

"Ah, that makes sense. Those bikes are fast."

"Let's see what we can find on him. Also, Cassie's roommate, Suri Bedingfield, seems to have suddenly moved out of their apartment and gotten a new job in Garwin."

"I'm on it. Anything else?" Ryan stressed the last two words.

Irritation flashed across Shawn's face. His jaw clenched tighter. "I'll keep you posted."

The silence on the other end of the phone went on for so long Addy began to wonder if they'd lost the connection.

Finally, Ryan spoke. "I'll be in touch."

Ryan disconnected.

Addy let out a deep breath. "So where to now?"

Shawn started the Yukon. "Let's go check out Cassie's apartment."

They made a quick detour to the office of the real estate agent who'd helped Cassie find her apartment. The agent hesitated to give Addy the spare key until Addy pointed out that she was technically a lessee since the landlord had insisted Addy be the signatory on the lease given Cassie's age and lack of rental history. The agent glowered but handed over the key.

Cassie lived in a yellow clapboard duplex in a residential area of the city. The cold air slammed into Addy the moment she stepped from the warm interior of the Yukon. Her eyes scanned the small, desolate front yard. The tufts of grass that had survived the winter weather were yellowed and crunched beneath their feet as they made their way to the front of the duplex.

A thought tickled at the back of Addy's mind, but she couldn't bring it into focus.

"You okay?" Shawn gazed down at her, concern in his eyes.

She smiled weakly, mustering a nod.

They climbed the steep, narrow staircase to the second-floor apartment, and Addy used the key to let them inside.

The apartment was small for one person. Having to share it with a roommate would have driven Addy insane. But Cassie had insisted on getting a roommate and paying her way, despite Addy's offers of financial help.

The apartment was freezing, but a musty smell still managed to linger in the air. The paisley sofa and armchair that had come with the furnished apartment remained, but it appeared Suri or Cassie had attempted to add some warmth to desolate space with cherry-red curtains over the living room and kitchen windows and a painting of a boat out to sea on the wall behind the sofa. Along the far wall of the space, three feet of countertop sat between an ancient range stove and an equally old refrigerator. The two cabinets overhanging the counter provided the only cupboard space. There was no dining table, and no room for one. Cassie and Suri must have eaten their meals on the sofa or in their bedrooms.

"Do you know which room was Cassie's?" Shawn asked, peeking into the room that opened up off the living room.

"Since it was her apartment, Cassie took the *slightly*—" Addy emphasized the word "—bigger room with a little more privacy."

Addy pointed and led the way down a short hallway to the second bedroom.

The room looked as if it had been stripped, possibly by someone moving out. An undressed mattress and box spring sat on a metal frame, an upright pine dresser across from it. The closet door stood open, several empty hangers dangling from the closet rod.

There were still months left on the lease, but from all appearances, the apartment looked to have been abandoned by its occupants.

Shawn searched the nightstand next to the bed while Addy explored the dresser, opening each drawer. Nothing. There wasn't so much as a sock in any of them. She reached inside the closet, pushing to her tippy toes, and fanned her hand over the top shelf, feeling for anything that might give her some clue as to Cassie's whereabouts.

Despite her five-foot-eight height, she wasn't quite

able to reach the back wall of the closet. Not wanting to miss any potential clue, she dropped back to her heels and rotated in a slow circle, looking for something she could stand on and see into the top of the closet.

On his knees, Shawn peered under the bed. Addy tilted her head, admiring how his jeans hugged his bottom. She wouldn't have thought it was possible for his tush to look better than it had in yesterday's tailored slacks, but the jeans were giving the slacks a run for their money. The man had a killer body.

Shawn turned, catching her off guard. Heat rose in her cheeks and flamed as a slow smile spread across Shawn's face. "What are you doing?"

"I can't reach all the way to the back of the closet. I'm looking for something to stand on." She ignored the pull to fan her cheeks, instead pointing to the nightstand he'd just searched. "Can you help me push that over here?"

Instead of helping her push the nightstand, he wrapped his arms around it and lifted it as if it was no heavier than a stapler.

"Where do you want it?" His flirty smile sent a tingle through her.

"Show-off."

He winked and wiggled his biceps in answer.

Another tingle, this time accompanied by flutters in her stomach and lower. She didn't usually find cocky self-assuredness attractive, but on Shawn? Majorly. Hot.

"Just put it in front of the closet. Thanks."

Shawn set the end table down and reached for her waist as if to hoist her to the top of the table, but she stepped back.

"I think I can manage."

He raised his hands in front of him and took a step back.

She braced a hand on either side of the nightstand and hoisted herself on top, knees first. The table wobbled at the addition of her weight.

Shawn's hand shot out, wrapping around her forearm and steadying her. His lips were only inches from hers. All she had to do was lean in an inch. Her heart pounded.

"This thing is a piece of junk. Take a look, and let's get you off it before it falls apart."

She swallowed hard and nodded, her heart still pounding. She needed to tamp down her libido before she spontaneously combusted.

Shawn held on to her arm as she pushed to her feet and peered into the closet.

Disappointment joined the flutters in her stomach at the sight of the dusty but otherwise empty self.

"See anything?" Shawn asked.

"No."

A cracking sound punctuated the statement. Shawn wrapped his arms around her, swinging her away from the closet. The nightstand crashed to the floor, and one of the legs rolled into the wall with a thunk.

Shawn made no move to put her down. His face flushed with desire and something else that she wasn't sure she was ready to name. She put it aside and did the thing she'd wanted to do since she opened the door to her hotel room and found him standing there this morning.

She reached her arms around his neck and pulled him into a kiss. Shawn's mouth moved against hers without hesitation. The touch of his tongue finally ignited a fire inside her, and all she could think about was how right it felt to be in his arms. He was strong and solid. Confident, cocky even, but kind. For the first time, she let herself consider what it might be like to come home to him and be kissed like this for the rest of her life.

That thought had her breaking off the kiss abruptly. It was one kiss. An admittedly amazing kiss, she corrected mentally, but not a reason to consider changing her life. She had a plan. Find Cassie. Close the Browning–Tuffs merger. Make partner. A relationship just didn't fit into that plan.

"I think you can put me down now."

Confusion clouded Shawn's eyes, but he lowered her to the ground.

"We should check out the rest of the apartment." Addy smoothed her wrinkled shirt and shifted past Shawn and out of the bedroom, avoiding looking him in the eye.

If he had any thoughts about her abrupt change in attitude, he kept them to himself. It was unfair to have kissed him like that when she had no intention of letting anything between them blossom. Maybe she should apologize. But with one glance at the hardened features of his face, she knew that an apology would not go over well right now.

She sighed to herself. He was angry with her, and she deserved it for leading him on. It was something she'd have to deal with. Later.

Addy made her way to the kitchen, Shawn trailing behind her and detouring at the end of the hall into the smaller bedroom that had been Suri's. She opened the refrigerator. Empty. She hadn't expected to find anything inside, but the cool air was a welcome respite from the flames heating her body. She moved to the range and opened the oven door, once again unsurprised when she found it empty.

Addy was the cook in the family, finding it calming and satisfying to start with nothing but raw ingredients and transform them into something that she could share with her friends and family. She doubted Cassie had ever turned on the oven, but that made it the perfect hiding place.

She finished her search of the small kitchen with the cupboards, which held the plates, cups and pots that had come with the apartment. The cabinet drawers were similarly appointed, holding only silverware.

"There's nothing in there," Shawn said, exiting the second bedroom.

"Nothing here, either," Addy responded, frustration ringing from each word. "I guess we can get out of here."

Shawn lifted the ruffled sofa skirt and looked underneath. This time she made a point of not looking at him as he did.

Shawn stood and went to the middle of the room. His eyes passed over her, then stopped just to her right. He crossed to the small kitchen space, his eyes fixed on a point on the ceiling.

"There's an attic or crawl space up there." He pointed to a square cutout in the ceiling. A short string dangled from a hook on one side.

Shawn jumped, grabbing the string. The door swung down. A set of folding stairs had been attached to the inside, and Shawn unfolded them.

Addy stepped forward, ready to ascend the ladder and see what, if anything, was up there. She doubted very much Cassie would have stored anything inside, but she wasn't leaving the apartment without searching every inch of the space.

Shawn held out a hand, blocking her forward movement. "You should let me do it. We don't know how sturdy this old ladder is or what we'll find up there."

Tension rolled off him, and Addy understood what Shawn had not said. He was worried about finding Cassie's body in the attic.

Shawn reached around his back, drawing a gun from his waistband.

He climbed the ladder, gun held in front of him with one hand, the other steadying him as he climbed. He stopped slightly more than halfway up, twisting so he could see behind him and sweeping the gun from left to right.

"There's something up here." He returned the gun to his waistband at his back, signaling that whatever was in the attic wasn't a threat.

Her heart thudded at the possibility that the worst had happened and they'd just found Cassie.

Shawn climbed farther up the ladder, disappearing inside the attic. After a couple of minutes his head appeared. "Stand back."

A dark gray garbage bag landed at Addy's feet, followed by a second garbage bag moments later.

She knelt, opening a bag as Shawn made his way back down the ladder slowly, a box in his hands.

The trash bags contained women's clothes—jeans, tops, suits, skirts. Addy pulled a faded pink T-shirt from the pile.

"These are Cassie's clothes," Addy said, rooting around in the bags, finding more familiar pieces of clothing.

"And this box looks like it's full of some of her other things." Shawn lifted a sterling silver picture frame from the box open in front of him. Cassie, Addy and their father at Cassie's high school graduation.

Addy came to kneel next to Shawn, taking the picture from his hands. "Cassie would have never moved without taking this photograph with her."

Addy looked from the photo to Shawn, fear lassoing her heart.

"I think you're right. There are other things in here that I don't think she would have left behind."

Addy scrutinized the objects in the box. A journal with brightly colored swirls on its face. A cell phone charger, although the cell phone appeared to be absent. Cassie's comb, brush and several other grooming implements. All things that she'd have taken with her if she'd been moving back to New York or anywhere.

"I think we have to call Sheriff Donovan," Shawn said, standing. He reached a hand down to her.

She took his hand and let him help her up. "You think he's going to care? He's dug in on the Cassie-moved-away theory."

"He doesn't have much choice but to care. This stuff directly contradicts that theory." Shawn waved his hand over Cassie's belongings.

Addy wasn't so sure of that. Sheriff Donovan had had days to search the apartment and discover this stuff, and he hadn't. Prior experience with men like the sheriff told her that he'd most likely see their discovery as an encroachment on his authority, a sign that they didn't think he'd done his job, which he hadn't.

The sound of footsteps on the stairs outside the apartment drew both their attention before she could voice her concerns. The window in the living room faced the side of the adjacent building while the one in the kitchen looked out onto the small patch of grass at the back of the building. None of the windows in the apartment faced the front, where a visitor was most likely to park, which meant the occupants had no idea who was coming up the stairs.

Shawn reached behind his back for his gun with one hand and gave her a little push toward the hallway with the other. "Get into Cassie's bedroom and lock the door."

Addy moved to the hall but didn't go as far as Cassie's room. She pulled her phone from her back pocket, ready to dial for help.

A fist pounded on the door. "Sheriff. Open up."

Shawn peered out of the small keyhole in the door, his gun still in his hand. "It's Sheriff Donovan."

Addy let out the breath she'd been holding and put her phone in her pocket.

Shawn tucked his gun into the waistband of his jeans and opened the apartment door.

Sheriff Donovan's eyes landed on Shawn, and he grimaced. "What are you doing here? You're trespassing."

"We're doing no such thing," Addy said, moving to Ryan's side. "I'm the cosigner on the lease to this apartment, and I have a key." She pulled the key from her pocket and held it up for the sheriff to see.

"We were just about to call you, Donovan." Shawn swung the door open wide, stepping aside to let the sheriff in.

The lawman's expression was doubtful as he stepped inside the apartment. "You were? Why?"

"Addy and I took a look around to see if Cassie left any clue as to where she was going. We found something."

The sheriff's gaze narrowed, moving between Addy and Shawn. "Suri Bedingfield let me search this place when you made the initial missing-person complaint, Ms. Williams. All your sister's belongings were gone."

Addy planted her fists on her hips, fury swelling. "Maybe that's because you didn't look well enough." Donovan's eyes glinted darkly, but she didn't care. "We found my sister's clothes and personal items in the attic above the kitchen." She pointed.

"You were with Ms. Williams when she found these things?" Sheriff Donovan's gaze swung in Shawn's direction as if her word alone wasn't sufficient.

"Yes," Shawn responded calmly.

"Did you look in the attic when you did your search?" Addy demanded.

Sheriff Donovan glanced at the bags and box on the floor. "There was no reason to climb up there. Your sister's roommate claimed she'd moved out. Why shouldn't I have believed her?"

"Because I'm her sister, and I told you Cassie wouldn't have left town without telling me about it first." She struggled to keep her anger in check, knowing that yelling at the sheriff wasn't going to help her case with him. Still, her words came out louder than she'd planned.

"Look, Ms. Williams, we can't go chasing down every grown woman that up and leaves town."

Her frustration with the sheriff neared the tipping point.

Shawn's hand came down around her shoulders, and he spoke before she did. "Well, now you have evidence that suggests Cassie didn't just leave of her own will. Or are you suggesting she intended to move back to New York but left personal effects like her graduation picture and journal behind?"

Sheriff Donovan looked as if he wanted to argue the

point, but thought better of it. "I'll have one of my deputies come process those things for evidence. But I need you two out of here before you compromise the scene any further."

That was the last straw. Donovan hadn't done his job, so she'd had to do it for him, and he had the nerve to suggest that she'd compromised Cassie's missing-person case.

Addy stepped toward the sheriff, aware of his hand going to the butt of his weapon as she did, but too angry to stop herself from speaking. "If we hadn't come here and searched—"

Shawn reached for her hand, drawing her back toward him. "You'll let us know what you find, Sheriff," he said a little too loudly, cutting her off.

The sheriff didn't answer, just jerked his head toward the door.

Shawn pulled her from the apartment, his back never turned completely to the sheriff.

At the bottom of the steps, he turned to her, his mouth turned down in a frown. "You need to be more careful around Donovan."

"Don't you start with me." She was in no mood for a lecture, but the trembles rolling through her body weren't just anger. The import of what could easily have happened hit her. She marched to the Yukon.

"You have been Black in America your entire life, correct?"

"I. Said. Don't. Start." She grabbed the car's door handle and pulled. The door didn't budge.

She rested her forehead against the passenger window, unsure if she could have hoisted herself into the car if she'd gotten the door open. The adrenaline and rage high she'd been on when she'd confronted the sheriff receded, leaving nothing but the fear that she would never see Cassie again.

"I'm sorry. I know getting into it with the sheriff was stupid. I just..." A sob escaped at the same time the tears began rolling down her face.

Shawn wrapped his arms around her, cradling her into his chest.

The fear and concern she'd been holding inside for days erupted like a volcano. She couldn't stop it and instead gave in to it, holding on to Shawn like he was her lifeline, because for those few minutes he was the only thing holding her together.

After several minutes, she drew back out of his arms. "I'm sorry." She swiped at her eyes.

"Don't be. If the situation were reversed and one of my brothers was missing, I would have fallen apart a long time ago. Even if it was Ryan."

She let the ends of her mouth turn up at his paltry attempt at a joke.

"Let's get out of here." He beeped the car unlocked.

Addy slid to the side to let him open the passenger door for her. Propping a foot on the running board, she pulled herself into the car.

Shawn didn't immediately close the door, his attention focused on the front right tire. "Damn it."

He shut the door and the car beeped, an indication that he'd locked her inside.

She leaned forward in the leather seat, watching as Shawn crouched by the tire, running his hand over the thick rubber before moving around the front of the car and examining the tire there before getting in the car.

"What's wrong?"

"Someone punctured both the front tires."

Addy glanced back at the door to the duplex. "Sheriff Donovan?"

"We can't prove it," Shawn said, shooting a glance at the sheriff's nearby SUV.

The sheriff had parked his cruiser next to the Yukon. It would have been easy for him to slash the car's tires before heading inside. It probably wouldn't have taken more than half a minute to puncture both.

Shawn started the car. "All of West's vehicles have run-flat tires. I'll have to get new ones today, but I want to get us out of here right now."

"You think the sheriff wants to keep us here for a particular reason?" Addy asked, her heart jumping into her throat.

If the sheriff intended to hurt them, she'd nearly given him an excuse inside.

Shawn put the Yukon in gear and backed out of the parking space. His eyes met hers as the car rolled forward. "I don't know, but we aren't going to stick around to find out."

Chapter Nine

Shawn drove them back to the hotel and made a call to roadside assistance. A tech arrived within the hour and quickly changed the tires on the Yukon. Addy retreated to the bedroom in the suite.

She'd planned to get a quick nap, but her brain wouldn't shut down long enough to allow sleep to come.

Someone had put Cassie's things in that attic, most likely to make it look like Cassie had left town. As Cassie's boyfriend, Ben was a prime suspect, and his nervousness this morning added to Addy's suspicion of him. But Ben wasn't the only suspicious actor here.

Suri was missing in action. She still hadn't returned Addy's call. According to Sheriff Donovan, Suri had also reported that Cassie had moved back to New York. But it seemed unlikely that all Cassie's clothes and personal items would have made it into the attic without Suri knowing anything about it. Cassie and Suri had only met after Cassie placed an ad for a roommate with an online home-share company. The company had conducted background checks on both Suri and Cassie as part of their policy and Suri's had come back clean, but what did that mean, really? She was glad Shawn had thought to have his brother check into Suri. She had no doubt West would be far more thorough than the home-share company.

Addy's stomach clenched at the thought that Cassie might have been sharing a home with someone out to get her.

Addy's phone beeped a notification that she had a new voice mail. She listened as Jarod fumed about her needing to get back to the office now. As he fulminated, she scrolled through her emails, finding that Jarod had sent several new ones in the last couple hours.

She exited voice mail and dashed off a hasty email reassuring Jarod that she had things under control. She swung her legs over the side. The thought that had been floating just out of reach when she and Shawn arrived at Cassie's apartment crystallized.

She crossed the bedroom and opened the door.

Shawn looked up from the computer in his lap. "Have a good nap?"

"I couldn't sleep. I just kept wondering what it means that we found Cassie's stuff and still no Cassie."

"We're doing everything we can. We'll find her." The determination in his voice reassured her.

"What are you doing?" Addy crossed the room.

Shawn tapped several keys as she sat beside him. "Ryan sent the background checks I asked for on Ben and Suri."

"Yeah? Anything interesting?" She leaned into him, trying to see his screen, but the reflective coating over it made that impossible.

"Here. You won't be able to see it unless you're looking at it head-on." He shifted the laptop from his lap to hers.

The report on screen had Suri Bedingfield's name on

top, followed by her birth date, place of birth and other personal information.

"The interesting stuff is on the third page. Ry was able to get a current address in Garwin, but what's more interesting is that she's living in a condo that rents for fifteen hundred dollars a month."

Addy felt her eyes go wide. "How in the world?"

"How much was rent on the duplex?"

"Just under nine hundred a month."

Shawn laced his fingers behind his head. "So Suri went from paying four fifty a month in rent to over a thousand? And her new job. It's not in food service." Shawn leaned forward, pointing to an area at the bottom of the screen. "She's working as an office manager for a sprinkler manufacturer."

"How? Becky said Suri worked for her since she'd dropped out of high school. Why would this company hire her to manage their office with no management experience?"

"That's an excellent question," Shawn said but offered no answer.

A myriad of thoughts collided in Addy's mind. "Part of the reason I couldn't get any sleep was thinking about whether Suri could have had a hand in Cassie's disappearance." Addy waved a hand at the computer screen. "This, none of this, makes any sense."

"I think we should take a ride to Garwin tomorrow."

"Can't we go tonight?"

Shawn ran a hand over the shadow of stubble on his jaw. "I can't. I have a meeting I have to go to tonight, and I want to look into Suri a little more before we question her."

Addy crossed her arms. "What about the report on Ben?"

"The associate's degree in business is legit. He's got a couple pops on his record for marijuana. Using, not selling. I'd bet there are a few more on a sealed juvie record somewhere. But nothing that stands out."

She set the laptop aside and got to her feet. "But the way he acted this morning? And now with finding Cassie's stuff hidden in the apartment. That proves he and Suri were lying about Cassie moving." She fisted her hands on her hips.

"It doesn't prove anything." Shawn stood. He held up a hand. "I'm not saying Donovan and the others are right. But Cassie could have put those things there herself. We have no proof she didn't."

Frustration swelled in Addy's chest. She had to be back in New York in two days, and so far she'd only managed to find more questions and absolutely no answers.

"I remembered what was bothering me at Cassie's apartment. Her scooter is missing."

"Scooter?"

"Cassie bought a little scooter to get to and from work. It wasn't in the apartment's parking lot."

Shawn ran a hand over his head. "We should call Donovan and see if we can get him to put out an APB on the scooter."

Addy frowned. Their last encounter with the sheriff hadn't gone well. "You really think he'll help us?"

"I don't know, but it can't hurt to ask. After we do that, I want to go talk to Ben again."

She glanced at her watch. "It's quarter after four. If we hurry, we might still catch him at Spectrum. I can call the sheriff on the way."

"Great. Just give me a minute." Shawn rose and disappeared into the bedroom.

She scanned a few more pages in the report on Suri, then moved the mouse to the task bar. The cursor hovered over Ben's report, but the document next to it caught her eye.

She left clicked, bringing up a background report bearing her name.

It contained more information about her than she'd have thought possible for someone outside law enforcement to get—where she lived, worked, even banked. The report contained details of her father's illness and death; even a copy of her divorce settlement appeared as an attachment at the end of the document.

Comment bubbles appeared throughout the document identifying their author as Ryan West. Little notes about one thing or another in her life. She scrolled through them, stopping at a note made in the paragraph highlighting her father's $100,000 life insurance policy and the amount of debt her divorce and her father's illness had left her with.

100k reasons for A to disappear C? Ryan had commented.

A wave of anger rose inside her that turned unexpectedly sharp as she read Shawn's typed response.

Look into who gets the money.

The rational side of her brain attempted to interject reason. One amazing weekend together six months ago didn't give Shawn a reason to trust her. He didn't know her, and when a person went missing it was most often at the hands of those closest to them, right?

Still, she found it hard to be rational. Hurt stabbed her in the chest.

Shawn thought she was capable of hurting Cassie. It felt like a betrayal.

The bathroom door squeaked as it opened.

She minimized the report with her name and brought Suri's back on screen.

"Ready to go?" Shawn asked.

"Yeah, sure." She set the laptop aside and got to her feet.

A crease bloomed above Shawn's brow. "You okay?"

"Fine. We should go before Spectrum closes."

Chapter Ten

The temperature had fallen another ten degrees by the time Shawn and Addy arrived at Spectrum just before five. He'd spoken to Ryan while Addy had attempted to take a nap. Ryan had agreed that finding Cassie's things wasn't a good sign, but he hadn't been ready to let go of the theory that Cassie might be somehow involved in the chip fraud.

He'd given serious thought to coming clean with Addy about the possibility that Cassie's disappearance had something to do with a multimillion-dollar scheme to sell fraudulent computer chips. In the end, obligation to the client won out, and he said nothing.

Not that Addy appeared to want to talk to him. She'd been silent for most of the drive, only speaking in response to a question or statement from him, and only with the briefest of responses.

He'd been around enough women to know when one was angry, although he couldn't imagine why she'd be angry with him. If anyone should be upset, it should be him.

When she'd kissed him, he'd stupidly allowed himself to think, for just the briefest of seconds, that they might have a chance. But then she'd pulled away like his lips had turned to molten lava and had avoided even looking him in the eye.

The least she could do if he'd done something to upset her was to tell him.

"Something bothering you?" he asked in a clipped tone.

"No, I'm fine," Addy answered without taking her eyes from the scenery passing by outside the car window.

Fine. If she didn't want to talk, they wouldn't talk. He wasn't in any rush to get kicked in the teeth again, anyway.

He parked the Yukon in the same parking lot from that morning, and he and Addy made their way to Spectrum offices.

Unlike earlier that morning, no one sat behind the reception desk.

"That's fortunate. Let's go on back. Maybe we can catch Ben off guard."

They walked side by side, but he made sure to keep a respectable distance between them. Addy stayed in step with him but didn't look his way as they made their way through the corridors of the office.

The floor was emptier than it had been earlier in the day. The door to Ben's office stood open, but it was empty, the lights off. When did this guy work?

"Can you act as a lookout while I search?"

"Lookout? You sound like we're about to pull off a heist," Addy said, the corners of her mouth turning up slightly.

He felt some of the pressure in his chest loosen.

Addy stood near the door while he went to Ben's desk.

He wiggled the mouse next to the desktop computer. The screen came to life, demanding a password.

He turned the keyboard over and searched under the desk. Despite the many high-profile hacking incidents in the past several years, people still did asinine things like taping their passwords to their computers and desks. It appeared Ben wasn't one of those people, but he didn't lock his desk drawers, not that there appeared to be a need for him to. The drawers were empty except for the usual office products—pens, a box of paper clips, a letter opener. In the larger bottom drawer, Shawn found three legal pads, still in the cellophane wrapper. He'd only been in the job a matter of weeks, but it certainly didn't seem like Spectrum had given Ben a ton of responsibility.

Shawn went to his knees and reached upward, running his hand over the underside of the top drawer. He hadn't expected to find anything but wasn't surprised when his hand moved over a small square envelope taped to the underside.

He pulled the envelope free and opened it.

A computer chip with the Intellus logo stamped on it fell into his hand.

"Someone is coming," Addy hissed, stepping away from the office door.

He put the chip back in the envelope and shoved it into his back pocket. Using one hand, he grabbed a square Post-it pad and pen from the desk. He hunched over the desk as if he'd been writing out a note to leave for Ben.

"What are you doing in this office? Who are you?" A slender man with unnaturally bronze skin available only in a tanning salon stopped in Ben's office doorway.

"I'm Addy Williams. I'm Cassie Williams's sister. This is my friend Shawn West."

Shawn straightened, waving the sticky note he'd

quickly scrawled in the air. "We were just leaving a note for Ben."

As if a light had been switched on, the man's frown turned into a smile. "I'm Lance Raupp, vice president of Spectrum Industries."

Lance stretched his hand out to Addy while his eyes swept over her body in obvious examination.

"Martin Raupp's your father?"

Lance's eyes flashed surprise. "Have you met?"

"Earlier today."

Shawn rounded the desk, his jaw tightening in irritation. Lance held on to Addy's hand much longer than was appropriate. Shawn stopped next to Addy, thrusting his hand out.

Lance frowned but dropped Addy's hand and shook Shawn's in a tight grip.

Lance took his hand, smirking as he did so, Shawn's pique and the reason for it apparently not lost on the man.

"We spoke to Ben this morning, and we were hoping to catch him for a few follow-up questions, but it looks like we missed him," Addy said, taking a step closer to Shawn while putting more distance between herself and Lance.

"I'm sure Ben will do whatever he can to help you locate your sister, but I believe he went home early today." Lance turned a charming smile on Addy.

"Maybe you can help, then," Shawn said.

Lance's gaze narrowed on Shawn. "Spectrum is a small company, but I can't say I knew Miss Williams."

"But you were aware she'd gone missing? How is that?" Shawn asked.

"As I said, Spectrum is a small company. Word gets around. I was under the impression Miss Williams moved back to her hometown of New York City." Lance pulled at the cuff of his left sleeve.

"She didn't," Addy said flatly. "We have reason to believe she didn't leave Bentham on her own, if she left town at all."

Lance raised an eyebrow, shooting Addy a curious look. "Really? And what, may I ask, gives rise to this belief?"

"Did Sheriff Donovan interview you?" Shawn asked without acknowledging Lance's question.

Lance gave Shawn a probing look, no doubt an action that had made many a man squirm. Unfortunately for Lance, he was not one of those men. Shawn met the other man's gaze with equal scrutiny.

"No. No doubt he saw no need to do so. Miss Williams was an intern. Caroline Webb, my human resources director, was her supervisor."

"Would you mind if we spoke to Ms. Webb again?"

"I know the sheriff already talked to her, but I'm sure she'd be happy to speak with you." This time his smile was tight and forced.

"Everyone seems willing to buy into the theory that Cassie just woke up one day and left town. But as you said, she was a solid, dependable worker. Wouldn't she, as a solid, dependable employee, have given notice to her employer?"

"I don't know. I'm sure you know your sister better than I do." Lance turned away from Shawn, sliding another smile at Addy.

Shawn fought the desire to punch the man in the face. Thankfully, Addy didn't seem to be buying Lance's routine.

Her eyes narrowed on Lance. "You're right, I do know

my sister. Even if Cassie had decided to move home, she would have given notice. An email or phone call would have only taken minutes."

In the several silent moments that passed, Shawn read the change in Lance. He realized the charming shtick wasn't going to lead to Addy falling all over him. Abandoning it, he adopted what Shawn suspected was a much more natural countenance. Superiority.

Lance glanced at the expensive Rolex on his wrist. He'd schooled his facial features into an expression of boredom.

"I don't know what to tell you," he said while tapping his right foot.

Shawn had spent enough time studying people to know a nervous tic when he saw one.

Lance looked back at Addy, his expression not nearly as friendly as before. "I'm late for a meeting."

"Lance," a voice called from the hall. "Here you are." Martin Raupp appeared at the door to Ben's office. "Oh, Ms. Williams, Mr. West, so nice to see you both again. Has there been any news on Cassie's whereabouts?"

"I'm afraid not," Addy answered.

Martin took both her hands in his. "Please know I am keeping her and you in our nightly prayers."

"Thank you," Addy said.

Shawn's gaze danced between the two Mr. Raupps. Martin Raupp appeared to be genuinely concerned about his missing employee. Unfortunately, the apple seemed to have fallen far from the tree with respect to the man's son.

"Lance, we're late for the meeting with the distributor." Martin's bushy eyebrows rose.

"I'm going to have to ask you to leave Ben's office

since he's not here." Lance stepped aside, gesturing for Addy and Shawn to leave the office.

They moved past Lance out of the office, and he snapped the door closed.

Shawn spoke just as both Raupps began walking away. "If you could just remind us of the location of Ms. Webb's office before you go."

Lance did a slow turn, facing Addy and Shawn once again. "I think she's also left for the day. Maybe you can give her a call tomorrow and set up a time that works for all of you." Lance's smile didn't reach his eyes.

The likelihood that all they'd ever get was Ms. Webb's voice mail was one hundred percent.

"That was interesting," Addy said, watching Lance and his father turn the corner at the end of the hall.

"You can say that again. Come on. I've got to get you back to the hotel."

Darkness had descended on the town while they were inside, and the temperature had fallen even farther. They hustled to the Yukon. Neither spoke until they were inside with the heat blasting away the frigid air.

"We need to go see Suri Bedingfield," Addy said as Shawn pulled into late-afternoon traffic. "She and Ben are the ones who said Cassie left town. If we can't find him and make him tell us why they lied, we have to find her and make her tell us."

"Tomorrow morning."

"Tomorrow? Garwin is only a forty-five minute drive."

He shot her a sidelong glance. "I have somewhere I need to be this evening."

"But if we can get Suri to admit she lied about Cassie leaving town, Sheriff Donovan will have to take her disappearance seriously."

"We will. I just can't do it tonight."

"What? I—"

Her phone rang, interrupting whatever she'd planned to say. She scrambled for the purse at her feet, pulling the phone from the outside pocket quickly, her face awash with hope. Her face fell when she saw the screen. "Damn it." He watched her punch the ignore button.

"We'll go to Garwin first thing in the morning and talk to Suri before she leaves for work."

Addy stared out of the passenger side window, saying nothing further. Anger poured off her.

He pulled into a parking space in the hotel's lot and turned to her. "I'm sorry, but I can't miss this meeting." He reached for her hand, and she turned toward him. "It's for the case I'm in town on. This will give you a chance to catch up on work."

Addy pulled her hand back. "No, I understand," she said, getting out of the car.

His jaw clenched as he got out of the driver's side and rounded the car. They fell in step next to each other, headed for the hotel entrance.

"Addy, wait."

She marched on. "You've spent most of your time helping me, and I'm grateful, but you have a job to do," Addy said.

The stiffness in her body made it clear she was still upset, but there wasn't anything he could do about it. "First thing tomorrow. I promise."

Shawn got Addy safely ensconced in the suite before heading out again. He felt bad that they couldn't go to Garwin to talk to Suri this evening, but he only had two days until the fraudulent chips were supposed to be delivered. He'd been neglecting the Intellus case.

His first stop was to a twenty-four-hour courier service. He suspected the chip he found in Ben's office was one of the knockoffs, but he needed the computer gurus back at West to make the final determination. The courier service assured him that they could have the chip at West's New York offices by 10:00 p.m. that night.

He dialed the number for West's tech department.

"Sup?" Tansy Carlson answered the phone. He could see her short, spiky pink hair and array of silver lip rings in his mind's eye. Tansy was one of West's best computer technicians. He quickly explained the situation. Long nights and unusual hours weren't out of the ordinary for West's employees, and Tansy assured him she'd be on hand to receive and process the chip as soon as it arrived.

He ended the call and headed to the address for Spectrum's factory.

The factory was located twenty minutes outside town on a street lined with dingy gray warehouses.

Shawn drove around the perimeter of the building. A brass plaque next to the front entrance denoted the factory as a "Carrier-Forest LLC property." He made a mental note to research the LLC when he returned to the hotel and continued to circle the building.

A tall chain-link fence encircled the property. Security cameras pointed at the front and side doors, as well as the doors leading from the building to the loading dock. That didn't mean much. Anyone capable of using Spectrum's distribution line to create fraudulent chips wouldn't have much difficulty getting around the security cameras.

Shawn parked on the street at the far edge of the factory property, out of sight of the cameras. Workers began trickling out of the employee entrance at exactly five thirty, and by five thirty-five, men and women streamed from the building in pairs and small groups. A young white blond man and a stockier man with dark skin and black hair headed for the far corner of the parking lot.

The blond reached for the door handle on a beat-up red pickup truck with a white-paneled door and called over the top of the truck, "Hey, Jorge. Got time for a drink?"

Jorge pointed his keys at a newer black pickup truck with chrome wheels, beeping it unlocked. "The missus is visiting her sister this week. I'm a free man." Jorge threw his arms open wide and grinned.

The blond laughed as both men got into their respective pickup trucks.

Shawn put the Yukon in gear and followed the trucks a short distance to a sports bar.

Music streamed from overhead speakers, and televisions strategically placed around the restaurant and over the bar beamed various sports events in closed caption.

About half the tables in the dining section were full, and a half dozen people sat scattered around the large bar.

Shawn grabbed a seat two stools down from the Spectrum employees he'd followed.

They'd ordered beers and chatted loudly enough for Shawn to hear their conversation.

Mostly work stuff. He overheard the blond refer to Lance Raupp as a jerk, a determination Shawn couldn't argue with. The stockier guy seemed to prefer to gossip about a coworker's extramarital affair.

The blond guy left to use the washroom, and Shawn turned to Jorge. "You guys work at Spectrum?"

Jorge cut his eyes toward Shawn, a wary look creasing his brow. "Yeah."

"I couldn't help but overhear. Man, I applied for a delivery job weeks ago, but I haven't heard nothin'."

Jorge cocked his head to the side and angled his body so he faced Shawn. "Yeah, it can be hard to get in the door."

"Even harder if you have a record. Did a year and a half for selling dope, only to get out and find out they made the stuff legal?" Shawn twisted his lip into a disgusted sneer that was only partially practiced. It really was messed up how many Black and brown people languished in jail for doing what legislatures in an increasing number of states now made millions of dollars in tax revenue on.

"Yeah, ain't that a trip. I got a cousin in prison right now for selling the same stuff the gringos in Massachusetts are making bank on." Jorge tipped his beer at Shawn. "Different rules for them."

Shawn signaled the bartender for another beer and leaned toward Jorge as if he was about to reveal the secrets of the universe. "The job I applied for, it's loading boxes onto delivery trucks. I've worked for big-time companies like Spectrum before. Not all the guys on the loading docks show up in the company books. You know what I mean?"

The leather-faced bartender slid an open bottle in front of Shawn without stopping, moving to the other end of the bar.

Jorge eyed Shawn, assessing.

Shawn held the man's gaze, waiting for Jorge to decide whether to trust Shawn.

The blond guy returned before Jorge rendered his final judgment.

"Hey, you ready for round two?" The blond clapped a hand on Jorge's shoulder.

"This is Shawn," Jorge said, pointing. "Shawn. Granger. He works with me at Spectrum. Shawn was just asking about working at Spectrum. You know, the kind of work Alvin does sometimes."

Jorge slid a look at Granger.

Granger's bushy blond brows lowered. "We don't know nothing about that. Try human resources."

"No problem." Shawn raised his hands. "If you say Spectrum is a hundred percent legit, it's a hundred percent legit."

Jorge snorted. "I wouldn't say that."

"Jorge."

Jorge waved his friend off. "Spectrum sometimes hires off the books. I'd usually throw the work my cousin's way." Jorge shrugged. "I can't promise anything, but I can let you know if I hear anything."

The blond man scowled and took his beer to the other end of the bar.

"Can't ask for more than that." Shawn jotted his phone number on a napkin and passed it to Jorge.

He shot the breeze with Jorge for a while longer before leaving the bar.

He knew putting off talking to Suri Bedingfield until morning had disappointed Addy, but at least his trip to the bar had been fruitful. If Spectrum used off-the-books labor, they'd most likely use it to move their fraudulent chips. Hopefully, Jorge would call tomorrow with an illicit job offer Shawn would be more than happy to accept.

He stopped off at the diner and picked up a piece of

apple pie as a peace offering to Addy before heading to the hotel.

His phone rang as he exited the Yukon and headed inside. He pressed the button on the speaker hooked around his ear.

"Hey, Ryan. I'm making progress on the case." He spoke before his brother could.

He filled Ryan in on finding the chip with the Intellus logo in Ben's office and the conversation he'd had with Jorge.

"That chip is a good find, but it won't be enough by itself." Ryan voiced Shawn's earlier conclusion.

Shawn stepped off the elevator and headed toward the suite.

"I know. I plan to track down Ben Konstam tomorrow and lean on him hard to get him to talk."

Shawn held his key card against the black box affixed to the room door. Two beeps sounded, and the red dot on the door turned green.

The darkened living room had him dropping the pie to the floor and reaching for the Glock in his waistband before he crossed the room's threshold. It was only eight thirty, far too early for Addy to have gone to bed.

"Addy?" He held his gun low but at the ready.

"What's wrong?" Ryan demanded.

Shawn didn't answer his brother.

He flicked on the lights, taking in every inch of the room in moments. The bedroom door was open.

His heart beat wildly, but he listened past it, ears perked for any sound in the suite.

He moved forward quickly, checking the bathroom and the closet.

The suite was empty.

"Shawn? Talk to me. What's going on?"

He forced the words past the lump that had formed in his throat.

"Addy's gone."

Chapter Eleven

Snow began to fall as Addy left the Bentham town limits, leaving the streets slick and turning the forty-five-minute trip between Bentham and Garwin into an hour-and-a-half drive. Sitting alone in the suite after Shawn left, the sense that she was running out of time to find Cassie had grown until it nearly overwhelmed Addy. She was grateful for his help, but there was no reason she had to wait for him to talk to Suri.

She'd only had a quick glimpse at the Garwin address in the background report West had done on Suri Bedingfield, but she'd remembered it easily.

Skirting the New York–Massachusetts border, Garwin was twice the size of Bentham but still much smaller than New York City. Three decades ago, the city's politicians had successfully courted a midsize pharmaceutical company, which had established its headquarters in Garwin. Other businesses sprouted up to support the influx of new residents, making Garwin an important small city in the area. The Garwin City Council must have used the same holiday decorator as Bentham—strings of white lights twisted around the base of every lamppost, with red-and-green happy-holidays banners as toppers.

Addy found an open parking spot on the busy street

in the heart of downtown Garwin, across from a modern glass-and-chrome high-rise. It looked like Shawn was right about Suri's new apartment being an improvement over the duplex she and Cassie had shared.

Addy's phone rang as she exited the Mustang. She didn't need to look at the screen to know the caller was Shawn.

For a brief moment, she contemplated not answering, but she didn't want to worry him unnecessarily. She stopped on the sidewalk next to the car and connected the call. "Hello, Shawn."

"Are you okay? Where are you?" The panic threading his words sent a stab of guilt through her.

"I'm fine. I'm in Garwin on my way to talk to Suri."

Shawn swore. "Have you talked to her yet?"

The wind whistled by, buoyed by the tunnel created by the high-rise buildings on either side of the street. She pulled her coat tight against the gale. "No. I just got to her apartment. I haven't gone in."

"Good. Don't. We don't know if she had a hand in Cassie's disappearance. She could be dangerous."

"I doubt she's going to do anything to me in her apartment. It's a big building. Lots of neighbors to overhear and a doorman who would notice if I didn't come back down."

"Addy, just wait for me. I can be there in an hour."

She shook her head, dashing behind a white minivan and across the street. "I'll be fine, Shawn. I've got to go."

Addy ended the call before he could argue further and headed toward the apartment building. No point arguing. She was here, and she wasn't going to wait another minute to get answers.

She already felt as if a clock ticked over her head,

every passing minute leading her further and further away from finding Cassie. Every fiber of her being screamed that Cassie was still alive, but the same intuition told Addy that Cassie wouldn't remain that way if she wasn't found soon.

She tugged open the heavy glass doors and crossed the white marble–tiled floors to the doorman's station.

A lanky young man in a turban and a doorman's uniform smiled as she approached. "Good evening. May I help you?"

"I'm here to see Suri Bedingfield."

"Your name, ma'am?" the doorman asked, reaching for the phone on his desk.

Addy gave her full name and waited while the phone rang. After several rings, the doorman replaced the receiver in its cradle. "I'm sorry. It seems Miss Bedingfield isn't at home presently. Would you like to leave a message for her?"

Addy looked at the phone still in her hand. A text from Shawn waited, but she ignored it and looked at the time. Fifteen minutes after seven. Suri could just be working late.

"No. No, thank you. I'll try her again later."

She jogged back across the street to her car. Sliding in, she turned the engine back on and cranked up the air. She'd already made the trip; it wouldn't hurt to wait awhile.

She dashed off a text to Shawn while she waited.

S not home yet. Waiting to see if I can catch her.

The number of pedestrians streaming by on the sidewalk diminished considerably as Addy waited for Suri to return home.

Twenty minutes into the wait, with no response from Shawn to her text, the phone rang. She answered without checking the caller ID, fully expecting the person on the other end of the phone to be a furious Shawn. Instead, she got a furious Jarod.

"Addy, finally. We need you back here now," Jarod barked.

Addy bit back a swear. "Jarod, we talked about this. It's Tuesday. I'll be back in time for the meeting on Thursday."

"You said you'd be available, and you haven't been," Jarod snapped. "I'm not confident you're ready for this meeting. The presentation slides are all wrong. They need to be redone, and you need to be in the office tomorrow by nine."

There were nearly sixty associates in the practice group who could rewrite the presentation, which was perfectly fine the way it was. Not to mention Jarod could do more than shake the client's hand and take all the credit if he really felt that more should be done.

She shook her head even though she knew he couldn't see her. "I can't do that. Transfer the project to another senior associate if you feel that's best."

"Transfer," Jarod sputtered. "The clients love you. How do you expect me to explain your absence to them? No, I expect you in the office tomorrow at nine," Jarod said, his tone indicating he expected that to be the final word. Outside, the moon came out from behind a cloud, spraying light across the windshield.

It suddenly became crystal clear to Addy just how much Jarod and the firm would require her to sacrifice to make partner.

Her stomach flip-flopped wildly, but her voice held steady. "I quit."

An SUV swooshed past her parked car, but the other end of the phone line remained silent for several long seconds.

"Addy, think about this," Jarod said in a tone that was softer and far more conciliatory than it had been a moment ago. "You're a year away from making partner. Everything you've worked for. This is about your career here."

"No, Jarod. This is about something more important than my career. This is about finding my sister." She hung up the phone without giving her boss another chance to speak.

Her hands shook.

A voice screamed in her head to call back. Apologize. Smooth things over. But she knew the only way to make things right was to show up at Covington and Baker tomorrow at nine, and that was something she just could not do.

She tucked her phone into the side pocket of her purse and tried to focus on what needed to be done to find Cassie.

Thirty more minutes passed before Addy finally spied Suri strolling down the sidewalk toward the building.

Addy had only met Suri once, when she'd visited Cassie not long after she'd moved to Bentham. She'd been pleasant but standoffish, mostly staying in her room when Addy and Cassie were in the apartment. Then, the slight blonde had worn her hair long and mostly up in a messy bun. Though Suri and Cassie were the same age, Suri looked years older and perpetually tired.

Even from a distance, Addy could see that Suri had

undergone a significant makeover. She'd lightened her dark blond hair and cut it into a stylish angled bob. Suri's sleek black suit and strappy heels looked to be designer.

She waited until Suri entered the lobby of her building and disappeared into the elevator before exiting her car a second time. She started around the front of the car and pulled up short as a large dark figure moved in from her right.

Addy yelped, tripping backward over the curb.

A hand shot out, steadying her before she fell. "Take it easy. It's just me."

"Jeez. You scared me. What are you doing here?"

The tic in Shawn's jaw returned. "You took the words right out of my mouth."

"Look, I get you have a paying client to answer to, but my sister could be in serious trouble. I will not wait around while you chase down some cheating husband or whatever."

Shawn's nostrils flared. "That's not fair. I've been right there with you looking for Cassie."

Addy averted her gaze, guilt tripping through her. He was right. He and West Security had gone above and beyond helping her look for Cassie.

She held up a hand. "Look, can we discuss this later? We're both here now, so let's just go talk to Suri."

His jaw twitched, but he stepped to the side, sweeping his arm out in an "after you" gesture.

They crossed the street and entered the lobby of Suri's building.

The doorman smiled anew as Addy approached. "Would you like me to try Miss Bedingfield again?"

"Yes, please."

This time Suri answered the phone, but from the doorman's facial expression, she wasn't happy to hear who her visitors were.

Before the doorman could hang up the phone, Addy leaned forward over the top of his high standing desk. "Suri, we found Cassie's things in the attic of the apartment. You can talk to us or you can talk to the police. Your choice."

The doorman's mouth fell open at the mention of the police.

"Let them up," Suri said from the other end of the line.

Shawn and Addy stepped out of the elevator on the tenth floor and headed to Suri's apartment halfway down the hall.

The door swung open at the first knock.

Suri had changed from her work clothes into a pair of cutoff shorts and an Atlantic City tank top. The scowl on her face was a contradiction with her beach-friendly attire.

"I don't know why you're here. I already told Sheriff Donovan everything I know."

"I don't think that's true," Addy said. "Can we come in?"

Suri's scowl deepened, but she stepped aside so Addy and Shawn could come in. She closed the door and crossed the room.

"Who's he?" Suri asked, falling onto a lime-green couch in the small living/dining space.

Addy sat at the opposite end of the couch while Shawn leaned a shoulder against the wall separating the kitchen from the living area and crossed his arms over his chest.

"He's a private investigator helping me locate Cassie."

Suri's eyes roamed over Shawn like a predator sizing up its prey.

Addy's dislike for the young woman deepened.

"We know you lied about Cassie leaving town, and we can prove it," Addy said. Maybe not the subtlest approach, but she was low on patience.

"I didn't lie," Suri spat.

"Then why did we find Cassie's clothes and other things in the attic of the apartment you two shared? Cassie wouldn't have moved without taking her things."

Suri squared her shoulders, but Addy read the fear in her eyes before they darted away. "Maybe. I don't know anything about that."

"So someone broke into your apartment and packed up all Cassie's things without you knowing a thing about it?" Addy struggled to keep her voice even against her rising fury.

Suri shifted, pushing her back against the arm of the sofa and putting as much room as possible between them. Still, her voice rang with defiance. "Cassie did talk about moving back to New York."

The *but* hung heavy in the air.

Addy glared silently.

Suri sighed. "The last couple of days before she left or whatever, Cassie was worried or something. She didn't tell me what it was about, but I think she was mad at Ben, or maybe they broke up or something, because she wouldn't take his calls and I know they hadn't been out on a date in a while."

"Why didn't you tell the sheriff about this?" Shawn asked.

Suri shot a look at him, then moved her gaze to the window. One shoulder went up. "I forgot."

Addy leaned forward across the sofa into Suri's personal space. "That's not going to fly."

Suri pushed to her feet and crossed to the television. Snatching a pack of cigarettes and a lighter from the stand, she lit up, blowing a ring of smoke up to the ceiling. "Look, I didn't want no trouble then, and I don't want any now." She jabbed the cigarette in Addy's direction.

Addy stood. "Then tell us the truth."

Suri rolled her eyes. "Fine. Whatever. That guy Teddy came by like two weeks ago and told me to say Cassie had moved back to New York. If you ever meet Teddy, you'll know why I did what I was told. That guy is deranged." A shudder rocked Suri's bare shoulders.

A picture of Teddy's menacing dark eyes popped into Addy's head.

"Okay, what about Cassie's clothes being in the attic?"

"I don't know anything about that. For real," Suri said when Addy shot a disbelieving look at her across the room. "Teddy said Cassie had left town and her stuff was gone. That's all I know."

"That's not all." Shawn spoke again.

Suri took another drag on her cigarette, blowing it in Shawn's direction.

He didn't blink. "How'd you get your new job and this fancy apartment, Suri?"

"That's none of your business." Suri ground her cigarette out on the side of the TV stand, not for the first time from the marks on it.

"It is if you had a hand in killing Cassie Williams," Shawn shot back.

Everything in Addy revolted at the idea, but she kept quiet and let Shawn press Suri. She recognized the question needed to be asked, and she wasn't able to do it.

Suri's eyes went to slits. "I didn't kill anyone."

Addy swallowed hard, pushing her words past the

lump in her throat. "Why lie, then? Cassie was gone. If you were really afraid of Teddy, why not tell the police what you know?"

"'Cause I have to look out for myself. I'm not a rich girl slumming it before I go off to MIT. When Ben came around offering me a real job and this apartment, I knew it was in exchange for keeping my mouth shut." Suri shrugged. "I didn't see a better offer coming my way, so I took it."

It was obvious Suri was jealous of Cassie. But what kind of person lied about another's disappearance? Her sister could be hurt or worse, and Suri didn't care at all. Her casual disregard for Cassie's safety sent anger pulsing in Addy's veins.

Addy hopped up off the couch, crossed the room and got in Suri's face before Suri processed the action.

"Without a thought for Cassie?" she hissed. "Don't you care at all that Cassie could be in serious trouble?"

Rage nearly blinded Addy. Her hands balled into fists at her side.

"Hey, I said I didn't have anything to do with Cassie disappearing or getting killed or anything like that. For all I knew she did move back to New York."

"Where is Cassie?" Addy yelled, grabbing Suri by the shoulders and shaking the slighter woman. "What did you do to my sister?"

"Get off me." Suri struggled, trying to push her away, but fueled by a combination of pure fury and fear, Addy's grip on the woman was strong.

Shawn crossed the small space in two steps, dropping a heavy hand on Addy's shoulder. "Let her go, sweetheart. She doesn't know anything more that can help us."

Addy let her hands drop from Suri's shoulders.

Shawn wrapped his arms around Addy's shoulders, and she leaned into him.

"I'm calling the cops," Suri screamed, backing away to the other side of the room. "She assaulted me in my own home."

Somehow she doubted Suri would follow through on the threat, though. Although she would be within her rights to file charges. For the first time in as long as Addy could remember, she had completely lost control.

Shawn gave voice to Addy's thoughts. "Do that. I'm sure they'd be interested in what we have to say about why we came to see you, Miss Bedingfield."

Suri's whole body shook, whether with anger or fear, Addy wasn't sure. Maybe a bit of both. "Get out."

Shawn shot Suri a hard look. "Come on, Addy. Let's go."

Shawn grabbed her arm, but Addy dug her heels into the floor.

Addy locked eyes with Suri. "If my sister is hurt, Teddy will look like a teddy bear compared to what I'll do to you."

Chapter Twelve

Addy had hoped to make it back to the hotel before Shawn. A little time for her nerves to settle before the inevitable argument would have been nice, but the Yukon rode the Mustang's bumper the entire way back to Bentham.

Shawn moved to her side the moment she got out of her car.

"What were you thinking, going to see Suri without me?" A couple passing by them in the parking lot glanced their way, the pace of their steps increasing as they did.

"Don't you think we should have this conversation in private?"

Addy turned and headed for the hotel without waiting for his response. Shawn fell into step beside her, and they rode the elevator in silence. With each passing floor, her anger grew.

Who was he to be angry at her for going to see Suri? Yes, he was helping her, but she was a grown woman. She didn't need his permission to go anywhere.

Not to mention he and his brother seemed to think she might have something to do with Cassie's disappearance in some bid to inherit Cassie's portion of their father's insurance. A thought broke through her fury. Maybe Shawn coming to her aid when he did, injecting himself into the search for Cassie, wasn't a coincidence at all. Maybe he wouldn't tell her about his case because she was his case, and he was investigating whether she had something to do with Cassie's disappearance. But who would have hired him?

The insurance company, maybe, but the small amount of insurance her father had held would hardly warrant an investigation. The money hadn't even covered a third of his medical bills. And the company had already paid out. No, that made no sense.

Still, she couldn't shake the feeling that Shawn's offer to help find Cassie wasn't one hundred percent altruistic.

Shawn opened the door to the suite and let Addy pass into the room.

She rounded on him before the hotel room door clicked shut. "I don't know who you think you are, but I don't take orders from you."

He tossed the key card on the table and met her head-on. "I didn't order you to do anything. We agreed we'd go see Suri together in the morning."

"We didn't agree to anything," she shot back, pointing a finger at him. "You said you had something else to do. Fine. I didn't. The only thing I care about is finding Cassie, and I'll do whatever I have to do to do that, with or without you."

"You could have been in real danger confronting Suri alone. The lies we already know she's told could put her in jail for a significant amount of time. If it turns out she knows more than she's saying or had a hand in Cassie's disappearance, that gives her even more incentive to keep you quiet."

Addy threw her hands in the air. "I can take care of myself."

"I didn't say you couldn't, but it's stupid to run head-first into a potentially dangerous situation without backup when you don't have to."

"Backup? Are you referring to yourself? Because I'm starting to question if I do, in fact, have backup?"

Shawn's expression hardened. "What the hell does that mean?"

"Tell me about the case that brought you to Bentham." She fisted her hands on her hips.

"I told you I can't. The client wants to keep it confidential."

"I saw the background check you had West do on me."

Wrinkles appeared on Shawn's forehead. "The background—Addy, we do background checks on all our clients. It's standard operating procedure."

"Except I'm not a client. You showed up at my hotel room with this serendipitous offer to help me find my sister. Why? Why do you even care if you have another case you're working on?"

She watched his jaw clench. "I explained that. I needed a cover that explained why I was in town, and I knew West could help you find Cassie."

"Is that the only reason?" Addy kept her eyes trained on Shawn's face, looking for any hint of deception.

"Addy, why don't you just ask the question you want to ask?"

"I saw your and Ryan's comments about my father's insurance payout. You think I had something to do with Cassie's disappearance. Is that why you're helping me?" The words spilled out of her mouth. "To keep tabs? Prove I hurt my sister for money? Well, if that's your plan, you're going to be disappointed. I would never hurt Cassie. I have no idea where she is, but I don't need someone who doesn't trust me to help me find her."

Addy turned on her heels and stalked into the bedroom. She took her suitcase from the closet and tossed it on the bed before moving to the dresser.

Shawn stopped in the bedroom door, watching her throw her clothes onto the bed.

"For the record, I never thought you had anything to do with Cassie's disappearance." The heat she'd heard in his voice moments ago was gone.

His words were like a pin to the balloon of anger she'd been sailing on. She dropped down on the bed next to her suitcase. "I saw your comment. Motive, question mark." She drew a question mark symbol in the air with her finger.

He sat next to her. "Money is always a motive."

"One man's change is another man's treasure?" She smiled weakly.

"Something like that," Shawn said, returning her smile. "But even if I found a note written in your handwriting saying, 'make Cassie disappear,' I wouldn't believe you'd hurt your sister."

Addy's lips cocked up, and she sent a sideways glance at him. "Now I have to wonder how good a PI you are."

Shawn chuckled. "Okay, maybe in that circumstance I'd start to wonder."

Addy dropped her head into her hands. She wanted to trust him, but she felt fried, unsure whether to trust her instincts. She wasn't even sure her sister was still alive. Wasn't sure she'd ever know what happened to her. She was in no state to judge whether what she felt for Shawn was real or whether he was using her to some end he wouldn't tell her about.

"The case you can't tell me about, is it about me or Cassie? Is somebody, the insurance company or some long-lost relative I don't know about, paying you to find out if I had something to do with Cassie's disappearance?" Her heart squeezed as the words crossed her lips.

She couldn't be sure, but she thought she saw something pass over his face. Whatever it was, it passed too quickly to name.

Shawn pushed the suitcase out of the way and took her hands in his, looking into her eyes.

"Addy, I promise you. I know you love your sister and had nothing to do with her disappearance. I am not investigating you."

The sincerity in his eyes caused her heart to stutter. She'd refused to get close to anyone after her divorce, throwing herself into her job so she wouldn't ever be hurt the way her ex-husband had hurt her again. And what did she have to show for it? No husband and, now, no job. But here was Shawn, still standing by her side, helping her to find Cassie even after she'd pushed him away. Somehow he'd worked his way past her defenses.

She eased closer, raised her hand to cup his chin and kissed him.

He kissed her back, tugging her closer. The sweep of his tongue sent electric shocks through her. After a heated minute, he pulled back.

"We should stop. I don't want you to do anything you regret."

Her entire body screamed that she wouldn't regret being with him. Even after their weekend together, when she'd vowed not to let it happen again, she'd never regretted being with him. She wasn't sure that was possible.

His rejection stung. She scooted back on the bed, putting more distance between them. "You're right. I'm sorry."

Shawn reached out and cupped her cheek. "You have

nothing to be sorry for." He rose from the bed and headed toward the bedroom door before turning back. "Sleep tight, princess."

He shot one last look across the room before shutting the door behind him.

Chapter Thirteen

Shawn spent the next several hours reading the background reports Ryan had sent on Suri and Ben and left a message asking for a tour of Spectrum's chip factory.

He also pulled a background report on Lance Raupp. From the superior attitude to the way he'd looked at Addy, the man had seriously rubbed him the wrong way. Ben had the necessary access to pull off the fraud, but Shawn wasn't convinced he had the smarts to pull it off. Lance, with a bachelor's degree in business and a minor in computer engineering, hit all the right notes.

No matter how hard he tried, Shawn's mind kept going back to Addy.

She'd been clear about why she didn't want to get involved. He didn't want to be like her ex, putting her in a position where she felt like she had to choose. He wouldn't do that to her. She'd regretted their first night together, and he couldn't, wouldn't, let her make that mistake again.

He laughed softly, mirthlessly. This was the first time he couldn't get a woman out of his head. He was honest with the women he saw, promising nothing beyond dinner, maybe dancing and a night of fun and pleasure. Some he saw for more than a night, but never much more.

Never long enough for any ideas of longevity, much less permanency, to set in.

But look at him now.

One night with Addy six months ago and…and he hadn't been with a woman since.

He'd teased Ryan in the early days of his romance with his now-wife, Nadia, mostly because that's what brothers did. But a part of him had also seen the kind of love Ryan felt for Nadia—the all-consuming need to be with another person, to make that person happy—and he'd wanted it for himself. He wanted it with Addy.

His phone rang, mercifully pulling him out of his thoughts.

It was after midnight. He didn't need to look at the screen to know who called.

"Got the chip," Ryan whispered.

"Why are you whispering?"

"Nadia is asleep." Ryan's wife had just entered her third trimester, and Ryan could barely stand to leave her side. "Analyzing it now. Should have something for you by morning."

"Okay. Thanks."

"What's wrong?"

Ryan could read him better than anyone. Add in that there was only an eighteen-month age difference between them, and it was almost as if they were twins.

It also made it nearly impossible to keep anything secret from Ryan.

"Nothing. I just… Addy. Nothing." Shawn's frustrated sigh was so loud he looked to the closed bedroom door to make sure Addy hadn't woken.

No sound came from the other side.

"Blue balls." Ryan laughed.

"Good night, Ry."

Ryan hung up.

Shawn put on his pajamas and brushed his teeth.

He skipped pulling the sofa out into a full bed and instead grabbed a blanket and two pillows from the closet near the door and stretched out on the couch. He'd slept in much worse accommodations, and he didn't want to take the chance that moving the furniture would wake Addy.

He'd almost fallen asleep when the bedroom door opened with a click. Shawn sat up on the couch.

"Everything okay?"

Long, silky brown legs showed from under a pale green sleep shirt.

His groin pushed against the front of his pajama pants. He could only hope the darkness of the room hid his desire.

"Yes, I…" Addy took several steps toward the sofa.

Shawn got to his feet, meeting her in the middle of the room.

He curled a hand around her arm. "Addy, what is it?"

She reached up and stroked Shawn's cheek lightly. "That weekend together wasn't a mistake."

His breath knotted in his chest. Whatever he'd expected her to say, it wasn't that.

"It was a rare time I felt free to just be. No job. No responsibilities. I could just be me."

Addy curled her arms around his neck, going to her toes and feathering kisses along his jawbone and down his throat. "And you saw me."

A groan tore from his throat. "Addy."

His resolve was evaporating fast.

She pulled back far enough to lay her hand over his lips. "I know what I'm doing, and I know what I want. I want to not feel scared. I don't want to think. I want to just feel. I want to feel pleasure. I want to feel you. Make love to me, Shawn."

Her lips, soft and sweet, took his in a hard kiss filled with intent and desire.

He slid his hands to her hips and carried her into the bedroom.

No other woman had stirred in him the feelings Addy did. He wanted her, not just physically, but he wanted to be with her. To sit beside her. To talk to her and hold her hand. To laugh with her and fight with her. And not just while they were here in Bentham. For the first time in his life, he wanted to build something real—with Addy.

He just hoped she felt the same way.

Chapter Fourteen

Addy awoke to the sun peeking around the curtains in the room and the bed next to her empty.

The last time they'd slept together, she'd been the one to slink away in the dark of night. Now she knew what it felt like to wake up the next morning alone. Of course, Shawn probably preferred it that way.

It left Addy with a sense of loss and more doubts than she knew what to do with. Not about what they'd done, but about where they'd go from here. Last night had been incredible. After they'd rested a bit, he'd awoken her with kisses down her spine and they'd gone at it again, this time in the voracious way of lovers long kept apart. He'd driven her to heights she'd only read about in the campy bodice rippers she'd sneaked out of the library as a teen. She cared for Shawn more than she should, far more than was prudent.

Trepidation spread through her.

Beyond the personal, she wasn't sure what their night together meant with regard to him helping her find Cassie. Would he decide it was best if they didn't spend any more time together, afraid that she might get too attached?

Too late.

No. Whatever they'd shared, she wouldn't let it stop

her from finding Cassie, and she had to admit she needed Shawn's help. Even if things were awkward, she was an adult, and she could handle it.

And if he wanted to return to her bed tonight?

The sounds of the door to the suite opening and Shawn moving around in the other room interrupted her musing.

She tossed the covers to the other side of the bed and crossed to the bathroom.

Sometime in the night, she'd donned her nightshirt again, but that didn't stop her from wrapping herself in the white terry-cloth robe that hung on the back of the bathroom door. She ran a brush through her hair and brushed her teeth and stepped into the common area of the suite.

"Good morning." Shawn flashed what could only be called a satisfied smile.

Her entire body flushed, and she tore her gaze from his, padding over to the table where he'd set two large paper coffee cups.

She reached for the cup on the left. "Good morning."

He took the cup from her hand before she took a sip, replacing it with the second cup. "You still want to track down Ben this morning?"

Addy took a long sip of coffee, letting the blessed nectar fully awaken her brain. "Uh-huh. Absolutely."

"Okay, then. The coffee is from the continental breakfast downstairs, but I figured we could get breakfast at the diner we ate at yesterday. I need more sustenance than a bagel after the workout you gave me last night."

The unexpected comment had her choking on her coffee.

He patted her back until she caught her breath, a sexy smile on his stubble-roughened face. "I…yes. Breakfast is good. I'm going to grab a quick shower. Maybe we can stop by the sheriff's office, too. We need to make sure Sheriff Donovan knows Suri lied about Cassie leaving town and that Ben and that creep Teddy are somehow involved in all this."

"I left a message for the sheriff last night. We'll follow up after speaking with Ben."

Addy returned to the bedroom and quickly showered and changed into jeans and a black-and-white-striped top. While she got ready for the day, she tried not to think about last night, which only led to her reliving every amazing moment—and there were many over the several hours Shawn had spent in her bed.

Heat curled in her belly.

She was not looking for a relationship, Addy reminded herself. Last night was magnificent and she wouldn't mind a repeat performance, but she was in Bentham to find Cassie. That's what she needed to focus on.

Her stomach fluttered as she reentered the living room area of the suite.

Shawn looked up from the laptop he tapped away on. "You ready?"

Her stomach growled in answer.

At just after seven in the morning, Bentham's rush hour wasn't quite in full swing yet. The diner was nearly full, but Becky seated them immediately in a booth in the back next to a window facing the surface parking lot where Shawn had once again parked the Yukon.

They ordered, and their food was delivered to the table quickly.

She dived into her pancakes and bacon, eating until the pains in her stomach subsided. Shawn had ordered pancakes and bacon, too, but unlike her golden flapjacks, his pancakes were a muddy brown and surrounded by stringy pink wisps of meat.

She frowned at his plate. “What kind of pancakes are those?”

He grinned. “Whole wheat. And Becky even rustled up some turkey bacon.”

She shook her head. “That’s just sad.”

He laughed at the same time a black BMW swung into the parking lot outside the window.

Ben emerged from the car in a long camel-colored wool coat. As he closed the door, a black motorcycle pulled to a stop behind the car, blocking Ben from leaving.

The motorcycle rider straddled the bike and flicked his visor up. Teddy Arbury.

“Look.” Addy pointed to the scene beyond the window.

Ben crossed his arms over his chest, a sour look on his face.

“I wonder what they’re arguing about?” Shawn said, setting down his fork.

“With those two, it could be anything,” Becky said, slipping up to the table to drop off their check and refill their coffee cups.

Shawn glanced over at Becky. “Why do you say that?”

“Teddy and Ben. They’ve been friends since high school. Bad seeds, both of them.” Her face twisted in a grimace.

Based on her last encounter with Teddy, Addy could understand why Becky didn’t care for Teddy. But Ben? Addy knew why she didn’t like him. He didn’t seem to care at all that Cassie was missing, which was suspicious as far as Addy was concerned. But Becky was referring to something else.

"Ben's a bad seed? He's an executive at a thriving computer company."

Becky tipped her head down to glare at Addy. "Executives can be bad seeds, too."

"Yes, of course," Addy answered, feeling chastised.

Becky shot her one more glare before continuing, "They went to high school together. An odd pair on the surface, but underneath they're more alike than not. Both selfish and entitled. Ben's money always got him out of the consequences, and I think that's why Teddy hitched his wagon to Ben's horse. You know where one goes, so goes the other."

The three of them watched as Teddy stabbed the air between him and Ben with a finger before roaring off on his bike. Ben walked out of view of the window, and Becky moved to refill the coffee cups of the couple at the next table.

"I'd love to know what that was all about," Shawn said, shifting to get his wallet from his back pocket.

Ben walked in and strode to the counter as Shawn spoke.

"I'm more interested in the tension Suri mentioned between him and Cassie," Addy answered, scooting off the bench. "Either way, let's not waste the opportunity to ask him."

Shawn followed as she wove between the booths and tables to Ben's side.

A young red-haired waitress handed Ben a paper cup, smiling coquettishly. Ben winked and turned away, stepping back in surprise when he saw Addy standing in his path to the door.

"Oh, Addy. How nice to see you again," Ben said in a politely distant voice.

"We finally tracked down Suri Bedingfield. She was under the impression you and Cassie argued right before Cassie went missing."

Ben smoothed the blue tie around his neck. "I can't begin to fathom why she'd think that. Cassie and I were no longer together, but we parted on good terms, as I told you."

Ben's expression remained placid, but he swallowed hard.

She cocked her head to the side and put on a faux-pleasant tone. "Yet Suri seems to think otherwise. Why is that?"

"You'd have to ask her," Ben said with a plastic smile.

Addy could feel the tether she had on her temper fraying fast. She moved closer to Ben's table, crowding into his personal space. "We also found Cassie's things thrown into garbage bags and stuffed into the attic at her apartment. You know anything about that?"

"I can't say I do," Ben said, his voice hard.

Addy bent forward, putting her face within inches of Ben's. "I know you're lying. I know you had something to do with my sister's disappearance." She slammed her hand down on the table. "Where is my sister?"

It took everything in her not to hit Ben. To pound on him until he told her where to find Cassie.

Shawn grabbed her arm and inched her away from the table.

Ben took the opportunity to slide out of the booth. "Look. I've told you what I know." He glared at Addy. "I don't like being harassed."

"I'm sure you can understand how upset Addy is," Shawn said in a conciliatory voice.

Ben's gaze slid to Shawn. "I need to get to work."

"Pretty early to be going into the office." Shawn cut Ben off as he attempted to move around Addy to the door.

"Yes, well, I need to head out to the factory before going into the office."

"Hey, why don't we go with you?" Shawn said, cuffing Ben's shoulder. "You did promise a tour."

Ben frowned. "I don't know."

"Then we won't be in anyone's way," Shawn said with an unnaturally bright smile.

Ben's frown deepened, but then he nodded. "Let me just make sure it won't be a problem."

Ben moved several steps away and pulled out his phone.

Addy's eyes narrowed on Shawn's face. "Why are you so interested in the Spectrum factory? It has something to do with the case you came to Bentham to investigate, doesn't it?"

Addy watched as Shawn's gaze moved from Ben to her. "You know I can't tell you about that. I can drop you off at the hotel."

"I'm going with you."

Shawn's brow furrowed. "I don't know if that's a good idea."

Addy's stomach twisted. Shawn was still keeping something from her, and she'd never fully trust him until she knew what it was.

"I don't care." He started to argue, but she cut him off. "Look, we can kill two birds with one stone here. I know you have confidentiality issues with this other case, but I hope by now you know you can trust me."

"I do trust you."

That simple declaration made her happier than she had time to examine at the moment. "Good. So there's no reason I can't go. Cassie was there at least two days a week. Someone may know something that could help us find her." Addy cut her eyes toward Ben. "And I want to talk to him some more. I think he knows more than he's saying about where Cassie could be."

She caught Shawn's glower out of the side of her eye but ignored it.

"You want to follow me?" Ben said, returning.

"Sure," Shawn said without enthusiasm.

A zing of electricity shot through Addy when Shawn put his hand on the small of her back as they followed Ben out of the diner.

Ben got in his BMW, and Shawn followed him from the parking lot.

"You really think Ben isn't connected to Addy's disappearance?"

Shawn followed the BMW onto a two-lane county road leading south. "I don't know. I just don't think we should jump to conclusions. Especially not based on evidence from Suri Bedingfield."

"Her sudden move to Garwin is suspicious, as is that fancy apartment."

Shawn's gaze moved to the rearview mirror.

"Exactly. And she had just as much opportunity, if not more, to hide Cassie's things in that attic."

She released a heavy sigh. "I just want to find Cassie."

He reached for her hand without taking his eyes off the road and squeezed. "I know, and we will."

He moved his hand back to the steering wheel, his eyes flicking to the mirror again and his jaw tightening.

"Why do you keep looking in the mirror with that worried expression?" She turned in her seat to see what he was looking at. There was very little traffic on this road, only Ben's BMW in front of them, a motorcycle coming up fast behind them. "Is that Teddy? What's going on?"

"Make sure your seat belt is on," Shawn answered.

She watched as the motorcycle advanced on the Yukon.

The motorcycle followed dangerously close. What was this idiot doing? He would rear-end them if he didn't slow down. "Shawn?"

Addy's adrenaline spiked. She faced forward in time to see Ben's BMW speed up on the street in front of them.

Shawn pressed the accelerator, switching lanes to avoid a slow-moving white-paneled van.

The motorcycle switched lanes behind them, speeding up to keep pace. The road ahead of them was clear, but a drag race down the highway was still dangerous.

Addy reached into her purse for her phone.

The motorcycle put on a burst of speed and pulled up next to them on Shawn's side of the car.

Addy tried to look past Shawn at the person driving the motorcycle, but she could only catch a glimpse of the face of a white male with a dark beard before Shawn hit the gas, throwing her back against the seat.

A succession of pops sounded at the same time Shawn yelled, "Get down!"

She froze, struggling to make sense of the sounds she'd heard and where they were coming from to heed Shawn's warning.

The popping sounds came again, and this time her brain processed exactly what they were. Bullets.

Addy shrank down in her seat so her head dipped below the passenger side window. She still held her phone in her hand. She quickly dialed 911, relating where she and Shawn were and that they were being shot at.

Shawn veered wildly to the right and onto the shoulder of the road. On either side of this section of the highway, there was nothing other than miles and miles of land.

Shawn got them back onto the pavement and put on another burst of speed in an attempt to outrun the bike. The motorcyclist kept pace behind them, but close enough that a sporadic volley of shots pinged off the back bumper. A bullet smashed through the back windshield, and a scream tore from Addy's throat.

Shawn ducked down, sending the Yukon swerving wildly. "Are you okay?"

She slid farther in her seat, nearly sitting on the floorboard. "Yes. But he's trying to kill us!"

"It certainly seems so."

Shawn swore, his gaze locked on something ahead of them.

She pushed upward enough to see through the front window.

A sharp curve with a steep drop-off loomed up ahead. The roadside sign cautioning drivers to slow down whizzed by, followed closely by another deeming the speed limit thirty-five miles per hour.

They were moving at well over twice that suggestion, and the continued shots coming from behind them cautioned against slowing.

Shawn gripped the steering wheel tight enough to turn his knuckles white. He tapped the brakes as they rode into the turn at a still much too fast speed.

The gunshots had stopped, but there was little time to give thanks.

The cyclist drew even with them again and swerved to the right. Metal screamed as the passenger side of the Yukon scraped along the barrier.

"Hang on!" Shawn stomped on the gas, sending them shooting forward again.

They were still in the curve, but a straight stretch of highway loomed in front of them.

The motorcycle slammed into the back of their car, sending them spinning.

Shawn struggled to regain control of the Yukon as it sailed across the center line. Luckily, there was no oncoming traffic.

They slid from the road, the driver's side of the car scraping along the barrier until they made it to the end.

But the Yukon didn't stop. It careened backward through the tall grass along the side of the highway, miraculously halting just before they would have plowed into a line of trees.

"Are you all right?" Shawn's voice sounded like it was coming from underwater.

Addy looked at him. A large gash slashed his temple, sending blood dripping down the side of his face. The sight sent a wave of fear through her, almost as strong as the one she'd felt when she realized Cassie was missing. But he was conscious and talking, so that was good.

"I'm okay, I think." She wiggled her fingers and toes and mentally scanned herself for injuries. A sharp pain radiated from her side, but it didn't feel too bad. She was dazed, but like Shawn, she hadn't lost consciousness and counted that as a win.

"I can't get out. My seat belt is stuck, and the door is jammed." Shawn pulled on the seat belt, but it didn't give.

She tried her seat belt, unsnapping it easily. Somehow the airbags hadn't inflated, which was a godsend, because if they had, they wouldn't have been able to see that they weren't out of the woods yet.

They'd stopped some twenty yards from the road near the end of the curve in the highway. From their vantage point, she could see a green pickup idling at the side of the road up ahead.

Fear and adrenaline rushed through her. She bent forward, scanning the floorboard beneath her feet, running her hand under the passenger chair, looking for her purse. It wasn't there, which meant her Ruger inside it wasn't there, either. The force of the crash could have easily sent it sliding to the rear of the car or even out of the now-missing passenger window.

"Where's your gun?" Addy asked without taking her eyes off the truck.

Shawn followed her gaze to the truck.

"In the glove compartment."

Addy prayed the glove box would open and breathed a sigh of relief when it did.

A black-and-silver pistol lay in the glove compartment next to a full magazine.

She grabbed the gun, inserting the magazine and checking that the safety was off.

"What are you doing?" he asked, attempting to reach for the gun but wincing.

"Preparing to defend us if it becomes necessary."

The bike lurched forward, swinging into a U-turn as she spoke. The truck began slowly moving in their direction on the wrong side of the road.

Where the hell were the police? It seemed like it had been hours since she'd called 911, although her rational mind told her it had been only a minute. That had been all it had taken to be shot at and driven off the road. She knew in her gut the police wouldn't make it in time to save them.

"Lean your chair back," Addy said, crawling over the console separating them. There was no need to let down the window. There was no window anymore.

"It's too dangerous. Let me do it." Shawn attempted to reach for the gun in her hand. The fact that she could easily swat his hand away told her everything she needed to know about which of them should hold the gun.

Addy scrambled over his legs. "We don't have time to argue about this."

Addy positioned herself so she had a clear shot at the cyclist.

The motorcycle crawled closer. The rider's arm rose, a gun in his hand.

The driver was male, but Addy still couldn't get a good look at his face.

She stopped trying and focused on the gun.

Her grandfather's voice rang in her ears.

It's all muscle memory, baby doll.

Sweat beaded on her forehead.

The driver raised his gun. She drew in a deep breath, then let it out as she pulled the trigger.

The driver's scream echoed over the empty highway. His gun fell onto the asphalt.

Addy kept the gun trained on the truck as its tires squealed. The rider turned toward her, the absolute hatred on his face sending a chill down Addy's spine. She recognized Teddy.

The motorcycle sped away.

"He's gone," Addy said, crawling back into the passenger seat. "It was Teddy Arbury."

Shawn swore.

She could hear the sounds of sirens in the distance.

"Sounds like help is on the way," Shawn said, peering through the windshield.

"Good." Addy handed the gun to Shawn. She didn't think Teddy would come back, but the calculation as to who was better off defending them if he did was rapidly changing. She reached under her shirt, touching her abdomen. She came away with her fingers covered in blood. "I think I need it."

Chapter Fifteen

Shawn paced the hospital waiting room.

The EMTs had whisked Addy away while the fire department cut him out of his seat belt. He'd waived treatment and had a deputy drive him to the hospital. He'd been so desperate to assure himself that Addy was okay that he'd forgotten to lie and say he was her fiancé or husband when the nurse had asked. Now no one would tell him anything about Addy's condition because he wasn't immediate family. He was nearly out of his mind with worry.

Shawn turned to head back the length of the room and spotted Donovan.

"This is quite a mess you and your lady friend got yourselves into," Donovan said.

"Not one of our making," Shawn growled.

"So you told my deputy. I retrieved Ms. Williams's purse from the vehicle. Thought you might want to hang on to it for her." Donovan handed Addy's purse over. "I'm afraid your vehicle is going to be a loss."

Shawn glanced inside the purse, checking to make sure her gun was properly secured in the purse holster.

One of Donovan's eyebrows cocked higher than the other.

"She has a New York permit to carry," Shawn said.

Donovan lifted his chin. "I know. If she didn't, she'd be headed straight for my jail from her hospital bed. How is she?"

He ran a hand over his head. "I don't know. No one will tell me anything because I'm not related. But there was a lot of blood. I think she might have been shot."

Donovan took pity on him. "Hang on. I'll see what I can find out," he said, exiting the waiting area and striding toward the nurses' desk.

Shawn was monumentally pissed off at himself. He'd messed up big-time, putting the only woman he'd ever cared about in danger. Nearly getting her killed.

Bile rose in his throat at the memory of seeing her covered in blood. That Teddy had been the one to fire the shots absolved him of nothing. It was his fault for putting her in the situation in the first place. He should have known better.

Shawn had given Ben an opening, and he'd taken it, setting them up to be shot. Had someone at Spectrum found out why Shawn was really in town? Or were the bullets meant to stop Addy from looking for Cassie? Maybe both?

If Addy hadn't been such a crack shot, they both would have been killed.

Another memory of Addy slumped next to him in the passenger seat of the Yukon, her hands covered in her blood, flashed through his mind.

It had been close. Too close.

Footsteps fell in the hall, the sound growing louder as they did. Someone was headed his way. He looked up, expecting to see Donovan, and was surprised to see Ryan and Gideon instead.

He'd called Ryan soon after arriving at the hospital,

but unless they'd learned how to appear by magic, there was no way Ryan and Gideon should be standing in front of him right now.

"What are you doing here? How are you here?" Shawn asked, rising and meeting the other two men in the middle of the room.

People had always commented on how similar the West brothers looked. A half inch shorter than Shawn, Ryan was stockier and preferred to keep his face and head cleanly shaven. But compared to Gideon, he and Ryan were downright diminutive.

Six foot six and roughly the width of a sedan, Gideon had muscles with muscles. He'd served in the military with Shawn's oldest brother, James. Even West's contacts and investigative powers hadn't successfully turned out a full background check on Gideon. No doubt the missing periods in Gideon's life would stay that way until the United States government wanted it otherwise. But James had vouched for his friend and fellow soldier, and that had been more than enough. Gideon had quickly proved himself an asset to the firm.

"We were on our way when you called. How is Addy?" Ryan dropped a heavy hand on Shawn's shoulder.

Gideon, the quintessential man of few words, only nodded.

"I don't know. No one has told me anything." Shawn expelled a breath. "Why were you on your way to Bentham?"

"We got the report back on the chip you found in Ben Konstam's office. It's a fake."

"I'm not surprised. I'm sure Konstam is also behind Addy and me being shot at," Shawn replied.

He'd given Ryan a quick and dirty summary of the

shooting in their call, but now he elaborated on the chance meeting with Ben at the diner and that he and Addy had been following Ben to the factory when they were shot at.

"I want to know where Konstam and Arbury are now," Shawn said, aiming a look at Gideon.

Gideon nodded briskly, moving to the other side of the waiting room and pulling out his cell phone. Gideon had cultivated an extensive network of contacts and snitches that had come in handy on more than one West investigation. If anyone could get a bead on Konstam and Arbury, it was Gideon.

"The fake chip alone isn't enough to prove the bad chips weren't manufactured by Intellus," Ryan said. "Intellus wants us to get enough evidence to show the authorities and the public that they aren't responsible. We need to show that Spectrum is making these chips and falsely using the Intellus logo to undermine their brand."

That was easier said than done. The only way to definitively show that Spectrum was behind the fraud was to get into the factory. Since they only had a couple of days, if that, to get the proof they needed, an undercover operation was out of the question. That meant they'd have to get into the factory and document the fraud without being discovered. They'd pulled off similar operations before, but the tight time frame made doing so riskier than Shawn would have liked.

Before he could voice his concerns, Donovan strode back into the room. His step faltered for just a moment at the sight of the three men before he recovered. It wasn't the first time the three of them together had had that effect on others.

Shawn stepped around Ryan and spoke to Donovan. "Did they tell you anything?"

"She wasn't shot. A piece of glass from the broken window lodged in her side. They got it out and are stitching her up now."

Relief flooded through him like ice-cold water on a hundred-degree day.

"Who are your friends?" Donovan asked, his gaze homed in on Ryan.

Shawn introduced Ryan and Gideon to Donovan. The men shook hands, and Donovan turned back to Shawn. "Why don't you tell me what happened out there?"

Shawn recounted the call from Ben this morning and being ambushed on the drive to Spectrum's factory.

Donovan shot him a skeptical look when he got to the part where Addy shot the motorcycle driver.

"She shot the gun out of his hand?"

Shawn couldn't keep a proud smile from spreading across his face. "Technically, I think she shot him in the forearm, but yes, she shot him and he dropped the gun."

"While the motorcycle was moving?" The question came from Ryan, who seemed just as skeptical as Donovan.

Gideon, who'd rejoined the group of men while Shawn recited the chain of events, maintained a poker face. If Gideon was surprised or doubtful, he never showed it.

Shawn's smile grew wider. "It was a damn sight to behold, but it saved our lives. Teddy Arbury tried to kill us."

Donovan scratched something in his notebook. "How can you be sure it was Teddy?"

Shawn explained seeing Teddy on his motorcycle outside the diner not long before the attack. "It looked like the same bike."

Donovan frowned. "But you're not sure? You didn't see the face of the shooter?"

"No." Shawn scowled. "I didn't. But Addy did."

Donovan scratched a note on his pad. "And how do you know Edward Arbury?"

"I don't. The first time I met him, Addy and I were at the diner and Teddy cornered her coming out of the ladies' room. He made a veiled threat about backing off investigating Cassie's disappearance, and I stepped in. It didn't go any further than that, mostly because the waitress put Teddy in his place, and Addy and I left right after."

"And you have no idea why Teddy would have approached Ms. Williams?"

"I didn't then. Did you get my message about the chat Addy and I had with Suri Bedingfield?"

This time Donovan frowned. "I got it. Want to explain what you were doing in Garwin?"

Shawn checked his temper and walked Donovan through his and Addy's questioning of Suri, leaving out his mad dash to get to Addy and her assault of Suri.

"So Miss Bedingfield just admitted to you two that she lied?" Donovan's eyebrows rose until they nearly touched his hairline.

"We asked some very pointed questions. Ms. Bedingfield correctly deemed it to be in her best interest to answer truthfully. I might be more skeptical of Suri's story if Ben Konstam hadn't just set us up."

Donovan narrowed his eyes. "What do you mean, set you up?"

"We were following Ben from the diner to the factory."

"So Edward Arbury and Ben Konstam are working together to get Ms. Williams to give up the search for her sister. Why?"

Shawn felt, rather than saw, Ryan tense beside him.

He knew how Ryan felt about keeping the client's confidence, but it was time to bring Donovan in on his real reason for being in town.

Shawn explained Intellus's discovery of fraudulent chips marked with their logo and how they'd hired West to root out the source.

Donovan's lips puckered with irritation. "You should have told me what you were up to—"

Ryan interrupted before Donovan could continue his dressing-down. "You have your obligations, and we have ours."

The two men stared at each other with twin scowls.

"Ben made a call before we left the diner. I'd bet good money if you pull his phone records you'll find that call was to Arbury."

They didn't have time for posturing or hurt egos. It was becoming increasingly clear to Shawn that Ben Konstam was the key to whatever was going on.

"Your suspicion isn't enough to pull Konstam's phone records," Donovan said dismissively.

Shawn felt a vein along the side of his neck throb in annoyance. "Did your office get an emergency call from Ben about the shooting? He had to have seen us getting shot at."

Donovan's brow furrowed. "No. The only call we got was from you."

First Cassie disappeared and now he and Addy were shot at. Not to mention the attempted mugging the night Addy got to town. He was convinced the events were related. He hadn't gotten a good look at the attacker's face, but his size and weight were similar to Teddy's. The situation had escalated, and they still had no concrete idea why. It seemed unlikely that the chip fraud he was investigating and Cassie's disappearance weren't connected somehow. But if Cassie was a participant in the fraud, why had she disappeared? The obvious answer was one none of them wanted to think about, but with every passing day, it became harder and harder to overlook.

"I think Ben and Teddy had something to do with Cassie Williams's disappearance and the fraud and are trying to hide it now."

Donovan exhaled loudly. "Yeah, it's looking more and more like that."

Some of the tension that had built up inside him evaporated. At least Donovan was considering the possibility.

"Addy's convinced Cassie is alive."

Donovan shook his head. "I'm sure you know how hard it is for family members to accept these things. Especially if there isn't a body."

"I know, but Addy is a reasonable person. If she believes Cassie could still be alive, we'll keep looking."

Out of the side of his eye, he saw Ryan frown.

Donovan ran a hand through his hair. "I can't stop you, as you well know, but whatever is going on here is dangerous. Think about that." Donovan directed a pointed look at Shawn. "In the meantime, I've put an all-points bulletin out on Teddy Arbury, and I've got a deputy on the way to Garwin to see if Suri Bedingfield will come in to give a statement."

"What about Ben Konstam?"

"I'll talk to him," Donovan clipped out.

A balding man in round-rimmed glasses and a hip-length white lab coat entered the waiting room. The stitching on his coat read Dr. E. Jackson.

His eyes scanned over the four men in the room. "Shawn West?"

"That's me." Shawn approached the doctor, his heart rate picking up speed.

The nurses had been adamant about not being able to tell him anything about Addy's condition. If the doctor was looking for him now, did that mean that the worst had happened?

"If you'll come with me, you can see Ms. Williams."

Shawn paused long enough to get the keys to the car Ryan and Gideon had driven to town and the approximate location of where they'd parked. Ryan and Gideon planned to pick up a rental and head back to the hotel.

Shawn followed Dr. Jackson down a long, bright white hallway with signs directing them at various intervals to the ER, ICU and cardiac areas of the hospital.

"I thought I wasn't allowed to see Addy," Shawn said, lengthening his stride to keep pace with the doctor. Though he was about six inches shorter and thirty years older than Shawn, Dr. Jackson moved swiftly down the hospital hallway.

Dr. Jackson rolled his eyes. "Strictly speaking, you're not. But Ms. Williams has been demanding to see you since she got here. I just finished her stitches, and I'm concerned she's going to pop them trying to get out of bed and get to you, so..." He threw up his hands, stopping in front of a blue-curtained area. "I'm working on her discharge papers now. I'll be back with them in a moment."

Shawn pulled the curtain back.

His breath caught in his chest when he saw Addy lying on her back, her face ashen. She'd pulled up the green scrub top she wore and was examining the bandage on the left side of her stomach.

She glanced up at him and smiled. “Hi.”

“How are you feeling?” He came to a stop at the side of the bed.

She pulled the hem of her shirt down. “Like I got stabbed in the side with a piece of glass.”

“Don’t joke.” He smiled weakly for her sake, but he couldn’t remember ever being more afraid than he’d been when the EMTs had driven her away from the scene of the shooting. He kissed her forehead, then, as softly as he could, her lips.

She grabbed his hand when he moved to pull away and squeezed. “You were trapped in the car. I was worried, too. How’s your arm?”

He raised his arm over his head and rolled his shoulder. “A little sore, but nothing a few industrial-strength aspirin couldn’t handle. That was some shooting.”

Addy’s right eyebrow rose higher than the left. “I told you I grew up on a ranch. I know how to shoot.”

“West has employees who are ex-military who couldn’t have made that shot.”

Addy shot him a lopsided grin. “I’ll host a class for them when we get back to New York.”

She glanced around him at the large circular desk, where two nurses and Dr. Jackson stood. An electric menorah decorated one end, and a small Christmas tree stood on the other.

“Did he tell you when he’s going to let me out of here?” Addy jerked her head in the doctor’s direction.

“He’s working on the discharge papers now.”

“Good.” Addy swung her legs over the side of the bed. “Ooh. Ah,” she grimaced, grabbing her side.

“Take it easy.” Shawn put his arm around her and helped her up from the bed.

He tamped down the rage that swelled at Addy's pain. Teddy better hope Donovan found him before he did.

Dr. Jackson returned with Addy's discharge papers, a prescription for painkillers and instructions to have her primary care physician look at the stitches in a week.

"Has the sheriff picked up Teddy yet?" Addy asked as they exited the hospital.

"Donovan is looking for him."

"Good. Teddy must have followed us from the diner."

The hospital's visitor lot wasn't large or anywhere near full, so he spotted the dark blue SUV easily. Shawn opened the passenger door for Addy. "The question is how he knew when we would leave the diner."

He watched realization spread across Addy's face. "Ben set us up."

"It looks that way."

Addy edged into the SUV slowly.

Shawn gritted his teeth, watching her breathe through the pain.

"Suri would have told them we talked to her. We need to find Ben now. If he and Teddy are desperate enough to try to kill us, there's no telling..." Addy's voice trailed off.

He stepped into the space between the car and the open door. "I know you believe Cassie is alive, but, sweetheart, it may already be too late."

Addy put her hand on his arm. "I'm not in denial. I can't explain it. I know she's alive, and I have to keep looking until I find her."

Her expression was equal parts earnestness, determination and fear.

The knowledge that she could be wrong, that it could already be too late for Cassie and to avoid Addy's heart breaking, made his chest tighten. He wanted desperately to protect her from the possible pain, but he knew he couldn't.

Shawn leaned forward and placed a soft kiss on her lips before backing up and closing the door.

As he drove them to the hotel, he thought about the fact that Addy would never be able to move on without knowing what happened to Cassie, one way or the other. And if that's the closure she needed, he'd make sure she got it.

Chapter Sixteen

Shawn exited the pharmacy with the painkillers Dr. Jackson had prescribed for Addy, a bottle of water and plastic wrap.

He could see Addy through the car's windshield as he approached the SUV. Her head rested against the seat, and her eyes were closed.

He felt a slap of anger. He'd get Addy settled in the suite, and then he planned to find Ben Konstam.

His phone beeped as he got into the car. A text from Jorge, the Spectrum employee he'd spoken to at the bar the night before.

We need a guy to help load the trucks. 6pm7. You in?

It was after three, which didn't leave him, Ryan and Gideon much time to figure out strategy, but this was their best chance for getting the evidence Intellus needed to prove their innocence.

Shawn sent back a single word. In.

Jorge texted Shawn an address he recognized as the Spectrum factory.

"Something important?"

He looked up from the phone and into Addy's eyes.

Even banged up, she was the most beautiful thing he'd ever seen.

"A possible break in the other case I'm working on." He popped the top on the pain pill bottle, handed her one and then opened the bottled water and gave that to her as well.

She swallowed the pill and half the bottle of water before speaking again. "I know I've taken up most of your time, and I haven't said thank you. Thank you."

He swept a lock of hair from her cheek, tucking it behind her ear. "Finding Cassie is my priority, I promise you."

His heart raced when she leaned her cheek into his palm.

"I doubt your brother feels the same way," she said, looking at him from beneath long lashes.

"Let me handle Ryan."

She pressed a kiss to his palm. He leaned forward, dipped his head and caught her mouth in a sweet, gentle kiss. He could have sat there forever kissing Addy, but his phone rang.

"You on your way back?" Ryan spoke without preamble.

Shawn put the car in gear, backing out of the parking space. "Yeah. I had to stop by the pharmacy first, but we're about ten minutes out. Got a text from a guy who may be able to help on our case."

He glanced across the car at Addy, but her eyes were closed. He still hadn't told her about his suspicion that Cassie might be involved with the ring producing fraudulent computer chips.

With each passing moment, keeping that information from Addy felt increasingly wrong.

"We can talk about it when I get back," Shawn said, ending the call.

He navigated the streets of Bentham back to the hotel. Addy hadn't stirred. He hated to wake her, but carrying her was out of the question. Not only because he was sure the gesture would mortify her, but his shoulder, while nowhere near as bad as her injury was, still throbbed. He'd bought a bottle of extra-strength Tylenol when he'd picked up Addy's prescription and planned to take one as soon as he got to the suite.

Hopefully, the pain medication would keep most of the pain at bay, because he'd be loading who knows how many trucks come six this afternoon.

"Addy. Addy, sweetheart, wake up. We're at the hotel."

She woke slowly, which he assumed was partly a result of the pain medication she'd taken. The pharmacist had warned that it could leave her drowsy.

He gave a moment's notion to calling Ryan or Gideon and asking them to carry Addy in, but banished the thought almost immediately. No way was he going to let another man carry his woman.

His woman.

He'd never once thought of a woman as his before. He'd been a part of protection details on more people, more women, than he could remember, and with each one he'd felt a duty to protect that went beyond collecting his paycheck. This was different, though. As cavemannish as the idea was, the need to protect Addy specifically was primal—and more than a little disconcerting, because he knew that if anything ever happened to Addy, he'd be lost.

He shook himself out of his introspection and helped Addy from the car and up to the suite. He helped her remove her shoes and get into bed. She was asleep before her head hit the pillow.

He snapped the bedroom door closed and took out his phone.

"We're back," he said when Ryan answered.

Ryan hung up without a response, and less than five minutes later, a knock sounded on the door.

"We've got to keep our voices down. Addy's asleep," Shawn said, letting Ryan and Gideon into the room.

"She okay?" Gideon asked, taking a seat at the table.

"Yeah. The glass cut deep but missed everything vital," Shawn answered.

Ryan crossed to the couch in the room and sat. "Good. Now, what's this about a text?"

Shawn caught Ryan and Gideon up on his strides in Intellus's case: his trip to the bar last night, the conversation with Jorge and his subsequent text offering Shawn a job loading Spectrum trucks this evening.

"That doesn't leave us a lot of time to prepare," Ryan said, waking the tablet he'd brought into the room with him.

"No, it doesn't, and since I don't want to leave Addy alone, it means there'll only be two of us," Shawn countered.

Ryan frowned without looking up from the tablet. "We don't have a lot of time to get the evidence we need for Intellus. If Addy stays in the room, she should be fine by herself."

Gideon leaned back in his chair, folding arms the size of tree trunks across his chest. A rare smile breaking out across his face. "I hear she's a hell of a shot."

Ryan laughed, but Shawn didn't join in.

"She's on painkillers. Teddy targeted us this morning, and we have no idea where he is. I checked with the hospital while I waited on word about Addy, and no one with a gunshot wound to the arm checked in."

Ryan's serious expression had returned. "Donovan would have alerted hospital staff to notify him if Teddy came in. He won't show up there."

"Probably not, but we can't be sure he won't come here trying to finish the job. It wouldn't be hard to figure out what hotel we're in, and we don't know if Teddy is onto me for looking into the fraud or if he wants to keep Addy from searching any further for Cassie," Shawn said.

"Could be both." Ryan stroked his chin. "We still don't know that Cassie Williams isn't involved in the fraud, but it's safe to assume Ben and his buddy Teddy are knee-deep in it. Could be that they want to stop your investigation and Addy's."

Shawn shook his head. "I don't know Cassie, but she and Addy seem close. I can't believe she'd allow Teddy to hurt her sister."

Ryan shot Shawn a dark look. "It wouldn't be the first time one family member turned against another. Especially when money is in the mix."

Shawn had seen enough close friends and family members turn on each other to know the truth of Ryan's statement. His gut told him that Cassie wasn't involved in the fraud. Still, that didn't mean she wasn't aware of it—knowledge that could put her life in danger.

"Gideon can stay with Addy. You can handle surveillance and serve as backup." Shawn sat on the couch next to Ryan.

Gideon nodded his acceptance. Ryan's only answer was a frown.

Annoyance rumbled through Shawn. He and Ryan

needed to have a long talk when they'd closed the Intellus case. Ryan might be president of West Security, but Shawn was as much an owner as he was. It was past time for Ryan to start acting like it.

For now, Shawn focused his attention on the tablet. He described the exterior layout of Spectrum's factory and where would be a good spot for Ryan to hide with the video camera. Shawn would be wearing a body camera and mic that would catch the Spectrum employees if they discussed the fraud. It was also his responsibility to get a shot of the chips that were being shipped. That would be hard if the boxes were already sealed, but he'd manage.

Ryan's job was to get the long shot of the dock while the boxes were being loaded and document which trucks the boxes went into. Hopefully, between them, they'd get the evidence they needed to prove Spectrum was behind the fraudulent Intellus chips tonight.

Then he could focus solely on finding Cassie.

They refined their plans and strategy until five, when Ryan left for the factory to get set up without anyone seeing him. They were lucky the days were shorter. Ryan was a master of hiding in plain sight, but the cover of darkness would come in handy. It was probably also why Jorge and his crew were starting the loading so early instead of later in the evening. If the employees cleared out in streams at five thirty like they had the day before, the factory would be deserted by six.

At five minutes to six, Shawn pulled into the small parking lot at the back of the factory near the loading docks. Jorge, Granger and two other white men waited on the docks.

Shawn put on square-framed glasses that hid a camera and mic and climbed out of his car to meet the men where they stood.

"Glad you could make it, amigo," Jorge said, extending a hand.

Granger shot a suspicious look at Shawn and ambled away to the other side of the loading dock while Jorge introduced the other men, Harris and Leon, the assistant manager.

Once he and Leon settled on a price for his labor, Shawn and the other men got started loading the three trucks.

By the end of the first hour, his arm ached, but he'd been able to peek into several boxes, finding nothing except computer chips marked with the Spectrum logo. A second hour passed, and he finished loading the boxes without finding any evidence of fraudulent chips.

Shawn pocketed the cash Leon handed him and drove back to the hotel.

Ryan parked beside him and slammed out of the Expedition. "Please tell me you got something?" He crossed his arms over his chest.

Shawn's irritation spiked upward at Ryan's attitude. "Nothing." He handed Ryan his glasses. "The chips I saw looked legit. They were all marked with Spectrum's logo."

Ryan's nostrils flared. "Damn it, Shawn. We're running out of time here," he snapped.

Shawn felt his jaw clench. He mimicked Ryan's stance by folding his arms over his chest. "We both know how these things go. Sometimes you spend hours on a stakeout or days working a contact and get nothing. It's not the first time."

Ryan stepped closer. "Intellus is sure the next shipment of fraudulent chips is going to hit the market in the next day or two, and they won't be able to keep it out of the press this time."

"I know that. I'm doing everything I can," Shawn ground out. He'd been putting off broaching the idea of telling Addy the whole truth, but if they weren't able to find evidence that Spectrum was behind the fraud, it would come out, regardless. He didn't want Addy to find out that way. "Look, Cassie is tangled up in all this somehow, maybe as an innocent, maybe as a player in the fraud. Either way, I think it's time to tell Addy everything."

Ryan shook his head. "We promised Intellus we'd keep this quiet."

"And we are. I trust Addy. She's not going to run to the press."

"You've known her for, what, a day? Two days? Come on, Shawn." Ryan snorted.

Shawn stepped into his brother's personal space. "Why don't you just say what you mean? It's not Addy you don't trust. It's me."

"Don't put words in my mouth," Ryan snarled.

"I don't have to. You've been second-guessing, checking up and generally riding my ass like I'm some rookie from the get-go. When's the last time you questioned how Gideon executed on one of his cases?"

"Gideon doesn't get distracted. You're more worried about saving a girl who might not need saving so you can impress her sister than you are about our client."

Shawn's hands balled into fists. Growing up in a household full of testosterone-led males, physical fights weren't unheard-of. It had been a long time since he'd punched one of his brothers, but at the moment, he itched to clock Ryan. Maturity held him back.

Instead, he stepped in closer to Ryan so they were only inches apart.

"Then I guess I'm more like you than either of us realized," Shawn said.

Nadia, Ryan's wife, had been a client of West Security when they'd gotten together.

Ryan glared.

For a moment Shawn again thought they might come to blows, then Ryan let out a deep sigh. "We don't have time to argue. We still need proof Spectrum is behind the fraud."

Shawn took a step back, a tacit agreement to a truce. "Then I suggest we go up and plan out our next steps. If my instincts are correct, the girl you think might not need saving and the fraudulent chips are connected. And if we're running out of time, so is she."

Chapter Seventeen

Shawn and Ryan found Addy and Gideon finishing dinner when they returned to the suite. The first thing Shawn noted was that sleep seemed to have done a world of good for Addy. The ashen pallor that dusted her face in the hospital was gone, and she attacked the Thai noodles on her plate with her usual vigor.

She turned a brilliant smile on him, sending a punch of desire through him.

"We got enough for both of you," she said, pointing to the takeout containers in the center of the table.

He smiled wanly and dropped into the chair next to her, reaching for the food. "Thanks."

Addy shot him a questioning look, but he focused on the curry chicken in front of him.

Ryan picked up the last takeout container. "I'm going to bring this back to my room."

"I'll head out, too," Gideon said, rising and tossing his empty container in the garbage.

Moments later, Ryan and Gideon were gone.

Addy tilted her head, looking at him. "It couldn't have been anything I said."

"It's not you. Ryan's pissed at me. Don't worry about it." He speared a piece of chicken and chewed.

"I guess whatever you two were up to tonight didn't go well."

He shook his head. Finding Addy awake meant he, Ryan and Gideon weren't able to talk about the Intellus case. He was sure Ryan would take care of bringing Gideon up to speed, but they'd have to wait until they could be alone to plan their next steps.

Not that he knew what the next steps should be.

He was confident Ben was at least aware of the fraud. The chip he'd found in Ben's desk seemed evidence enough of that. But was he in on it? And how did the fraud connect to Cassie's disappearance?

Addy seemed content to let him eat and ruminate. His phone ringing broke the silence in the suite.

"Shawn West."

"I didn't have anything to do with you getting shot at." Ben's shrill, almost frantic voice rang out.

Shawn put the call on speaker, motioning for Addy to stay quiet as he did.

"I have a really hard time believing that, Ben," Shawn replied, his voice hard.

"I didn't, I swear. I mean, Mr. Raupp saw that note you left for me asking for a tour of the factory. I called to ask him if it was okay to take you on a tour of the factory, but I didn't know he'd send Teddy after you."

Lance Raupp. It made sense. Ben was in the perfect position to orchestrate the fraud, but he lacked the mental firepower to pull it off. Not like Lance, who was smart enough to organize the scam and offer up Ben as the fall guy.

Of course, Ben's declaration of complete innocence rang hollow. Ben had taken that two-lane county highway on purpose, leading them right to Teddy. But arguing with him wasn't going to get Shawn what he wanted, so he put it aside for now.

"This whole thing is out of control," Ben screeched into the phone. "I just wanted to make some extra cash."

"What's out of control? Why would Raupp send Teddy Arbury to shoot at us?"

"Oh, man. This is really bad. Teddy, that guy isn't all there."

"Ben?" Shawn was quickly losing patience with the conversation.

"Look, all I did was package and deliver some fake computer chips. No big deal, but then Cassie figured out what was going on and Raupp said she needed to be dealt with."

A strangled squeak came from Addy's throat. Shawn squeezed her hand and lifted a finger to his lips, indicating she should remain quiet. He didn't want Ben realizing she was listening in and clamming up.

His instincts had been spot-on. Cassie was mixed up in the fraud, but she'd discovered it—she hadn't been a part of it.

"How did you deal with her?" Shawn asked.

"Me? I didn't do anything but help Suri get a job out of town. Teddy is the one who dealt with Cassie."

Tremors shook Addy's body.

Shawn prayed the answer to his next question wouldn't break her. "Is Cassie still alive?"

"I… I'm not sure. I think so," Ben stammered.

Addy's breath released in an audible whoosh.

"I overheard Raupp and Teddy talking about keeping her alive until the next shipment of chips goes out. Look, I need your help. I know you're some big-shot PI from New York City. The last shipment goes out tonight. Once those chips are delivered, Raupp won't want to keep either of us alive."

Could Ben be playing them again? Shawn hadn't been able to look inside every box he'd loaded earlier that evening, but none of the ones he'd opened had contained fraudulent chips. Their best bet was to get their hands on Ben and get the whole story as soon as possible.

"Where are you?" Shawn asked.

"I'm… I'm at my grandmother's old place—it's been empty for years. I figured it was a good place to hide under the radar for a while, but Raupp is bound to look here eventually. I need to get out of town."

"What's the address?" Shawn grabbed the hotel notepad from the television stand. He jotted down the address while Addy keyed it into her phone's GPS.

"You have to come get me," Ben demanded.

Addy turned her phone screen outward so Shawn could see it. The GPS put the address about twenty minutes away from the hotel.

"Sit tight," he said ending the call and immediately making another.

"What's wrong?" Ryan asked when the call connected.

Shawn filled his brother in on the call from Ben. Before he'd finished, a knock sounded on the suite door.

"Could be another trap," Ryan said, striding into the suite.

Gideon followed with a large black duffel bag that Shawn knew held a number of devices useful for various excursions.

"That's why I need you and Gideon to go with me."

Ryan set the laptop he carried on the table and went to work. Shawn knew he was pulling up maps of the area as well as real estate info and whatever other information he could find on the address Ben had given them.

"Ben said Cassie was still alive," Addy added. She'd been silent since Ben's call. Shawn hadn't pushed, allowing her space.

Shawn took her hand in his. "Ben has a lot of reasons to lie right now."

"I've got to hang on to hope."

The last thing he wanted to do was to take away her last fragment of hope. If this was another ploy by Ben to attack them, they'd cross that bridge when they got to it.

"Let's go, then," Addy said, looking from Gideon to Ryan before her gaze landed on Shawn.

Shawn shook his head. "You're staying here."

"No way. I've come this far, and I will see this to the end."

"I put you in danger once already today." He put a hand on each of her shoulders, turning her toward him. "It's not going to happen again."

Addy gripped his wrist. "Shawn, I am a grown woman. I understand there are risks, and I'm willing to take them."

He shook his head.

"If you leave me, I'll just drive myself."

His mind worked overtime to come up with a way to keep her at the hotel. Given Teddy's determination this morning, Shawn wasn't comfortable leaving Addy at the hotel alone, anyway. He wasn't taking any chances this time. He needed Ryan and Gideon for backup when he approached Ben. Taking Addy with them would keep her close, and if she waited in the car while they secured Ben, she should be safe.

"You'll go with us, but you have to do what we say. It's the only way we can be sure you'll be safe."

Addy's mouth turned down, but she nodded.

Ryan's gaze moved from the computer screen to Shawn. "Gideon and I picked up a rental after we left the hospital. We can follow you two to the house."

Minutes later they were in their respective vehicles and rolling toward Ben's grandmother's house. A light snow fell as they drove, reflecting off the car's bright headlights.

Ben's grandmother's neighborhood was older, built when homeowners expected more than an arm's-length worth of land between their home and their neighbor's. The houses that lined the street in a neat row of symmetrical brick squares were worn and time battered, the occupants more concerned with survival than home repair. Here and there, multicolored lights had been strewn around a tree or an inflatable Santa waved from a front yard.

Shawn parked the SUV behind Ryan's rental three houses down from the address Ben had given him.

Ryan and Gideon met Shawn and Addy in the darkness between the two cars.

Ryan glanced from Addy to Shawn. "How do you want to play this?"

"I'll go through the front." Shawn looked at Ryan and Gideon. "You two come through the back."

Ryan nodded and opened his hand. Three small earpieces sat in his palm. Shawn and Gideon each took one.

"What about me?" Addy asked.

"You stay in the car," Shawn said, fitting the earpiece in his right ear.

"I already told you—" Addy began.

"And now I'm telling you. You stay in the car until we clear the house. I'll come get you when we know it's safe." When she looked like she was ready to argue, he softened his tone and added, "Addy, please."

She scowled. "Okay. But I want to be there when you talk to Ben."

"Done," he promised, relieved that she'd agreed without further argument. No matter what, he was determined that she would not be hurt again.

Addy returned to the car, and he waited until he heard the door locks click into place before motioning for Ryan and Gideon to take up stations around the house.

The exterior of Ben's grandmother's home was covered in chipped, faded white stucco. Rotten wood fencing encircled the overgrown front yard.

Shawn walked along the crumbling concrete walkway, his eyes scanning back and forth for shapes lurking in the adjacent yards or too-curious faces in neighboring windows.

An American flag rippled on the house next door, but unsurprisingly he saw no one. It wasn't a neighborhood where it paid to be curious.

He waited for Ryan and Gideon to round the side of the house before climbing the front steps to the porch.

Just in case someone was watching, Shawn kept his gun in its holster under his jacket. He knocked on the front door. "Ben? It's Shawn West."

Nothing but silence answered from inside.

He attempted to peer through the window at the side of the door, but it was covered with years of grime, making it impossible to see anything inside.

Shawn knocked again, then tried the door. It opened easily.

"Front door is unlocked," he said, knowing Ryan and Gideon would hear through their earpieces. "Going in."

Shawn stepped inside, pulling his gun.

The cold temperatures had done nothing to quell the smell of garbage and animal feces that permeated the air. Only abject fear and desperation would lead a person to seek shelter in the house.

"Front room clear," Shawn said.

"Coming in the back door." Ryan's voice came through Shawn's earpiece.

"Ben? Are you here?" Shawn called out again.

He inched past the faded burgundy velvet couch in the den and the aged yellow linoleum flooring in the kitchen. Almost everything in the house was covered in a thick layer of dust, but the kitchen table had been wiped clean, and a single plate and cup were in the sink.

In his line of work, Shawn had learned to trust his instincts, and he had a bad feeling about the current situation. It smacked of a setup, but if there was even a small chance that Ben knew where to find Cassie, it was a chance they had to take.

"Basement's clear." Ryan's voice came through the earpiece.

"Kitchen clear. Holding here," Gideon responded.

The home's two bedrooms were at the back of the house.

"Ben? It's Shawn West," he called, identifying himself again in case Ben was afraid to come out of hiding.

The house was still.

He and Ryan converged at the opening to the hallway leading to the bedrooms and a single bath in the house.

Ryan motioned, signaling he'd clear the first room.

Shawn nodded and moved to the second door on the right.

A heavy wooden dresser lined one wall and a woman's dressing table sat against the other. A four-poster bed stood between them. A single pillow and a tousled blanket lay across the otherwise unmade bed.

Ben lay on the floor at the foot of the bed. Shawn swept the closet quickly to make sure no one hid in the room.

It looked like Ben had been wrong about no one looking for him at his grandmother's, but he'd been right to be scared. It had taken less than thirty minutes for Shawn and Ryan to get to Ben's grandmother's house, but they'd still been too late.

Shawn crouched next to Ben. The bullet hole in Ben's head left no doubt that he was dead, although the still-congealing blood indicated he hadn't been that way for long.

"The house is clear." Ryan's voice came in stereo through the earpiece and from behind Shawn.

Shawn stood and moved aside, giving a clear line of sight from the door to Ben's body.

Whatever Ben knew about Cassie or the fraudulent chips, he'd never reveal now. Ben's killer had gotten to him quickly. And by all appearances, they had just missed Ben's murderer.

How had the killer known where to find Ben and that he'd been about to tell all?

Shawn scanned the small room for Ben's cell phone but didn't spot it. The killer might have taken it with him in an effort to conceal his communication with Ben. They'd probably never know. If Ben's killer had his phone, he'd certainly destroy it the first chance he got.

Shawn and Ryan backed from the room. They made it back to the living room as Addy came through the front door.

Shawn swore. He stepped in front of Addy, putting his hands on her shoulders to keep her from barreling down the hallway they'd just come from.

"Where is he? Did he tell you where Cassie is?" Addy craned her neck to see around Shawn.

He looked down at her. "You can't go back there, Addy."

Addy's expression was fierce. "Move, Shawn." She tried to shake his hands off, but he held firm.

"Listen to me. Ben's not talking to anyone. Addy, he's dead."

She froze.

"No. He…he can't be. He knows where Cassie is. He knows."

He pulled her to him, holding her as her shoulders began to shake with sobs. "I'm sorry, sweetheart. I'm so sorry."

Chapter Eighteen

Shawn shot Addy another concerned look. The last of several since they'd left the police station. He mercifully hadn't tried to engage her in conversation. She didn't have it in her to talk anymore right now.

Sheriff Donovan had been apoplectic when he'd arrived at the scene. He'd threatened to arrest all four of them and probably would have if he could have found any cause. At the station, the sheriff had asked a hundred questions a dozen different ways, even after she'd told them she hadn't seen anything. After hours of questioning, he'd finally let them go well after midnight.

Addy felt hollowed out, yet she wanted to scream.

They were so close. Deputies had found Cassie's scooter in a shed in the backyard, but no sign that Cassie had been at the home.

She was sure Ben had known more than he'd told them, maybe even where Cassie was being held.

"I'm not going to find Cassie. She's probably… I'm probably too late."

"Don't say that." Shawn reached a hand across the middle console, but Addy pressed into the side door. "We're doing everything we can, and we'll keep doing everything we can."

"I'm always too late." She'd been too late in noticing her ex-husband pulling away. Too late seeing how sick her father had become. And now, too late to save Cassie. The words looped around her heart.

The SUV jerked as Shawn slammed into a parking space in the hotel's parking lot.

He turned to her and took her by the shoulders. "Stop! You're doing the best you can."

"That's just it. My best is never good enough! No matter what I do, the people I care about just keep leaving me, no matter what I do."

Shawn wrapped his arms around her. She clung to him, shaking with silent sobs. She couldn't remember ever crying as much as she had in the last several days. But for a few precious minutes, she put down the mantle of the strong sister and daughter and let herself fall apart. It probably meant something that she felt comfortable doing so with Shawn, but she'd have to save that analysis for a time when she wasn't having a nervous breakdown.

After several minutes, she gathered herself. They walked from the car to their room, Shawn's arm around Addy's shoulder, hers around his waist. As much strength as she drew from Shawn's presence, what she really wanted and needed was time to sift through her emotions alone.

Addy crossed to the bedroom, turning back to look at Shawn before going in. "I'm going to take a shower." She needed a nice long soak in the suite's Jacuzzi tub, but she'd have to wait until she got her stitches out. The injury to her side throbbed, and she desperately needed a painkiller.

In the bedroom, she grabbed the pill bottle from the bedside table and swallowed two pills with a glass of water from the bathroom sink. Her torso muscles still felt like a tight rubber band on the verge of snapping. Until that night it had been easy imagining Cassie was still alive. But Ben's murder moved the entire situation into a new, much more dangerous place.

She started the shower, then padded into the bedroom while the water warmed to grab a change of clothes from her suitcase. She could hear Shawn's and Ryan's voices, low but still audible through the closed door. They weren't arguing, exactly, but the tone of the conversation was tense. She pressed her ear to the bedroom door, catching more of the conversation.

"I honestly don't know. I'm sure Ben is involved in both the fraud and Cassie's disappearance, but there's no hard evidence the two things have anything to do with each other," Shawn said.

"Cassie Williams knows computers, and she worked at Spectrum. She could be in on the fraud, too," Ryan responded.

His words reminded her that Ben had mentioned something about delivering fraudulent chips when he'd called. That must be the other case Shawn was in town for. But what did Cassie have to do with any fraud?

Addy swung the door open and marched into the living room.

Ryan sat on the sofa, Shawn across from him in an armchair.

"Are you insane?" Addy fisted her hands at her sides, glancing from Shawn to Ryan. "Cassie would never have gotten involved in any fraud."

She noted that the utter surprise on their faces would have been comical in another situation. But at that moment, she was too angry to laugh at anything. She turned to Shawn. "Is this the case you've been working on? Have you been investigating Cassie?"

Shawn rose from his seat. "I'm not investigating Cassie." He glanced at his brother before training his gaze back on Addy. "I'm investigating the production of fraudulent computer chips. We think Ben is somehow involved."

"And Cassie?" Addy took a step backward, putting space between them. She felt like the pieces of a puzzle had just snapped into place in her mind, and she finally saw the whole picture. "That's what this has been all along. You helping me but really trying to find Cassie because you think she's involved in your other case."

"That's not true." Shawn moved toward her.

She shot both hands out in front of her, stopping his progress.

"I considered whether Cassie could be involved in the fraud, but I never believed it. Addy, you have to believe me." Shawn's gaze beseeched her.

He sounded sincere, and her heart cried out for her to believe him.

"We have to consider the possibilities," Ryan said from his perch on the couch. "Whether you want to believe it or not, your sister has the knowledge to do something like this. The disappearance could be her way out." Ryan crossed his arms over his chest.

Addy shook her head. "You have no idea what you're talking about."

Shawn cut off the rest of her rebuke. "Someone at Spectrum is behind the fraudulent chips—I think it's safe to say that's the case—and they've been manufacturing the frauds for a while, starting well before Cassie began working with the company."

"Maybe they recruited her? It is somewhat strange for

a young woman to move from New York City to a relatively small town. Or Spectrum could have just gotten lucky when Cassie walked in looking for a job." Ryan continued to argue his point.

Ryan didn't know her sister like she did. Cassie was kind and gentle. She believed in doing the right thing, even when it was difficult. She never would have taken part in fraud.

"What about what Ben said when he called? Lance Raupp kidnapped Cassie."

"We can't take anything Ben said at face value," Ryan answered.

"You just want to believe the worst of Cassie to give your client a scapegoat."

Ryan didn't respond.

The drum of the still-running water in the bathroom filled the silence. Addy turned back to the bedroom. She shut off the shower in time to hear someone knocking on the suite door. Hurrying back to the living area, she caught Gideon strolling into the room.

"I just got a tip on Teddy's whereabouts." Gideon stopped in the center of the room, looking at them each in turn. "What's going on?"

"Nothing. Whaddya got?" Ryan answered.

Addy wasn't finished with this conversation by a long shot, but with Ben dead and not enough evidence to pressure Lance into coming clean about his part in whatever was going on, Teddy might be the last hope for finding Cassie alive.

Gideon's expression remained skeptical, but he let the matter drop. "Teddy is holed up at a girlfriend's place the next town over. My source says he has a bullet hole in his arm." He quirked an eyebrow at Addy.

Ryan moved back to the couch and pulled the laptop into his lap.

Gideon, Shawn and Addy followed suit, each one pulling a chair over from the dining table. Gideon relayed the information he'd gotten from his source. Addy had seen the town name on an exit sign on the highway between Bentham and Garwin. As far as Gideon's source knew, Teddy was still there.

Ryan called up a satellite map of the address, and after several minutes of strategizing, the guys settled on a plan of approach.

"Okay, what time are we leaving?" Addy asked, looking from one brother to the other.

Ryan gave a hard shake of his head.

"You can't come with us," Shawn said.

Now Addy stood, too. "Cassie's my sister, and I am not going to sit around while she's out there needing my help."

"This is not a place you want to be," Ryan said.

"It's not safe. Teddy shot at us once already," Shawn agreed.

She wanted to argue with him. She could probably wear him down until he gave in, but to what end? Her side still ached, and all she'd do was slow them down. What she wanted, what she needed, was information that would help her locate Cassie. If hanging back was the best way to get it, then she'd do what she had to do.

"Fine."

Shawn reached for her hand, stopping her before she walked away from the table.

"We will find Cassie."

She prayed with everything in her that he was right.

Addy finally got into the shower after Shawn and Ryan left to track down Teddy. The hot water helped loosen up the muscles in her body. From being shot at to finding Ben dead, cords of tension wound around her muscles. She stood under the shower until the hot water ran tepid, then got out. Try as she might to turn off her thoughts, her mind kept going back to Ryan's ridiculous suggestion that Cassie could be involved in fraud.

Cassie was a sweet, kind computer nerd. She wanted to make technology accessible for everyone, to use it for the common good. She wouldn't be involved in stealing from members of the community she loved being a part of. Cassie had once returned to the grocery store to pay for a bag of chips a cashier had forgotten to ring up. Cassie would have gone straight to the sheriff if she'd known about any fraud.

But what if Addy was wrong? Was the big-sister lens through which she saw Cassie painting a picture of Cassie that was rosier than what the rest of the world saw?

She grabbed clean underwear from her overnight bag and put it on before shimmying into pajama bottoms.

Her cell rang on the bedside table. A local number she didn't recognize.

"Hello."

"Addy?"

The weak but familiar voice sent Addy's heart into her throat.

"Cassie! Cassie, where are you?" Tears of relief streamed over her cheeks, leaving wet splotches on her shirt.

"Ms. Williams, you and your sister have been far more trouble than either of you are worth, so if you want your sister, come get her." Addy's pulse raced. The cultured voice that flowed through the line was Martin Raupp's.

"Where is she?" Addy stripped off her pajamas and pulled on the jeans she'd worn that day.

"Our old fabrication facility on Route 29. I'm willing to let your sister go, but if you involve the police, well, I'll have nothing to lose then. Understood?"

Addy snatched her purse from the coffee table and headed for the door of the suite.

"How do I know this isn't a trap?" She headed out the door as she spoke.

"You don't."

The line went dead.

Addy ran down the hall, forgoing the elevators for the stairwell. She hit the heavy door with enough force to send it flying open and pounded down the stairs, the phone still in her hand.

She ran across the parking lot to the Mustang, sliding behind the wheel while she dialed Shawn's number. Her heart pounded hard enough that she wouldn't have been surprised if he heard it on the other end of the line.

His phone went straight to voice mail.

She let loose with a string of swears and barreled out of the parking space. "Shawn, Raupp just called me. Cassie is alive. He's holding her at his factory on Route 29. I'm headed there now."

She prayed she wouldn't be too late.

Chapter Nineteen

The ride to Chatham was quiet. Shawn attempted to push his pique aside as Ryan drove. Confronting a man who'd already shot at him once was dangerous enough without negative emotions clouding his judgment. It was hard. Every protective instinct he had had been triggered as Ryan and Addy argued. He wasn't objective when it came to Addy—he couldn't be. He loved her.

"Listen, what I said earlier about you being distracted. I was out of line questioning your work ethic." Ryan broke the silence.

Shawn shook his head. "Now is probably not the best time for this conversation."

Ryan shot him a half smile. "We don't know exactly what we're about to walk into. I don't want you mad at me." As usual, they were on a similar wavelength.

"For real," Ryan continued. "You're an asset to the company, and I don't say that enough."

"Thank you. And look, I know I could step up more on the administrative side of things. You have a new wife and a baby coming. When we get back, I will do better."

Ryan rolled his eyes, but there was humor in them.

"You'll have to show me the ropes, of course, but I'm

serious. If I want you to treat me like a co-owner, I need to act like one."

"Okay. Okay. Let's not get ahead of ourselves. I'm still the president of the company, but I appreciate you stepping up. I'm going to want to spend some time with Nadia and the baby after she's born."

"It's going to be so fun to watch you with a daughter one day." Shawn laughed.

As they drove closer to the address Gideon's source had given them, the houses they passed appeared more run-down and the businesses fewer and fewer. They both sobered.

As they neared the location, the tension in the car ratcheted up. Given that Teddy had tried to kill him and Addy this morning, they planned to approach with guns drawn, but the seedy, run-down nature of the surrounding neighborhood only accentuated the potential danger.

Shawn drove slowly past the three-story brick apartment building where Teddy was supposedly lying low. A dirt yard fronted the structure and wound its way around to the back where residents parked their cars. A dirty vertical window traversed the center of the building, revealing an interior stairwell. There were lights on in several of the apartments on either side.

It was a few minutes after 2:00 a.m. They had no idea if Teddy was still inside the apartment, but if he was Shawn was determined to make the man talk.

Shawn pulled into the parking lot behind a neighboring apartment complex, and the three of them got out of the car.

They each checked their guns, then slid on tactical vests. They fit their earpieces and did a sound check before moving toward the building.

It wasn't the first time they'd worked together, and they each knew their role. Shawn approached slowly from the front, keeping to the shadows. Ryan circled, approaching from the back. Gideon hung back, keeping an eye out for anyone coming up behind them.

Ryan came around the building, meeting Shawn at the front door.

"One exterior exit at the rear. Requires a key to enter from the outside," Ryan said.

"I'm on it." Gideon's voice came through the earpiece.

"We're going in the front now," Shawn said, following Ryan through the unlocked front door.

The unit Teddy hid out in was on the second floor. They stopped in front of unit twenty-three, Ryan to the right of the door and Shawn to the left.

Shawn counted to three, mouthing the numbers so he didn't tip off the occupant of the apartment to their arrival.

On three, Ryan kicked the door open, sending it crashing against the wall.

The apartment was a studio with a small kitchenette tucked into a corner.

Teddy lay on a threadbare brown couch barely off the floor. On the floor next to the couch sat an old flip cell phone, a nearly empty bottle of rum and a Glock.

For a moment Teddy stared, wide-eyed like a deer caught in headlights, as Shawn came through the door and advanced toward him. Then he lunged for the gun.

Shawn got there first, kicking the gun under the couch and grabbing Teddy's injured arm.

"Ahhh!" Teddy cradled his arm against his chest.

Ryan cleared the small bathroom and came to a stop

next to Shawn. They waited a moment for Teddy's caterwauling to quiet.

Shawn kept his gun trained on Teddy. "Teddy, we have some things we need to discuss."

"I ain't saying shit to you." Teddy pushed himself into a sitting position using his good hand. He'd used a belt and a dirty white T-shirt to make a tourniquet for his arm. His legs splayed open on the couch, his beady green eyes cloudy and unfocused as a result of pain and booze. The grayish pall of his skin suggested he'd lost quite a bit of blood.

"Now, now, Teddy. There's no call for that kind of language," Shawn said.

"You shot me!"

This was interesting. Teddy hadn't noticed it was Addy shooting from their vehicle. They might be able to use that information later, but for now, he was happy to have all Teddy's anger focused on him.

"So we're just going to ignore that you were shooting at us first. That's cool. I'm willing to let bygones be bygones, Teddy. Who shot who is so this morning. What I want to know is where is Cassie Williams?" Shawn said.

"Screw you, man," Teddy spat out. Then his mouth curled up into an ominous smirk. "You're too late, anyway. The delivery is going down now, and Raupp's going to kill the women right after."

Icy shards of fear spread through Shawn. "Women?"

Teddy laughed sinisterly. "Raupp's decided to get rid of both the Williams sisters. That oldest one has really pissed him off, and she's a threat to his operation. He won't tolerate that."

Fury and fear tangled in Shawn's stomach.

"Where? Where would Lance hold them?"

Teddy smirked. "You don't have a clue."

Shawn's heart raced in fear, but he held the gun steady and put two bullets in the bottom front panel of the couch between Teddy's legs.

Out of the corner of his eye, he saw Ryan move to cover the apartment door, in case the shots brought curious neighbors. In a neighborhood like this one, it wasn't likely that a couple of muffled shots would lead anyone to call the cops, but they knew better than to take chances. Cops meant questioning, and if Teddy was telling the truth, he didn't have that kind of time.

A string of swears burst from Teddy's mouth. He covered his groin with his good hand. "What the hell? You almost shot off my junk."

"The next shot I won't miss," Shawn said. "Where are they?"

"You won't get there in time, anyway."

"Then it hardly seems worth losing your manhood over, but it's your call." Shawn raised the gun a fraction of an inch higher. "I won't ask again."

Teddy's eyes widened in fear. "All right, all right. Raupp called your girlfriend about a half hour ago. Told her to meet him at the factory if she wanted to see her sister alive. He told her to come alone, but he's expecting you."

Shawn glanced at Ryan. "We've got to go."

Ryan jerked his head toward Teddy. "What do you want to do with him?"

"We can't wait for Donovan." Shawn pulled a pair of handcuffs from his vest. He hauled Teddy up from the couch and pushed him toward the kitchenette.

"Sit," he ordered Teddy.

Teddy lowered himself to the scarred linoleum with a grimace.

Shawn snapped one side of the handcuff around Teddy's wrist and the other around the handle on the stove. "We can call Donovan to come get him from the car."

Teddy pulled at the stove. "You can't leave me like this."

"Be grateful, Teddy. You were this far from becoming a eunuch," Shawn said, closing the apartment door.

Shawn pulled out his phone and dialed Addy's number as they burst from a side door out into the trash-strewn yard surrounding the apartment building. Gideon met them at the SUV.

Addy didn't pick up, but she'd left a voice mail message. His blood chilled as he listened to the message.

"Martin Raupp. He's got Cassie. Addy's gone to meet him."

Ryan swore and started the SUV. "Martin Raupp? The father?" Ryan swore again. "That's what Teddy meant when he said we don't have a clue. We were looking at the wrong Raupp."

Shawn called out the address Addy had left on the voice mail, and Ryan plugged it into the GPS. "I know this address, but I can't place it." He frowned and dialed Tansy.

Ryan gunned the SUV out of the parking lot.

"Sup?" Tansy answered.

"On my way to an address. It's familiar, but I can't place why." Shawn gave Tansy the address and listened as computer keys clacked on the other end of the line.

Less than a minute later, she spoke. "It's the address for that building Spectrum previously leased. It was in the initial research I gave you on the company. There's a recent real estate listing putting it up for rent, so looks like it isn't in use."

He remembered now. Carrier-Forest LLC. He'd planned to research the property, but so much had happened since he'd rolled into Bentham, investigating a warehouse that Spectrum no longer used had slipped his mind.

He saw now what a mistake that had been. Empty property made for an excellent place to hold someone against their will.

"It's empty, but who owns it?" Shawn asked, although he suspected he already knew the answer to that question.

"Hang on," Tansy replied. A moment passed before she spoke again. "Deed's in the name of Madeline Raupp."

"Damn. I should have caught that," Shawn said after he'd signed off with Tansy.

Martin probably counted on no one thinking about a property Spectrum no longer operated out of.

"We gotta get there now. Raupp has got to be desperate by now. His entire scheme is crashing down around him."

Ryan pushed the SUV to go faster.

Shawn checked the safety on his gun as the neighborhood flew by outside the car's windows. "If Raupp has touched a hair on Addy's head, I'll send him straight to hell."

Chapter Twenty

Addy found the factory easily. A large, faded for-rent sign stood sentry at the entrance to the empty parking lot fronting the drab single-story square building. The weak glow from the one functioning lamppost near the building's door did little to cut through the darkness.

Ignoring the faded white lines marking the asphalt, Addy pulled to a stop directly in front of the spiritless gray building. A large metal loading door was set into the wall of the building next to the glass-fronted main entrance.

Martin stepped out of the glass doors as Addy stopped the car. She reached for her purse in the passenger seat, slinging it across her body.

Martin stepped outside, sticking close to the cover granted by the alcove entrance. Security on either corner of the building sent light bouncing off the silver pistol in Martin's hand. He peered at the car, then scanned the parking lot beyond. "Where's your boyfriend?" Martin's words dripped with disdain.

On his way, I hope, Addy thought. "I came alone." She swallowed the fear clogging her throat. "Where is Cassie?"

Martin scanned the expanse of the building again.

"Inside." Martin stepped aside and motioned to the door with the gun. "Now."

Addy passed Martin, ignoring his smirk.

Any furniture in the space had long since been removed, leaving only threadbare gray carpeting and a chipped and scarred reception desk.

"Down the hall to your left." Martin prodded her in the back with the gun.

Addy flinched, her grandfather's voice floating through her head. *It's never the gun's fault. It's always the idiot who's holding it.*

They walked down a long laminate-tiled hall, the click of the heels of Martin's loafers the only sound in the cold, otherwise empty corridor. Despite being in the process of committing any number of felonies, he'd managed to dress the part of genteel businessman in tailored brown slacks and a crisp white button-down.

"In the office on your left," Martin said, motioning to a closed door.

Addy glanced over her shoulder at him. If this was a trap, she could be walking to her death.

But the voice she'd heard on the phone was Cassie's, which meant her sister was alive or at least had been twenty minutes ago. If there was any chance Cassie was inside this room, she had to go in.

Addy reached for the doorknob, turning it slowly. She pushed the door open and froze.

Cassie sat in a desk chair, her left wrist cuffed to a large black filing cabinet. Her hair was a rat's nest of tangles and knots, and her face was slimmer than it had been the last time Addy saw her, but she was alive.

"Cassie!" Addy raced forward, kneeling so she could wrap her sister in a hug.

"Addy, I'm sorry." Tears rolled down Cassie's gaunt cheeks, her shoulders shaking on a sob.

"No, honey. Don't be sorry. None of this is your fault. We're going to get out of here."

The sound of the door snapping closed drew both their attention. Addy's gaze fell on Martin Raupp, whose gun remained trained in their direction.

"I'm sorry, but I think you know I can't let that happen."

Addy straightened and put herself between Martin and Cassie. Cassie peeked around Addy's side, her hand slipping into Addy's. "You said you would let Cassie go."

Martin shrugged. "I lied. I've got to make a very important delivery tonight, and you girls are going with me."

"Why? Why not just leave us here and go? Too many people know you're behind the fake computer chips. Your fraud is over."

"You're so confident you're right," Martin sneered. "From where I'm sitting, the only people who know anything are staring down the barrel of my gun. And both of you are going to disappear. For good this time," Martin said.

A wave of fear crashed through Addy, followed by the determination that she couldn't let Martin Raupp win. Cassie had managed to stay alive for nearly two weeks. Addy just needed one shot at Martin to bring him down.

"At least answer me this," Addy asked to keep Martin talking and buy time. "Why? You're a well-respected businessman. Spectrum is a successful business. Why risk everything you've built?"

"Call it diversification. Spectrum is a little fish in a very big pond. Frankly, there's a great deal of money to be made in cyberfraud. Plus, there's the added bonus of destroying the competition."

"Greed and jealousy," Cassie said.

Martin's face twisted in anger. The hate-filled glare he shot Cassie made Addy's mouth go dry. Cassie's grip on her hand tightened.

"None of that explains why you kidnapped my sister," Addy offered quickly. The last thing she wanted was to make him angry.

"Your sister stuck her nose in where she shouldn't have," Martin spat.

Cassie glared back at Martin. "Ben showed me one of the fake chips. He was drunk and he told me all about the fraud."

"Idiot," Martin snarled. "I should have known better than to bring him in on it, but I needed delivery drivers who had, shall we say, malleable ethics to make the extra deliveries off the books. Then he blackmailed me into giving him a management job." Martin's snarl morphed into a cold smile. "I didn't mind killing him at all."

"I told Ben he should go to the sheriff. That what Martin was doing could get him in a lot of trouble when it came out, but Ben wanted the money." Cassie shook her head forlornly.

Martin scoffed. "Sheriff Donovan. I'd be surprised if Donovan can spell fraud, much less be able to spot one. He's only interested in two things—upholding the illusion that there's no crime in Bentham and getting reelected. Three guesses who his biggest political donor is." Martin's smile grew wider.

Cassie wheeled the office chair she sat in so she was beside Addy. "Ben wouldn't go to the sheriff, so I decided to go myself. But I wanted some proof. He caught me going through his files after work." Cassie jutted her chin in Martin Raupp's direction.

"That dolt Ben had just told me you knew about the fraud. I was trying to figure out what to do about it when I saw you going through the files. I knew you wouldn't be bought off. I had my little friend here." Martin gestured with the gun. "And I was able to persuade Miss Williams to partake in a little staycation in my basement."

Martin looked pleased with himself.

"And you had Ben and Suri Bedingfield tell the sheriff Cassie had moved back to New York." Addy filled in the rest of the blanks. Cassie's gasp told Addy she hadn't been aware of that part of the story. "Did you think no one would come looking when Cassie didn't make it back home?"

Martin flicked his wrist, looking at his watch before focusing back on Addy. "Don't you watch the news? Women traveling alone going missing is nothing new. Even if a relative came looking, that had nothing to do with me or Spectrum." Martin's eyes darkened. "I guess I underestimated you. It won't happen again."

He took several steps to the left, away from the door. "Big sister, you get over there." He waved Addy toward the corner of the room opposite Cassie.

Addy hesitated. Martin was clearly done with talking, but it wasn't clear exactly what he planned next. Attempting anything was risky in the small room, particularly given Cassie's limited mobility.

"Now! And keep your hands where I can see them," Martin growled.

Addy did as he said, moving to the side of the desk. A few sheets of computer paper and a glass paperweight the size of a large marble were the only items on the desktop.

Her heart thundered in her chest as she watched Martin approach Cassie. If he turned just a little more, she might have a chance.

Martin stopped short of turning his back on Addy. He pulled a handcuff key from his pocket and tossed it at Cassie without taking his eyes off Addy. "Uncuff yourself."

Yes! They had a much better chance of overpowering Martin together. Cassie was weak, but Addy knew her sister would fight for her life. Knowing her sister, Cassie was probably more than a little pissed off at Martin Raupp.

Cassie fumbled with the key in her nondominant left hand. Martin kept his gun trained on Addy, but his irritated gazed flicked to Cassie. "Hurry up!"

As discreetly as she could while Martin wasn't looking, Addy reached for the paperweight. It didn't look like it would do much good as a weapon, but maybe she could use it as a distraction.

It took several more tries, but Cassie finally got the cuff off. She rubbed her bruised, raw wrist.

Martin gestured with the gun. "Head for the hallway. Both of you."

Cassie stumbled toward Addy. Although she didn't appear to be hurt physically, she was weak. Addy wrapped her arm around Cassie's waist and helped her to the door.

"To the right. We're going to the loading docks," Martin said.

They walked through the corridor, following Martin's directions, the overhead security lights illuminating the way.

Two oversize red doors loomed at the end of the hall. A sign affixed to the one on the right declared this the entrance to the factory floor. Another sign on the left cautioned that the area was for authorized personnel only and that protective gear must be worn at all times.

"Go on," Martin prodded.

Addy held on to Cassie with one hand and pushed the metal bar in the middle of the door with the other.

The space on the other side of the doors was dark.

Martin was obviously familiar with the space. He reached for the wall to their left, the dim light that trickled in from the door he still held open illuminating a panel of light switches on the wall.

Martin flicked each of the switches in turn, but nothing happened. The room remained shrouded in darkness.

It was now or never. Addy launched the paperweight toward the far end of the factory floor. The distraction worked as she'd hoped. Martin turned with the gun toward the sound of the glass breaking. Grabbing Cassie by the shirt, Addy half pulled, half dragged her behind an enormous machine to the right of the door and along an aisle of equipment.

She had no idea where they were going or if there was another exit from the factory floor.

She could hear Martin swearing at her and Cassie and at the lights that he still struggled to get on.

She reached into her purse, wrapping her hand around her gun and unclipping it from its holster.

Addy didn't know whether to wish for the lights to come on or remain off. As much as the darkness hampered their advance to freedom, it also made it that much more difficult for Martin to find them.

"Are you familiar with the layout of this place?" Addy asked quietly, still half dragging her sister.

"No," Cassie whispered, wincing. "I've never been here before."

Cassie cradled her arm, and although Addy couldn't see an injury there, she knew firsthand that didn't mean there was none. The wound on her torso stretched and stabbed with pain.

They kept moving around large pieces of equipment and turned a corner.

Martin, wherever he was now, had gone ominously quiet.

They'd made it to the far wall of the large space when the harsh fluorescent overhead lights sprang on.

Addy pulled Cassie down behind a nearby machine and peered around it.

She didn't see Martin or any doors that might lead to safety, but she did spy a red-and-white exit sign hanging from the ceiling. Unfortunately, it was on the opposite side of the factory. To make it to that side, she and Cassie would have to cross an area of the factory that offered no machines to hide behind.

As she considered how they could make it across the open area, Martin stepped into it, blocking the path to the exit.

"This is a waste of time, you know. Better to go quietly, gracefully, than to engage in this battle you cannot win," Martin shouted.

His eyes roamed over the space. He didn't know where they were, but that could change at any moment.

Addy looked at Cassie. She'd sunk to the floor, her back to the machine they hid behind, her breathing labored.

Rage tore through Addy. She had no idea what Cassie had been through in the past several days, but she'd survived.

Addy would be damned before they'd give up now.

She helped Cassie to her feet, taking most of her sister's weight.

If they could just get to that door, maybe even get out of it without Martin noticing…

They picked their way around the machines, using Martin's increasingly unhinged taunts as a guide to areas to avoid.

They'd made it to the point where they'd have to cross the space that provided no cover when Martin fell ominously quiet.

Addy's heart rate kicked into warp speed. Was he setting them up? Watching and waiting until they stepped out into the open, giving him a clear shot at them?

Addy reached for the front of her shirt, but several things seemed to happen in that instant.

Cassie's legs gave out, sending the full weight of her body into Addy. Addy wrapped her free hand around her sister's waist, keeping her off the floor.

At the same moment, the door to the factory that Martin had used to lead her and Cassie onto the factory floor burst open. Shawn and Ryan swept in. Any relief Addy felt at seeing them was short-lived.

She sensed more than saw Martin step out from behind the machine to their left.

He grabbed Cassie by the hair, yanking her from Addy's unstable grip with enough force to make Cassie cry out and Addy stumble to the side.

Addy turned and faced the man who now held a gun to her sister's head. Out of the corner of her eye, she could see Shawn and Ryan advancing toward them quickly.

"Back up!" Martin's gun hand shook. "Back up now, or she's dead."

Shawn and Ryan stopped, but their guns remained pointed at Martin.

It might have been fear or adrenaline, but Cassie's wide eyes were more alert than they'd been since Addy had found her handcuffed to the filing cabinet. Hopefully, that rally would last long enough for all of them to get out of this with their lives.

Martin trained his wild gaze on Shawn and Ryan, giving Addy cover to slip her hand into her open purse unobserved.

"This isn't going to go your way, Raupp. Drop your weapon," Shawn said.

They stood in a lopsided triangle of sorts, Shawn and Ryan at one end and Addy at the other. Raupp and Cassie formed the tip at the top of the triangle.

"You're in no position to give orders. Drop your weapons or this pretty little thing's brains are going to be all over the floor."

Cassie flinched as Martin's grip on her hair tightened.

All the air fled Addy's lungs. Killing Cassie made no sense, but Raupp had rolled right on past rational a while ago. His scheme was all but over, and he was on his way to prison for a very long time. He had nothing to lose.

Addy kept her eyes locked on Cassie's face, but out of the side of her eye she saw Shawn and Ryan share a glance.

Do it! Please do it! This could be just the distraction she needed.

As if he'd heard her telepathy, Shawn said, "Okay."

They both held out their guns and began slowly lowering them to the ground.

Addy's gaze never left Cassie's face. Shawn and Ryan weren't the only siblings communicating without words.

As they slowly lowered their weapons, Cassie nodded slightly and wrenched away from Martin. She threw herself to the side with enough force that Martin was left with a clump of hair in his hand as Cassie fell to the floor.

Addy didn't hesitate. She pulled her gun from her purse and fired a single shot.

Martin jerked, his face registering a moment of surprise. He looked down at the blood spreading across his chest, letting his gun fall from his hand.

Ryan rushed toward Martin.

All Addy could see was Cassie. "Cassie!" She rushed to her sister's side, making it there at the same time Shawn did.

"Are you two okay?" Shawn's eyes never left Addy's face, though he'd directed the question at both of them.

Addy nodded. "He didn't hurt me, but we need to get Cassie medical help now."

Shawn gave her one more long look, assuring himself she knew that she was okay before pulling out his cell phone and stepping away.

"I'm fine," Cassie said, but the weakness of her voice belied the comment. Tears spilled over Cassie's cheeks. "I knew you'd find me."

Addy pulled her sister into an embrace. The sisters held on to each other for several seconds before Cassie spoke again. "Did you kill him?"

Addy looked over her shoulder.

Ryan had ripped off the bottom of Martin's dress shirt and was pressing it against his wound. Shawn held his cell phone to his ear, requesting police and medical assistance.

"I think he's still alive," Addy said, turning back to her sister.

Addy sent up a quick prayer. Even after everything he'd done, she didn't want Martin dead. Didn't want any man's death at her hands.

Shawn returned, crouching beside Addy. "Donovan and medics are on the way."

Addy raised her palm to his jaw and stroked the stubble blooming there. "Thank you."

He leaned into her touch. "For what?" Shawn smiled. "Once again your shooting saved the day, sweetheart."

Chapter Twenty-One

Cassie sat up in the hospital bed, a huge smile on her face. She had a presence. Shawn watched the corners of Gideon's mouth turn up a fraction, a rare phenomenon. The young woman had to have some kind of magical powers.

Shawn felt a light touch against his arm and looked into Addy's brown eyes as she came to a stop next to him just inside the hospital room door.

"Dr. Rose says she'll be fine in a day or two." Addy frowned. "At least physically. He suggested I find her someone to talk to about the whole ordeal."

Martin and Teddy hadn't physically hurt her, but psychological damage had the potential to be even more devastating.

"Therapy might not be such a bad idea. For Cassie or for you," Shawn said pointedly. Addy had gone through a trauma of her own—nothing close to what Cassie had suffered, but a trauma, nonetheless. He'd held her in the hour after Cassie had been brought into the hospital while she'd cried out the fear she'd been holding inside for nearly two weeks.

"Maybe." Addy moved her gaze from his face to her sister. "Maybe Cassie and I could go together."

Shawn put his arm around Addy's shoulder, pulling her in tightly against his side. Where she should be.

At least as far as he was concerned.

They'd both confessed to having feelings for each other, but they hadn't exactly had time to discuss what that meant for either of them.

He knew what it meant for him. He wanted a future with Addy, but he knew she wasn't positive she could achieve her professional goals and maintain a relationship. He didn't think she needed to choose, but would she come to the same conclusion?

Someone cleared their throat.

Shawn and Addy turned in tandem to find Donovan behind them. "I came to see if Miss Williams is up for giving her statement now."

Shawn, Addy, Gideon and Ryan had given their statements at the scene, but the EMTs had taken Cassie off to the hospital before she could give Donovan a complete statement. She had made it clear that Martin Raupp and Teddy Arbury had held her hostage for the last twelve days and that she suspected her ex-boyfriend Ben had been in on her kidnapping. Martin had also had her sign the phony resignation letter. She'd still have to flesh out some details for Donovan and testify if there was a trial, but Raupp would likely spend the rest of his life in jail.

Shawn felt Addy's body tense, and he was sure she was seconds from telling Donovan off. She still hadn't forgiven the man for taking such a hands-off approach to Cassie going missing.

"I'm fine to give my statement now, Sheriff." Cassie spoke up.

Addy shot Donovan a dark look but stood aside so he could enter the room and go to Cassie's bedside.

"If you don't mind, Miss Williams, it may be easier to do this in private." Donovan's eyes roamed over each of the men in the room and Addy before settling back on Cassie.

"I want my sister and Shawn to stay."

Donovan frowned but nodded his acceptance.

"I'll be in the waiting room," Ryan said.

Donovan retrieved a notebook from his breast pocket and flipped to a clean page. "Why don't you start from the beginning and lay the whole thing out for me in your own time and way."

Shawn and Addy had been able to deduce some of the pieces regarding what had gone down with Spectrum and the falsified chips, but the details about Cassie's kidnapping remained fuzzy. Shawn was as interested as Donovan in finding out exactly why and how Cassie had ended up in the middle of a million-dollar fraud.

Cassie let out a deep breath. "I really don't know where to start, Sheriff. At first, the internship at Spectrum was great. The people were nice. I was learning a ton, just like I'd hoped when I delayed starting school and work." Cassie looked to Addy, almost in confirmation that this was the goal.

Addy smiled and nodded her agreement.

"As an intern, I did most of the filing. You know, the grunt work no one else wants to do, so they save for the lowest woman on the totem pole." Cassie grinned.

"I'm familiar with the practice." Donovan returned Cassie's grin.

"Anyway, after a while, I noticed some discrepancies between what was on the written inventory forms that came from the factory floor, the number that was in the computer and how many chips appeared to be coming off the assembly lines on the days I worked at the factory."

Donovan scribbled notes on his pad while Shawn and Addy listened with rapt attention.

"I'd been dating Ben for six weeks or so by this time, so I brought it up to him." Cassie frowned. "He got really nervous. Said I didn't know what I was talking about and blew me off." Her frown deepened. "I was already realizing he was kind of a jerk, and I was ready to break it off with him, anyway. Two days later, he came to my place uninvited. He'd been drinking a lot, from the smell of him. That was the last straw. I broke up with him, and he lost it. He went off on how I thought I was better than him and smarter than everyone, but he was the smart one. He said he was going to be rich soon, and I'd come crawling back."

"You should have called the sheriff," Addy said, rage dancing across her face.

Donovan nodded in agreement.

Cassie shook her head, looking down at her hands in her lap. "I thought it was the alcohol talking. I'd have thrown him out, but I didn't want him driving. He eventually wore himself out, and I told him he could sleep it off on the couch. He tripped over the leg of the coffee table, and a computer chip fell out of his pocket. I knew right away something was wrong. It had an Intellus logo on it. I picked it up before he could get to it, and everything kind of fell into place in my brain, you know."

Cassie looked from Shawn to Addy to Donovan.

Donovan blinked several times, his face a blank. "I'm sorry, I don't know anything about computers, except they don't like me and I don't like them. Can you spell it out for me?"

Cassie smiled at Donovan, and Shawn could have sworn he blushed a little. Addy's little sister was a charmer, even when she wasn't trying to be.

Then again, no one could be more charming in his book than the eldest Miss Williams.

"Tons of products, from your phone to your watch to any number of everyday household appliances, have at least one kind of computer chip in them," Cassie said, visibly warming up to the subject. "The manufacturers of these items don't make the chips themselves. They purchase them from companies like Spectrum and Intellus. Now imagine one in every five or ten or even a hundred products starts consistently failing because of the chip inside? As a manufacturer, that impacts your company reputation, and you're going to find another chip supplier."

"Like Spectrum if you've found that Intellus's chips are faulty." Donovan nodded, his pen tapping the notebook in his hand.

"Chip fraud is the fastest-growing form of fraud in the world right now." Cassie leaned her head back against the pillows.

"To the tune of billions worldwide." Shawn jumped into the conversation. "By selling faulty chips with Intellus's logo, Raupp was not only pocketing a small fortune, he also almost decimated the reputation of his competition."

"Okay, I think I understand. Let's go back a bit. What happened after you picked up the chip Ben dropped?" Donovan focused on Cassie again.

Cassie's forehead scrunched. "I don't remember exactly. I think I told him I was going to go to you, Sheriff. He must have hit me with something, because I felt a pain in the back of my head, and when I woke up I was in this little room. I didn't know where at first, but later I realized it was a panic room."

Donovan nodded. "We found a panic room in the basement of Martin Raupp's mansion. We're processing the house now."

"Mr. Raupp or that guy Teddy brought me food once or twice a day, but otherwise they left me there. I think the food was drugged. I tried to eat as little as possible because I was always so sleepy after eating."

Donovan slid a sidelong glance at Shawn. "We've arrested Mr. Arbury."

When Shawn had called Donovan to let him know they believed Martin Raupp was involved in Cassie's kidnapping and that they were on their way to the Spectrum factory where they believed he was holding her, he'd also told Donovan where he could find Teddy Arbury.

"Two days ago you called your sister?"

"The bathroom in the panic room flooded a few days before. The smell was awful." Cassie's nose crinkled, and her face twisted in disgust. "On the second day, I woke up after lunch, my hands tied behind my back, in an office. They'd moved me so they could have the bathroom fixed."

"How did you get a phone? And why didn't you call 911?" Donovan asked.

"If there was a phone in the room to begin with, they'd taken it out, but I was able to work one of the desk drawers open, and I found my wallet and cell phone inside. I used the facial recognition to unlock it and voice commands to call Addy, but I was still groggy from whatever they'd put in the food. Mr. Raupp must have heard me talking."

Donovan scratched the back of his neck and shifted his weight uncomfortably. “I’m sorry, but there is no good way to ask this next question, Miss Williams.”

Addy’s back straightened under Shawn’s arm. She squeezed Cassie’s hand in support.

“Why do you think Martin Raupp kidnapped you instead of, well, instead of—”

“Killing me?” Cassie visibly swallowed.

“Well, yes, ma’am.”

The fire that ignited in Cassie when she’d begun talking seemed to have fizzled. “I don’t know.”

Shawn spoke up. “This is just speculation, but we think Raupp knew Intellus was onto the fraud. They weren’t sure exactly who was behind it, which is why they hired us, but we were closing in. The death of a Spectrum intern would have invited scrutiny that Raupp probably wanted to avoid until after he’d put the fraudulent chips out into the market.”

Donovan shook his head. “That makes sense. We may never get a for-sure answer. Neither Raupp nor Teddy is talking.” Donovan closed his notebook. “It’s hard to imagine something like this happening in my town.” Donovan patted Cassie’s knee. “I think that’s all I need for now. You get well,” he said before leaving the hospital room.

“Did Dr. Rose answer all your questions?” Cassie rolled her eyes at her sister.

Addy reached for Cassie’s hand and gave it a squeeze. “Yes, he did. He wants to keep you for observation overnight, but he said you can go home tomorrow morning.”

“Yippee. I am so ready for home. New York home.”

“And I’m so ready to have you back home in New York.” Addy smiled at Cassie.

"Shawn." Ryan's voice came from the doorway.

"Be right back." He planted a kiss on Addy's temple and earned a cheeky eyebrow raise from Cassie before exiting the room.

He and Shawn moved farther down the hall, away from the door. From the hard set of Ryan's jaw, he wasn't going to like whatever his brother was about to say.

"Intellus wants a debrief ASAP. In person. We can be on a flight out in three hours if we leave now."

Shawn's head was shaking before Ryan finished his last sentence. "I can't leave Addy right now."

Ryan crossed his arms over his chest. "Addy and her sister are fine. Didn't I hear her say they were headed back to New York tomorrow?" When Shawn didn't reply, Ryan added, "Intellus is our client. You were the principal on this. No one else is going to be able to debrief as well as you."

"Go."

Shawn turned at the sound of Addy's voice behind him. Shawn shook his head. "I'm not going to leave you to deal with everything on your own."

Addy's shoulders rose, then dropped. "What everything? Cassie and I can get ourselves back to New York."

"I don't think—" He stopped when Addy stepped in close to him, wrapping her arms around his waist and looking up into his eyes.

"Go. I'll be here when you get back."

He placed a light kiss on Addy's lips. "Promise?"

Addy's smile was blinding. "Absolutely."

Chapter Twenty-Two

Dr. Rose discharged Cassie from the hospital at eight the next morning. They didn't even bother to stop at the sheriff's office and pick up the things Addy and Shawn had found in Cassie's attic. By eleven they were back in New York City.

Addy felt like it was the first time she'd taken a breath since Cassie went missing.

For three days after they got home, her entire focus was on taking care of Cassie. Her independent sister let her hover for two days, but her patience with the mothering had worn thin.

Cassie was out now, at a friend's house, working on getting some sense of normalcy back. Addy had received several recommendations for therapists. She and Cassie agreed that seeing one together could go a long way to helping them both heal. They had their first appointment next week.

On the second night they were back in New York, they'd gone out for a nice dinner and had a long talk about the future. Cassie admitted she planned to turn down MIT's acceptance and attend university in the city. Addy couldn't be happier to keep her sister close, and considering Addy was now unemployed, she appreciated that Cassie's decision to attend school in the city took a lot of the financial pressure off.

Now here she was, less than a week before Christmas, sitting at the small desk in the corner of her bedroom, ostensibly to put out feelers, hoping to set up some job interviews in the new year. But she'd spent more time thinking about Shawn than searching job sites. They'd shared several short text conversations and two even shorter phone calls since he'd left the hospital headed for Silicon Valley. She missed him more than she could have imagined. In the few short days they'd spent together searching for Cassie, she'd fallen totally and irreversibly in love with Shawn West, despite her best efforts.

During their conversation last night, Shawn had told her that he might need to stay in California for another week.

The separation disappointed her, but it was the distant tone in his voice that scared her. She couldn't help but wonder if, now that the adrenaline had worn off, Shawn was reconsidering a relationship with her.

She inhaled deeply, let it out slowly and focused on the computer in front of her. She'd put out feelers and had received a surprising invitation to discuss a job opportunity from Brandon West, Shawn's brother.

Brandon West's firm was small, just him and a couple of paralegals, based on his website. But the work they did was innovative. They were a long way from offer and acceptance, but joining his firm would mean reimagining what her career could be. She wasn't sure if she was ready for that, so she hadn't responded to his email yet. The description of his firm and the work he did was intriguing, but she wasn't sure how she felt about working with Shawn's brother. Especially if she and Shawn didn't work out.

The doorbell rang.

She opened the door and froze.

Shawn stood in front of her.

"Hi." He smiled, but it was shaky and unsure. Very un-Shawn-like.

Her heart fell into her stomach, but she forced a smile onto her face. If he was there to call things off, she'd accept his decision with grace.

"Hi." The word came out thinner, breathier than she intended.

They stared at each other for a long moment before Shawn spoke. "May I come in?"

"Oh, yes, of course," she said, moving aside so he could stride past her into the apartment.

"What are you doing here?" she asked, closing the door and leading Shawn into the living room.

"I just followed one of your neighbors in. He didn't even look at me."

"That's not what I meant. You said you needed to be in California for another week."

"I know, but right after we got off the phone, I realized that the place I truly needed to be was with you."

"Really?" A smile so wide it hurt Addy's cheeks spread across her face.

Shawn's smile mirrored her own. "I think I knew it six months ago, when I caught you undressing me with your eyes across the reception hall at my brother's wedding."

She scoffed, but her smile didn't dim. "I was not undressing you with my eyes."

Shawn arched an eyebrow, his eyes blazing with heat. "Well, maybe you can do that later, then?"

A laugh bubbled out of Addy. "So I guess we're giving this relationship thing a whirl, then."

"For as long as we both shall live, princess. For as long as we both shall live."

* * * * *

COLTON 911: TEMPTATION UNDERCOVER

JENNIFER MOREY

To Allie, my ever-faithful Australian shepherd,
who gives us big smiles or furry hugs and
a few well-placed kisses

Chapter One

While not the big-box elegance of a chain bookstore, Mostly Books had its own charm. Rows of new and old books spread across three-quarters of the space, and the coffee counter with three small tables and a quaint seating area took up the rest in the front. Ruby Duarte rang up an order for a gray-haired woman. Her co-worker, Melvin, got busy making the iced latte. It was usually just the two of them working the morning shift.

Having taken care of five patrons, all but the gray-haired woman enjoying their coffee in the seating area and one of the tables, Ruby moved to the corner of the counter that faced the windows. She liked watching people passing by, going about their day. A woman and her young child walked along the sidewalk in shorts and summer tops. An early August day in a suburb of Chicago, it was shaping up to be hot and muggy.

The bell above the door jingled, and a man stepped inside. He was dark-haired and a touch over six feet tall—and vaguely resembled her ex, Kid Mercer. For an instant she stiffened, and her heart flew into a panic until she reminded herself that the man couldn't be

Kid because Kid was dead. Other than his height, the man's similarity to Kid ended. Kid's hair was lighter, and this man had brown eyes. Ruby had to admit her ex still haunted her.

She breathed through her nose relaxing her nerves. The man wasn't Kid, but that didn't mean one of his associates wouldn't come searching for her. She was always on alert for that.

Ruby went to the register and took the man's order. As she worked, the bell jingled again, and this time a familiar face entered. She was again struck by his good looks, a tall drink of Chris Hemsworth, dark blond hair a bit long and ragged, closely trimmed beard and hazel-green eyes magnetized her. He even walked like the sexy man. His mouth crooked up when he saw her. He came in almost every day before he started his shift at the Foxhole pub down the street.

So far they had only exchanged small talk and hadn't really gotten to know each other. They talked weather and current news and things that happened while he bartended and the goings-on at the Mostly Books store. He seemed nice, though. She had a good vibe about him. That didn't mean she'd let her guard down. She'd just escaped a dangerous relationship and wasn't about to put herself through anything like that ever again. She'd had a good vibe about Kid, too, and look where that had gotten her.

"Hi," he greeted in that deep voice that always tickled her soul.

"Hi yourself."

Last time he had joked with her about his lack of a

green thumb and that he'd bought a plant to reassure himself that he was capable of taking care of a living thing other than himself.

"How's the plant?" she asked.

"Not dead."

She smiled.

"I think it's growing," he added.

"That's a good sign."

She had asked him where he lived, and he said in an apartment above the Foxhole. The Foxhole was a fairly upscale pub, but she'd heard some questionable people frequented the place.

"Maybe I'm dad material after all," he said.

Ruby thought of Maya, her five-year-old daughter, and wondered if she would ever want him to meet her. She was extremely protective of Maya, especially since her daughter had finally adjusted to living with her and not the girl's father. Ruby had made great progress with her, and the therapy helped ease the tension in the girl. It broke her heart knowing what Maya must have gone through living with a criminal like Kid Mercer. Although Ruby had never given up trying to get her daughter back, Kid had too many dangerous men surrounding him, and she couldn't get close enough to snatch her.

"Coffee?" she asked Damon.

As always, he ordered a plain black coffee.

"Working the lunch shift today?" she asked as she processed the transaction, keeping the talk neutral between them. He was earlier than usual.

"Actually, no. I have the day off," he said, leaning an elbow on the higher counter next to the pay area.

"Oh, out on the town today?"

"Not exactly. What time do you get off work?"

Her heart did a little flop of excitement. Was he going to ask her out on a *date*?

"Two."

"Would you like to go have ice cream with me?"

She looked outside at the steamy day. She did like ice cream, and she could get something with fudge. And being curious about this man who had come in so many times, she'd like to get to know him more. It was high time she had some fun, anyway, and she wasn't due to pick up Maya until after class tonight.

"Okay."

He grinned. "Great. I'll be back at two. We can walk there, so you don't have to worry about getting into a strange man's car."

He wasn't exactly a stranger. She knew his name was Damon Jones, and he knew hers. They knew some details about each other but nothing too personal.

Melvin handed Damon his coffee. A fiftysomething man with kind blue eyes, Melvin was a humble soul who loved the outdoors. Ruby thought he should work for the forest service rather than serve coffee. He told her once he liked the social aspect of his job.

Damon took the cup and looked at Ruby. "See you soon."

"Looking forward to it." She smiled, and he grinned back flirtatiously.

She watched him leave the store, glad he didn't see her check out his fit butt in those light blue jeans.

"He finally asked you out, huh?" Melvin asked.

Ruby became aware of him next to her, so caught up in her Chris Hemsworth–fantasy man that she hadn't noticed.

"I guess so. If you call having ice cream a date," she said.

"Oh, it's a date all right, and about time. He's taken it really slow with you. He's been coming here, what—six months now?"

It had been about that long. Damon said he'd been working at the Foxhole pub for the last nine months. And he had taken things slow, something she appreciated. She didn't know if he had done that for himself or for her. Ruby could be rather transparent, something that worked against her at times.

"Yes."

"I was beginning to think he'd never ask," Melvin said.

He'd been paying that much attention? Another customer arrived, and it was a while before the afternoon slowed. She hadn't stopped thinking about Damon.

At two, she went to the bathroom to tidy herself up. When she emerged, Damon stood inside the entrance, waiting. He saw her and grinned. She smiled back, feeling so good about this. Damon was a good man. She just knew it. Things were finally looking up for her.

DAMON HAD TWO primary objectives in his DEA undercover case. One, get to know Ruby Duarte, and two, infiltrate her ex-boyfriend's criminal syndicate. Kid Mercer had frequented the Foxhole, holding meetings there with his followers. Damon sometimes heard them discuss problems with drug-trafficking routes. They hadn't known he listened, of course. Mercer had been a dangerous man with many followers, more than Damon could count. His syndicate had been enormous in the Chicago underworld and still wasn't completely dismantled.

Damon had spent the first three months watching Ruby, getting to know her routines and work and school schedules. Then he began going to the bookstore that also served as a coffee shop, initially not saying anything to her except *thank you*. Over the last four months, he had gradually worked up a friendly rapport with her. He had immediately sensed extreme guardedness in her, which is why he was taking things slow.

He had caught on to an underlying attraction to him, as attested by her occasional nervousness. She had begun flirting back with him after about two months. He had gotten her to reveal a little about herself, even though he already knew pretty much everything about her. She lived in the Woodlawn area, where he also had a house. She was twenty-six, and he was twenty-nine. She liked people-watching. She was going to nursing school. He avoided talking about past relationships because once he asked if she'd ever been married, and she had responded with a curt *no*. The subject clearly was sensitive for her.

Now she walked toward him, dark wavy hair down

from her ponytail and light brown eyes twinkling with attraction.

He held the door for her, and they began walking down the street.

"How was the rest of your day?" he asked.

"Uneventful. It always slows down after around noon."

Today he would stop carrying on the small talk. Early on he had joked with her, saying she must love books to be surrounded by them every day. She had said she did, but she was going to school to become a nurse. He had told her he worked as a bartender down the street.

"How is nursing school?" he asked.

"Good. I have a long way to go, but it's good."

"Where do you go?"

"Chicago State University. I had help in getting a grant, otherwise I don't think I could have afforded it," she said. "And I know I couldn't do it without my mother. She watches Maya while I work and go to school."

"Maya?" He knew about her daughter, but they hadn't talked about her in his role as a bartender.

"My daughter." Ruby beamed maternal love and pride. "She's five."

"An adorable age."

Ruby laughed a little. "Most of the time. She can be a real pistol when she wants her way."

They walked in silence a while before she asked, "Do you like kids?"

"I love kids. Hope to have some of my own someday."

That seemed to please her, her eyes smiling and lips curved up slightly. "Maya is deaf."

"Really?" He feigned surprise.

"Yes. Since she was two. I had to learn sign language. She does really well. She learns quickly. My smart girl." She smiled.

"Can she read lips?" he asked.

"She's getting better at that, but lip reading is challenging at best."

"Does she get by okay?"

"She does fine. She is strong and makes friends with other kids. I don't think it will hold her back in life."

"Maybe she takes after her mother."

She smiled again. "She might be a little tougher than me."

Reaching the ice cream shop, Damon held the door for her again. They ordered and took their containers of peanut parfaits to a table. Damon sat across from Ruby, realizing he must be rusty with dating. He had been so involved with his work that he hadn't dated in a long time, long before starting his undercover job here. At a loss for words being with this remarkable, beautiful woman, he ate a few bites, looking at her every once in a while, noting the details. How her eyes sparkled, her tan skin radiated her beauty. She was tall for a woman, too, probably five-eight. And slender.

"So, Mr. Jones, tell me about yourself. How'd you wind up bartending?"

"Damon. I thought it was cool after high school."

"You never wanted to go to college?"

He really did not like lying to her. He decided to tell

a partial truth. "I make a good living bartending, and I meet lots of people."

She didn't seem satisfied with his answer, as though she wondered if he had no aspirations in life. Did she not respect a man who held a job as a bartender?

"If you did go to college, what would you study?" she finally asked.

He debated telling her another partial truth. What would it hurt? He pretended to think a bit.

"Criminal justice."

She smiled. "That's a far cry from bartending. Why criminal justice?"

"When I was a kid I was fascinated by superheroes. Getting the bad guys." That was the truth. Growing up with a father like his, he had wanted to be the opposite of what Erik Colton represented.

"Did your parents encourage you to go to college?" she asked.

"My mother died when I was seven, and my father wasn't around much, so no, I wasn't encouraged by them."

"Oh. I'm so sorry. My father died when I was ten. It's hard to lose a parent when you're a kid."

"Yes. My dad's ex-wife raised me, and she did encourage me. She was a good mother to me." He felt good about not lying. He would just avoid saying names.

"Do you have any brothers and sisters?" she asked.

"I have two older brothers, one is my half brother." He'd refrain from going into detail about his newly discovered cousins and all the affairs that had produced other children. They were the children of his grandfather Dean's twin sons from his first marriage. Damon's grandmother, Carin, was always after a way to hoard money. Her latest scheme exposed a claim to the Dean Colton fortune. She had somehow produced a will that named Erik and Axel Colton rightful heirs. Damon had never felt close with her and, as with his father Erik, had a strained relationship with her. He had never felt a need to obtain wealth, just satisfaction in what he did with his life.

"Why wasn't your dad around much?" Ruby asked.

He couldn't say much about that without risking his undercover investigation. "Let's just say he wasn't dad material."

"He had an affair with your mother?" Ruby asked.

That was a delicate question. "Yes."

Ruby turned her attention back to her ice cream.

"What about you?" he asked. "Tell me about your family."

She swallowed a bite and looked at him. "I have an older sister and brother. We stay in touch."

"They aren't from around here?" he asked.

"Wisconsin."

"You're a Wisconsin girl? What brought you to Chicago?"

"I moved here with my boyfriend," she said, and got a faraway look.

She must be referring to Kid Mercer. "Is that your daughter's father?"

She nodded, obviously not happy to be discussing this. Her eyes avoided his, and she seemed to withdraw.

"Is he involved in your daughter's life?" he asked.

Ruby shook her head. "He died."

"Oh. I'm sorry..."

"Don't be." She pushed her ice cream aside. "I should go pick up Maya."

It was only three. She said earlier she had until five.

"I'm sorry. I didn't know you don't like talking about him," Damon said.

"It's all right. It is a mood-changer, though." She smiled, albeit forced.

"Is your family still in Wisconsin?"

"My mother is here. She moved here shortly after I did, and that makes Chicago home."

She must be close to her mother. Seeing she still wanted to leave, Damon didn't try to keep her any longer. "I'd like to take you out again, maybe for dinner," he said.

She smiled, although the residual distaste over bringing up her ex still lingered. Actually, *distaste* wasn't the right word. *Apprehension* was more appropriate. She was afraid. As well she should be. Mercer was dead, but his band of criminals weren't.

"I'd like that," she said.

Damon was both elated and filled with guilt over misleading her the way he was. He had way too much interest in her. He had a job to do, and yet, this felt like a real date. When he should be pretending, he didn't have to. Honestly, he felt attracted to her the moment he met her. He thought he could keep that under control, but now, being with her like this, he worried he wouldn't be able to. What was worse? Pretending or not? Either way, the day would come when she'd learn his true identity. She'd be hurt. And so would he, if he allowed any feelings to grow.

He walked with her back down the street.

"Have you been following that story about the Coltons?" she asked.

She did so to make conversation, but she had no idea the bombshell she had just dropped on him. Luckily, the media didn't focus on Damon and his brothers. They focused on Erik and Axel Colton, and Carin, of course. So far. Damon wasn't in the limelight while he worked undercover, and his brothers were more concerned over the damage Carin would cause if her suit were successful. Damon himself was curious of his new cousins and had no interest in taking anything from them.

"No, not really," he said.

"They have cousins they never knew about, and Dean Colton's mistress from way back when is going after their inheritance."

"Sounds like an evening soap opera," he joked.

Ruby laughed. "Money attracts all sorts, apparently."

"I'll say."

"Money was never that important to me. I was more interested in finding someone I could be happy with. I mean, everybody needs money to survive, and I don't want to be the one who struggles to live comfortably, but it doesn't have to be in excess."

"I couldn't agree more," he said, having had similar thoughts about his father and grandmother. He felt a bond grow between them, as though they were magically linked in this moment. And the attraction he had so far been able to temper began to slip from his grasp.

They reached the bookstore, and Damon faced her.

"I'm glad we did this," she said.

"Me, too." The urge to kiss her overcame him. It should be a tactical move, but seeing her full lips and eyes that no longer held that haunted look, he'd do it for more than that. He couldn't deny it. Managing to restrain himself, he kept it chaste and leaned in for a kiss on her cheek.

Getting a whiff of her sweet scent and being so close to her beautiful eyes, something changed in an instant. He could see the heat go into the way she looked up at him. He shifted just a bit and pressed his mouth to hers. Soft at first, the lightning-fast reaction in him and what he felt in her response made him kiss her harder.

Ruby slid her hand up his chest to the back of his neck and kissed him with equal fervor. A few seconds later, she began to withdraw.

Stepping back, she put her hand to her mouth and stared.

"Yeah," he said. "I wasn't expecting that, either." What an understatement. They were explosive together. How was he supposed to conduct his investigation with that kind of knowledge?

After a few seconds, she lowered her hand and pointed toward the bookstore. "Now I really need to go."

"Yeah. Good idea." In a few more seconds he'd be doing his best to take her home with him.

"M-my car is parked in the back."

"I'll walk you there." Although it was still afternoon, he didn't like the idea of her alone in the back of the building, which was essentially an alley.

"No, no." She briefly waved her hand. "I'll be fine." With her palm toward the sky and eyes going up, she said, "Daylight."

He chuckled. "Sorry. Chivalry isn't dead for me." And it wasn't. He just needed to meet a woman who appreciated that about him. Or, at the very least, recognition that it wasn't an attempt to rob her of her independence but, rather, respect her for her exquisite beauty, inside and out.

Damon had given up trying to find that a long time ago, but it was still nice to fantasize.

"It is for most men," she said, smiling.

Still grinning, he said, "Dinner tomorrow night?"

"How about Friday? I have class tomorrow night."

"Okay. You want to give me your address so I can pick you up?"

"Pick me up here."

She still didn't trust him. He could deal with that. "Seven," he said.

"Seven it is."

She smiled and breathed a few deep breaths. He felt

the same, still breathless. What would happen after dinner on Friday…?

Snapping out of that fantasy, he remembered Mercer's followers. Ruby wasn't aware of Damon's knowledge of the danger she could be in.

"I'll walk you to your car," he said.

Her smile warmed, obviously touched by his show of what she perceived as chivalry.

They walked in silence with enticement charging the air. Too soon, they reached her car door. She faced him.

"Well," she said, "until Friday."

"Not unless I come get my coffee in the morning," he said.

She breathed a short laugh, one full of sexual awareness.

Things would be a lot different now. Their acquaintance had gone from platonic to a wide-open road of possibilities.

"Thanks for walking me to my car." Still smiling, she got into the driver's seat and looked at him as she started the engine.

Damon stuffed his hands into his pockets and couldn't subdue an answering grin, knowing it was flirtatious and revealed how good he felt because of her, because of being with her the way he had been this afternoon.

She lifted a hand in farewell, and he took his right hand out to answer. He stood there for several seconds, long after she disappeared down the street. Turmoil churned in his guts. These feelings were too strong after just one innocent date. He was undercover, and she was his primary target for gaining the upper hand on Mercer's criminal followers. The two would surely clash into an unfavorable ending—for him and for Ruby.

Chapter Two

Damon had taken Ruby to the movies once and dinner twice. Now he took her to Matthiessen State Park, about an hour-and-a-half drive from Chicago. He planned on a picnic and maybe a hike afterward. People who weren't from Chicago probably would never guess there was a place with beautiful rock formations, trees and wildlife a relatively short drive away. Growing up in Wisconsin, she and her family would take vacations up north. Her grandparents had a house on Long Lake. This place reminded her of that.

Reaching the picnic area, Ruby helped Damon spread a tablecloth and unload the cooler and a bag he used in lieu of a basket. The table was secluded in trees, and she could hear a stream nearby. A careful look around and she could see water through branches and undergrowth. A path had been trampled down where others had gone to partake in the beauty or perhaps fish. The path where they had just walked was visible but about fifty yards away. She could see people passing by, but this was a private place.

"Have you been to this spot before?" she asked. How had he known to bring her to this table?

"I did some reading and got a map. A very friendly park ranger told me about this table," he said.

"It's so beautiful." And so much more special with him. Their dates had progressively drawn her closer to him, or at the least, much more interested in taking this further. She sensed he felt the same. One could never be sure at this stage of a relationship, however. What she felt might not have the same meaning to him. And she had vowed never to let her guard down until she was 100 percent certain she was with the right man.

"What did you make us?" Ruby had never been with a man who prepared her food. Kid had either taken her out or brought food in.

"Club sandwiches with avocado, chips, coleslaw and fruit," he said, handing her a paper plate with a wrapped sandwich. "Nothing extravagant."

Extravagant enough for her. The gesture was what counted. She took out two sodas and the coleslaw. The coleslaw had come from a deli, but the clubs were homemade. He grinned. "I'm not a very good cook."

Laughing lightly, she sat on the bench across from him.

Eating a bite of the delicious sandwich, she said, "You're an excellent club-sandwich chef."

"Thanks. Just don't ask for anything gourmet." He chuckled at her teasing.

"I bet you could follow a recipe if you had to." Anybody could do that.

Content just being with him, Ruby took in her surroundings, listening to birds and the stream and feeling a soft, warm breeze under a clear blue sky.

"I haven't been to a place like this in so long," she said.

"What other places does this remind you of?"

"My grandparents had a house on Long Lake in Wisconsin. We used to go there all the time. Then my dad died, and everything changed. My mother took us there but not as often. She was pretty heartbroken. We all had a hard time getting past that."

"What happened to him?" Damon asked.

"He got brain cancer," she said. "Brain cancer is ruthless and indiscriminate. We found out, and he lived less than a year. None of us had time to process his illness, and then he was gone. Just gone." Ruby shook her head slowly and looked out across the park, remembering how terrible the whole ordeal had been.

"That must have been awful," he said. "I'm sorry." He reached over and put his hand over hers.

She met his eyes, appreciating the gesture. The *I'm sorrys* never helped. His touch did.

"We seem to have loss in common," he said. "Not the connection I'd prefer, but..."

"You mean your mother?" she asked.

"Yes. She was alive and well one moment, and in an instant, she collapsed and died," he said. "I don't know what's worse, having time to struggle through a terminal diagnosis or losing someone close to you quickly."

"I don't, either. I suppose I'd have to think of the person who is about to die. Going quickly, they don't suffer."

"They also don't have time to get their affairs in

order. I would hate to leave things unsettled for my family to deal with."

"I think it would be easier if none of us had to die at all," she said with a smile.

He chuckled. "Immortality, never aging." He nodded. "Yeah. I could do that."

They ate in silence awhile.

"Where are you from in Wisconsin?" Damon asked.

"A little town called Neenah."

"And your mother followed you here?"

"Yes. She lives with me now. Having Maya around really helps her. She loves being a grandmother," Ruby said. "She never had any interest in remarrying."

"Some people get it right the first time," he said.

"They did. My sister and brother and I had a really great childhood up until my dad died. I have so many fond memories. My parents never argued. They talked things through. They were strict but not overly so. They wanted us all to be disciplined and develop good life habits."

Damon fell silent, and she sensed he didn't like talking about his childhood. "Do you have any good memories?"

"Sure. My brothers and I were close. We did a lot together. Rode bikes. Played sports. We were ordinary boys."

"Have you ever been married?" she asked.

"No. My father and uncle taught me how to get it wrong. I don't plan on doing that."

Ruby liked the sound of that.

"What happened with Maya's father?" he asked.

Why was he so interested in that? Was he being

cautious and only wanted to know why they ended? Or did he have another motive?

"Why do you want to know?" she asked.

Lowering his head, he looked contrite when he met her eyes again. "Sorry. Just curious, I guess."

"Curious?" He seemed more than curious. He seemed to want details, and that she could not give him.

"Yes. I can see it's upsetting to you," he said. "But I don't want to push you. Really. I'm sorry."

After studying his face a while and unable to determine if he was being genuine, Ruby stood. "We're done with lunch, right? How about that hike you promised?" She forced a smile.

Damon stared at her for a few seconds. "Yeah. Sure. Let's put all this away and go for a hike."

Ruby felt a flash of guilt. Did he deserve an explanation? She was beginning to have very strong feelings for him. If he was as good and decent as she sensed, she didn't want to blow it. But talking about Kid reminded her of how terrified she had been when she was with him and how afraid she'd been of his friends. Damon must see her fear. She was beginning to feel obligated to tell him about her ex-boyfriend, Maya's father, which was absurd because she didn't have to tell him anything. She was just getting to know him. Maybe she just needed more time. And more time with Damon appealed to her no small amount.

DAMON WALKED BESIDE Ruby in a state of frustration and guilt.

His personal feelings for her were seriously interfering with his ability to conduct his investigation. He had spent so much time trying to melt her defenses, and yet she showed no signs of softening. And more and more, he was becoming convinced she didn't know enough to be worth all of this effort. He also worried his efforts were too personal and not in the best interest of the undercover case.

While he suspected Ruby didn't know anything about Kid's operation, he had to be sure. He was getting pressure from his boss to move the case forward and to do that he needed to determine if in fact Ruby did know something. In order to do that, he needed to know more about her relationship with Kid. He needed to get her talking.

As they hiked along the path, passing rock formations and trees, Damon struggled to find a way to broach the subject of Kid again. She got so upset every time he tried, he wondered if he should let it go and not push as he'd said earlier. But this investigation was going nowhere as long as she refused to open up about the creep. He stopped walking, making her do the same. He put his hands on her shoulders. "Ruby, I know you don't like talking about your ex, but it makes me wonder why. Can you at least tell me why?" he asked.

After looking past his shoulders a while, she finally said, "I just don't like talking about him."

That wasn't enough. He already knew that. "But why, Ruby?"

"He wasn't a good man."

"In what way? Was he abusive?"

"Please don't ask me about him anymore."

"I just want to know about him," Damon said.

"Well, I don't want anyone to know about him. He almost ruined my life. And Maya's. I'm glad he isn't around anymore."

"What happened to him?"

Ruby's lips pursed, and she turned back toward the direction they had come. "I'd like to go home now."

Damn. He'd pushed her too hard. Or had he? She was always so reluctant to talk about Kid. Vague, even. Why? The only logical answer was fear. Someone had to make her face her issue with the man.

He caught up to her. "I can see you're afraid, Ruby. That's why I can't let it go. I'm concerned about you."

Ruby stopped, and they faced each other again. She seemed to search his face for some kind of sign. What was it? That he was being honest? Thankfully, he was.

"Don't be. I'm all right."

He angled his head dubiously, raising his brow in a lighthearted way.

She smiled slightly. "As long as people don't keep asking me about Kid, I'll be all right."

That wasn't what he wanted to hear. "I don't mean to upset you. I don't mean to keep badgering you. But you should talk about him, what happened between you. It might help you, not hurt you."

"I'm not ready for that," she said.

What she didn't say was she wasn't ready for that *with him.*

"Fair enough, but that's not going to make me stop worrying about you," he said. "I've grown to care about you, Ruby."

Her eyes softened even more. "I care about you, too."

He heard the truth in her voice and already knew the truth had tumbled out of him. A warm energy mingled between them. He saw it in her eyes and the tiny curve to her lips. He felt the same reaction in him.

Taking her hand, he walked with her down the path, glancing over at her and catching her own glances.

Back at Damon's Jeep, he began to feel letdown that this day would now come to an end. They had already loaded the picnic supplies in the back. He opened the door for her, but put his hands on the frame to stop her from getting in.

She tipped her head up and faced him.

He put two fingers under her chin, seeing her eyes flare with surprise and heat.

"There's only one thing that will finish this day to perfection," he said.

"What's that?" She played along. She must know what he intended and wasn't resisting.

"This," he murmured, leaning in for a brief, soft kiss. But what he meant to be brief lasted many seconds. The world around him dropped away. All he felt were Ruby's warm, soft lips against his.

When he would have probed for more, he drew back. Baby steps with this one, he reminded himself.

She stared up at him for a timeless moment before she seemed to drift back down to earth.

She patted his chest once, lightly, nervously. "I wasn't sure I was going to do this today, but now I think I will."

"Do what?" he asked. "Kiss again?" He grinned.

"No." She didn't smile. "I want you to meet Maya."

Now, that was progress. "I'd love that."

"I should warn you...she's an excellent judge of character," Ruby said.

"I should pass the test, no problem," he said.

"I hope so." She briefly bit her lower lip. "Why don't you come over to my house for dinner tomorrow night?"

"What time?"

"Five? Are you working?"

"Not tomorrow. Five it is. What should I bring?"

"Nothing. Just an appetite."

"You're a very demanding woman," he said, letting his arm drop to make room for her to get in the Jeep.

"Just wait till you meet my daughter."

Chuckling, he closed the door and walked around to the driver's side. Maybe, just maybe, he'd get her talking. Once she trusted him completely, she would feel safer. As those thoughts came to him, the guilt set in again. What if she didn't know anything as he suspected much of the time? She would be hurt when she found out who he really was.

RUBY WASN'T SURE what troubled her more: her inability to talk about Kid, or Damon's persistent interest in the topic. He said he was concerned about her. She believed that. She was concerned about herself and Maya. But she just didn't feel comfortable talking about Kid. First, she was embarrassed at having gotten involved with a man like that. Second, getting pregnant had been an accident. She had used birth control but still got pregnant. Third, he was a scary, dangerous man with lots of men who followed him and thought she knew more than she did.

Leaving the state had been an option, but Ruby had refused to run. She liked Chicago. Maya was settled here and safe. Ruby's mother liked it here. They were close to Wisconsin and could visit family often, but she would not run.

Her mother knew all about Kid and agreed with her. Bethany, or Bette as those close to her called her, had the stamina and strength of a mama grizzly. Something Ruby had inherited—despite her inherent transparency—and Maya had as well. A tiny mite, Maya showed signs of that spirit even at her young age. Ruby was so proud.

"What's got you all smiles?"

Ruby stopped chopping vegetables for the salad to see her mother walk into the kitchen. The house was actually rented in her mother's name, a tactic to protect Ruby and Maya. So far, they had not had any uninvited visitors.

Bette always wore colorful clothes, flowing and figure-slimming. Her dark hair was cut short. She had dark eyes and smooth, olive skin. Ruby had gotten her hair and skin from her mother and her light brown eyes from her father.

"Hi, Mom." Ruby leaned over and kissed her mother on the cheek.

"Can I help?"

Ruby had a big cutting board on the kitchen island and a bowl she was gradually filling with vegetables.

"The grill needs to be lit and the ribs seasoned," Ruby said. "I have water warming for the corn. Baked beans and a salad, and we are ready for an all-American dinner."

"Sounds lovely. Where is Maya?"

"Your cute little granddaughter is in her room playing with her dolls."

"I'll start the grill and go get her."

Just then, the doorbell rang. Ruby stopped chopping carrots.

"I'll get that first," Bette said.

Ruby resumed chopping, but her heart skipped a few beats. This evening would change the course of her future. She just knew it. Having a man she trusted meet her precious daughter was no small event. Damon didn't know how important this was to her, how much of a privilege Ruby considered this to be. Maybe after tonight, he would.

NOT MANY THINGS made Damon nervous, but he was right now. This evening could take his relationship with Ruby into much deeper intimacy. Meeting her daughter meant a lot. He was going to get to know her family. Would this entwine him more than he was prepared for?

When the door opened and he saw a woman who must be Ruby's mother, his foreboding flared to life. He should have remembered her mother would be here.

He felt as though he was intruding where he didn't belong. He wasn't who either of these people thought.

"Mr. Jones?"

"Damon. You're Ruby's mother?" he said.

"Yes. I'm Bette. Come on in."

He entered their home. It wasn't a large house. It was older, probably built in the fifties. Stairs led up to a covered porch, and now he stood in a small entry off the living room. Wood floors throughout, ahead was the dining room and to his left double French doors led to a sitting room with a bookshelf.

Damon followed Bette through a wide archway into the dining room. That opened to a remodeled kitchen with wooden stools before an island. The house was small but charming, which suited Ruby.

She turned from chopping a tomato and said with a smile, "Hi."

She was so beautiful. "Hi."

"I see you met my mother," she said.

"Yes."

Bette had left the kitchen.

"Would you like anything to drink?" Ruby asked.

Damon looked around for Maya and didn't see her. "What are you having?" he pointed to her glass of dark liquid.

"Iced tea."

"I'll have a glass of that." He stepped into the kitchen. "I'll get it."

"Glasses are up in there." She gestured with her knife to a cabinet. "Pitcher of tea is in the fridge."

He got a glass and put some ice in it from the dispenser on the refrigerator door. Then he poured himself some tea.

Hearing the sound of Maya bounding down the stairs and feet pattering on the floor, Damon turned in time to see her enter the dining room and kitchen. Tall for a five-year-old, she was slender and would surely grow into a beauty like her mother. It made him wonder what his own children would look like. What would Maya look like had he been her father? He hadn't thought much about starting a family, but seeing Ruby's daughter seemed to light something in him, possibilities. Curly brown hair up in a high ponytail that swayed as she moved, her adorable light brown eyes found him. She stopped short, looking suddenly shy. She went to her mother as Bette appeared around the wall. Maya peered around the back of her mother at Damon, who found the whole display utterly charming.

"She was full of energy today," Bette said. "Until now."

"She's always wary when she meets new people." Ruby signed, *It's okay. He's a friend*, then put the bowl of salad in the refrigerator.

Damon knew a little sign language. He hadn't told Ruby that yet.

"I had to ask her to put her toys away. She's hungry and looking forward to ribs," Bette said.

"She'll eat anything."

Maya signed, *Can I have a soda?*

"Sure," Ruby said, signing at the same time, but Damon caught on that Maya could read lips. Ruby took out a soda and gave Maya the can. Then she crouched and signed, *This is my friend Damon.*

Maya looked up at him and signed, *Hello.*

He signed, *Nice to meet you.*

Ruby stood. "You know sign language?"

Seeing her pleasantly surprised look, he said, "Enough to get by."

"Why did you learn?" she asked.

"That's impressive," Bette said. "Ruby's never met a man who can sign."

Ruby sent her a warning look, as though her mother had just given her nod of approval for her to have Damon as her new boyfriend.

"I knew someone who was deaf, a long time ago," he said, hoping she wouldn't ask further. He had learned because he found it useful when he encountered deaf people in his line of work as a DEA agent, whether they be criminals or witnesses.

"A friend?" she asked.

"Yes," he said, again hating that he had to lie.

"Are you still in touch with him? Or her?"

"Him. And no, we drifted apart." The man had been a witness. Not being able to communicate with him had cost him too much time. That's why he had learned sign. "I also happen to have an interest in languages." That was true. "I speak Spanish and a few other languages."

"Wow. Impressive," Ruby said.

Her mother raised her eyebrows and smiled at Ruby.

"So you do have aspirations in life," Ruby said, teasing.

What are asps? Maya signed.

Damon chuckled with Ruby and Bette.

Ruby signed, *Aspirations. They're like wishes.*

I wish I had a daddy, Maya signed to the room at large.

The innocence in her quick glance at Damon cut through him. He had no illusions over what the young girl must have gone through when her father kept her from seeing her mother. Not to mention the line of work he did. The bad people he associated with. A child that age would not have the mental capacity to know it was wrong. She had probably been confused. To her, her father loved her, and she had likely worshiped him. The parent–child relationship was all unconditional until the kids reached an age where they became aware of their individuality. Maya also loved her mother and must have missed her intensely. But being just five, she had no defenses. She hadn't understood the awfulness of being taken from her mother, and now she had no father. Damon wished she had never gone through this. But of course, when she grew up she would realize.

Damon signed, *I'm sure your mother will meet someone nice someday.*

Are you nice?

I like to think so.

Her sweet eyes studied him a while. *Do you like my mommy?*

Yes, I do. He looked up at Ruby with a grin.

"Come on, Maya." Ruby sent Damon a flirtatiously warning look and then took her daughter to the table, where she had a coloring book.

After grappling with guilt over what could be construed as using a five-year-old to get information, Damon grilled the ribs. The activity and the festiveness of it helped take his mind off the true purpose of his presence here. He caught Ruby eyeing him every once in a while, as though reading his mood. Did she know he had tried to get information about Maya's father, or did she wonder how he felt about being involved with a woman who had a child? He suspected it was a little of both. Clearly the subject of her ex was totally and completely off-limits, but why was she so adamant about it? Was she embarrassed? Scared, for sure, and Damon didn't blame her. Mercer and his gang of criminals were dangerous people.

"She's a cute kid," Damon said as he helped her prepare the back patio table.

"I like her just a little," Ruby said with a smile.

Bette had gone inside to get the salad and Maya.

When everything was ready and Maya plopped down on a chair at the table, Damon sat across from her, leaving the chairs beside her for Ruby and Bette. Seeing she had brought her coloring book, Damon leaned forward a bit.

What did you draw? he signed.

Maya signed back, *A horse.*

Damon looked at the black horse and noticed how Maya had stayed inside all the lines. *That's very good. You could be an artist someday.*

Maya smiled big. *My mommy was an artist when she was a kid.*

"Wow." Damon turned to her. "Why did you give it up?"

"It was just something I did growing up. A hobby. I guess you just get busy as an adult." She turned to her daughter. "And then you have children of your own." Ruby ran her forefinger down Maya's tiny nose, and the girl looked at her mother with love in her eyes.

Damon envied the bond they must have, one that must have grown stronger after being separated for so long. He wanted to know that kind of feeling and to be a part of a family. He had always known he would start a family some day but had never made any concrete plans. Meeting the right woman was the most important element, and he had not met anyone who had made him start to think seriously about that.

Until now, maybe. He looked at Ruby, who caught his gaze.

Ruby blinked as though sensing the somberness of his thoughts. The moment warmed, and Damon had to turn away. Bette saw them and had that approving glint in her eyes.

Unabashedly biting into a rib, Maya watched Damon as she messed up her face and fingers with barbecue sauce.

Damon dug in right along with her, deliberately getting sauce on his face and hands. That made Maya laugh. She bit into the rib again, smearing more sauce. Damon chuckled. The kid was absolutely adorable. What impressed him the most was her deafness didn't seem to deter her at all. At such a young age, her future dawned before her.

"Your daughter is quite intelligent," he said to Ruby.

Ruby beamed with the compliment. "She is. She

learns fast. She is going to be a smart girl. She's already smart."

He imagined people who were deaf had to adapt, be more alert than most. "It's nice to see a kid adjust so quickly to being deaf," he said.

"We don't think of it as a disability, and I work hard at guiding her to keep thinking that way."

"You must be such a good mom," he said, meaning every word. "There are moms, and then there are exceptional moms. I think you are one of the latter."

"She is a great mom," Bette said. "She learned from the best."

Ruby smiled at her mother, while Maya spooned some baked beans and shoved them into her mouth, giggling and watching Damon. She must have caught at least some of what he and her mother talked about. He played along, taking a huge bite of beans.

Beans make you fart, she signed.

Ruby put her hand on Maya's arm. Maya looked at her, and Ruby shook her head. Then Ruby signed, *Manners.*

Maya calmed and resumed eating without fooling around. When she looked at Damon, he winked, for which he was rewarded a cute and secretive smile.

The warm and loving connection he felt just then made him check himself. He didn't want to lead these two remarkable people into a false reality, but at the same time this felt so personal and…right. What a tragedy that he should meet this nice family and begin to have thoughts of joining them when there was no possible way that could ever happen. When Ruby found out who he really was, she would not forgive him. He would never see any of them again. Best not to get too attached. Maybe that was easier said than done, especially now, after Maya had wormed her way into his heart just by meeting him.

He saw that Ruby had caught the exchange, and she smiled in a way that told him without a doubt how much she liked the way he got along with her daughter. Oh boy, was he ever going to be in trouble.

Chapter Three

Two men sat at the bar drinking the beers Damon had served them. As he worked, Damon could not stop thinking about Ruby and Maya. Bette, too. She would probably make a great mother-in-law. Maya was a special kid. And Ruby…

She was beautiful inside and out. She raised Maya with loving discipline. Damon couldn't stop his feelings from intensifying. He wanted things he had never wanted this much before. He wanted to be with Ruby. He wanted to be a part of Maya's life. This all seemed so absurd, since he had only spent one evening with Maya. Maybe it had more to do with Ruby and the strong attraction he had for her. He had to stop that. He had a job to do. The sooner he wrapped up the undercover case, the less damage he'd do to everyone, himself included.

Frustrated and troubled over the way Ruby refused to talk about Mercer, however, Damon wondered if he should just listen to his gut and ask his boss if he could be removed from the case. It wasn't the first time he'd had this thought. After meeting Maya and seeing how much it meant to Ruby, he contemplated it more seriously. He could quit the bar and tell Ruby everything. Maybe he'd have a chance at earning her forgiveness by withdrawing from the case. Then he could explore their relationship for real. He hadn't seen her in a few days and had had plenty of time to think things over.

The only problem was Ted Reyes had been killed by Mercer's gang, and Damon had personal reasons for going after them. Ted had been a close friend and colleague. He had had a confidential informant, and the two of them had been caught together. It had been assumed that the informant had been discovered by Mercer's other associates and followed. Both of them had been killed, and the shooter had gotten away. Damon hadn't been there but wished he had been, even though there had been no reason for him to be. He had been freshly assigned to this undercover case. He couldn't give up now. He had to bring down the one who'd murdered Ted and the criminals who had ordered the hits.

Damon wiped down the bar after a customer had left, glancing over at a table of three men having beer late in the afternoon. They were Mercer's men, and they had been watching Damon. Word had spread that he was interested in making extra money. The owner of the Foxhole tolerated them and maybe even supported their cause. Damon hadn't witnessed him taking kickbacks, but he had good rapport with most of the members.

The three over there frequented the pub the most. After Kid was killed, Damon had overheard them talking about a man named Santiago. Just that. Santiago.

He didn't go by any last name. Apparently he had taken over control of the syndicate. They all called themselves the Nightcrawlers. Worms as far as Damon was concerned. A bunch of reprobates.

Damon suspected Orlando Braxton was the one who'd killed Ted. Six feet tall, longish dark hair, he had brown eyes with a sort of dead stare, never showing any kind emotion. He must be a mean one. Also at the table was Curtis Morgan and Sonny Cooper. They seemed to follow Orlando. After some surveillance, Damon learned those three were Santiago's top men and likely the ones who carried out orders to kill and who oversaw drug deals. They were the men Damon had been targeting to win their trust. He hadn't gotten very far with that, which only added to his inclination to ask to be removed from the case and pursue Ruby.

Just then, he saw Orlando look over at him again and then stand, say something to his pals and start walking toward him. Really? Orlando was going to come over and talk to him? Maybe his luck was about to change.

Orlando approached the bar and took a seat on a stool in front of Damon.

"What can I get you?" Damon asked.

"Beer."

Damon went about pouring him a mug.

"Thomas tells me you do a little business on the side," Orlando said.

Thomas was the owner of Foxhole. "I do. I hear you do, too."

"Maybe."

"Maybe we can help each other," Damon said.

"My boss wants to talk to you," Orlando said. "He's on his way right now. When he arranges for a meeting here, it's expected that the meeting takes place."

Damon understood that all too well. The front door opened, and a man entered. Damon recognized him as someone who came in infrequently but had conversed with some group members and others he didn't know. He only came here for meetings. Damon figured that out just now.

"Ah. Here he is now," Orlando said.

"All right."

"He'll come to the bar. Make sure it's vacated of other customers." Orlando glanced over at the one remaining drinker.

"Of course," Damon said.

Orlando walked away, intercepting Santiago and speaking briefly to him. Damon went to the lone customer.

"Your drinks are on me tonight. Go find a table."

The man looked at him for a few seconds, then glanced toward the door and the table where the other gang member sat. Without a word, he raised his glass of booze to Damon in thanks and walked away.

Damon had learned much of Santiago's operation over the last several months. He began by befriending the members who made up the lower hierarchy of the organization. The people who moved drugs or guns. The people who sold them on the streets. Many of them came to Chicago for meetings. Some operated outside the United States.

The international runners diverted legally purchased

weapons from debarred countries. They bribed government officials to move them through those countries without licensing. Government workers didn't make much money, so cash payments were common. They also targeted government stockpiling facilities. The US runners did the same, but it was a lot tougher here when it came to stockpiles. Santiago had made deals with corrupt arms manufacturers.

And then there was his drug operation. That was where he really made most of his money. He had people who transported product across the San Ysidro and Laredo ports of entry and, he was sure, by other methods, such as underground or by boat or plane. It was a big operation.

Damon waited as Santiago walked with the confidence of a ruthless killer to the bar. Alone and without backup possible, Damon had to steel himself into his role as a small-time drug dealer looking to make an alliance with the ruling gang in the community.

Santiago was around five eleven and fairly trim in his fifties. His eyes were dark and beady and lacked emotion of any kind. "Damon Jones?" Santiago said.

"Yes."

"I'm Santiago."

"I know who you are."

"Oh?" Santiago sat. "And how do you know me?"

"I've seen you come in, and Orlando told me you were coming to meet me."

Santiago reached into his expensive-looking inner-jacket pocket. Damon concealed his concern and readiness to respond until he saw the man pull out a pack of cigarettes. There was no smoking allowed in the Foxhole, but Damon didn't object as the man took out a lighter and lit one.

After Santiago puffed a billow of smoke and lowered his hand with the cigarette between two fingers, he asked, "What do you know about me?"

Damon bent to retrieve a short glass and put it near Santiago's burning cigarette to serve as an ashtray.

Santiago's eyes met his in shrewd appreciation.

"What can I get you to drink?" Damon asked.

"Your best whiskey, straight."

Damon gave him what he asked for. "Santiago? You have a last name?"

"Just Santiago."

That was all he wanted Damon to know. Or maybe he did really only go by that name. Everyone knew him as Santiago. As a drug dealer, he was likely proud having one name associated with him. With his commanding, almost six-foot-tall good looks, it suited him.

"I've had my eyes on you over the last few months," Santiago said.

"I've noticed." Damon played it cool. Santiago and his trio of watchdogs would know a lie. Damon had planned for this moment, when he could face the leader and convince him he could be trusted—when he couldn't. This could turn out to be a major break in the case.

"Tell me about yourself," Santiago said.

Damon reached into the reserves of background he'd been trained to recite in situations like this. "What do you want to know?"

"Where did you grow up, and how did you end up here, working at the Foxhole?"

Nothing like getting right to the point. Damon found he liked that about the man, despite his degenerate nature. "I grew up in Detroit and moved to Chicago as soon as I graduated high school. My dad left when I was a kid, and my mom worked two jobs." Telling the lies was so much easier when the recipient was a criminal. "I worked as a bartender at a few other places before finding the Foxhole…and Thomas."

"Thomas is a good man."

Of course he would have that kind of opinion about a man who looked the other way when illegal activities were going on. Those activities had cost Ted his life. Damon had had to face Ted's family after he was killed. He had to quell his anger over the injustice.

"*You* found the Foxhole?"

"Yes. I liked its patronage." That should tell Santiago that Damon had searched for the right place of employment to facilitate his side job, fictitious but essential to the case.

"Its patronage." Santiago was testing him.

"You know exactly what I mean."

Puffing on his cigarette and tapping the ashes into the glass, Santiago studied him.

Taking the hint, Damon expanded on his explanation. "I had a gig back in Detroit, but here in Chicago I've noticed the marketing opportunities are limited." He paused. "I don't want to tread where I'm not welcome, but I'm more than a little interested in investing. I don't want to lead. I want to make some extra cash is all, and like I said, I don't want to tread where I'm not welcome." That should be neutral enough to avoid anyone else hearing him and convince Santiago he was for real.

Santiago met his gaze with deadness similar to Orlando's. "I respect that in a man. Orlando has told me you are cautious. I also respect that. You've left subtle messages of your interest in joining my organization… but are you trustworthy?"

"I never said I wanted to join your organization. I just don't want to start a turf war." Damon shrugged with his hands outspread in a peaceful gesture. "It's just me. I like making extra money, that's all."

Santiago didn't respond. Damon knew he might not accept a connection like that, one that was so individual.

"I'm sure you checked me out," Damon said. "You know my background. Aside from that, every business deal comes with some uncertainties. I'll work with you on terms until you know you can trust me."

Santiago smiled. "That, my friend, might be manageable." He drained the entire glass of whiskey and set the glass down. "But for us to engage in business, there is something I need from you."

This was the part Damon disliked about undercover work. When criminals asked him to do distasteful things.

"How much do you know about Ruby Duarte?" Santiago asked.

Damon should have expected something like this—to involve Ruby. "What does she have to do with anything?"

"We know you've been seeing her."

Of course they did. They had eyes on him. Damon had seen them from time to time. He expected that. He had planned for it. But Ruby's safety was paramount to him.

"I have, just recently." Damon intended to plant a seed of doubt in Santiago's mind. "She works down the street at a coffee shop I go to."

Santiago's brow lowered. "You don't know her association with me?"

"With you?" Damon feigned ignorance. "I'm sorry. I don't know what you're talking about. What association?"

Santiago remained silent.

"Are you planning to use her against me? Like a soft spot?"

Santiago chuckled. "That's always a possibility. Everyone has their weakness."

"I just started seeing her. I'd hardly call that a weakness," Damon said.

With a hard, unreadable look that would be threatening to most people, Santiago met his eyes in silence for several seconds. What was going through his mind? For one, Damon made it clear Ruby wasn't his weakness—thereby protecting her—and for another, he had given this gangster the impression he didn't know Ruby very well.

"Do you know Kid Mercer?" Santiago asked at last.

"Not personally, but I know who he is and that he was killed by a cop." He withheld any further knowledge until he could glean what Santiago was after.

"Ruby was his lady," Santiago said.

"Oh. I get it now," Damon said.

"With his death there have been some changes."

Damon nodded. "One would expect that. I've been wondering who took over in his place. It's good to know the man who did. At last."

Santiago smiled again, though not really genuinely. "I have a proposition for you."

"I'm listening."

"You're in a unique position," Santiago said. "If you really want to do business with me, I need you to help me find out what Ruby knows about Kid's activities before he died."

Join the club. That's what Damon had been trying to do from day one. "What exactly do you want to know?"

Santiago glanced around. The bar was vacant, and only two tables were occupied, one with Orlando and his crew, the other with two men engaged in what appeared to be an intent conversation.

"Just what I asked... What does she know about Kid?"

Damon realized he'd have to give this man something. He had to be careful. Anything he revealed could put Ruby's life in danger, and Maya's.

"I have noticed something," Damon said. "I've asked Ruby about her daughter's father, but she's been close-mouthed about it—to the extreme."

Santiago nodded. "She knows more than she lets on."

"What do you want me to do?"

"Get her to talk." Santiago leaned back, more relaxed as he must have begun to trust Damon. "Mercer had a stash of guns and ammunition."

What? Damon had to hide his astonishment. He and his team knew nothing of this.

"My organization depended on the revenue from the sale of them," Santiago said.

"I can understand that," Damon said.

"And we need them. Now."

Damon nodded. "You want me to find out where they are, and then we can do business?" Damon asked.

"Yes." Santiago looked satisfied. His dead eyes actually came to life for a brief few seconds.

Damon's mind reeled. This had to be why Ruby was so afraid, why she never talked about Mercer. New resolve came over him. He would fight hard to get her to open up. Not just for the sake of his undercover case, but more so to save her and Maya.

RUBY HAD ANOTHER evening to herself. Maya and her mother were asleep, and she enjoyed a cup of tea and a book—or she tried to.

Damon had to work late again, and he'd be at the pub until after two in the morning. They had been seeing each other almost every day. Ruby was afraid to let herself feel what she knew was bursting to be free from her heart. Heck, she probably had already done that.

Ruby had thought a lot about why she was so against talking about Kid. Yes, she was humiliated and felt like a bad mom for her inability to protect the one person who meant absolutely the most to her, but Damon seemed like someone she could lean on. It was the latter that had her so reluctant to trust him. He *seemed* trustworthy…but was he? He was a bartender, but he was clearly capable of more. That's what bothered Ruby the most. Instinct warned her not to let him in too deep. She had that feeling early on, just a few months after he had started coming for coffee. Why was she so attracted to him? He didn't seem to fit his current profession.

Aside from his sexiness, he had intelligence. And an affinity with kids. With her daughter. And her mother. And her… Ruby herself. He was kind and sure of himself.

She had felt similarly about Kid when she had first met him. Kind, charming, good-looking. He had convinced her he had the same long-term goals. Family. Security. Love. He had seemed to have a lot to offer. She had wondered about his profession as a nightclub owner, but his business had a good reputation and was upscale. Her main concern was how much time he would be away from her. And any kids they had. But he had reassured her—convincingly—that he would delegate accordingly so he could have regular hours. Ruby had believed him.

Now here she was, involved with a man who was a bartender—not a nightclub, but still too similar. Kid had been a charming snake. She couldn't say Damon was a snake, but he had charm. The biggest difference between them was Damon wasn't as secretive as Kid. Kid had a scary distance about him. She had learned the magnitude of that too late.

A knock on the door startled her. She checked the

time. Just after nine. Alarm sent her into defense mode. Her daughter and mother were asleep in the house. It was late for a visitor.

Carefully and silently she made her way to the door. Peering through the peephole, she saw Damon.

Why was he here at this hour?

She opened the door a crack.

"I'm sorry to have come here so late and unannounced," he said. "I had a weird conversation with someone tonight, and I needed to make sure you were okay."

A weird conversation? "Who?"

"A guy named Santiago."

Ruby didn't know anyone by that name.

"Let me in so we can talk." Damon looked around as though fearful he'd be seen. Ruby didn't want that, so she opened the door.

Her heart now raced with unknown possibilities. The unknown was always the most terrifying.

They went into the living room, where she didn't feel like sitting. She folded her arms and faced him.

He put his hands on his hips and took in her stance, not appearing to like it. "Santiago is part of a drug organization, and he knows you and I are seeing each other."

Her jaw lowered and shock ravaged her. She had never heard that name before. Kid had surrounded himself with people who had nothing to do with the complexities of his business. She had never met the men who worked closest with him. Kid had made sure of that. He had lured her along his deceitful path for as long as he could.

"Who is Santiago?" she asked.

His head angled as though he thought she should know. When she said nothing, he said, "Apparently he took over for Kid Mercer. Your ex."

Her mouth opened, in further shock. Thoughts and questions bombarded her. "Wha…why are you talking to people like that?" Never in million years would she have expected this. Why was this coming out now—with Damon? Was it a coincidence? What were the odds? Now he was connected to Kid's gang? And her?

"I bartend at a place they frequent."

"Down the street?" She had moved, but she hadn't moved far. She had moved far enough away from Kid's nightclub. Just her luck that his gangers took a liking to the very same pub where Damon tended bar.

"He approached me," Damon said.

Damon hadn't known Kid's gang members went to the Foxhole? Was it only after the man named Santiago had contacted him that he had learned Ruby had had a relationship with a drug dealer? Ruby had to gather her aplomb. And failed. This was serious. She thought of Maya and what this could mean for her precious little girl and nearly lost control.

"But…how does he know we're seeing each other? How does he know me?" She heard her own fear in her voice. She began to tremble. This was exactly what she had always dreaded: Kid's men coming after her.

"I don't know, but they don't seem like the type to

let things go very easily. I was uncomfortable talking to the man."

Ruby had no doubt about that. She fidgeted with her fingers. What was she going to do? Maya…

"When are you going to tell me about your ex?" Damon asked. "This doesn't seem like a good situation we're in."

"I left Kid as soon as I found out what he was into. He and his friends aren't part of my life anymore." That wasn't exactly how it had gone, but she had planned on leaving him and taking Maya with her. And she couldn't be certain that part of her life was over. Kid still haunted her, even in death.

"What was he into?"

"Drugs." Oh, she so did not want to let that part of her past into her life now. She had worked so hard to get Maya therapy and to move on, to make her and Maya's life better, safer. With the help of January Colton and Detective Sean Stafford, that had seemed like an attainable dream. Now she wasn't so sure. Her fears seemed to be coming true.

"Anything else?" Damon asked.

She looked at him, dazed and confused as to why he'd ask that. Then she grew apprehensive. What else could there be? Did he think she knew more? "Isn't drugs enough?"

Damon studied her a while. Did he doubt her? Why would he care?

Then he stepped toward her, looking apologetic. He opened his arms to her. She didn't resist or try to stop him. She needed comfort. She didn't know who she could trust, but Damon was the one person she felt she could. More than anyone else, anyway.

He gently took her into his arms, his hands rubbing her back. "Don't worry. I'll handle him."

He would handle a drug dealer? "How? He could be extremely dangerous."

"I've dealt with his kind before," he said.

She leaned back to look him in the eyes. "You have?"

His hesitation set her on alert.

"I'm a bartender," he said. "I've worked in places that attract that sort of people."

That seemed like an adequate explanation, but Ruby had a feeling he was hiding something. "Why bartending?" She couldn't shake the feeling he was doing more, that he had more ambitions than that.

After a brief hesitation that raised her suspicion higher, he said, "I was young. I went into the service industry and ended up bartending. It seemed like a good thing at the time."

He was still young enough to change all that. "Do you see yourself moving on to something else?"

His mouth crooked up on the right side. "Of course. I don't want to serve drinks the rest of my life." He chuckled.

His lightness eased her wariness. "What do you dream of doing?"

"Dream? I don't dream. When I decide to do something, I do it," he said.

She certainly liked his confidence and believed he

meant every word. "What are your choices? What do your aspirations tell you?"

"I've thought about law enforcement."

She moved back a step, surprised by his declaration. "Really?"

"Yeah. I get tired of watching bullies and criminals. Sometimes I wish I could do something," he said.

She smiled, liking him even more now. He did strike her as the upstanding type, the type who would go up against the Kid Mercers of the world.

"I didn't know Kid was a drug dealer until it was too late. He duped me. Don't think for a minute that I don't berate myself for allowing that to happen. But if I hadn't been with him, I wouldn't have Maya."

"Don't be too hard on yourself. Those people are good at lying and cheating their way through life. They don't care about anyone other than themselves and their own personal gains."

Ruby stepped close again, going back into his arms. "Tell me more about you," she said with a tone that spoke her heartfelt wishes. He'd shared some details about himself, but it all seemed…rehearsed. She hadn't realized that until now.

Ruby wanted to know him. She wanted to know everything about him.

When his expression closed, a foreboding certainty came over her that there were things about him he hadn't shared. She began to withdraw, her defenses rising higher. She did not need another bad mistake. Another really, really bad mistake.

"I'm who you see me as," Damon said.

He moved even closer, but Ruby stepped back, too apprehensive of the unknowns about him.

But he drew her to him, hooked an arm behind her. She found herself pressed against his impressively hard-muscled body. Her hand automatically came up and landed on his chest.

"All you need to know right now is the only thing that matters to me is you, your safety, and Maya's," he said.

All she needed to know?

Before she could rebut, he pressed a commanding kiss on her mouth. Electric sparks spread and tingled. Ruby lost all coherent thought. She only felt Damon, his hands on her, his mouth working magic with hers.

He slid his hand farther around her and pulled her against him. She looped her arms around his shoulders and angled her head to get more of him. He responded by deepening the kiss. The play of tongues made her hotter for him. If this went much further, they'd end up in bed. Or on the floor. Right here.

But then his hands covered the side of her breast. Heat shot to her abdomen. She did what she had been dreaming of doing ever since she'd first seen him. She pressed her hands to his hard stomach and moved up to his chest. She felt his broad shoulders and returned to his chest before treating herself to his back and finally his rear.

He lifted his mouth from hers and met her eyes, his breath mingling with hers and his eyes hot. With her hands still on his rear, she began to feel him grow hard. This was not like her, not after Kid. She did not get bold with men. She'd gone on some dates, but she had not gone this far with anyone since then.

Slowly, he brought his mouth to hers again, this time not ravaging. He made love to her, soft and thorough. Their lips matched in movement and poignancy.

Ruby slid her hands around to his front and reveling in his fit torso again before placing one hand on his shoulder and sinking the fingers of her other into his hair. He had magnificent hair. Shaggy in the right places.

Turning with her in a half circle, he backed her up against the dining-room wall. Then he pulled up her shirt. So out of her mind with desire, Ruby lifted her arms and away went the shirt. She unbuttoned his shirt and parted it. Then she planted kisses on his chest, running her tongue over his nipples and going lower to his abs.

He unclasped her bra, and it slipped off. She rose up, and he looked at her bareness. His rapt attention thrilled her and turned her on even more. He touched her, and she put her hands on his forearms, feeling the muscles work lightly as he caressed. He lifted her, using the wall as support, and put his mouth over one breast.

Ruby wrapped her legs around his hips and closed her eyes to lovely sensation. She dug her fingers into his hair again.

Kissing his way up her neck to her mouth, he kissed her with more purpose. Hard and driving. Ruby met his verve with her own, reeling with how spectacular she felt.

Damon began to move his erection against her. She was on for him. In the next few moments they *would* be on the floor.

Ruby had to stop. "Damon."

She sounded so breathless.

He withdrew and looked at her. She saw the raging passion in his eyes and knew it mirrored hers. They were combusting on desire for each other.

He had however, gotten her mind off Kid's gang—if only for a few moments. A few glorious, startling and maybe even scary moments. What lay ahead for them now? What wasn't he telling her?

Chapter Four

Ruby was so glad Damon insisted on staying the night. He slept on the couch and had acted as though he had been just as shaken up by the kiss as she. It wasn't so much the kiss, it was the potency of it.

He was already up when she appeared in the kitchen, making what appeared to be pancakes.

"You're going to spoil her rotten," Ruby said.

He chuckled. "I love pancakes."

"Who doesn't love pancakes?"

"My fat cells." He patted his stomach.

He hardly had anything to worry about. She had felt those hard abs when he pressed her against him. The man was definitely fit.

"Is Maya up?" he asked.

"I'm going to let her sleep in. She looked too sweet to wake up."

He smiled. "She is something. Does she miss her dad?"

Ruby knew he was curious about her ex. He must be doubly curious now. She didn't like talking about her past with Kid, but it was time to tell him. She trusted him enough now.

"I think she misses her father, but somewhere in her little heart she sensed he wasn't a good man. Kids have a way of looking up to their parents no matter what."

"I know you were afraid of Maya's father," he said. "I knew early on. Your face says a lot, whether you realize it or not."

"My mother always told me I was a terrible liar."

"Honorable people are terrible liars," he said.

Gee, thanks. She sighed, dreading talking about Kid. It soured her stomach and brought back feelings she never wanted to remember or feel again.

"I didn't know Kid very well when I got pregnant," she said. "It was an accident…getting pregnant. But Kid was elated. I thought it was the beginning of something wonderful. A family. A man to love." She grunted derisively. "Boy, did I ever get that wrong."

"Everybody makes mistakes," he said.

She looked at him. "Not everyone makes that big of a mistake."

"What do you mean?"

She averted her head, embarrassed at what she considered extreme stupidity. "After about two years I began to notice things."

"It's okay, you don't have to talk about this. I know it upsets you."

"No. It's okay. You and I are close enough now, and I want you to know." She reached out and put her hand on his arm.

He appeared touched by what she said. Then he blinked a few times. "That means a lot to me, Ruby."

She smiled a little and then dropped her hand to rub her forehead. Then she continued. "Kid was so secretive about his business, which I always found odd. He owned a nightclub. What was so sensitive about that?" Folding her arms, she looked around the kitchen, not liking the memories flooding her. "His livelihood should have been my first warning. He was rarely home, never at night. Every time I asked him about his work, he got defensive. Then one night I overheard him talking to someone in his home office. They were discussing a drug deal."

This would reveal just how debauched her choice in a man had been. And what had led to her failure to protect Maya. She had felt like a terrible mother.

"Kid Mercer was a drug dealer," she said. "A high-ranking one. He was also an arms dealer and became very powerful. I was appalled. My only thought was of Maya. I had to get her out of there." Ruby lowered her head, on the verge of a surge of tears.

"You don't have to do this, Ruby," Damon repeated.

He sounded so caring, as though he cared more about her than knowing her history.

She shook her head. Looking up at him, she said, "This feels right. Telling you. It's hard, but it's right."

She met his eyes, which appeared as traumatized as she felt. She fell for him even more in that moment. He was such a good and decent man. So different from Kid's lying and violent ways.

"Kid caught me trying to leave with Maya," she

said. "He had his men take Maya from me and forced me to leave. He kept my own daughter from me for almost three years."

"That's terrible. What kind of person would do that?"

"An unscrupulous one. One who has no empathy. A criminal," she said bitterly. "I got her back after police shot and killed him in an altercation. He was going to be arrested and resisted. Mightily." She wiped her cheek as a tear slipped past her defenses, and she lowered her head.

Damon tipped her chin up. "I'm sorry you had to go through that," he said. "You don't have to be afraid anymore, Ruby. I won't let anyone harm you."

He pressed his lips to hers in what seemed to be a comforting kiss but ignited into something completely different. Looking into his kind and honest hazel-green eyes, she recalled their kiss last night and had an instant desire to share another.

"I'm not afraid when I'm with you. You make me feel safe," she murmured. "Like this is a good thing."

"I feel the same."

"You've had a bad relationship before?" she asked.

He nodded ruefully. "I was engaged once. I found out she was sleeping with another man. It's your typical heartbreak story, except she really did a number on me. I don't like thinking about her, much less talking about her."

"Have you been with anyone else since then?" she asked.

"Not like that. I've dated since then, but not with

anyone that would last…and not for a long time." He met her eyes as he finished the last of his sentence. The importance of mutual respect clearly meant the same to each of them.

A wave of strong attraction engulfed Ruby. He was such a man. A real man. "Well, maybe knowing each other will get us both past our bad decisions." She felt so good saying that.

"I'd like that," he said in a raspy voice.

With nothing further to say on the matter, Ruby let the chemistry between them warm up before moving closer and touching his lips. She kissed him lightly but lingered a while to let him know how invested she was in him right now. She slid her hand up his chest, seeing the flare of heat in his eyes. He held her around her back, not too tight, a loose and gentle embrace. Patient.

At last the kiss ended, and she could breathe again. Ruby looked up at him, dazed and giddy with new romance. She hadn't expected the kiss to be so strong last night. This morning it was tender and full of promise.

Hearing Maya approach, Ruby moved back from Damon to see her rubbing her lovely light brown eyes, her medium-brown hair all messy from sleep.

Mommy, I'm hungry.

"Well, it just so happens that Damon made us pancakes." Ruby signed as she spoke.

Maya brightened in an instant. *Cool!*

Damon put their plates on the table, and they all sat like a real family. Ruby had never been happier in her entire life. Seeing Maya watch Damon, she knew he would make a great father for her. Could her life finally be headed to a good place?

DAMON DIDN'T FEEL right about continuing to see Ruby. A few days had passed, and he missed her way too much. He could tell she genuinely liked and trusted him. She wouldn't have confided in him about Kid otherwise. He had met her daughter, someone more precious to her than anyone else on the planet. He was honored that she had opened her heart to him, but his duplicity would not go unpunished.

By now, she was probably wondering why he hadn't called or come by. She was probably also afraid. Maybe feeling alone. Another arrow for his heart. What she didn't know was he was keeping an eye on her. Well, not him but another agent. Tonight he sat with a nature program playing at a low volume and a calming cup of tea. One of those herbal numbers. It wasn't working.

His phone rang, and he saw it was his brother Nash, a year older than him. His spirits lifted. An architect with a Chicago firm, Nash had found success and purpose in his life. He had been close to their mother and had taken her death hard. But Nicole had been there for both of them. She had been a great mom. Damon doubted Nash would have had the drive to become an architect without her loving guidance.

"Hey, bro," Damon said.

"Checking in on you, danger-seeker," Nash said.

Although he teased, Damon knew his brother meant his high-octane job as a DEA agent. "How are you doing?"

"Fine. Working a lot. You?"

"Fine. Working a lot."

Nash laughed, and so did Damon. This small talk wasn't like them.

"Dad called," Nash said. "Surprised me until I realized he must have an agenda."

"Grandfather's will?" Damon asked.

"He didn't say it directly, but he played nice with me, like he was trying to smooth over our relationship to prepare me for whatever he wants. It disgusted me."

Growing up, Nash had had difficulty with their father's apathetic parenting. There had been a lot of yelling and neglect. He was all right now, but he had no soft spot for Erik Colton.

"We can always block his calls," Damon said.

"What? And miss the entertainment?"

Damon chuckled. "That's a healthy way of looking at it."

"Uncle Rick is the only father I ever had," Nash said.

"I feel the same." A memory struck him. "You remember the first time you called Nicole *Mom*?" Nash hadn't had an easy time adjusting to their mother's death.

"I was in high school."

"Took you long enough."

Nash laughed a little. "She's an amazing person."

"You seeing anyone?" Damon asked.

"No. The good ones are already taken. You're probably closer than me. Women dig agents."

"No, they don't. Not the good ones." Ruby didn't

like him because he was an agent. She didn't even know he was one.

"Yeah," Nash said soberly. "But hey, that's not why I called. Our cheating grandfather's real family is having a postholiday party, and we're invited."

"What?" It was August.

"Yeah. They want to get to know us better. If you weren't so deep undercover you would know."

It was true. He hadn't been to his real home in months. "They want to get to know us?"

"Yes. And I think it's a noble gesture. None of us kids have been on board with Grandmother's unquenchable vengeance for being the rejected mistress."

"Very eloquently put, brother."

Nash chuckled.

"Are you going to make it?" Nash asked.

Doing so could ruin his cover. "I don't know. I hadn't really thought about it."

"You should be there. We have a huge family now. And our cousins seem to genuinely want to know us."

Damon had picked up on that, too. He didn't want to miss a family event like that. He wanted to get to know the people he had not known existed until recently.

"I'm working," Damon said.

"That's all you do is work. I'm not asking for days or weeks. Just one night. Come on. Let's go together. You, me and Aaron."

Aaron their half brother, who was every bit a full brother to Damon and Nash. "I'll try."

"No. You commit right now. You're going."

Damon did want to go. The party was this Saturday.

He had that night off. Besides, he needed some time away from Mercer's men and Ruby. And Maya. That whole family-feeling he had with them.

"All right. You and Aaron pick me up, brother." He'd be careful not to be seen leaving or coming home. It wasn't his usual practice to mix his personal life with work—especially when he worked undercover, but he needed a break. And he wanted to know more about the cousins he had only recently learned existed.

DAMON STOOD IN Farrah Colton's Tuscan-inspired mansion, feeling a little awkward among the cousins who were basically strangers. He also worried he'd taken an undue risk coming here while working an undercover case. He had been careful not to be followed, but there was always that chance he'd be discovered.

What Damon knew about his new cousins was limited, but they were the progeny of Damon's grandfather Dean Colton and his wife Anna. Damon's siblings were the children of Dean Colton and his mistress, Carin Pedersen. Damon found it ironic that Dean's wandering lust had been passed down to his sons—all four of them, two sets of twins. What were the odds? Dean must have had a massively dominant twin gene in him. Ernest and Alfred's mother was Anna, which made Damon's cousins legitimate. Damon's uncle Axel and his father Erik were the illegitimate sons of Dean's mistress, Carin.

Damon, his brother Nash and their half brother Aaron had only recently been introduced to their legitimate cousins. They had always known their grandmother had had an affair with a prominent Colton, but that side of the family had never been part of their lives. Damon, like his brothers, had not thought much on it—until their conniving, bitter grandmother had come up with a scandal to use her sons as a tool to take an inheritance that didn't belong to them.

"Do you think this is as weird as I do?"

Damon glanced over at Nash and held back a sudden urge to laugh. "Weird. Yes. I was just thinking there are a lot of twins in our family."

Nash did laugh but kept it low. "We're in the house of one twin."

Farrah Colton's twin was Fallon. Farrah had married Alfred, and Fallon had married Ernest. Both husbands had been murdered. From what Damon understood, it had been a random killing. A couple of nineteen-year-olds knocked off some people on a spree. It was freakish. Ernest and Alfred were leaving work late and were shot. Senseless. He had been so busy, he hadn't had time to delve into the details. He had been more interested in the people, his extended family. Family had always been important to him. But his head spun with all the drama on top of discovering he had such a huge family.

"They're doing very well." Nash glanced around the elegant furnishings.

"Do all of them live like this?" Damon asked.

"I don't know. I assume so." The inheritance had been quite large.

Damon glanced around at the throng of people. There were many from the community in attendance, but Coltons made up the majority. He felt like he had been dropped into the middle of a *Succession* episode. It was so not his thing. But he never backed down in the name of doing what was right, and what was right here was not taking money that didn't belong to him or anyone in his immediate family.

"Do you know who our cousins are?" Damon asked.

Aaron appeared to his left just then. "I just got all the introductions." He looked across the room. "Farrah's three daughters are over there. Simone, Tatum and January." He searched the room and stopped his gaze on a man standing near a bar with an attendant standing behind it. "That man over there is Heath, the oldest of Fallon's kids."

Seeing them, Heath walked over. "You must be Damon and Nash." He looked from Nash to Damon.

"I'm Damon."

Heath reached out a hand, and they shook. Heath had dark blond hair and shadowy stubble. He studied Damon directly with dark blue eyes.

"Good to meet you." He turned to Nash and shook his hand. "I already met Aaron, here."

"Heath is president of Colton Connections," Aaron said. "They do inventions."

Damon had heard that. "Your family is very successful."

"So is yours. Aaron told me he owns some gyms and Nash here is an architect. You're a DEA agent. That's impressive."

Damon thought it was generous of him to say such nice things when his father and uncle were trying to clean them out of their inheritance.

"Why don't I take you around to meet everyone?" Heath said to both Nash and Damon. Then he turned to Aaron. "You're welcome to join us if you like."

"I'm good. I'll go talk to Myles and Lila. They just arrived."

Damon saw his cousins on their side of the railroad track enter the room. "We'll catch up with them later." He was glad to see them. They were all very close, and their stepdad was like a father to him and his brothers, had been ever since their mother died.

Heath led the way toward an athletically built blonde and another fit body, a male with dark brown hair.

"Hey, Heath," the woman said, giving him a hug. "Are you commandeering the room like you do at work?"

Heath chuckled. "Just being social. This is Damon and Nash Colton." He turned to the aforementioned men. "This is my sparky sister Carly and my brother Jones. Carly is a nurse at the University of Chicago hospital. Jones owns the Lone Wolf Brewery. We were all so excited to have an opportunity to get to know our new cousins."

"We were," Carly said.

"None of us knew anything about you," Jones said, reaching out a hand to shake Damon's and Nash's hands.

Carly didn't do the same, but her welcoming smile

said all that needed to be said. Again, Damon was overwhelmed with how friendly these people were. Could it be they had loving parents who cared more about their well-being than money?

"You are all being very gracious given the circumstances," Damon said.

"From what I've seen, you aren't the ones on the offensive," Heath said. "It's your fathers, Erik and Axel."

"The one to truly blame would be our grandmother," Nash said. "We're kind of the bastard sons of a bastard son."

Nothing like putting it bluntly…

"I'd rather think of it like we're all family here," Carly said, this time without a smile. She meant it.

For the first time since arriving, Damon felt relaxed. Like he and his brothers belonged.

"Thank you for saying that," Damon said.

"You better be careful with this one. He's a DEA agent."

"A real badass," Jones said.

"I'm not a badass. I just think doing what's right and protecting people is important," he said.

"He was raised by someone who taught him what was wrong," Nash said. "As was I."

The three others laughed good-naturedly.

"We figured you had that attitude, and we can't say we're glad, because it's your dad and grandmother," Heath said. "They are family. Just know that we have felt similar conflict in our family."

"You had a good father," Nash said.

"Yes, but not so much for a grandfather," Heath

said. "Our dads were definitely good. Innovative and inspirational."

Damon didn't say he wished he could say the same. Now wasn't the time or place to have that kind of discussion. Maybe later as he felt out the rest of the cousins.

Heath's fiancée came over to join them, and Nash got into a discussion with the two of them. Damon excused himself and headed over to where Farrah's three daughters stood talking and laughing, holding champagne flutes.

All three smiled as he approached.

He introduced himself.

"This is Simone and Tatum, and I'm January."

"Nice to meet you. I might have trouble remembering who is who after this."

The three laughed, and he smiled. "I do know you're all Farrah's children." And they were all attractive just like their mother. Simone had chin-length brown hair and blue eyes, Tatum had long, gorgeous blond hair and blue eyes like her sister, and January had long wavy blond hair and green eyes. She looked like a model, despite being around six or seven months pregnant.

"We've heard so much about all of you," January said. "It was so shocking to realize we had so many cousins."

"It was shocking for us, too," Damon said. "I was flattered to be invited here tonight." They certainly didn't have to do that. It was a nice gesture.

"We all wanted to get to know you."

Despite the circumstances? "We wanted the same." He glanced around at all the other Coltons. "You all must be like siblings rather than cousins, being born from twins."

"Yes." January's eyes brightened. "We are all very close."

"I'm close with my brothers. We also have a really awesome uncle. Rick Yates. He was like a father to us."

"Oh, that's great," January said. "Well, it's all of our wish to get to know you all and have a family relationship if that's possible."

"After meeting you, I think it is," Damon said. "And on that note, I wanted to tell you in person how sorry I was to hear about your father and his brother."

"Thank you," January said. "It's been very difficult."

"I get the impression your father and his brother were much better men than my father and uncle," he said.

"Well, it is true our father and uncle were respected men. We don't want you to feel bad about how your father and uncle behave. One could argue it isn't their fault, given the way they were raised," Tatum said.

"Yes, and our grandfather isn't exempt from blame here," Simone said.

He had cheated on his wife, yes. And his sons hadn't. Not the story on Damon's side of the family.

"My brothers and I have talked, and we intend to try and stop Carin from railroading you. We all know it isn't fair, and none of us want or need the money. We are all financially comfortable. We aren't those types of men." There: he had said what he'd planned to say.

All three women bestowed him with adoring, appreciative smiles.

"Why aren't you married yet?" January asked.

He thought of Ruby and wondered why she had popped into his head at that moment with the mention of marriage. He pushed it out of his head. He did not wish to go there yet.

"I am. Soon to be divorced."

"Oh, well…whoever ends up with you is one lucky lady," Simone said.

"I could say the same about you, except it would be one lucky man."

"Try three. They're all taken."

Damon turned to see a man with light brown hair approach. He leaned in and kissed January.

"This is my fiancé, Sean Stafford," January said, beaming as Sean put his arm around her. "He's a detective for Chicago PD."

She also sounded proud. Damon didn't see that kind of love very often, but it radiated off this couple.

"I take it you are married?" Damon asked the other two women.

Tatum smiled. "Not yet." She pointed a few feet away where a group of men stood talking. "The one in the middle is my boyfriend. He also works at Chicago PD, but he's in Narcotics. The slightly taller one is Simone's. He's an FBI agent. So you see, you'll fit right in as a DEA agent."

Nice. Lots of law-enforcement types in the family.

"What do you ladies do for a living?" They didn't strike him as the kind of women who would settle for letting a man take care of them. They were too stong and confident.

"Simone is a professor of psychology, and Tatum is a chef who owns True."

"I've heard of that restaurant," Damon said. It was a good one.

"I'm just a lowly social worker," January said.

"She's being too humble," Sean said. "January cares a great deal about the children she helps."

The more Damon learned about his new cousins, the more he realized what good people they were. He considered it his lucky day and was glad he had taken the risk in coming here tonight.

Seeing his brothers together with their cousins from the so-called other side, Damon said, "Will you excuse me?"

"Of course," January said. "I'm sure we'll be seeing more of each other from here on out."

"I'd like that." He left feeling good about his future and gaining an extended family. More than ever that seemed important. Tantamount, actually. He wore a closemouthed smile that could burst into a full-out, white-toothed happy thing.

Lila and Myles were together now. Not talking to others at the gathering. Damon had a backward thought that his instincts as an agent, working undercover cases, had allowed him to see they were as out of sorts as him. Even with his absolute fascination with his other cousins, he was still in covert mode. That could be good or bad. He voted for the good, since that would give him the best leverage with Ruby once she discovered his true identity. And she would. That was inevitable.

He closed off those thoughts. He needed to gather around the family right now.

Lila hugged him, and Myles next.

"How are you doing?" Lila asked.

"Good, actually. What do you think of all this?"

Nash and Aaron walked up, standing next to Lila. It felt like a wrong-side-of-the-tracks communion.

Damon looked out through the throng of people in the rich environment. He knew his brothers and cousins did the same, picking out their privileged cousins. Damon had no ill feelings. No instincts that told him these people were bad—like his father and uncle.

"I think we should fight the suit," Aaron said.

Damon looked at him, and Aaron met his gaze.

"And I mean *really* fight it."

"With them," Nash said, giving a nod to the groups of cousins targeted by Carin.

Damon chuckled, feeling good about all of this and connected in ways he had never been before. He only wished Ruby could be here with him.

With that thought, he was reminded of his duplicity and how impossible it would be for them to be together if she ever found out who he really was.

He inwardly corrected himself.

When she found out who he really was. His only hope was controlling how and when she did.

Chapter Five

Ruby was on cloud nine. No. Ten, eleven or twelve. Whatever number could be assigned to how astronomically good she felt. She walked up the beautifully lighted path toward Farrah Colton's front entry, two white pillars supporting a gabled roof. The Tuscan-style house was a mansion to Ruby. She had never been here before, nor had she met Farrah. January was her daughter, who had invited Ruby to this epic, if not iconic, postholiday party.

January had cousins she never knew, and they'd all be here tonight, but the Coltons had invited many others. The main objective, as January had told her, was to get to know her long-lost cousins. This was a party to break the ultimate ice. Christmas in August!

Ruby was in the perfect mood for a celebration. Her spirits couldn't be higher, and Damon was responsible. He was a good and strong and honorable man. Nothing like Kid Mercer. Ugh. That was such a horrible time in her life. Damon had turned that all around in the months she had known him.

And Maya adored him.

Her heart soared with joy over that. Her mother–daughter bond was finally intact, and she believed she had found a man who could fill the final void. A real father for her daughter.

And a real husband for her…

She stopped those thoughts. She had to be cautious. A good marriage to a handsome and loving man seemed like a fairy tale. Could it be she'd have that with Damon?

Walking toward the front entry, Ruby felt like a princess in her best dress, which would pale in comparison to probably most of the other women at the party tonight. A white flowing sleeveless, it was a good replica of something expensive. Her heels were soundless against the crafted concrete pathway, thanks to good soles.

A butler let her in. She entered the party, a little late in getting there. Maya hadn't wanted her to go, and she had to do some comforting first. Her mother had gotten her set up with a cartoon, and she would be going to bed soon.

Arriving by herself was disconcerting. She didn't recognize anyone. She only knew January and Sean. Searching for them, she didn't see them through the crowd of people. As she expected, most were dressed elegantly. There was a lot of money here tonight. She had never been to a party like this. Kid had thrown some elaborate ones, but they had all been odd, at least to her. That was the word she had for those events. *Odd.* The people had a nice facade, but the vibes had always been…dangerous. From their body language, which had always been on the tough side to the way they dressed, some in leather, some with body piercings and tattoos on their faces, and nearly everywhere else visible, and men with bold jewelry. She had always been uncomfortable, even apprehensive.

Sean was the kind of detective who truly cared about not only the victims of crime but the families affected by it. He had done her a big favor when he had gone after Kid and tried to arrest him. Kid had been shot and killed in the altercation. Ruby wasn't upset at all. With Kid gone, she could have her daughter back. Both Sean and January had developed a close relationship with Maya. They cared about her a great deal and would have adopted her until they learned the girl had a mother who was alive. They had not only helped her get her daughter back, they had given a heavenly hand. They had gently reunited Maya with her mother.

She spotted them standing in the huge and opulently beautiful living room. Although richly decorated, it had a warm feel.

Ruby smiled big, genuinely glad to see January. She leaned in for a hug. "It's so good to see you."

They were the same height. January was blonde, and Ruby was dark-haired. Ruby felt as though January could be something of a sister to her. And an aunt to Maya. Ruby had already made her and Sean her daughter's godparents.

"You look fantastic!" January exclaimed, moving back with Ruby's hands in hers and looking her over.

"Not nearly as fantastic as you," Ruby said. January wore a knee-length sparkly cocktail dress that didn't hide her pregnancy. Ruby looked down at her round tummy. "How are the twins?"

January put her hand on her stomach. "They're active. And I mean it. You look great."

"Thank you."

"How is Maya?" January asked. "I miss her so much."

Ruby would have to arrange to bring Maya around her more often. She had been so focused on her daughter's well-being that she thought of little else.

"She's doing really well," Ruby said. "Thanks to you and Sean." She looked at Sean to include him.

"I just did my job," Sean said.

He had saved Maya from a dangerous man. Ruby's ex.

"No, really," Ruby said. "The therapy you helped me set up did wonders for Maya. I feel like she's a normal child now. She chatters more. Plays more. Laughs more. And she isn't having so many bad dreams."

"That's great, Ruby. She's a sweet little girl."

Ruby couldn't agree more. "I'm almost grateful she was so young when Kid took her from me. I hope she doesn't remember much of it, if anything, especially the terrible things she must have seen." Things no child should have to witness, the biggest one being the murders in the warehouse where police had found her hiding.

"Oh," January said, her hand going to her heart, indicating how touched she was.

"We'll plan a barbecue or something so you can spend some time with her." January knew sign language and had been instrumental in bringing Maya out of a bad situation and helping Sean solve his case.

"We won't miss it," Sean said.

"Not for anything," January added. "How is school going? Are you managing all right? Is there anything you need? I feel like it's been so long since I've talked with you."

"School is going great. My mother watches Maya while I work and attend classes. She is really getting the hang of being a grandmother. And Maya just loves her. It feels like I am part of a family. A real family. At last." Ruby thought of Damon and hoped the beaming happiness she felt just then didn't show too much on her face.

January studied her face with a knowing smile. "Are you seeing anyone? That's a look that says you are."

Drat. She never was good at hiding her feelings. She wasn't sure she wanted to talk about Damon. They were still so new at their intimate relationship. Well, maybe not *that* new, after nearly having sex the other day and being acquainted for several months.

"Yes. I am," Ruby admitted.

January's mouth opened with a soft gasp. "Who is he?"

"This sounds like it's going to be girl talk," Sean said. He kissed January on her cheek.

She looked into his eyes, and Ruby could feel their love in that exchange.

"I'll catch up with you later," Sean said.

"Okay." January kissed his lips, and Sean lingered a bit before moving away.

After he left, January faced Ruby. “Okay, I want details. Tell me everything about him. How did you meet? What’s his name? Is he cute?”

Ruby laughed lightly. “He’s a bartender at a pub down the street from where I work. He’s been coming in for coffee for months, and we’ve gradually gotten to know each other. And I wouldn’t call him cute. He’s extremely handsome, though.”

“Wooo, look at you. It’s all over your face that you really like this guy,” January said.

“Yes. Our schedules are very different, but we’ve managed to see a lot of each other.”

“So he kept coming for coffee, huh?”

“Yes.” Ruby remembered the first time he came in. She was struck by how tall and handsome he was, in a rugged sort of way. When he ordered his coffee, she had melted at the sound of his deep voice. “He stared at me but didn’t ask me my name. He came in a few times a week, and we’d have small talk, until eventually he asked my name and told me his. He would always have funny stories to tell about what happened at the bar the night before. They were much better than mine about the goings-on at Mostly Books.”

“He sounds nice. Takes it slow?”

“He took it very slow, which I needed. It’s almost as if he knew.”

“Some men can be intuitive that way.”

Ruby couldn’t help smiling. “He is the exact opposite of Kid.” At least she hoped. She still harbored some hesitancy there.

“So you’re dating now?”

"Yes." Ruby beamed some more. "We've been on quite a few dates, and he's met Maya. He knows sign language. Can you believe that? And Maya likes him. He's good with her."

"Ruby, that is wonderful. You deserve a good man."

Just then Sean returned. That hadn't taken him long. But he had someone in tow. A somewhat older woman. Short curly dark brown hair, she was almost as tall as Ruby and January and wore a long flowing white dress.

"Sorry to interrupt, ladies, but there's someone I want Ruby to meet. Farrah, this is Ruby, Maya's mother," Sean said. "Ruby Duarte, this is January's mother, Farrah."

"Ah." January had told her the party would be held at her mother's house. "You have a very beautiful home."

"Why, thank you." Farrah sounded as genuine as her daughter January.

"My mother owns an interior-design company with my aunt, Fallon," January said. "They're twins. I don't know if I ever told you that."

Ruby didn't recall if she had. "That seems like a really creative profession." She could have cringed at how unintelligent that comment sounded.

"January told me so much about you and Maya," Farrah said. "I'm so happy things are going well for you now."

"If it weren't for January and Sean, I don't know that I'd be where I am."

Farrah turned adoring eyes to January, obviously

proud. Then she looked back at Ruby. "I don't mean to brag, but I did raise three incredible daughters."

Ruby heard the sincerity and didn't take it as bragging. "Thank you for inviting me to this party. I'm truly honored."

"We wouldn't have it any other way," January said.

As with any grand party where there were so many prominent people, Farrah was whisked away by a man Ruby didn't pretend to know, much less his importance. There must be many here who were influential in town.

"Something to drink, Ruby?" Sean asked.

"I'll find my way to the bar." She didn't plan on drinking alcohol. She had a daughter to go home to.

Sean and January took up talk with another couple she again didn't recognize. She began to feel out of place, like a single person who intruded on the interactions of two couples who obviously were familiar with each other.

"Excuse me," Ruby said.

January turned her head and smiled. "I'll catch up with you."

Her friendliness always made her feel so welcome. When she first learned where her daughter was, she had been so worried she'd never get the little girl back. Social workers were involved. She had feared her association with Kid would be her lifelong ruin. But to her great relief, January had given Maya a safe refuge, and Ruby had been reunited with the one thing that meant the absolute most to her.

Ruby looked around. Maybe there was a lone person somewhere she could strike up a conversation with.

She was in a roomful of people who were way out of her class. She had expected this party to be extravagant, but nothing could have prepared her for not only the number of invitees but also the wealthy elegance. January and Sean were so humble. Ruby bet most of the others in this throng weren't.

She meandered her way to a bar set up just for this party. "Ginger ale, please."

The black-coated bartender gave a nod and got her a glass full of ice and the soda, plopping in a straw and a festive umbrella.

Ruby turned and moved to a tall cocktail table, taking out the umbrella and covertly putting it there. Sipping from the straw, she scanned the crowd of chattering rich people amid classical music playing at an appropriate volume. This was so not her scene. She liked classical music, but she wouldn't play it at home. She was more of a pop and country girl.

She decided to entertain herself by just watching everyone. She'd stay long enough to be polite and then leave.

Taking another sip, her roaming gaze caught sight of someone familiar.

What?

She knew that face. That was…

Damon.

What was he doing here? A bartender from the Foxhole…*here*? It didn't fit.

Confusion gave way to a shock wave. His presence here meant something was wrong. He didn't belong here. She could argue neither did she, but what were the odds he'd be at a Colton party?

Her heart slammed. Her breathing became restricted. She could not process what this meant. She didn't want to. She didn't want to face it. Not after all the magic.

A cocktail waitress approached, holding a tray. "Can I get you anything?"

Ruby pointed to Damon. "Do you know who that man is? The one with dark blond hair and a short beard."

"That's Damon Colton. Like all the other Colton men, everyone else notices him, too."

Ruby shook herself into coherency. "I-I'm sorry. Did you say *Colton*?"

"Yes. I'm surprised you didn't know. Everyone knows who all the Coltons are. Especially the men." The waitress winked. "Are you doing all right on that drink?"

"Y-yes." She felt her whole world tilt and whirl as though in a horrible cesspool, just as it had the day Kid had taken Maya from her. The taste of betrayal was familiar.

"Are you all right?" the waitress asked.

"Yes. I-I'm fine."

"You look like you just saw a ghost."

Ruby didn't respond, and the waitress walked away with a concerned look.

Just then Damon turned after laughing at whatever he and two other men were talking about. His gaze caught hers, and he froze. His white-toothed smile faded. They stared at each other for a timeless moment. Then he put his beer down on a table and started toward her.

Ruby's first desire was to get away, to get him out of her life. He had obviously been lying to her for months. But she needed some kind of explanation in order to put this behind her.

As he strode toward her, his handsome manliness speared her with loss. All that she knew about him was a lie. Her heart longed to feel good about her attraction to him, but it was only physical now. He wasn't who he had said he was.

"Ruby?" He stopped before her. "What are you doing here?"

Her shocking pain gave way to indignant affront. "Excuse me? What are *you* doing here, Damon *Colton*?"

His wary, questioning look smoothed into resignation. "I wanted to tell you."

"Tell me what? That you've been lying to me all this time?"

"I work for the DEA. I'm an agent and my case is to investigate Kid Mercer's gang. I've been working undercover. Blowing it could cost me my life."

Ruby nodded cynically and looked away, not really seeing all the people enjoying themselves while her world crashed and burned. Undercover agent. Kid's gang. Bartender working down the street from Mostly Books…

It had all been planned. He had gotten the bartending job at the Foxhole because that's where Kid's gang hung out. Ruby hadn't known that, but Damon must have. He must have also known she worked down the street.

She returned her gaze to him, numbness beginning to come over her. "I let you meet my daughter."

Damon blinked slowly, his guilt showing. "Ruby, I never meant to hurt you. I wanted to tell you so many times."

"But first you needed me to tell you what I knew about Kid," she said.

"That was initially the plan, but after I got to know you—"

"Stop." She put her hand up. "Don't try to tell me it was real."

"It was. Not at first, but—"

"You infiltrated my life as part of your investigation. You got the job at the Foxhole, and you came into Mostly Books to worm your way closer to me."

Damon looked defenseless now. He said nothing. What could he say to the truth?

"You asked me out on a date. You *dated* me!" And they had very nearly had sex. Thankfully, it hadn't gone that far.

"That part wasn't a lie," he said.

"Oh, so you didn't ask me out to further your investigation?" she snapped.

Damon sighed hard. "Ruby, I did have to carry out my investigation."

"And asking me out on that first date was part of it." She wanted to force him to admit it.

He sighed again, this time shorter and in two frustrated breaths. “All right. Yes, but—”

“That’s all I need to know.” Ruby marched away, searching for January. She had to keep it together long enough to get out of here.

“Ruby, wait.” Damon took her arm and stopped her.

Pain seeped back into her as she met his magnetizing hazel-green eyes.

“I asked you out on a date to try and get information about Kid, but the date itself wasn’t part of that. You and I were not part of that. You have to believe me. I know you felt it, too.”

Oh, that drove a knife through her and ground out her heart. She yanked her arm away.

“You should never have let it go as far as it did while you were making me believe you were someone *else*!”

He had that defenseless look again. He couldn’t argue that point. He never would be able to.

Ruby turned and went to January, whose smile faded when she saw her. She walked to Ruby, and the two stood face-to-face.

“Ruby, what’s wrong?”

“That man I told you about?” Ruby turned her head to where Damon still stood, watching. “He’s the bartender at the Foxhole. He’s a DEA agent, and he’s been working undercover to investigate Kid Mercer’s gang.”

Despite her best effort, tears burned her eyes.

January looked from Ruby to Damon and then back to Ruby. “I didn’t know, Ruby. I mean, I knew he worked for the DEA, but I didn’t know anything about his investigation. Neither did Sean, or he would have told me."

"It's not your fault. Damon lied to me."

"And hurt you. I can see that. Would you like to go somewhere private to talk?"

Ruby shook her head. "I just need to go home. I wanted to thank you again for inviting me. I'll be in touch so you can see Maya again."

"Maybe you shouldn't drive. I can arrange for someone to drive you."

"No. I'll be all right." Ruby smiled woefully. "If I survived Kid, I can survive anyone."

"I'll call and check on you in a few days," January said.

"Okay." Ruby appreciated her friendship, especially now.

Walking toward the front door, Ruby glanced at Damon, who watched her go. Each step away from him sealed her fate. No more Damon. No more dreams of a happy family. Ruby just wasn't destined to have that in her life. She had Maya, and that was enough. She'd keep telling herself that, anyway.

ALL DAMON COULD do was watch Ruby walk out of his life. So many things went through his head. Only pain and regret went through his heart. There was nothing he could say to her that would make her understand. Not right now. She needed time. But that meant she'd be alone. In danger. He'd worry about her every waking moment.

He caught sight of January approaching. *Here we*

go, he thought. Another reprimand. He wished both women knew he didn't need it. He had already reprimanded himself more than once.

"What happened?" January asked. "Ruby was really upset."

"I know. I didn't mean for her to find out this way," he said. "I couldn't tell her."

"She really liked you, Damon. She told me about you."

She had? "What did she say?"

"She said you were the opposite of Kid."

"I am definitely the opposite of Kid." He supposed he should be glad she at least thought that about him. Maybe not anymore, though.

"Sean and I knew you were working the Mercer case, but we didn't know you were undercover," January said.

"That's the whole point of working undercover. You don't tell anyone." At least his sense of humor was still intact.

"I didn't think Ruby was involved, but now, in retrospect, I should have. She was with Mercer. She had a child with him. The DEA would want to find out what she knows about him."

"Would you have warned her if you had?" Damon asked.

January seemed to ponder that a moment, averting her gaze and passing a glance around the lavish room. "I'm sorry to say, but yes, I think I would have. You probably broke her heart."

Damon didn't doubt he'd hurt her. He regretted that

to his core. He had dreaded the day she'd find out the truth. He just hadn't expected it to come this soon.

He looked around at all the Coltons and felt removed from it all. Gone was the celebratory mood he'd felt before. He was still shocked over the unlikelihood of Ruby knowing anyone here—or the unlikelihood he had perceived. He hadn't even considered the possibility.

"She beamed when she was talking about you," January said. "She thought she'd met a really great guy."

She thought right, but getting her to believe that now might be impossible. "I didn't pretend about that. I did need information from her, but her and I? That was real."

"Well, did you get the information you needed?" she asked, seeming satisfied by his declaration but doubtful as to Ruby's happy ending.

He grunted. "No. I don't think she knows anything."

January put her hand on his upper arm. "I hope you can find a way to win her back. She deserves someone good."

She still thought he was good? "Thanks for the vote of confidence. I'm going to need it."

"That you are." January smiled and left him standing there contemplating the road ahead. The curvy, uphill road. What was he going to do? He couldn't leave her to her own defenses, not with Santiago on the prowl.

RUBY STEPPED INTO a quiet house. It was just after nine. Her mother must have gone to bed. Ruby was relieved.

She needed to be alone. After kicking off her shoes and setting her purse aside, she went to Maya's bedroom door. She always liked the door open. A seashell night-light kept the boogeyman away.

Walking to the bed, she sat beside a soundly sleeping Maya and lightly brushed some hair off her face. Leaning over, she kissed her soft cheek. And then just watched her sweet, peaceful slumber.

At least Ruby would always have her.

Going downstairs, she went into the kitchen and made a cup of chamomile tea. Once that was ready, she took it to the living room and sat on the sofa with her legs curled under her. Holding the steaming concoction that normally would relax her, she knew it would not tonight.

She left the television off, lest she wake her mother. Left alone with her thoughts, she was overwhelmed with how duped she'd been by Damon. He was certainly good at his job. Did he only work undercover? If so, his whole outlook on life would be so warped. He worked with criminals like Kid. Pretending to be just like them. Well, if a man pretended for too long, he became just like them, didn't he?

Ruby had been so cautious. She had no regrets over the due diligence in screening a man who wasn't good for her. She hadn't done anything except protect herself and her daughter. But what was a girl to do when the man she met presented himself as someone full of integrity, when in fact he was just a good actor? A role player with a staunch resolve to solve a case—no matter the toll it took on the innocent.

Who was he?

A Colton. That's pretty much all she knew about him at this point.

January was a Colton. She was a good person. Was Damon? Despite his lies?

It did not matter. Ruby had been through hell with Kid. She had her daughter back. Dreams of a husband who would be father to her daughter and make them a family were gone. She had been foolish to think she could have that. She had been foolish to trust anyone with Maya's future. More than that, she had been selfish.

Maya had been through enough. Ruby had almost sacrificed her again. That was unforgivable. Ruby would not—not ever—trust anyone ever again.

Someone knocked on her door.

Alarm chased through her. Was it Damon? She sat where she was for several seconds, waiting for a second knock.

It never came.

It was late for someone to knock on her door. Apprehension brought out the mama bear in her. She'd be damned if anyone would ever take her daughter from her again.

Getting up, she quietly made her way to the door. Sliding the peephole cover aside, she peered through it and saw no one outside.

She went to the front window, staying to the side

of the frame. As she slowly leaned over, she parted the blinds just enough to see. Nothing stirred outside. Outdoor lights illuminated the street. Neighbors always had their houselights on. Ruby saw nothing move.

She looked toward the entry. From here, she couldn't see if anyone stood at the door.

Taking a deep breath, she went to the front door and peered through the peephole once more.

No one.

Maybe it was a late package delivery. She unlocked the door. Opened it a fraction. Saw no one was there. She looked down and saw a note under a small rock, flapping in the breeze.

Searching around again, she opened the door enough for her to crouch and retrieve the note, quickly bringing it in and closing and locking the door.

She lifted the note.

We are watching you.

Ruby's hand trembled with the obvious threat. What perplexed her was she already suspected she was being watched by Kid's cohorts. Why did they feel the need to make this kind of announcement? She didn't understand. If they thought she knew something valuable that only she would be able to provide them now that Kid was dead, why send this anonymous and quite late message?

They must be aware she knew Kid was involved in drugs. Did they assume she knew more about his business dealings? If so, her life and her daughter's life were both in greater danger than she'd originally projected.

What was she going to do?

Stay up all night, for one. Try not to obsess over Damon's betrayal for another…

Chapter Six

Ruby finding out his true identity couldn't have happened at a worse time. Santiago's not-so-veiled threat that he had to find out what she knew put her in great danger. Alone, with a five-year-old, she couldn't know the risk. Not the way he did. That was one thing. The other… What were the odds she actually *knew* a member of his family? He was still poleaxed over that. He couldn't have predicted that if he had tried. He hadn't seen that coming, not by a long shot. When he had first spotted her standing there at the party, he couldn't believe his eyes. At first he thought she just looked like Ruby, dressed to the nines and stunningly gorgeous. But, oh no. It was Ruby. Her icy eyes had bored into him.

Disbelief had given way to shock, and that had given way to dread. He didn't blame her for not wanting anything to do with him. He would have reacted the same way. He had reacted the same way when his ex, Laurel, had slept with another man. She had told him it wasn't the first time she had kept two or three men on the side. Her lame excuse had been that she needed lots of sex. When he told her he was capable of satisfying her, she said she liked variety—as in more than one on the side. It was a living fantasy for her. Having sex with one man knowing she had just been with two others and in the next day or two she'd be with a third turned her on.

Well, that very well might be, but it wasn't fair to the person with whom she pledged fidelity. Damon had gone straight to the doctor to check for diseases. Why had she even agreed to marry him? She had even tried to convince him they could have a healthy, albeit open, marriage.

He'd told her to get lost.

Then he had begun a long road to recovering from his gross misjudgment of character. He was trained to read people, to predict their behavior and act accordingly. She had duped him completely and totally. Granted, he had been young and new at his job, but he should have recognized the signs.

That was why he couldn't blame Ruby. When he had watched Ruby leave, he knew he had to give her time. He gave her two days before trying to call. That was this morning. She didn't answer. If he ever earned her respect and trust back, it would be a miracle.

Damon was sitting on Nash's back patio, sipping beer with the outdoor television playing a baseball game. He wasn't much into watching baseball, but the sound was cheerful. It had been a couple of days since the party. The atmosphere, the game or Nash's manicured backyard and stone patio didn't lift his mood. As an architect, his brother had bought this craftsman bungalow and fixed it up. The place had loads of charm.

"What's got you all in the dumps?" Nash asked, returning from inside to take the chair beside him, separated by a small table with a bucket of iced beer. There was a round patio table with an umbrella next to them.

Damon glanced over, surprised his mood showed. He normally didn't expose himself like that.

"My case," he said simply.

Nash observed him as only a man who knew his brother would. "I haven't seen you this way since Laurel showed her true colors. Who is she this time?"

The sound of someone opening the patio door spared Damon from responding. But only for a moment.

Rick Yates stepped out onto the patio, bringing with him his trademark air of upbeat positivity. Five ten with a full head of gray hair and a goatee, he said, "Nash said you were going to be here, so I had to come by. We haven't seen much of you in the last several months."

"He's been working a case," Nash said.

"Is it over? Did you get some more bad guys?" Rick asked, moving a patio chair closer to them and sitting.

"Not yet," Damon said. "You know I can't talk about my undercover cases."

"Yeah, but you can talk about the woman you met on it," Nash said.

"You met someone?" Rick asked. "Is she pretty?"

"He doesn't want to talk about it," Nash said, teasing.

"Oh, come on. You're with family. What's wrong, Damon?" Rick asked.

Sixty years young, Rick Yates was more of a father

than his own had been to him. Erik's twin Axel had married Vita, who divorced him and married Rick, and it had been all about family ever since. Rick loved big gatherings and often had Sunday barbecues.

"Nothing," Damon said, annoyed.

"Oh, now, you know your uncle won't fall for that. Come on. Out with it."

"It has something to do with his case, but he has the look of a man besieged by thoughts of a woman," Nash said, his handsome face grinning.

Damon loved his uncle, but some things were best left alone. He didn't say anything.

Nash leaned toward the bucket of beer and took one out, cracking open the top.

"How's the plant nursery going?" Damon asked, an obvious ploy to steer the topic away from him. He owned Yates's Yards plant nursery with Damon's aunt Vita. They sold garden plants and flowers and other landscaping items. The business sat on six acres, with the nursery in the front and a big house behind that. Damon loved all the fruit trees.

"Nice try. You know it's going good. Now, out with it."

Uncle Rick would not let it go now. Damon was resigned to his fate and said, "Ruby Duarte was involved with a criminal whose organization I'm investigating. She found out I'm with the DEA."

"Ahh," Nash said. "So you and she are an item now, huh?"

"Were. She doesn't want anything to do with me."

Rick sobered. Damon was glad he wouldn't tease.

That was Rick. He cared deeply about his family and what happened in their lives.

"I'm happy to hear you found someone who makes you want to keep her, Damon. The ones who make you feel like that are worth every effort. Look at me and Vita."

He and Vita did have an awesome relationship, and it was obvious Rick loved her.

"Well, I'm afraid I blew it with her," Damon said. "I know what it feels like to be betrayed by someone I thought I knew. That's how she's feeling right now."

"That doesn't mean you should give up," Rick said.

Damon looked out across Nash's big backyard. A hawk circled above, searching out some poor, unsuspecting rodent. Ruby wouldn't talk to him. He had tried calling today, and she hadn't picked up.

"What's her story?" Rick asked.

"She's beautiful inside and out and has a five-year-old daughter," Damon said, knowing he was only scratching the surface of what made Ruby Ruby.

"Walking into a new family can be good. It was for me. Look how you both turned out."

Rick had a way of making family gatherings festive and full of warmth. The bigger the party the better, as long as it was all family. Vita's daughter was Lila, and her son was Myles. Lila managed an art gallery, and Myles was married and had a son. He was a lawyer.

"I told her my name was Damon Jones and I was a bartender," Damon said. "Then she showed up at Farrah's for the party. Apparently she knows January." Damon stewed over his bad luck once again.

"She was bound to find out one way or another," Nash said. "She'd have been upset no matter what."

"How does she know January?" Rick asked.

Damon could see by his expression he thought that was extraordinary, just as Damon had.

"I don't know." That was another reason why he wanted to talk to her.

"Well, the sooner you get to patching things up with her, the sooner she'll start to trust you again," Rick said. "Trust is everything."

"Thanks for reminding me," Damon said.

"Tell us more about her. What does she do?" Rick asked. "Does she have family here in Chicago?"

"She's in nursing school. Her mother lives with her, and she has a brother and sister in Wisconsin. That's where she's from." There was a lot more he could say about her, that she was kind and warm and stunningly beautiful, but he didn't say it.

"Call her. If she doesn't answer, then go to her house," Rick said.

Damon took out his phone and called Ruby. As with all the other times, she didn't answer. He held up the phone. "No answer."

"Then, go to her house," Rick said. "I've waited a long time for you to find a woman you can love. I won't let you stand by and let her slip through your fingers. Go get her!"

DAMON TOOK RICK'S direct advice and drove to Ruby's house the next day. He told himself it was mostly out of concern for her safety, but his heart said it was much more than that. He missed her to the point of pain. His heart hurt. The depth of his feelings for her caught him off guard. He wasn't prepared for this. He had never felt this way before. He needed Ruby. He needed her in his life. That frightened him, but he could not stay away.

He rang the bell. As he expected, she didn't answer. He knew she was home because her green Toyota Prius was in the driveway. After a third ring, he began pounding on the door.

"Ruby?" he said loudly. "I know you're in there."

Nothing.

He pounded again, longer this time. "I'm not leaving until we talk!"

After a few seconds, the door opened, and Ruby's mother appeared. "She's being stubborn."

"I get that about her. It's one of the things I like about her."

Bette smiled. "I've been trying to get her to listen to your side, just so you know."

Damon grinned. "It's good to know I have someone in my corner."

"Well, I wouldn't say I'm in your corner, but I did get a strong impression that you were a good man. You're a DEA agent. You are no criminal. My Ruby deserves someone on the right side of the law."

"That I am, ma'am."

Bette opened the door wider and stepped aside. "She's in the kitchen."

"Don't do it, Mother," Damon heard Ruby snarl.

"He's on his way."

Damon walked to the kitchen, finding Ruby with her hand on the kitchen island, looking displeased.

"We need to talk," he said.

"I've said all I need to say, and I don't want to hear anything more from you," she answered.

Damon walked up to her, deliberately standing close, hoping to melt some of her stubborn resolve. She tipped her chin up and eyed him defiantly.

This was not going to be easy. "I'm sorry I had to lie to you."

"I don't even know you," she said.

"I told you. Not everything was a lie. I told you about my family. I just didn't tell you their names. And my name is Damon. Just not Damon Jones."

"No, it's *Colton*."

"All right. I did go to college. I got a degree in criminal justice."

"Oh, gee. Lucky me."

Damon angled his head. "I also told you about Laurel."

"Your ex-fiancée?"

"Yes."

She contemplated him a moment. "Damon, I can't just flip a switch and start trusting you again. I fell for Kid not knowing who he really was, and I almost did again with you. I completely believed everything you said. How am I supposed to know you're a good person? You were acting the whole time."

"I am a good person. I'm a DEA agent. I told you the truth about my fascination with superheroes. What I didn't tell you is the reason why. My father, Erik

Colton, is not a good person. He only cares about himself and material possessions and money. I grew up envying superheroes. And my Uncle Rick was more of a father to us than my own." These were things he'd wanted to tell her before now but couldn't. "You see, my dad is a twin, and his brother is my uncle, but my aunt divorced him and married Uncle Rick. My brother Nash and I are the sons from our father's affair with our mother, who did die when we were kids—another thing I didn't lie about. Nicole was married to Erik and took me and Nash in after Mom died. She raised us as her own."

"January told me some of the story about your family," Ruby said, sounding more relaxed. "It's big."

"Yes, and getting bigger now that we have met our new cousins," he said.

He met her eyes and could feel her struggle with forgiving him. He didn't expect her to immediately. He just had to make sure she was safe.

Just then, Maya came bounding into the kitchen. She had on blue jeans and a T-shirt that said *Her Royal Fiveness.* And her brown ponytail swayed.

Hi, Damon, she signed, eyes bright with vitality and happiness.

"Hi, Maya." He signed the greeting as well.

I'm glad you're back.

Damon signed that he wasn't back. He just needed to talk to her mother.

Ruby touched her daughter's head, getting her to look up at her. *Go watch your cartoon.*

Maya turned to Damon. *Come back.*

I'll try, but it's up to your mom.

Maya tipped her head up to see her mother. *I want him to come back.*

Ruby pointed toward the living room and signed, *Go watch your cartoon.*

Maya did as she was told. Damon was touched by her kinship toward him. He had never had a child look up to him like that.

Alone with Ruby, Damon had a point to make, and he hoped to lower Ruby's guard enough to let him protect her.

"Are we finished?" Ruby asked.

"Not quite. I need to talk to you about my case," he said.

Ruby turned to a cutting board where she had been in the process of making a salad. "I can't help you with that."

"I need to be sure you're all right," he said.

Ruby looked out the patio door. What was she looking for? Mercer's men? Did she fear they'd come after her? She should.

"I am all right."

"Ruby..." How could he convince her she shouldn't be alone right now?

"You still haven't solved your case. How will I know you aren't still trying to use me?"

"I never intended to *use* you, Ruby. You have information about Mercer that I need."

"Do I?"

He went to stand beside her. "Truthfully, I wondered about that. I didn't think you knew anything that would help me make arrests. Then I began to have feelings for you, and I didn't like playing a role, deceiving you. That's why I considered being pulled from the case."

"But you didn't."

"No, because this is bigger than me. It isn't only about arresting a bunch of murderers and criminals. I lost a friend and colleague because of them. He had a family and was a good man. He didn't deserve to be snuffed out like that."

Damon saw Ruby recognize his passion. He was a man of justice. He upheld right and hated wrong. He actively defended and fought them respectively.

"What happened to him?" she asked.

"He was shot when he met with a confidential informant. The informant was killed, too."

Her mouth frowned in sympathy. "I'm sorry about your friend. Truly, I am. I can see you're doing what you feel you have to do, and for good reason. I can't say I wouldn't do the same."

While that all sounded encouraging, she had a tone that led up to a wordless *but*. He was doing what he had to do and that had included lying to her.

"Ruby, most of what I told you was the truth," he said.

She nodded. "Maybe. But when you were lying, I couldn't tell at all. I still can't tell the difference between you when you lied and when you didn't. All I know for sure is you are a really, really good liar."

"I have to be. If I'm not, then I'm a dead man," he said. Didn't she understand that?

"I thought we were headed for something meaningful."

"Maybe we are." He wasn't ready to commit to that yet. "Maybe."

Despite the fact it would probably be the nail in a coffin that represented the end of them as a couple, he could not mislead her. "Yes, maybe."

She seemed all the more disappointed. "I thought things were going well between us."

"They were," he said.

"No, I mean well enough to start thinking about the future."

What had she thought? That he would propose? Already? It had been seven months since they had first met, but just a couple of weeks since they'd begun dating, but Damon was not a man who dove into anything serious with a woman, not anymore.

"I had more than one reason for taking it slow with you," he said. "The case, and my engagement to a woman I should never have trusted."

Ruby scoffed at that. "Well, then you have an idea how I feel right now."

He was forced to acknowledge that. "I know what it's like to be betrayed. My relationship with Laurel was different than this, though. I thought she was someone other than who she really was, and she deliberately misled me."

"Like you did with me," Ruby said. "Sounds exactly the same to me."

"She lied about her past and about her feelings for me. I never lied to you about either of those things."

She studied him a while. "So you don't have any plans to be with a woman long-term?"

"Plans? No. I'm open to the possibility, but it will have to be right. I have to be sure. And it's too soon for us. Surely you can understand that. You didn't want to rush into anything, either."

"No, but it's been a long time."

Was she arguing they should become a committed couple?

Suddenly, she closed her eyes and waved her hands as though negating what she just said. "I'm getting off track." She looked at him with new resolve. "It's good you don't want anything lasting with me. I don't want anything lasting with you, either. I'll never be able to trust you, which I'm sure you can relate to. I bet you'd never trust Laurel again."

No, he wouldn't. "That's different. She was sleeping with someone else. Who wants to marry someone who has no principles when it comes to that?"

"Who wants to be with someone who made them believe they were a bartender when in fact they were an undercover agent?" she said.

Damon sighed. He'd get nowhere with her today. His first concern was her and Maya's safety.

"I think you should come and stay with me. You and Maya shouldn't be alone," he said. She might not trust him or like him much right now, but she had to see she was in danger.

"I'm not alone. My mother is here."

"You could be putting her in danger."

That gave her pause, he saw. She averted her eyes, brow lowering in consternation. She would be defenseless by herself. Her mother would be no help.

"She might be in more danger if she's here alone. What if they hold her hostage?"

"Is there somewhere she can go until this blows over?"

Ruby looked out the patio door again, then through the side kitchen window, where she must have a partial view of the street.

"Has something happened?" he asked. "You seem nervous."

"I've been nervous ever since Kid was killed," she said.

He watched her for a bit. She fidgeted with her hands, and fear joined the consternation in her eyes. He had seen her like this before, but now she seemed more concerned. "You would tell me if something happened, right?"

She put down the knife and turned to face him. "You mean like you told me things when I didn't know who you were?"

Frustrated, Damon sighed. "Ruby, come on. I'm worried about you."

Ruby met his eyes, and he saw a flicker of wavering stubbornness.

"Don't let what's going on between us stop you from being safe," he said.

"I can be safe without you. If I need help, I'll call 911."

"If you get the chance."

She lowered her head and folded her arms. He decided not to push her more. He was going into the bar tomorrow. He'd get a sense of how impatient Santiago was getting.

"At least call me if you need someone to be with you and Maya. And send your mother away."

"I'll send my mother away."

Damon heard doubt in her tone. She was considering staying with him. That was good. She had twenty-four hours to come to her senses. He'd lure Maya and put Ruby over his shoulder and carry her out of this house if he had to.

He moved closer to her and put his fingers under her chin, tipping her head just a bit. Enough to touch her lips with his. Just a brief reminder of how good they were together—and also of his determination.

When he finished, he held her gaze with his. "Most of it was real, Ruby."

"Was it?" Her gaze flitted between his eyes. "Or are you just very good at your job?"

She thought he was manipulating her right now.

"Let me prove it to you," he said.

"How can you do that? Propose marriage to me?"

Was she challenging him? Baiting him to see what he would say?

"I don't think we're there yet, Ruby." He still had trust issues from the last time he had proposed marriage.

"No, you aren't there yet, Damon, because you were never there. You never felt the same as me. You were doing your *job*."

"That isn't fair. I told you about Laurel, how she cheated on me. I never saw it coming. You aren't the only one who made a mistake with someone. You can't have that all to yourself. Other people have been hurt and betrayed, too."

"So are you saying you have no plans to get married and have kids?" she asked.

"No, that is not what I'm saying. I think I will eventually. I just haven't planned on when."

"You would know by now if you felt strong enough about me to at least consider it," she said.

"Have you?" he asked. He truly wanted to know. "Do you feel strong enough about me to consider it?"

She averted her face, and he had his answer. She wasn't any more certain than he. She had trust issues the same as him. Different circumstances, but their experiences had done the same kind of damage.

"Let's just agree to get along for now, all right?" he said. "I need to keep you safe, Ruby."

She looked at him for several seconds. "I'll think about staying with you until your investigation is over."

He nodded. That would have to be enough for now. "Thank you. I'll stop by tomorrow afternoon, then."

"All right."

He backed away from her. "Keep all your windows and doors locked."

"I will."

Damon turned to go, hoping it was safe to leave her alone. He didn't think so, but he knew she did need some more time. He'd drive by a couple of times tonight just to be sure. He didn't like leaving her like this. He also didn't like what their conversation today had dredged up. He thought he was long over Laurel's betrayal. Turns out it was still fresh. For the first time since the weeks after he'd discovered her treachery, he wasn't sure he'd ever be ready again for marriage.

Chapter Seven

Ruby struggled with Damon's suggestion to stay with him. For a very real reason, she wondered if she should not hesitate to accept his offer. He was right. She was in danger. Her daughter was in danger. But she had no recourse. Local police couldn't help her in the short-term. She had no friends well versed in dangerous people. She only had Damon's expertise. The note said Kid's men were watching her. It hadn't said they'd take any action. It hadn't said they'd harm her if she didn't deliver whatever they demanded.

She hadn't slept much last night. She kept getting up and looking out windows. Her mother had agreed to go stay with her brother and had packed and left this morning, her parting words still echoing.

"Go stay with Damon, Ruby."

She had called work and said she wouldn't be in the rest of the week. She also wasn't going to class. Her professors had agreed to let her make up the coursework.

Maya sat at the dining-room table coloring, and

Ruby was in the living room watching the news, trying to calm her nerves.

The doorbell rang, and she all but leaped off the chair. Going to the door, shock and fear zapped her. She recognized Sonny Cooper. He had been one of Kid's men. Average height with dirty-blond hair, his blue eyes were creepy. Fear palpitated through her.

"I know you're in there, Ruby. I need to talk to you," Sonny said through the door.

"What do you want?" she asked, picking up her cell phone from the console by the door. Should she call 911?

"Let me in," Sonny said.

Ruby remembered seeing all of Kid's men carrying guns. She tried to calm her nerves. Her heart raced.

"I can't. My daughter is here."

"All the more reason to let me in. If you don't, I'm going to break down this door."

She'd like to see him try. It was a metal door. But he could break a window and still get in. Or go around to the back and break in there. She didn't want to cause Maya any trauma.

"If you do that, I'll call the cops." She held up her phone and tapped in 911 without connecting the call.

"They won't get here in time to help you. Let me in. All I want to do is talk. I'm not going to hurt you or your daughter."

Said the snake to the cute and cuddly chipmunk.

Ruby glanced at Maya, who still colored as though an evil man were not on the other side of the door.

"I'll come outside." Ruby opened the door a crack

and glanced up and down the street. A neighbor was walking their dog, and cars passed.

She stepped outside and closed the door behind her.

Sonny observed her. "You're looking good."

What a sicko. "What do you want?" she demanded harshly. Her mama-bear instinct kicked in. She would do anything to protect her daughter.

"I want what my boss wants, and that is to find out where Kid stashed a significant amount of valuable guns and ammunition."

"I don't know anything about that. Kid didn't share his work with me."

That didn't seem to please Sonny much. "You know, I always liked you, Ruby. You were always nice to me."

"I try to be nice to everyone." No matter how despicable they happened to be. Being nice sometimes was a life-preserving strategy, but a man like Sonny wouldn't understand that.

"See, I think you do know something. And if you don't, then that adorable little girl in there probably does, since she was with Kid up until he went and got himself capped."

"Maya would have told me or her therapist, and she hasn't. She doesn't know anything. She's only five years old. Keep her out of this."

Sonny leaned close, his ice-blue eyes threatening. "This is a courtesy visit, Ruby. If you won't tell me where the weapons are, then tell that boyfriend of yours. Either way, I need to know."

"Is Damon working with you now?" she asked.

"In a manner of speaking." Sonny straightened.

What did he mean? Was he worming his way into Kid's organization? That made sense, since it was his investigation.

Sonny leaned close again. "You only get this one courtesy visit."

"Was that note a courtesy, too?" She probably should keep her tone polite rather than sarcastic, but she couldn't help it. She despised everything this man stood for. And a fighter rose up to protect her daughter.

"Yes, it was. Santiago asked me to first send you the note and then pay you a visit. The next time we cross paths, it won't be good for you. Give Santiago what he wants."

"I don't know where the guns are," she said with a raised voice. "I didn't even know Kid was dealing them."

"You know, Ruby," Sonny said. "Don't lie to me."

"I don't! You have to believe me."

Backing up, Sonny turned with one last spine-chilling look and walked to a car parked on the street, a driver waiting there.

Ruby went back inside, agitated, frustrated and scared. She saw Maya had noticed her disappearance. She stood by the front door, a questioning look in her eyes.

Where did you go?

Nowhere, Ruby signed back. *Someone stopped by to talk. They're gone now.*

I'm hungry, Maya signed.

"Okay. Let's get you fed." Ruby signed along with speaking aloud. Then she walked into the kitchen and began preparing lunch. All the while she kept mulling over what to do about Santiago. She had to find a safe place for Maya, and the only thing that came to mind was Damon.

Settling her daughter down at the table, Ruby cleaned up and stepped into the living room. Seeing the front blinds open, she went to close them. As she reached for the cord, she saw a familiar car parked on the street. Cigarette smoke floated up from the driver's window.

Ruby closed the blinds, shaken. They would be watching her all the time now. Unsettled, she didn't feel she had much of a choice. She could go to the police, maybe call Sean, but legally what could they do but stop by and check things out? She didn't want to impose on Sean and January. They had done enough for her.

Back in the kitchen, Maya had finished her lunch. She got her daughter's attention.

I need you to go pack a bag, Maya. We're going to stay with Damon for a while.

Maya's whole face lit up, and she laughed. Ruby loved the sound. But she adored Damon way too much. Her attachment to the man bothered Ruby. It also touched a deep spot in her heart where she had no control. She just had to stay focused. Maya's safety was a number-one priority. She would take her to Damon, at least temporarily, until she figured out another option.

Taking her cell to her own bedroom, she called Damon.

"Are you all right?" Damon asked when he answered.

"Yes, but one of Kid's men just stopped by asking about guns and ammo."

"Who?"

"Sonny."

"Damn. That's not good, Ruby." Damon sounded tense with concern.

"I know."

"Please come and stay with me," he said.

"That's why I called. Is it all right if we stay there until we find another safe place?" she asked.

Silence met her across the wireless connection. "You can stay here for as long as you need to," he finally said.

"Damon?" She said his name unbidden, her trepidation showing. She couldn't take it back now.

"I know, Ruby. Let's get you somewhere safe, and then we'll take it from there. I understand you don't trust me personally, but please trust me as a DEA agent."

His words rang true with her. This wasn't personal. She and Maya were in danger. "Okay."

"Just come to the bar. I have an extra key to my place."

Ruby ended the call, anxious to be gone from there and not alone and scared.

DAMON WATCHED SANTIAGO sitting at a table with Orlando, Curtis and Sonny. Orlando's dead stare showed no emotion as he looked from Curtis to Sonny. As the leader of the lesser ranked members of Santiago's organization, he exuded an aura of evil power. Curtis was the weaker of the members, shorter in height and a man of few words. Sonny was much more dangerous, a powder keg of easily triggered temper.

Earlier he had spoken to Sonny and Curtis and the two had left. Damon wondered where they had gone and hoped it wasn't to harass Ruby. Now Santiago and Orlando seemed to be having a chummy conversation.

Sonny and Curtis reappeared at the pub, going to the table and sitting. Sonny spoke to Santiago, who nodded in satisfaction. Then he looked over at Damon. Standing, he walked to the bar and took a stool.

"How are you today, Damon?" Santiago asked.

"I can't complain. And you?"

"I am well, except for my missing guns and ammunition."

Damon nodded.

"Have you made any progress with your girlfriend?"

"If you mean does she know anything about that, no. I asked her, and she doesn't know anything." Would his word be enough?

"My friend Sonny over there doesn't agree. He stopped by to talk with her, and she denied knowing anything to him as well, but he thinks she isn't telling the truth."

Great. Now they were going to turn up the heat on Ruby? No wonder she'd called and said she was on her way. At least he knew she was all right. Just scared, most likely. He'd do his best to make her feel safe.

"What if she is telling the truth?" Damon asked.

"That's what I need you to find out. Are you still seeing her?"

"Yes. In fact, she's going to come and stay with me now." Damon looked Santiago straight in the eyes.

"Ah. Then, things are progressing? She should be able to trust you to give you information. See that she does. Do we understand each other?"

"Yes, I believe we do." But did Santiago and his men understand that Damon would kill any one of them if they put so much as one finger on Ruby?

"She's only afraid someone will come after her if she tells them she knows where the items are. I don't want to harm her. I only want my guns."

His guns. That was priceless. He wasn't the one who'd bought them on the black market. "I'll do my best."

"You should do better than that, my friend. If you can't get her to talk, I will have to take matters into my own hands."

"Ruby can't reveal what she doesn't know, Santiago. I believe her. I can tell she isn't lying about that. She doesn't know."

Santiago leaned forward and patted Damon's shoulder. "Then, you will find a way to get me my guns and ammo, won't you?"

Now he expected Damon to magically produce guns? He shouldn't be surprised. A thug like him didn't listen to reason.

"I plan on giving you a sizable cut from the sale of them," Santiago said.

"Well, that certainly gives me some inspiration. You can count on me."

"I knew I could." Santiago glanced around. "I

haven't seen Ruby here. Are you sure the two of you are doing all right? Sonny said you haven't been with her every day like you usually are."

"We're fine."

"When she gets here, I'd like to meet her."

He wanted to meet Ruby? Certainly not for personal reasons. Santiago was no friend. He wanted one thing from Ruby and one thing only. Guns. And he expected Damon to deliver. Even if Damon had to snap his fingers to make them appear.

"All right," Damon said.

With that, Santiago stood and walked like a man who believed he controlled the world. Damon would work very hard to arrest them all before any of them could hurt Ruby.

ON THE WAY to the Foxhole, Ruby alternated between looking in the rearview mirror at Maya playing with a doll and driving and watching for suspicious cars. So far she hadn't been followed. It was almost four in the afternoon. She just wanted to get to Damon's home and feel safe.

Ruby's cell rang. Seeing it was January, she answered, putting the phone on speaker.

"Just checking up on you," January said.

"I'm fine." Ruby wished no one had seen her that night.

"You left so upset. I'm going to be looking in on you from time to time."

"Well, you'll have to look in on me at Damon's

apartment above the bar." Might as well get that out in the open.

"Wha—" January was clearly stunned. "You two patched things up?"

"No, not really." Not by a long shot. "Kid's men have been coming around, giving me veiled threats. I'm staying with Damon for Maya's sake." That was a partial truth. She truly did think he was her best bet for survival. "I would have called Sean, but it's Damon's case. He's more familiar with it and everyone he's been investigating."

"No need to explain. I'm thrilled."

She was?

"I don't pretend to know Damon super well, but what I do know so far is he's got a lot of integrity. Did you know he and his brothers and I think his cousins are going to help us fight Carin and her penchant for ruining Colton Connections?"

"No." He was going to do that?

"I don't mean to say anything bad about his dad and uncle, but it's just the way they're going about it, attacking us."

"Damon doesn't seem to have a close relationship with his father," Ruby said. "In fact, he grew up wanting to be the opposite of him."

January smiled and nodded. "I believe that. Hotshot, handsome DEA agent."

"You have Sean."

"Yes. They do share some similarities. I can't tell you how grateful we are that Damon and his brothers are going to help. I just don't want Erik and Axel to cost my entire family everything they've worked so hard to build. What they are trying to get will literally take everything from us."

"I heard about it," Ruby said. Hearing Damon had redeemable qualities went against her new perception of him. She had believed he did. She didn't feel like forgiving him yet but felt this was the wisest move to make at the moment.

Ruby arrived at the Foxhole. The dining area and bar was about half-full. She spotted Damon serving drinks, and his rugged good looks struck her. Somehow knowing he fought for justice made him more attractive to her. She wouldn't share that with him, though.

Ruby took Maya's hand, and they walked toward the bar. She was a little uncomfortable bringing her daughter into a place like this, but the Foxhole was more of a pub and not run-down. She hoped it wouldn't trigger some dormant memory and upset her. She seemed to be doing fine, looking around and studying people as she often did.

Damon saw her approach and finished with a customer. He said something to another bartender, who nodded. Then Damon walked from behind the bar and came to stand before her.

"Hi, Maya," he said.

Maya signed *hello* back with a big smile.

Then Damon surprised her by leaning in to kiss her mouth. "We need to make it look believable." His voice was low, breath falling against her skin.

They had to make it appear as though they were seeing each other? Why? Part of his cover, no doubt.

"I need to introduce you to Santiago," Damon said. "Are you up for that?"

Ruby wasn't a liar. Her face revealed too much. "No, I'm not up for that!"

"All right. Let's get you both settled in, and then you can come back down later." He glanced over at Santiago as though worried they'd create an unpleasant scene.

Ruby became angry. "I'm not acting, Damon." She was well aware of her stance, but he had to understand he couldn't just turn on a switch in her and have her do his bidding.

He met her gaze. "You're right, Ruby, but we can't afford probing questions right now."

Maya tugged at her hand, and Ruby saw her worried face.

It's all right, Ruby signed.

Damon put his hand on her lower back and led her and Maya toward a back door. Through that was a storage area, and on the far left was a heavy wooden door. Damon punched in a code and opened it for her and Maya.

"I'll give you the code. Don't write it down anywhere."

He was in commando mode.

Inside the door was a remarkably clean and bright entry. A console had a vase of silk flowers. There were no windows. An intricately trimmed staircase turned to the left after three steps to a landing, where more stairs led to the second level.

Pictures of cities hung on the wall. Chicago, of course. New York. London and Paris.

Ruby was impressed. She was even more impressed when she reached the top of the stairs where another landing offered plenty of room for entry. Not only that, she could barely hear the noise from the pub.

She supposed gangs liked nice places, too. This wasn't a dress-to-the-nines establishment, but it seemed solidly constructed.

Damon opened the door for her and Maya.

As they entered she was again surprised. The apartment was like a warehouse, a loft conversion, with tall ceilings and open space. Two sitting areas, one with a huge television, and a modern kitchen with an island, and a dining room. She saw a hall to the left in the middle of the space. That must be the bedrooms and bathroom. There was another bathroom right off the entry.

"Wow. This is nice."

"I do have my standards."

Ruby heard his sarcasm and looked back at where he stood unable to suppress a soft smile.

His grin disarmed her so she focused on the accommodations. "Where will you have me and Maya?"

"Maya can have her own room, or you can stay in the same one," he said. "Let me show you."

He walked down the hall, and she took in everything. The clean white trim, the wood-floored bathroom with an open shelf of towels. The first bedroom burst with cheerful colors and a queen bed.

Maya made a gleeful sound and jumped up onto the bed with her backpack.

"Well, I guess this is your room," Ruby said, putting Maya's suitcase down.

"You have your own room," Damon said. "There are three bedrooms." He walked down the hall to a door opposite another.

Ruby went there. This room was decorated in softer tones, more of a seashell theme.

"Did you do all this?" she asked.

"It came furnished."

"It's nice for being above a pub named the Foxhole." She put down her suitcase on the bed. "Quiet, too."

"The owner told me it was constructed to be soundproof. He originally lived here with his family before they bought a house."

Lucky her. This would be a good place for a kid, away from the adult atmosphere downstairs. Ruby appreciated that.

"We need to go down and talk with Santiago," Damon said. "I called January, and she agreed to come over and watch Maya."

He must have done that after she had spoken with January and before she'd arrived at the Foxhole. January was probably the only person she would trust with her daughter, other than her mother. How thoughtful of Damon to choose her. January could sign.

"Why is it so important I meet him?" she asked.

"He asked to meet you. I told him I asked you to stay with me. I wasn't sure you would."

In other words, Santiago was not a man to be disappointed. Kid had been the same way. She had discovered that abhorrent thing about him too late.

The buzzer by the door went off. January was here. Ruby followed Damon to the door, where he pressed an intercom button and checked his phone. His doorbell was equipped with a camera.

"Hello, January."

She smiled and waved at the camera. "Hello."

Damon let her through the lower door. Ruby was impressed by the security. Like a big apartment building, he could buzz people in from inside his apartment, and he must have a security system in place. She looked up and saw a detector at the top of the door. She spotted other devices throughout the room, motion detectors.

Damon allowed January inside, and her beautiful smiling face appeared.

"Thank you for coming on such short notice," Ruby said.

"Oh, no problem. I feel lucky that I get to spend time with Maya," she said, hugging Ruby.

Ruby stepped back.

"Are you two going on a date?" January asked, moving farther into the home, looking around, presumably for Maya.

"Sort of," Damon said. "I want to introduce her to some people."

"Mercer's group?" January asked, clearly perplexed.

"Santiago made the request. But we shouldn't be talking about that," Damon said.

"Of course. I know the drill."

Sean was a cop, so she must be accustomed to the irregular hours and complexity of police work.

"Where's Maya?" January asked.

"She's in her room, probably already has her toys spread out. She loves going to new places."

January laughed fondly. "She's a very brave girl." She continued to look around, taking in the apartment. "This is a lovely home, Damon. It has a…family kind of feel to it."

"A family did live here before me," he said.

"He's being modest. Maya likes him," Ruby said, looking at Damon and saying with some angst, "a lot."

"What's not to like?" January said. "She liked Sean, too. It's good she's got some good men in her life to influence her."

Damon grinned at Ruby, probably loving the vote of confidence.

Okay. Enough of that. "Let's get this over with." Ruby stepped to the door.

Just then, Maya came out of her bedroom. Seeing January, her eyes brightened, and a big smile sprang forth.

January signed, *Hi, Maya.*

Maya reached out to her, and January crouched to take her into her arms. They hugged for a moment. Then January leaned back and smoothed Maya's hair back from her face.

"Look how pretty you're getting," January said.

Come play dolls with me, Maya signed.

January straightened and looked from Damon to Ruby. "I've been summoned."

Ruby laughed, adoring her daughter. "We shouldn't

be long. Can you stay for dinner? I know Maya would love that."

"Why, yes. I'll definitely take you up on that. Mind if I invite Sean?"

"Not at all."

Maya took January's hand and tugged her.

"Don't worry about us," January said, looking back as she walked with Maya toward the bedroom.

Smiling, Ruby led Damon down the stairs. At the bottom, he stopped her.

She looked up at him in question.

"This is going to be tricky, Ruby. I need to make sure you're ready."

"I'm ready. Don't worry." She didn't have to pretend to be attracted to him, if that's what bothered him.

"We have to appear to be a real couple."

"I know. We can exchange a look here and there, and you can hold my hand," she said.

"If I touch you, are you going to recoil?" he asked.

She wouldn't like that, but it was necessary, she supposed. "No. I'll play along, but only for Maya, to keep her safe."

"I think we should practice," he said.

"Practice what?"

"A kiss?"

Ruby stepped back. "We don't have to go that far, do we?"

"I hope not, but just in case..."

She eyed him, wondering if he was trying to maneuver his way back into her heart. He was already there, but she didn't need any more temptation.

"It's just to be sure, Ruby," he said, as though reading her.

After a moment more of thought, she finally nodded. "All right." She didn't want to blow this any more than he did.

Gently, he slid his arm around her and pulled her against him. The shock of her body against his startled her. The potency of her attraction and desire disconcerted her.

"Easy," he murmured, sexy and deep.

Her inner turmoil must show. When he moved his head closer, her heart flew. His lips pressed to hers.

Ruby tensed and tried to shove him away. It was too much. Too strong.

He released her, his brow went low with displeasure. "See, now that's the kind of thing that could get us both killed."

Ruby stepped back. "I never asked to be a part of your *investigation*, Damon. This is not who I am. It's who you are."

"No, you never asked, but you were a part of it from day one. Whether you knew it or not, you were a part of it. Your association with Kid put you in this situation, not me. What do you think would have happened if I hadn't been sent here to work undercover?"

She shivered with what he was suggesting. She and Maya would be in so much danger. She had felt in danger even after Kid was killed.

"I see your point. It's just…" She couldn't bring herself to voice again his betrayal.

"I know, Ruby." Damon's expression relaxed. He put

his hands on her shoulders. "I'm well aware you don't want me to touch you and you'd rather not be near me. Let's just play our roles and resolve this case. Then… then we can take it from there."

She didn't dislike being near him. That was actually a problem. She did like being with him, which wasn't good for her. She was still too out of sorts over the way he played her. Had he felt the same as her, or had he pretended? She didn't know what to believe. The way he said they'd take it from where the investigation left off gave her tickles of butterflies inside, but her mind was full of caution.

That set aside, they had to get through this evening safely, and that meant convincing Santiago their relationship was real…even if it wasn't.

"All right." She slid her hands up his chest to his shoulders. "Let's try that again." She rose up and kissed his mouth, then lowered and looked up at him with her best *I'm attracted to you* face. "How was that?"

His eyes smoldered. "Good." He stepped back. "A little too good." She smiled and went through the door. Damon followed but walked beside her once they appeared in the restaurant and bar. She recognized Sonny, who sat at a table with two other men. She presumed the older man was Santiago. He looked over as they approached.

She stopped next to Damon at the table.

"Ruby Duarte?" the man said.

"That's me." Ruby smiled, having to force it. These people were no different than Kid.

The man stood and extended his hand. "Santiago. Damon has told me a lot about you."

"Has he?" Ruby glanced over at Damon. Only he could read her thoughts. He'd talked a lot about her because she was an integral part of his investigation.

"All good, of course." Santiago smiled, and for a moment he could pass as an ordinary, friendly guy. He turned to his cohorts. "This is Orlando and Sonny."

"I've met Sonny before," she said tersely, then in greeting she said, "Orlando."

"Nice to meet you," Orlando said in a flat tone. His eyes were beady brown and dead. No doubt, he was a scary man.

"Nice to see you again, Ruby," Sonny said a little snidely.

"Please. Have a seat. Join us," Santiago said.

Ruby bet he was not this congenial most of the time. Kid had been the same way, playing nice when in reality he was an extremely dangerous man. She sat beside him, Damon to her right at the round table, one of the largest in the dining area.

The men went about talking business for what seemed an endless length of time. Santiago and his men talked about nothing that had any bearing on her safety, just a lot of bragging as far as she could tell. She checked the clock on a nearby wall and saw more than thirty minutes had passed.

When she faced them again, she noticed they all looked at her and their conversation had stopped.

"Damon tells me you work at a bookstore with a coffee shop?" Santiago said.

"Yes. And attending college for nursing," she said.

"Ah. A woman with a caring heart. No wonder Damon kept going back for your coffee."

Ruby smiled at Damon, who met her eyes with warming energy passing between them. That she didn't have to fake. She wondered if he did.

Turning back to Santiago, she saw that he had noticed the exchange and seemed skeptical.

"We were all saddened by Kid's death," he said. "He was a friend and a hard worker. Loyal."

Loyal. Ruby smothered a scoff. Loyal in breaking the law.

"Kid told me you left him a few years before that," Santiago said.

What was he getting at? Why was all of this important? "Yes."

"And he kept your daughter."

"Against my will, yes, he did. He forbade me from seeing her, although I tried." Ruby could not pretend she had obeyed or gone along with that. She glanced at Orlando, whose expression apparently never changed. Sonny eyed her smugly.

"I will say that he was upset you left. Heartbroken."

Really? He'd had an awful way of showing that.

"Keeping your daughter was probably his way of lashing out. It was an emotional reaction," Santiago said. "I hope someday you can forgive him. I realize having a child taken from you is difficult, but know that it isn't something Kid took lightly."

Difficult? The man was insane. Difficult didn't begin to describe what she had gone through. And

Kid deserved no forgiveness. Kid may not have *taken it lightly*, but he had done it out of spite and viciousness.

"She's getting past that, and Maya is doing very well," Damon said.

He must have sensed her steaming reaction.

"This is good," Santiago said. "I was beginning to wonder if the two of you were parting ways."

Ruby stewed inside. They'd been spying on her for a long time, and she had never known. She had suspected, that's all. She'd wanted more than anything to rid herself of Kid. Permanently. Even dead, he still terrorized her.

"I'm sorry," she said. "Why would you think that? And why would it matter?"

Under the table, Damon tapped her foot with his.

Santiago's entire demeanor changed. Ruby saw the evil emerge in his eyes and the way he leaned back in his chair and drove his gaze into hers.

"I don't think I need to explain that to an intelligent women such as yourself," he said. "But now that you mention it, we noticed the two of you weren't together last Saturday and weren't together after that until now. It's suspicious."

So he was the couples police on top of drug slash arms dealer? Why did he care? His weapons, of course, but why was it important for Ruby and Damon to be together? Because he thought Damon was playing her and he'd have a better chance of getting her to talk?

"Where did you go that night?" Santiago asked.

Ruby checked her rising ire and indignation. This was where Damon would tell her their lives depended on how she answered.

"I was invited to a party," she said.

"And you didn't take Damon?"

"We're just dating," Damon said.

"Yes, just dating, but you, Damon, weren't home that night, either. Where did you go?"

That told Ruby he'd had someone follow her and probably had someone watching Damon, but he had made sure he wasn't tailed. Santiago knew she had ties with the Coltons.

Good lord, this was getting diabolical. And way, way too dangerous.

"I went to see a friend," he said.

"Who's the friend?"

"Someone I've known since high school. He lives in California and came out to see his family. We spent some time together."

Ruby forced herself not to look at Damon. He was such a good liar. He sounded calm and confident, and seeing Santiago's face confirmed he believed him.

After a time, Santiago turned to Ruby. "I trust Damon's intentions, but I have trouble with yours."

The sting of fear shot through her. "I'm not sure I understand what you mean."

"I mean… Kid took your daughter from you. Have you infiltrated yourself into Damon's life in some sort of plot to have revenge?"

Her breath whooshed out of her.

"She didn't know me before I went to get coffee," Damon said.

"Yes, yes. I know. But once she knew where you worked, she might have devised a plan."

Oh, geez. That was so ridiculous. Ruby hoped her cynicism didn't show.

"She had no plan. She only wants to be rid of Kid and anyone associated with him. She lives in fear every day." Damon turned a pointed look toward Sonny.

Santiago smiled, and not with any humor. "That is good to hear." He met Ruby's eyes, which she was sure were hard and direct right now. "Since you don't know where my guns and ammo are, perhaps your daughter does?"

That was enough. Ruby shot to her feet. "How dare you!"

Santiago flattened his hands on the table, and his face grew ominous. "How dare I? How dare you speak to me that way!"

"You're suggesting my daughter was involved in what Kid was doing," Ruby said, not softening her tone at all for this reprobate.

Damon stood and took her hand. "Ruby?"

She glanced at him, incensed that he would allow this man to threaten her little girl.

"Not involved. I merely said she might have seen something."

While that might be true, Ruby would not stand for Santiago drawing Maya into any dangerous situation.

"She's *five years old*!" Ruby spat out at Santiago.

Santiago continued to regard her as though at any moment he would signal his men to take her out. "I am aware. But she was with Kid in his last years. You were not. She may have seen something. Perhaps you can ask her."

"I will do no such thing." Not the way he likely pictured that playing out. Ruby wouldn't ask her daughter where Kid hid a stash of weapons.

"My advice to you now is to consider very carefully how you proceed, Ms. Duarte."

Meaning she had better do as he asked or he might take matters into his own hands—take her daughter from her as Kid had done. That infuriated her.

She stepped around the table and leaned down, putting her face close to Santiago's. "If you or your men go anywhere near my daughter, I'll kill you," she hissed.

Santiago looked up at her face, his anger having faded. Now he only looked amused. He turned to his men, who had put their hands on their weapons, exposing them for her to see. With a shake of his head, his men concealed their guns.

Santiago looked at Damon. "She's a pistol, this one. But then, I shouldn't be surprised, given she was with Kid."

"You'll have to excuse her. She's very protective of Maya. We'll see what we can do, though. You have my word," Damon said.

He walked to her and took her arm in a gentle but firm grasp. "Let's go, Ruby." Then he turned to Santiago. "Until we meet again."

Ruby fumed inside, but she knew better than to incite a man like Santiago any further. She left with Damon, itching to have it out with him. She didn't have to wait long…

Chapter Eight

At the door requiring a code, Damon took Ruby's arm and gently turned her to face him. Leaning down and close to her face, he said sternly, "What were you *thinking* talking to him like that?"

He got it that she understood he had his cover to preserve, and she probably thought he had to understand she would not budge when it came to Maya. He didn't blame her for that. She'd lived around these thugs. She knew what they were capable of. She also knew the only language they listened to was violence.

"Anyone who even implies a threat to Maya will know my wrath," she said in an equally terse tone.

Letting go of her, he pinched the bridge of his nose. After he calmed himself, he lowered his hand and looked at her.

"Ruby, I'm not in the habit of letting pieces of work like Santiago run me, but I'm undercover here. The way you behave and the way you speak to a man like that could trigger his psychopathic nature. He's a violent narcissist. He could order you killed in an instant."

Ruby's head lowered. Then after a few seconds she

lifted it and looked into his eyes. "I know. How can you possibly not realize that? I was with Kid Mercer."

Damon held his hands up. "Okay, yes. I do know that, but you aren't a professional in dealing with these people. You were a victim. I'm the guy who's trying to put an end to them all."

He could see her concession. She agreed. And maybe she even liked what he said about ending them. Ending the violence. Ending their terror on innocent people. Damon's number-one goal was to stop it all. Hopefully, she liked that about *him.*

"You can't behave like that ever again," he said as gently as he could. She was a mama bear when it came to Maya, maybe even more so than most moms given her history.

"What do you want me to do?" she asked.

"No disagreeing or showing your abhorrence for the man. Never forget that I'm on your side."

She eyed him dubiously.

"Trust me, Ruby. Trust me as a DEA agent. If you can't trust me as an ordinary man, trust me as an agent."

Her doubt and distrust eased, he saw. And she said, "Okay. Deal."

Geez, this was going to be harder than he thought. Ruby was no pushover. A little transparent in an unabashed way. She never internalized what people thought of her. She had her thoughts and owned them. Her expressions gave her away because she didn't care to hide them. She was about as honest as a woman could be, which both endeared him and raised his defenses. He had thought Laurel was honest, too.

Entering the apartment, Damon saw Sean had arrived and both he and January were in the kitchen, fresh vegetables strewn over the counter and something delicious cooking. Maya saw them from her perch on the kitchen island and jumped down to rush to her mother. Ruby swooped her up and held her in a smiling hug. Then leaned back to look at her daughter's sweet face. Ruby kissed her nose.

"I love you," she said.

Love, Maya signed.

Ruby carried Maya to the kitchen and put her down. "It smells great in here."

Making fried chicken and mac and cheese, Maya signed, excited.

"Oven-fried," January said.

A little healthier. But kid-friendly.

"Also a salad and some mashed potatoes," Sean said. He wore an apron that matched January's.

"Did Sean bring the aprons?" Ruby asked.

"He brought everything to make dinner. We decided together." January looked at Sean and the two shared a warm exchange.

Damon thought how nice it would be to have that with a woman. While he felt he might be able to have that with Ruby, he had been through relationships in the past where he'd believed the same and ended up being wrong. So for now, he simply envied a couple who had found that rare love, shared by both. Damon didn't consider himself lucky in love. Especially with Ruby, at least right now.

When Ruby reached for the bowl of salad, Sean playfully swatted her hands away.

"Go sit down," he said. "This is our treat tonight."

Ruby laughed. "What did we do to deserve such pampered treatment?"

Damon enjoyed watching her easy charm and the way she moved, so graceful. Her figure didn't go unmissed, either. He always admired her shape. She had nice legs, long and fit in leggings today with a blouse that fell to just below her waist.

She directed Maya to a chair at the table, and Damon joined them, sitting adjacent to Ruby. Sean and January brought the food and soon they were all preparing plates, Ruby helping Maya with hers.

"When January told me you lived here, I got a little curious." Sean broke the silence other than the sounds of the process of eating.

Damon chewed some chicken and looked at him. He was always careful about his undercover work, but with his identity blown with Ruby and her connection to his family, he had no choice but to take a risk. Sean and January knew enough already, with Sean being a cop who'd worked a case involving Mercer. As a cop, Sean was no dummy. It hadn't taken much for him to ascertain the reason Damon was living here, above the Foxhole. He probably already knew Mercer's gang hung out in the pub.

"Don't worry, we know the drill. We won't say anything to anyone." Sean glanced over at January.

"Nope," she said.

It was no secret Sean was well aware of Kid Mercer and his followers. "I'd rather not talk about it," Damon said.

"I had the distinct pleasure of meeting Santiago tonight—playing my new role." Ruby turned a caustic gaze to Damon.

"I had to introduce her to the new leader downstairs." Santiago. He looked at Ruby. "It didn't go so well."

Ruby shoved her food around on her plate. "He started to ask if Maya knew anything about what her father did, and I got upset."

January's brow lifted. "Understandably so."

Damon didn't blame her for that, either, as he'd already concluded during their meeting with Santiago. He only wanted her safe. Maya safe. It drove him to anxiety sometimes. What if he couldn't protect them? She'd fight Santiago with all her might, but by herself she'd fail. Damon had spent months infiltrating Mercer's organization. She knew what they were capable of, but protecting her daughter might cloud her judgment.

"If you need any help, I've got experience with Mercer," Sean said.

That wasn't a mystery to Damon. "Thanks. I just might take you up on that. You've heard of Santiago?"

Sean glanced around. "Is this place bugged?"

"No." Damon grinned. "I sweep it regularly."

Sean nodded, clearly relating to Damon as an undercover operative. "Yes, I've heard of Santiago. Not the most congenial gent."

"Oh, he can put up a facade," Ruby said, scooping up a bite of mac and cheese at the same time Maya did, who giggled as she chewed.

"He says Mercer had a stash of armaments and has pretty much said Ruby knows where it is, whether she does or not."

"Which I don't," Ruby said.

"He expects us to find it."

"He thinks Maya knows where it is." Ruby rolled her eyes, elbow on the table, fork hanging from her fingers. "They've been harassing me. After the party I came home to a note that said, *We're watching you*. Who does that?"

Suddenly Ruby stilled and turned to Damon. She had not told him that.

"What?" he demanded. "They sent you a note, and you didn't *tell* me?"

"I told you Sonny came to see me," she said. "That was more threatening than a note."

"Don't keep anything from me, Ruby," he said, exasperated. "Why didn't you think that was important?"

"It *was* important. I didn't want to scare Maya," she said.

Why did she have to do that? He would have done the same. Not talk about danger in front of an impressionable child. Or not want to frighten Damon, so as to alert her daughter to that danger. Whatever it might be, Ruby's foremost thoughts were of Maya.

"Please, Ruby. Find a way to tell me when things like that happen," he said.

Ruby poked her fork into what was left of her macaroni. "All right. I will. But it isn't as if you haven't kept anything from me."

Sean chuckled. "You just found out he's undercover."

Ruby turned an incensed gaze to him. "It's not funny."

Sean held his hand up. "I'm not laughing because of that. It's just…it's obvious the two of you were meant for each other."

Ruby's mouth dropped open, and she looked at Damon.

"What?" Ruby said, clearly shocked.

"Don't mind him," January said. "He means no harm. We both went through turbulent waters like you two are. And I have to agree, it is obvious you both have feelings for each other."

"January…" Ruby protested, sounding as though she might as well say, *I thought you were my friend.*

"Mmm, this chicken is sooo good." She ate a bite and then sat up straight, dropping her fork and uttering, "Oh." She put her hand on her belly.

Sean put his fork down, too, and met her eyes.

"The twins must like fried chicken, too." January laughed softly, and the exchange between her and Sean was palpable.

Damon was almost uncomfortable. He wanted that with a woman. That love. He looked over at Ruby, whose mouth had dropped open slightly as she stared at the marvelous spectacle.

Sean put his hand on January's stomach, and they shared the movements of their children. The world had obviously dropped away as they basked in ultimate and soul-consuming love.

Without thinking on it too much, Damon moved his hand to cover Ruby's. She had to know how significant this moment was.

He turned to her. She closed her mouth and met his gaze, clearly flustered but awed at the same time.

His feelings for her were too strong for his comfort, but he'd be a fool not to consider what a future with her would look like.

"Sean and I had our hurdles to jump, too. My advice is to take it a day at a time," January said.

Jarred from the exchange with Ruby, Damon turned to the couple.

Sean put his hand on January's on the table.

Damon was sure he'd looked at Ruby that way. She had looked at him that way, too. If only he could be certain that his heart was safe with her and that she felt the same about him.

January looked at Maya and then Ruby and both signed and said, "We have an announcement to make."

That changed the mood. What did they want to tell them?

"January's baby shower is coming up," Sean said and January kept signing for Maya.

Ruby sucked in a breath and stood from the table. She went around the table and hugged January.

"Oh, congratulations!" Ruby exclaimed. "I know what it meant to you to have Maya live with you and to have the adoption thwarted by my return. I'm so happy that you're having twins!"

"I'll always have a soft spot for Maya." January looked at the girl fondly, signing that she would have twins.

Maya smiled big. She had crumbs on her mouth from the chicken she held in both hands.

"We're also eloping." January beamed.

Eloping? Damon couldn't believe it. He looked at Ruby and wondered if he ever had the opportunity to get her pregnant if she'd have a pair, too. Twins most certainly ran in this branch of the Coltons!

Ruby met his eyes and seemed to be wondering the same. Damon couldn't tell if it frightened her or if the idea tantalized her.

RUBY FINISHED CLEANING up after breakfast while Damon sat on the sofa with Maya. They had a Tinker Bell movie going, and Damon seemed genuinely into it. Maya sat close to him, snuggling. Damon had his arm across the back of the sofa and every once in a while looked down at what Maya was drawing in her art book. The two of them together tugged at her heartstrings. Kid had never been like that with their daughter. Maya had been more like a possession. He had been prouder of planting a seed than he had been of Maya as a little human being.

Damon moved his arm from the sofa and signed, *Wow, that is really good.*

Maya put her drawing book down and signed, *I love drawing.*

Are you going to grow up to be an artist?

Maya shrugged. *I don't know.*

Can I see what you've drawn so far? Then to Ruby he asked, "How long has she been drawing?"

"Ever since she could handle a crayon. That book is about a year old. She's had that through her therapy sessions. It's almost full now, though."

Maya gave him the book, and Damon started from the beginning.

Ruby walked over. It had been a while since she'd seen Maya's drawings. The first few were those an innocent girl would draw. Stick figures. Flowers. The sky, sun, dogs and a family. The family drawings sort of broke Ruby's heart. They were so idyllic. Nothing like what it had been with Kid, and then after when he had prevented Ruby from seeing her own daughter.

Then the drawings grew darker. Maya had created them after she had been found in a warehouse where three of Kid's gangers had been shot and killed. One of the men was helping to bring Kid down, and it was assumed the three were killed before they could talk.

Some of Maya's drawings were of what appeared to be a warehouse. Others were of her home but were all in dark shades, with evil-looking faces in a window or peeking up over a bed, all drawn like a five-year-old's rendition, cartoonish and sometimes difficult to decipher. Her therapist had used them in some of her sessions.

Maya became engrossed in the movie while Damon

turned pages. He came to one that had the recurring theme of a warehouse, this one with stickmen holding Ls as if depicting a gun. One had red lines shooting out of it. Ruby had been enormously disturbed that her daughter had drawn images of men shooting guns.

"She drew these just after I got her back," Ruby said. "It was when she was going through therapy. She never mentioned anything to the therapist."

"What do you mean? These look like guns," Damon said.

"They are, but Maya never elaborated on them. I don't think she wanted to talk about what she saw that night the three men were killed."

The next drawing was another warehouse, dark and foreboding from the mind of a troubled little girl, trouble her father had caused by merely being Kid Mercer. This one depicted more stickmen but had a table with what appeared to be a mound of guns. Maya had drawn what Ruby and the therapist had surmised was a puddle of blood under the table.

"I don't like looking at these," Ruby said. "I tried to take the book away from her, but she wouldn't let me. She keeps saying she isn't finished yet." Her drawings had gotten much better since she had drawn these, and Maya didn't go back to look at them. She only enjoyed drawing new pictures. Ruby thought it was remarkable that her daughter didn't like waste. She had to draw on every page before getting a new book.

The next few pictures were of mounds of Ls, some big, some small. In one, there was more than one table.

"These piles of guns seem important," Damon said.

"It's almost as if the shooting she saw in the warehouse triggered other memories of guns."

Ruby leaned closer. Maya had drawn several piles of guns. In the next picture, the piles were accompanied by squares, possibly representing boxes.

Damon looked up at her. "Do you think Maya could have seen piles of guns and boxes of ammo?"

Ruby contemplated him. She did not want Maya involved in his investigation in any way. But if she had seen the guns and ammo…

"I suppose so."

Damon glanced at Maya, who was still into her movie, then back at Ruby. "Look, I would never put Maya in any situation that would be dangerous or traumatize her in any way, but if she did see something, maybe she can tell us where."

Ruby considered that, appreciating that he had addressed the possible impacts on Maya. She wasn't sure what seeing these places again would do to her.

"Santiago will never know it was her who led us to it," Damon said.

That was certainly a plus. If a man like Santiago discovered Maya had drawn pictures of a stockpile of guns, there was no telling what he would do to get the little girl to reveal the location. As far as he was concerned, Damon and Ruby were searching for the weapons. He would never know.

After weighing the consequences, Ruby nodded. "All right. Let's ask her about these pictures."

Damon touched Maya's shoulder. She reluctantly turned from the television and looked at him.

He pointed to the piles of guns and then waited for her eyes to lift. *Do you remember drawing these?* he signed.

Maya looked down at the picture again, then at her mother, seeming suddenly withdrawn and uncertain.

It's all right, Maya. You can tell him.

Maya turned to Damon and nodded.

Damon signed, *Is it a real place?*

Maya nodded. And lowered her head. Clearly she didn't like thinking about this.

Ruby touched her chin. "It's okay, Maya. You're safe. Damon is just..." She signed *curious.*

Are all the places you drew real? Damon signed. *You've been to them?*

Maya nodded.

Did you see these guns? Damon asked.

Again, she nodded. Damon looked sharply at Ruby.

It's what Daddy always had. And his friends, Maya signed.

Ruby pointed to one of the piles. *Where did you see them?* Maya didn't seem as reluctant now, so Damon thought she was all right with talking about it.

Maya stared at it a while and then looked up at her mother. *I don't remember.*

Okay. That's okay. Thank you. You can watch your movie now.

Maya seemed glad to do just that, and soon she was absorbed in Tinker Bell's latest adventure.

Damon stood, and Ruby went into the dining area with him, where he faced her. "This could be our ticket out of this mess."

Ruby became agitated, her eyes worrying. "I hope you don't mean Maya could be our ticket out of this mess."

"No, of course not. But if she can recognize one of those buildings she drew, maybe we could find something."

"But I thought those men were shot and killed in a warehouse. If the guns were there, wouldn't Sean have found them?"

"Not if it's a different warehouse."

Maya had drawn different kinds of buildings. One looked like a warehouse and had been a recurring image. Others were just small rooms. Some even had childlike pictures hanging on the walls.

"The changing scenes tell me she was confused when she drew them, like she didn't know much about the place where she saw the guns," Ruby said.

"All right," he said. "We'll take this slowly. I don't want to rush her into bad memories, but maybe we could take her to some places that might resemble her drawings, places Kid would have gone," Damon said.

"All right. Let's start by researching the places Kid went, and then maybe tomorrow we can drive around."

"Okay." Damon kissed her forehead. "I promise to put Maya first no matter what." He looked over at the cute little girl with her single braid and honey-brown eyes.

Touched by the honesty she heard in his tone, Ruby took in his determined face and fell in love with him a little bit. Then an instant later, the notion of falling in love with him—or any man—frightened her.

Damon brought his laptop to the table, and Ruby sat next to him. He also had a notebook and pen, which he handed to her.

"Make a list of all the places you know of where Mercer went or might have gone," he said.

"Well, here. The Foxhole." She wrote that down.

"Santiago would have checked here already. The warehouse where Mercer's men were murdered is out, too."

"Okay." Ruby thought for a moment. "His nightclub."

"Santiago probably checked there, too," Damon said.

"He had meeting space there, his own private quarters. Maybe there was some kind of secret entrance in the basement or something," she said. "There's also a large shipping dock there, with storage areas."

"We can go there, just you and me. We don't need Maya to see that place again. We can drop her off at January and Sean's, whenever they're available."

Ruby smiled into his eyes. "You would make a really good dad."

The words tumbled out before she thought better of it. He looked into her eyes, and she felt him warming with the words.

"You're already a great mom," he murmured, this time angling his head and kissing her mouth.

Although brief and chaste, it packed an electrical punch Ruby had not yet felt with him. She should be jumping off the chair and telling him to never do that again. Instead, she stayed in the heavenly sensation only he could produce.

"Uh…um…" Ruby stammered.

Damon wore a seductive grin and his eyes heated, obviously enjoying her awkward moment. He must know what she felt.

"K-Kid also had a storage unit he never let me or anyone see," she said.

That statement cleared Damon's face of passion.

Ruby wrote *storage unit* on the paper. "And then, of course, there's his home." She tapped the pen gently against her chin. "His closest drug dealer was killed by a rival gang. Maybe he stashed them at his house. His name is Michael Wallace, and he had a wife. She might still live there."

"All right. Then, I'd have to find a way inside."

"We can go visit her. She knows of me. I could distract her while you look around."

"She wouldn't know there was a bunch of guns stored in her house?" Damon asked. "Maybe not if he hid them somewhere."

"I've never been to their house," Ruby said.

"We'll find it."

"He also had mistresses," Ruby said. "One of them might know where he put them, or have some ideas."

"Wouldn't Santiago already have spoken with them?" Damon asked.

"Maybe. And if he and his men searched, they didn't find any guns."

"Let's assume Santiago has already spoken with everyone close to Kid. No one knows where the guns are, so we can also assume that wherever they are, Kid is the only one who knew."

For the first time since finding out Kid's true character, Ruby felt confident she'd be able to put him behind her once and for all. She would be rid of him. For real. She wouldn't have to keep looking over her shoulder or always have it in the back of her mind that he—while he still lived—or one of his men would come after her. Kid and his men needed no good reason to take someone out. Even the slightest perception of disloyalty was enough to justify a kill.

And Damon would be the one to help her do that. She met his eyes, turning her head where they sat close at the table. She felt herself softening to him, knowing it could well be a big mistake. But would it be? What if he was right for her? What if he wasn't?

She could not be wrong again.

DAMON STEPPED INTO Kid's nightclub, aptly named the Nightcrawler. Kid hadn't broadcast his ownership of the club much. That had to be due to his use of it as a cover and a way to launder money. Decorated in bright colors beneath dim lighting, it smelled like stale alcohol. Tall tables filled most of the space, with a dance floor and stage centered toward the back. There was one long bar on the left and a smaller one on the right. There were few people here, as it was early.

"We aren't open yet." A dark-haired man appeared from a door beside the stage. "Frank didn't lock the door back up when he came in."

Frank must be an employee. Damon took out his badge. "I'm from the DEA. I was wondering if you'd mind if we took a look around."

The man stopped before them. "What for?"

"Are you the manager?"

"Nick Hansen. I'm the new owner."

"Oh, good. I'm investigating Kid Mercer's criminal activities. I need to have a look around."

"I was told police already did that months ago."

"I know. I just want to look again. It would really help our case against the gang members."

"Sure. No problem. I can show you around."

"We'll be fine. Just appreciate you letting us take a look." Damon gave a nod of appreciation, and he and Ruby walked farther into the club.

"The offices are up those stairs." Ruby pointed to an L-shaped staircase.

Damon could see she didn't like being here again. She led him into an anteroom where two sets of double doors were. One led to Kid's old office.

"It used to be a lot gaudier," Ruby said.

The space was large and had three desks and neon beer signs. A sofa was to the side.

"He had velvet sofas, and there were swords on the walls," Ruby said, scoffing. "He thought he was so important."

"This must be difficult for you," Damon said.

Ruby walked around looking at the room. "It feels different now. Cleaner. Not evil."

Seeing her at peace, Damon started searching for secret doorways. There was a bookshelf vacant of books but no hidden door.

He searched the rest of the office and then the conference rooms, now empty save one.

"I'll take you to the basement." Ruby led him to a doorway he already knew had stairs going down. He had planned on going there next. Kid must have had his own private passageway to the basement from here, probably to the club level as well.

It was a dark, narrow stairway, lit only by low-wattage bulbs spaced far apart. Damon wondered if Kid had gotten a rise out of that, especially when he'd led targeted enemies this way.

They passed a keypad-locked door that must provide entry to the club and descended farther. At another keypad entry, Damon checked the handle. The door opened.

He shared a look with Ruby. Apparently the new owner had nothing to hide the way Kid had.

Damon found himself in a well-lit storage area. This was where the club kept their supplies. There were crates and boxes everywhere. He imagined how it might have been when Kid ran the place. Not much different when it came to operations. What he looked for were hidden doors or safes or floor passages. He overturned rugs and moved items on shelves. There was nothing.

"Next stop—the storage unit," Ruby said.

Hearing her sigh, Damon went to her. He drew her against him and brushed some wayward strands of hair off her smooth skin. She was so beautiful.

"Thank you," he said.

Her eyes quirked as though in confusion.

"For coming with me here," he said. "I don't like

reminders of my past, either, so I know what this must be costing you."

She blinked a few times. "You have to stop doing that."

"Doing what?" he asked.

"Making me fall for you." She gave him a semi-firm shove.

He took the hint and stepped back, not missing the ground he had gained with her. They were walking into territory neither of them welcomed. Damon's heart directed him, as he was sure hers did, too.

Where it led them, only the brave could go. Damon had never been weak, and he suspected Ruby was of the same ilk. He hoped they both ended up on the same path.

Chapter Nine

Ruby noticed Damon checking and rechecking to make sure they weren't seen when they left the Nightcrawler and drove to Kid's storage unit. Damon insisted they leave his car at the club and take a cab. He walked with her several blocks before hailing one, telling her only then that he had noticed Santiago had someone tailing them. This was part of the plan. He was no fool.

Ruby had to fight off the tingling sensation of arousal the whole time.

Kid had kept all of his haunts close. His club, the Foxhole, his home, the storage unit. Even his mistresses lived close to his center of business. He must have put them up on his dime. Funny—or not—Ruby hadn't cared then, and she cared even less now.

It was getting late in the afternoon. The storage business wasn't busy in the middle of the week. It was an older establishment, something that may have appealed to Kid. Quiet. Off the beaten path. Mom-and-pop.

Reaching the storage facility, The cab driver parked in front of the one Kid had rented. They got out. The facility manager was waiting for them. Damon had obtained a search warrant. So the manager opened the unit and rolled the door up. Damon found himself looking at plastic-wrapped crates.

When Ruby stepped forward, he stopped her.

"This is when we have to make it official." Damon took out his phone and called his boss. They'd go through everything and keep it secret until the investigation was over.

Afterward, Ruby looked one way and the other, watching for Kid's men to jump out of the shadows.

"We weren't followed," he said. "You're safe."

Her shoulders lowered as tension drained out of her muscles. "You're sure?" She wanted to feel relief, but fear hung on to her.

"Very. That's why we took a cab. Santiago knows we went to the club and nothing more."

"So he'll want to know where we were," she said.

"We were at the club," he said.

Sirens and lights were a heavenly welcome sound and sight.

DAMON GOT RUBY away from the DEA team foraging in the discovery of drugs in Kid's storage unit. He hid his great disappointment that only drugs had been found, no armory. Although he was sure Ruby shared his sentiment, she was quiet, exhausted. He needed to get her back to his apartment. Their absence would not go unmissed by Santiago and his men.

He had the taxi driver drop them several blocks from the Nightcrawler. Ruby was clearly done. Emotionally and physically. Damon had called Sean, and he and January would keep Maya for the night. She would be safe there. Damon could not predict what might transpire tonight. Santiago would not know they had discovered the storage unit, but he would know they had vanished from the nightclub.

He hoped Ruby was up for his plan.

At the nightclub, Damon readily saw two of Santiago's men watching as they got into his used maroon Cadillac.

Expected.

Ruby didn't notice. He ushered her into the passenger seat and got behind the wheel. He watched the car follow them. It would take some clever driving, but he knew just the route.

Using his blinker, he turned left. The car followed.

"This isn't the way to your apartment," Ruby said.

"We have company." He looked in the rearview mirror, which compelled her to lean forward enough to see into the passenger-door mirror.

Damon made a right and then another immediate right. There was a parking garage, again another right, where he drove and sped up to maneuver the lane. This garage had two entrances. The other opened to another street. Damon drove there and made a right. The next left brought him back to the road he'd originally been on. He watched the rearview mirror. The other car never appeared.

"Wow, you're good," Ruby said.

Damon drove to the back of the Foxhole, and the two of them climbed out. It was getting late. Ruby yawned.

It had been a long day for her. He wanted to get her into the apartment and pamper her. She made him want to do things like that for her. He adored even her yawns.

Eyeing her fondly, he opened the door for her. The sound of people in the pub told him the bar hadn't closed yet.

Inside, he stopped short with Ruby when he saw Santiago and Orlando standing near the lower apartment door, waiting for them.

"Where were you?" Santiago demanded.

Ruby glanced at Damon, and he sensed her trepidation.

"We went to Kid's club looking for your weapons," Damon said.

"I'm aware of that. Where did you go after that?"

Damon put his arm around Ruby. "We wanted to be alone."

"You can be alone here." Santiago moved closer, inspecting them, or more like trying to dissect them.

"Can we?" Damon said in challenge.

"You didn't tell me where you were going or what you planned to do. My men lost you," Santiago said.

Just then, Sonny walked through the door. "He lost me on purpose."

"Your car was at the nightclub, and you were nowhere to be seen."

"We took a cab," Damon said.

"Why?"

"Why do you think?"

Santiago stared hard at him. "If you are trying to dupe me, you are making a big mistake."

Releasing Ruby, Damon stepped closer to him, standing a couple of inches taller. "Look, I don't like being followed. You said you want your guns—I'll get your guns, but you're going to have to call off your dogs."

Santiago glanced at Orlando with a nod.

Orlando moved on Ruby before Damon could predict what he would do. She gave a shriek as he grabbed her and put her back against him, holding a knife to her throat.

Ruby's eyes widened in terror.

Damon looked at Santiago. "Let her go." He swore he'd end this whole charade right now if he hurt Ruby. He was already afraid he'd do just that, if provoked. And Damon didn't think it would take much provocation for a man like him.

"This is what will happen if you do not cooperate, Damon. I'll take what you value from you. I want to know where you are and what you are doing at all times."

"Fine. Let's schedule a status update once a week like the corporate people do," Damon said. He had to fight to keep his cool. He'd accommodate the man, but Santiago also had to know he was no coward and he was not afraid of him or his men. "I'm sick of being followed. Stop tailing me."

Santiago held his gaze in that same deadly way. Then he looked at Orlando with another nod.

He released Ruby, and she ran to Damon, who held her to him. He took her hand and guided her in front of him toward the door.

"I want a status report at the end of the week," Santiago said.

"You know how to find me." Damon entered the code, careful to conceal it from Santiago and his men.

Inside, Ruby's head fell against his chest, and she breathed deeply a few times. "I was scared out of my mind."

"I wouldn't let anything happen to you. Santiago knows if anything happens to you now, he will never get his guns. He's just having a control-freak moment. And unfortunately, scare tactics are his way of maintaining that."

Ruby looked up at him, doubtful and tired. Damon realized she wasn't physically tired. She was tired of dealing with the fallout of Kid Mercer.

He understood now why she had so readily agreed to let Maya stay with January and Sean. Her number-one priority was Maya: she could not be exposed to anything relating to Kid's debauchery.

"Hey." Damon took her hands in his. "Maya is safe tonight. Let's get you relaxed."

Seeing the distressed response in her eyes, Damon held her hand and took her up the stairs. At the top he opened the door and ushered her in. Then he locked them inside.

"Go get comfortable," he told her. "I'm going to check the security system."

While she went to her bedroom, he did a security sweep and set the alarm. They were all alone tonight. Safe.

RUBY RAN A bath in the main bathroom. She found some stress-relieving bubble bath and poured an ample amount in the warm water. Damon had been sensitive to her low bandwidth for Kid's criminality. She was so grateful Maya was with January tonight. She was at her limit of endurance. Please, could she just get Kid out of her life?

She wasn't sure if Damon had put candles in here on purpose, but they worked magic on her nerves, along with the vanilla-scented bubbles. The flickering flames offered the only light, which she loved. She rested her head back on a bath pillow and closed her eyes to ecstasy.

A knock on the door brought her head up.

"I poured you some champagne," Damon said.

That did sound lovely. Ruby checked the bubbles. They covered her nakedness.

"All right. Come in."

Damon entered with two glasses held in one hand and a bowl of strawberries in the other.

"Why are you doing all this?" Ruby asked.

He sat on a chair near the tub and put down the bowl and then one of the glasses of champagne. "I figured you haven't gotten enough of this in your life."

"Pampering?" She reached for the glass, careful not to disturb the concealing bubbles.

"Yes. And…you've had a rough night," he said.

She wondered if he had another reason. He was, after all, in the bathroom with her while she reclined naked in the tub. He didn't seem to acknowledge that, though. He was being a gentleman.

It was true: she hadn't been treated like this in years. "I had a boyfriend right after high school who opened doors for me and brought me flowers," she said. Then laughed ruefully. "I should have hung on to him."

Then she would have never met Kid. She also would have never had Maya, and that was unthinkable.

"I'm glad you didn't." Damon moved to sit on the tiled edge of the tub.

At first Ruby was alarmed, but then the intimacy of him being there took over. She couldn't ward off the warmth he brought to her soul.

He lifted a strawberry. "I had one of these already," he said. "They're so sweet and juicy. It's what made me come in here."

"You wanted to share the experience?" she asked.

"Yes." He brought the berry to her mouth, and she took it and chewed. "Mmm." He was right. They were the perfect ripeness.

He ate one, too and handed her the glass of champagne. "There's a reason why people eat strawberries with their bubbly."

She sipped with him, unable to look away from his eyes.

After long seconds, he put down his glass. "I think I should join you."

She raised her brow. "What?"

"Yeah. You're getting the full effect of champagne and strawberries." He removed his shirt. "I feel left out."

She laughed despite the alarms going off in her head. He was being so fun-loving. And she couldn't deny temptation. She'd been fighting that even before she'd learned his true identity.

"Okay if I join you?" he asked.

"Yes." How could she refuse? She wanted him too much.

She bent her knees up and folded her arms around them while he dropped his pants.

And then all she could do was stare.

"What I should have done a long time ago." He climbed into the water and sat at the opposite end.

Ruby had gotten a good look at him. He was pleasantly endowed. She hadn't been with a lot of men and, other than statues and pictures, hadn't seen many naked men, but he was beautiful.

"Are you all right?" he asked.

"Uh…" She shook herself out of her stupor. "Yes. I think so."

"We're just taking a bath." He stretched his legs out on either side of her, knees bent to accommodate their length.

"Come here," he said, patting the bubble-topped water in front of him. Damon leaned forward, took her glass of champagne, and put it next to his and the bowl of strawberries.

"Just come here." He took her hands and pulled.

She slid in the water, and before she found her balance, he had her back against him.

"Okay," he said. "Now relax."

"Ha. Really?"

Damon picked up her glass and handed it to her. "Wait."

She waited, hotness pooling low.

He presented a strawberry in front of her mouth.

Ruby took it and then sipped champagne, hearing him do the same behind her, feeling his muscles as he moved. She leaned her head back against him.

"No pressure, Ruby, okay?" Damon put another strawberry in front of her mouth. She took a bite.

He ate the rest of it and then sipped the last of his champagne.

She drained hers as well.

With both glasses on the tiles of the large, oval tub, Ruby waited in heated anticipation for what he would do next.

She was afraid to move. To think. To feel. To anything. Feeling wasn't an option, she discovered. She felt powerful attraction for him.

He slid his hand around to her abdomen, setting her afire with the liquid caress. Then he lowered his face next to hers and nibbled her earlobe, his warm breath slow and steady and too, too arousing.

"Damon?" she was on thin planks that made up a bridge she could not cross safely.

"Shh," he murmured against her ear. "I won't do anything but this unless you want more. I won't hurt you. Not ever."

His words were like honey, warm and promising, but she had to be prudent. Smart. Cautious.

Didn't she?

Damon's hands ran over her body now, over her breasts, down to her abdomen and lower. A sound escaped her, a foreign sound. She had never made that sound with any other man. Damon pulled sexual hotness from her she had never felt before.

"Damon..." Ruby heard her breathless, lustful tone and tried to check herself. Her mind spun with uncontrollable feelings she could only describe as love, or the makings of it.

"Let go, Ruby." Damon kissed her temple and then her cheek, going down to the side of her mouth.

"Oh..." Ruby was losing control.

Or had she ever had that with him?

She turned her head to find his mouth. He met her, answered her, and she heard his satisfied groan.

"Damon..."

"Kiss me, Ruby..."

"Oh..." She did. She kissed him with all her heart.

Water sloshed. Her wet hand came up against his face, and his equally wet hand found her breast. She sought his tongue, and he gave it to her. They shared a tender play of loving intimacy.

After too many sensuously torturous moments of kissing, Damon ran his hands down her body, over her breasts and lower. He rubbed her. Ruby was taken aback by her instantaneous response. She had to break away from his passionate kiss to catch her breath.

"Damon..." If he didn't stop...

"It's okay," he murmured passionately.

The sound of his voice sent her tumbling over a sweet edge. She came so hard she cried out and arched her back involuntarily.

"Oh..." Ruby breathed deep several times. Then reality descended. "That has never happened to me before."

Damon wrapped his arms around her. "Good. I like firsts with you."

Ruby relaxed against him. She hadn't had such an intense orgasm with any man, ever. She melted against him, her head resting on his shoulder, taking in the low, flickering light from the candles.

Damon's strong, muscular arm moved, and he filled their glasses. Then he picked up hers and put the rim to her mouth. She sipped, closing her eyes. She felt him take a drink from the same glass and put it down.

"I want more moments like this with you," he said.

So did she. But she didn't voice it. Something was missing. He had pleasured her and not received the same. Searching her heart, she realized she wanted him to feel what she had. She felt him against her lower back, an invitation he couldn't hide. He was hard as stone. She could have another orgasm. That would be new for her. Two in one day…

This was so intimate. They could easily take this all the way. But what would sex with him do to her mental state—and her emotional state? Deciding to ignore the warning in the back of her mind, she decided to let what might happen happen. She had already been intimate with him. What damage could be done by pleasuring him the way he had her? Besides, it touched her tremendously that he showed such restraint—and respect for her.

She tipped her head up to see him. His eyes were warm with desire, but in a contented way.

"Are you all right?" she asked.

He grunted a sexy laugh. "Never better."

"I bet you could be better," she said.

He sobered at that. "Ruby, you don't have to. I can't help what's going on down there."

Of course, she knew that. She also knew it was her body against him—her that was making him respond. Moving to turn to face him, she straddled him and sat on his hardness. Then she kissed him, just lightly and just once.

His smoldering eyes met hers. "What are you doing?"

"What I should have done a long time ago," she said, mimicking him.

He chuckled.

She kissed him again, this time lingering and deepening the caress. He put his hand to the back of her head, fingers going into her wet hair. She had her hands on his shoulders. The contact with his erection heated her up. She rubbed herself against him, making him groan a little.

Ending the kiss, she met his eyes again, lifting herself up. He helped her position his erection so that she could slide down onto him. Shards of tingly sensations rocketed through her. She could not have predicted he would feel so good. She tipped her head back and closed her eyes, then began to move, rocking her hips gently. The friction drove her wild.

Damon held her hips and lifted her, then let her down onto him. He did this a few times before she took up the same rhythm, grinding on him as she sank down.

The tingling intensified until she no longer felt a part of herself. She was lifted into some other magnificent realm, where she came undone. Only then did she become aware that Damon had groaned and his breathing had quickened. He had reached his climax with her.

Ruby savored this moment with him. Nothing of their troubles interfered. It was only the two of them. She had never felt this cared for before. She dared not call it love.

Letting her head fall to his shoulder, she held on to the escape of being with Damon like this. But alas, earth came floating back. Then she looked at him. His eyes still lingered in what they had just shared. She sensed it had meant as much to him as it had to her.

Damon kissed her, soft and tender, packed with emotion. Ruby began to fret that maybe she'd gone too far. Maybe she should have at least waited.

More reality descended. The magic faded, and Ruby was left with the significance of this kind of lovemaking. He had deceived her for such a long time. Looking into his eyes, searching, she couldn't tell what he was thinking. Was he assessing her?

Disconcerted, she moved back from him. "The water is getting cold." Standing, she stepped out of the tub and retrieved a towel. He did the same.

Wrapped in the towel, she faced him. He grinned, clearly satisfied.

"This doesn't mean I trust you."

"Fair enough, but it's a good start." He grinned.

"It was just sex," she said.

"It felt like more than that, but we can go with that for now." He moved closer and kissed her again.

It carried with it a different sentiment, loving and

not so passionate. Ruby felt connected to him deeper than ever now. Disconcerted, she stepped back.

"I'm going to get ready for bed."

"All right. I'll see you in my bedroom," he said.

She glanced back. "Do you think that's a good idea?"

"I do. How about you?"

"I'm not sure."

"Well, why don't we try it? If you get uncomfortable, you can go back to your room."

She might be able to do that. She'd decide after she had her nightgown on.

"Ruby?"

She stopped at the bathroom door.

"You do know you're safe with me, right?" he asked. "And I don't mean just from Santiago. I mean with me." He gestured with a nod toward the tub. "With that."

"I didn't. Thanks for saying something." He had relaxed her. He wouldn't push her when it came to love and sex. She could take some comfort in that.

Some. But not in totality.

Chapter Ten

When Damon woke, his first awareness was that Ruby wasn't next to him. Why hadn't she stayed awhile to spend some time with him before getting up? He experienced a few seconds of regret before he realized what transpired last night had driven Ruby from his bed. Potent. Powerful. Almost incomprehensible. He'd felt it, and he knew Ruby had, too. That kind of love was as real as could be. Intangible. Rare. Beautiful. He was having a hard time dealing with that himself. The more he came awake, the heavier the impact became.

He had taken a big risk putting his heart out on a ledge. After spending months calculating his relationship with her, he had finally given in to instinct. Maybe it had all been worth it. If he could have a woman like Ruby for himself, he could have all he ever dreamed. He didn't have to pretend anymore.

However, the fact she'd left his bed spoke volumes. He hadn't expected her to do a one-eighty after their earth-shattering sexual encounter, but facing reality today didn't alleviate his disappointment.

He consoled himself by rationalizing last night happened because he had shed his barrier. Would he ever be rid of his distrust of women? He had taken things so slow with her, knowing the kind of man she had been with before and all she had gone through because of him, but he had also taken it slow because of his history, his experience with ultimate betrayal. And, of course, his investigation had taken precedence. He had allowed it to. From the moment he had first seen Ruby, something instinctual had gripped him. More than her beauty, something about her had filtered into him. Something sweet and innocent. He didn't like that thought. He trusted her as a person, but not with his heart. He didn't trust anyone with that. Not anymore.

But he still had an investigation to complete.

His plan was to make this as fun as possible for Maya. The less she knew about the reality, the better.

He showered, dressed and went out into the living area of his apartment. Ruby had her daughter planted in front of a bowl of healthy cereal and a Disney cartoon. Ruby had a cinnamon roll and a cup of coffee. Seeing him, she opened the oven and took out a tray of more cinnamon rolls.

Damon poured himself a coffee, feeling the tension emanating from her. He remained calm, but inside the stark reality that she could not face what had happened soured his stomach. He opened the refrigerator and took out an apple.

Taking a bite, he met her eyes. She watched him warily.

He took his apple and coffee to the table and sat.

She deposited a small paper plate with a warm cinnamon roll in front of him, then sipped her coffee and sat across from him, all the while avoiding eye contact.

"Are you all right?" Damon asked.

Her silent glance said no. And he should know no explanation was needed.

"Why did you get up before I woke up?" he asked, even though he already knew the answer. She was running the way his own instinct directed him to do. He would face it, though.

"We're going to take Maya to a festival. On the way there and on the way back, we're going to take her to places she may have seen piles of guns. We're going to make sure it's fun for her. Got it?"

"Got it." She smiled big.

She captivated him every time with that smile. Just by being herself, she lassoed him, despite any hesitation he might have. An invisible force kept him tied to her, his heart locked with hers. He would pursue her, but it might be the end of him.

RUBY SAT IN the passenger seat as Damon drove to the festival. She didn't say much, and neither did Damon, although he kept vigil of their surroundings and to ensure they were not being followed. He had taken a long route, so if anyone had tried to tail them, Damon had lost them. He made her feel so safe. Even as danger surely lurked, with him she felt protected.

That aside, Ruby knew Damon wasn't happy about having sex and her reaction to it. She wasn't, either, and suspected they shared the same conundrum. Different causes but the same outcome. It had meant too much to both of them. While Ruby had been prepared for something good with him, she could not have imagined the extent of unbridled passion. That frightened her. Damon must also be troubled, with his history. Now they were left with what they had begun with, hardened hearts, distrust and disillusionment.

Maya hadn't caught on to the drama playing out between them. In the back seat of Damon's car, she had her favorite doll and cooed adorably while immersed in play. There was a time when Ruby feared her daughter might not ever find her innocence again, after all she'd witnessed with Kid. But here she was, a five-year-old in her own world, oblivious to evil. Ruby was so grateful.

"We're coming up on Kid's second warehouse," Damon said.

Ruby looked at the crumbling brick building that decades ago had been a factory of some sort. It had very few windows. She had never been inside, but she knew Kid would have secured some space in there so no one could access his loot.

Reaching back, she tapped Maya's ankle. Maya looked at her, and Ruby signed, *Do you remember this place?*

Maya looked out the window as they passed the warehouse, then shook her head.

Have you ever been here before? Ruby signed.

No. Why are we here?

It's on the way to the carnival. It's just an old, abandoned building. Part of history.

I like history.

Maya did like history, but in her young mind that was how Walt Disney had become an icon. She wanted to go to Disney World and see the castle. She also had become captivated by women who made a difference, like a famous supreme court judge people liked to celebrate. Ruby had to explain what a *pioneer* was. She had loved that. Ruby smiled as she continued to watch her daughter, who had resumed her play, completely oblivious to what the warehouse meant, much less its connection to Kid.

"Let's go to the carnival and then go by Mistress Number One's house," Damon said. "We need to make these trips fun." He kept his mouth turned away from Maya, lest she read his lips and start asking questions about what a *mistress* was.

He continued to amaze her. He was so in tune with Maya and her mental health. He understood what she must have gone through living with Kid, not to mention being found hiding at a murder scene.

Damon parked, and the sights and sounds of fun engulfed Ruby as she walked with an excited Maya toward the carnival. The Ferris wheel dominated the distant picture, the roller coaster second. All the other rides were in motion and produced squeals and laughter. The aroma of fried food wafted stronger as they reached the entrance. Sugar-coated food, too.

Damon walked faster and then turned to walk backward in front of Maya. "What do you want to do first?"

Roller coaster!

Maya didn't need a voice to let them know her excitement. Ruby would never get tired of her daughter showing such genuine childlike innocence. She searched and found a kiddie coaster, a caterpillar with a happy, grinning face. Smiling, feeling like a kid herself, Ruby pointed in answer to Damon.

He took Maya's hand and started toward the ride. Ruby took her other hand and had a feeling of family come over her, a feeling of rightness. She let it wash over her for now. Maya mattered more than anything, and she was gleefully happy.

They stood in line, Damon on constant lookout for signs of danger. Maya wouldn't notice or understand why, but Ruby did. She eyed him inquiringly.

"We're good," he said.

She smiled her appreciation. It was so nice to have a day like this, an escape from threats, albeit temporarily.

The line moved forward, and they finally took their seats in a caterpillar car, luckily accommodating three. Maya sat in the middle. The roller coaster moved slowly, up gentle hills and valleys and around a few brief turns. It was by no means a thrill ride for adults. But Maya loved it. Her laughter rang out, touching Ruby and making her share a look with Damon, who clearly enjoyed this as well.

Ruby tried to subdue the feeling of unity. The ride ended, and Maya reached up to take Damon's hand. Then she took hold of Ruby's. She smothered a flash of jealousy that Maya had taken his hand first. She supposed Maya's fascination and, yes, her fondness for Damon had much to do with her action. He hadn't been hanging around them that long, so the newness hadn't worn off. He had quickly become her friend.

They walked through the crowds until Maya spotted a train called the Looney Tooter. The cars were designed after cartoon characters like Tweety, the Road Runner and Bugs Bunny. Maya would love that ride. Sure enough, she tugged them forward, her little feet running.

Ruby laughed and saw Damon smiling. They got in line at a charming train station and boarded with cheerful, animated music. Maya chose the Sylvester car, and their journey began. The tracks wound their way around the entire carnival. Ruby took in all the happy people and the sounds and lights. Although beneath a bright blue sky, the carnival lit up. The train stopped, and Ruby found she didn't want this afternoon to end.

They rode the Tilt-A-Whirl and the carousel and two other rides before Ruby spotted a food truck that was sure to have delectable sweets. She led Damon and Maya there. As soon as Maya realized where they were headed, excitement made her almost skip her way over.

Funnel cake? Ruby signed.

Maya nodded enthusiastically.

She ordered that and two cotton-candy lemonade slushies for her and Damon. She'd share hers with Maya.

"I like a woman who orders for me," Damon said.

"I'm curious to know if you like it as much as I do," she said. They went to a table under a white canopy where several other people gathered to eat and drink.

Maya sat between them on a bench. Damon sipped the slushy.

Ruby sipped, too and watched him, Maya happily munching on her funnel cake.

After making much ado of taste-testing, Damon looked at her. "It's delicious. Yet one more thing we have in common."

What else did they have in common? He could sign. They had both been scarred by past relationships. They had both lost a parent when they were young. And they had similar tastes in food. Ice cream and slushies.

"A carnival experience isn't complete without a Ferris wheel ride," he said.

Finishing their treats, Ruby took Maya's hand and started walking through the crowd. Maya reached up for Damon's hand and he took it with a fond look down at her. Ruby would never get tired of seeing that.

They arrived at the Ferris wheel and got in the short line. Getting into the seat, Maya was again between them. Damon rested his arm along the back, his fingers brushing Ruby's shoulder. She looked over at him and shared a silent, intimate moment. Being like this was magical. Ruby had not felt more a part of a family unit since before her father died.

She imagined what it would be like to have a man like him with her and Maya always. He'd watch Maya grow up, grow out of toys and into a young lady. First dates. Prom. Graduation. Maybe he would adopt her and give her away at her wedding.

She had not had any of these thoughts before. She hadn't had time with Kid, nor had she had any inclination to imagine that with a monster like him. But now…

Now a warm, glowing cloud of loveliness blanketed

her. She could see them having these types of outings on a regular basis, as a family. The temptation to fall into this fantasy was too strong to resist, so she stayed there through the ride. She enjoyed the sights of the carnival below and downtown Chicago in the distance. She also enjoyed the feel of Damon's hand on her shoulder.

The ride ended too soon, and they exited their seats.

"Well, I suppose it's time to go," Ruby said, disappointed that their time together would come to an end.

"One more stop." Damon went to a shooting game where there were giant stuffed animals.

Delighted, Ruby watched as Maya, jumping up and down, pointed to the unicorn.

The game host was a skinny fiftysomething man with an untrimmed beard. He looked rode hard and put away wet. He didn't smile—well, he sort of smiled, a halfhearted, toothless curve to his mouth. His dull eyes said he had plenty of regrets, probably the biggest one being deciding to travel with a carnival and not put down any roots. That's how Ruby would feel if she were in his shoes.

Damon paid for a few shots and took aim. He effortlessly gained the top score and won the biggest prize. Maya squealed and still jumped up and down, more of a bounce.

Ruby laughed as the game host handed Damon the unicorn and he passed it down to Maya. It was so big she could barely carry it.

"What a grand finale," Ruby said as they headed for the parking lot. But as they neared the car, the magic of the afternoon began to deflate. Damon was a man who had expertly fooled her. He had known everything about her before she ever met him. All of his charm in getting to know her had been a ruse. How could she ever trust a man like him, a man whose job it was to live a lie?

DAMON HELPED RUBY put Maya to bed, and the two of them went downstairs. They had gone by one of Kid's mistresses' house, and Maya didn't recognize it. They'd have another outing on another day.

He wasn't ready for bed yet, and he was sure Ruby wasn't, either. He could tell her mood had gradually dimmed as they'd driven to his apartment. He had fallen under the spell of enchantment, too. If he ever had a family, he'd make sure they did fun things like that together all the time. He had felt part of a family today. He couldn't think of anything more important in life than having that, a family. His job was extremely important to him, but that human connection trumped everything. He hadn't really considered that until now, how fulfilling being a part of a family could be.

Figuring Ruby needed to relax as much as he did, Damon took out a bottle of red wine and poured them each a moderate glass. He took them into the living room, where she was surfing channels with the remote. He sat next to her and handed her a glass.

With remote in hand, she looked up at him, hesitant at first, and then took the wine.

Noticing how she put all her attention into finding something to watch, he sensed her tension.

She settled on a history channel program about antiques. He liked her choice.

"I felt the same today," he said.

She scooted more toward the edge of the couch, sitting ramrod straight, and put the remote down.

"Being with you and Maya," he said. "It was so good."

Still, she looked straight ahead at the TV, without seeing it, he knew.

"It felt right, Ruby. Like being a family," he said. "I've never felt that way before."

Her foot bobbed up and down, an obvious sign of her discontent. Damon didn't relent. This was too important. They needed to talk about this, whether either of them wanted to or not.

"Can you deny it?" he asked.

Her foot stilled, and after several seconds, she looked at him, met his eyes. "No. But neither can I deny what a professional you are at your job. *Undercover man*."

He sighed and put down his glass. So much for trying to relax.

"I'm not sure I'm ready for this, either, Ruby, but we need to face what's happening," he said.

"What is happening, Damon? You're still in an active investigation. You're still playing a role. What am I to you? A vital part of solving your case? Of making your arrests?"

"You're more than part of my investigation. You weren't when this whole thing started, but you are now. You have to know that."

"That's the problem, Damon. This *whole thing* started with a great big giant lie. When I think about the possibility of being with you long-term, I wonder if I can ever trust you. Ten, twenty years from now, how will I ever know you're being honest with me? You could get tired of me and seek out something new, and I would never know because you are an expert liar."

"I'm not an expert. I play a role undercover because if I don't it could cost me my life. I am not an expert liar when it comes to real relationships. I didn't lie to you unless it would have put my life in danger. And I will never lie to you ever again. Now that you know about the investigation, there's no need for me to be secretive. I can tell you everything. You have no idea how much of a relief that is to me. I hated having to deceive you. I never felt good about that, especially when I became attracted to you on a personal level."

He watched her absorb his words and waver over trusting him, believing him.

"You could be lying to me right now. Your investigation isn't over. You need me to keep acting like I'm your doting girlfriend," she said. "You want us to have a fake relationship. I suppose that would be nothing new."

Damon scowled at that. There was no convincing her.

"We had sex, and today felt real to me," she went on. "I can't keep doing this, Damon. I think I should go stay with January and Sean for a while. This isn't good for me."

"No, Ruby. You need to stay here." Not only could

he not protect her, her leaving would send the wrong message to Santiago. He didn't dare say that, though. She would assume he was putting the investigation ahead of her.

"Sean can protect me and Maya," she said.

"He has to work. He can't be around you all the time." He hoped she would see that reasoning.

She averted her head, clearly considering the consequences. Surely she wouldn't put Maya in that kind of danger. January, too.

At last, Ruby turned to him again. "I at least need a break. I'm getting worried about Maya's attachment to you more than to me."

"What kind of a break?" he asked. "Do you want to take a day to think things over? I'm not comfortable with you taking more time than that." He'd be worried sick about her and Maya.

"Maybe a couple of days. A weekend."

"Ruby, I really would rather you didn't."

"Why, so we can keep playing these roles? It's gone too far, Damon. I can't keep Maya in this situation."

Damon could see there would be no reasoning with her tonight. Their glorious day was too fresh, and their sex too amazing.

"Hopefully, it won't be for much longer," he said. "But even after this case is closed, I still want to keep seeing you."

"I don't know about that. Maya is getting way too attached to you. And… I am, too." She averted her eyes.

"Okay," he said. "Let's get this straight." When she

looked at him, he said, "We both didn't mean for us to have sex."

"I agree," she said.

"I wanted to take things much slower, and I am pretty sure you did, too."

"I did."

"So let's get back to that. Let's be friends."

She half cocked her head, disbelieving. He didn't think they could be just friends, either. But he needed to reassure her.

"Okay, we'll cool things off for now," he said. "And I'll be careful with Maya. I don't want to rush into anything anymore than you do. I get you don't trust me, but if I'm being honest, I'd have to say I don't trust you, either. I don't trust any woman. It's part of my baggage from past experience."

She nodded. "I can go with that."

Damon caught sight of Maya tugging her mother's shirt. She signed, *Are you fighting?*

No.

It looks like you are.

We're having an adult talk, Ruby signed.

I like Damon. Don't take him away.

Ruby looked at Damon, clearly upset. He crouched before Maya. *Your mother and I are friends. We just have some grown-up issues we need to resolve. Everything is all right. Okay?*

Maya looked him directly in his eyes for a while and then gave a nod. *Okay.*

Damn, she was a smart kid. She was advanced well beyond her five years. And not only with intelligence.

She had strong self-esteem and Damon would not be surprised if she went far in life. He didn't think that would be possible, however, without strong family bonds. Love.

Damon looked up at Ruby and saw her worrying frown. Maya liked him, and she wasn't comfortable with that. He needed to convince her that leaving was not an option, even temporarily. But how would he do that?

Chapter Eleven

Ruby understood leaving was a risk, but she absolutely needed some time away from Damon. Moreover, she had to get Maya away from him. He had too much of an influence on her. She packed a duffel bag with everything she and her daughter would need for two nights at January and Sean's house. Sean was off duty, and they'd all be together. It felt safe. She hadn't told Damon. She had awakened Maya early and planned to leave before he woke. He'd only try to talk her out of this.

I don't want to leave, Mommy, Maya signed.

It's only for two nights. Don't you want to see January and Sean?

After her young mind contemplated that, she looked up and signed, *Yes*.

Ruby took her hand and glanced back to ensure Damon hadn't awakened. She didn't hear anything. Opening the upper door as quietly as she could, she took Maya into the stairway and, with equal quietness, closed the door. Going down the steps, she left the apartment and then the dark back room of the pub. The sun had yet to rise, so the outdoor lights were still on.

She kept looking back as she made her way to her car. There, she hurriedly unlocked it and opened the back door for Maya. After getting Maya buckled in the back seat, she put their duffel on the passenger side in the front and walked around to the driver's side. She stopped short when a man emerged into the reach of exterior lighting. She didn't recognize him. Average in height, he had dark sandy-brown hair and hazel eyes that held dominating confidence.

Before she could open the car door, he asked, "Where are you going?"

Fear raced through her, putting her on high alert. She glanced toward the back door of the pub. Had Damon awakened after all?

She faced the stranger, dredging up an outward appearance of courage. "Who are you?" He wasn't any of the men she had seen in the Foxhole.

"I'm someone Santiago calls when he needs to get his point across."

In other words, he was a hit man. Ruby grew frightened. She looked at Maya in the back seat. She was busy with a game on her tablet.

"Where are you going?" he asked again.

"None of your business. If you want to know, then follow me." She hated saying that, but she was so sick of being bullied.

He became displeased, judging by the frown. "Santiago will be patient only for so long."

"I can't help you. I'm sorry." She faced her car door.

He took her arm and turned her back toward him.

Ruby yanked free, growing more alarmed. This was a man who knew Kid, a man no different than him.

"I'm not your enemy," he said. Then his eyes took a creepy tour down her body and back up to her face. "In fact, I'd like to be something of a champion to you."

"What?" What did he mean? How could anyone like him be a champion, much less think of himself as one?

"You are a remarkable woman, Ruby. You are stunning."

Ruby turned and opened her car door. "I can't help you."

"We aren't talking about that now," he said. "I'm trying to tell you I can make this situation easier on you."

Ruby felt like throwing up. Did he actually mean if she welcomed his attention he'd protect her?

"How do you propose to do that?" she asked.

"We haven't been properly introduced. I'm Carl Whitmore. It's a great pleasure to meet you, Ruby. Kid didn't know how lucky he was. But now that he's gone, maybe you and I could go out for dinner sometime, and I could tell you how I can help you. I'm close with Santiago."

So, he thought he could persuade Santiago to leave her alone—if she went out on dates with him.

"I'm not interested in dinner with you." Was he crazy? She'd just been freed of Kid. What made him think she'd sign up for another horror show like that again?

"I'm hoping you'll change your mind. See, I can tell things aren't going well between you and Damon."

How could he tell? Just by her leaving in the wee hours of morning? "That's none of your business," Ruby said.

Movement at the back door of the pub drew her eyes there. Damon appeared and relief rushed through her.

The stranger looked there, and his expression changed from intimidating to angst-ridden. Clearly he didn't want this interruption. He must be one of the men Santiago assigned to watch her and Damon, except he had eyes for Ruby. Yuck.

Damon appeared beside her. "Carl. What brings you by?"

"I was just having a conversation with your girlfriend," he said. "If she's still your girlfriend. Looks like she's planning on being away awhile." He gestured toward the car behind her and Damon. "I saw her put in a bag."

"So what if she is?" Damon said. "What's it to you?"

"Santiago wants to know where she is at all times. You owe him something."

"It's time for you to leave," Damon said, stepping forward and towering over Carl, putting his body between him and Ruby.

No longer possessing that aura of dominating confidence, Carl looked up at him with a creepy but ego-challenged grin. "You can't escape Santiago."

"Santiago will get what he's looking for," Damon said. "I better not see you near Ruby again."

Carl sized Damon up and appeared to relent. He must be alone on his watch tonight and would be no match for Damon, who was much bigger and not afraid.

Lifting his hands, he stepped back. As he did so, he looked past Damon, sending Ruby a chilling gaze, as if to say, *This isn't the last time you'll see me.*

With goose bumps spreading over her arms, Ruby watched him go.

"I guess we can expect to see him some more," Ruby said, voicing her thoughts aloud.

"Yeah. All the more reason to keep up appearances and stay close to the pub."

Damon wore a worried face, and Ruby had no doubt about the gravity of her situation. She had thought she should be afraid before, but to now have that confirmed gave her a sick feeling.

"Get Maya and come back inside, Ruby."

His commanding tone had a strange effect on her. Kid had been controlling, but Damon was not doing that. He was being protective. He was being a dad. A husband. A family man. And he was absolutely right. She could not leave.

DAMON HADN'T SLEPT much the previous night. He was grateful Ruby had decided to stay with him, but she was a loose cannon. Her lack of trust sprinkled danger into his investigation and also for herself and Maya. No, he couldn't control her and didn't want to. He admired her spirit, her strength. He related to her reticence because he had experienced challenges in his life, too. He wished he could tell her this. If only she would believe him.

Yesterday they had spent the day avoiding each other. She played with Maya in the child's room for hours, until Damon had to go to work. He had thought of nothing else but her and Maya. Santiago and his men had not shown up last night. It had been quiet. Damon had been happy to be surrounded by normal people.

This morning, he made Maya strawberry French toast. Ruby hadn't awakened yet, and Maya had told him she was hungry. She sat at the table with her drawing book. He brought her a plate and put a cup of coffee down for himself, sitting across from her.

She looked up at him. *Why was Mommy going to take me to January and Sean's?*

They're her friends.

Maya picked up her fork and tried to pry apart a piece of French toast with her fork. Damon took her knife and fork and cut it into bites for her.

She stuffed a big bite into her mouth and happily chewed. Then after a while, putting down her fork, she eyed him. *Who was that man?*

Damon had to do some quick thinking. *He comes to the restaurant a lot.*

Mommy didn't like him, she signed.

"No," he said, signing as well.

Is he friends with my daddy?

He might have been.

Maya contemplated that before digging into her French toast again.

Just then, Ruby came out of her bedroom. She didn't look pleased with his early commandeering of her daughter's morning routine. He would not tell her it was Maya who had come into his bedroom and woken him. He had not gone to her mother.

He also wouldn't tell her about the earlier conversation he'd had with her daughter while he was making her breakfast.

Do you like kids?

"I love kids."

I can tell. Maya had smiled big, helping him mix the egg wash for the French toast. He had let her crack the eggs, picking out the broken shell pieces when she finished. He found the entire exercise beyond charming. He simply adored this kid.

Why don't you have any?

"I haven't been that lucky yet," he said, making sure she could see his mouth and ever impressed by her ability to understand him.

You have one now.

Damon had no idea how to respond to her declaration. He could vividly imagine living with her as a father figure. Ruby was the only question mark. Never in his life had he thought a child would touch him this way, a child that wasn't biologically his. Life sure was funny like that. Nobody could predict what lay ahead.

Ruby entered the kitchen, taking in Damon at the table with Maya.

"Strawberry French toast?" Ruby said sarcastically, eyebrow raised.

"With whipped cream," Damon said grinning at her expression.

I'm done. Can I go watch TV? Maya asked.

Sure, Ruby signed.

Maya went into the living room where she had dolls

spread out on the coffee table and the television tuned to a cartoon.

Ruby got a cup of coffee and some orange juice and came to sit where Maya had vacated.

After sipping some coffee, she picked up Maya's fork and took a bite of strawberries and French toast.

Damon watched her. He was good at making that because it was one of his favorites.

She looked at him after she swallowed. "This is good." She stabbed her fork in the air above the plate.

"Thank you."

"I love strawberries," she said.

"Me, too."

When she looked at him again, he felt that now-familiar and fiery chemistry ignite. Just because they both liked strawberries. No, it went deeper than that. It was her body language that told him before she spoke that she liked what he had made, and it was their eyes meeting.

He reminded himself of his plan to keep his distance for a while. Not just for her comfort but for his as well. They were volatile together. Man and woman with live wires ready to spark.

Ruby turned on her tablet and read something. It looked like the news. Damon watched her do that and eat the rest of Maya's breakfast. Every movement captivated him. Her lips. The lashes of her eyes. The slope of her nose. Her soft, smooth and clear skin. She had on a sleeveless blue-and-white knit top that emphasized her breasts and light blue jeans that fit her butt perfectly.

"There's a kite festival this weekend," she said. "They have face painting."

Something fun for Maya while they searched for the cache of weapons. "All right." That reminded him of a time when his mother by choice, Nicole, had taken him and his brothers to a kite festival that had also had face painting and balloon decorating, among several sweet food trucks.

"I went to a kite festival when I was a kid," he said, wanting to share the memory. "They gave you kite kits where you could design your own. I made a really bad depiction of Captain America." He chuckled.

Ruby smiled with him.

"I collected Iron Man and Hulk and other comic figures. I had countless comic books."

"I was a typical Barbie-doll collector," Ruby said. "And I loved Scooby-Doo and *Big Hero 6*–type movies."

Damon chuckled again. "You had a taste for superheroes."

"Scooby?" Ruby laughed.

"He was a hero. He just didn't know it most of the time."

Ruby fell silent in thought, but her smile remained, albeit mild. "My dad was my superhero. Then he died, and that fantasy died with him."

Damon nodded. "Yeah, I know that feeling. After my mom died, things weren't golden. My dad was—and still is—a terrible role model. That's what really drove me to go into criminal justice. The kid in me never let the idea of superheroes go. I'm glad for that."

"Are you in touch with your dad at all?" she asked.

"Not unless I have to. I met with him to try and talk him out of going after the Colton will. He sometimes injects himself into my life and will likely continue to."

He saw her register how sad that seemed to her. "I have a bad dad, but I had a good family after my mom died."

"And now it's getting bigger," she said. "That party seemed to bring you closer to your new cousins."

He appreciated her noticing. "Yes. My dad and uncle are corrupted by my grandmother. None of us kids wants to see them take what isn't theirs. My grandfather took really good care of Carin and her twins. She's just bitter now and will do anything to get revenge. I'm not proud of that."

Ruby's eyes warmed, and she put her hand on his from across the table. "Of course you aren't. You aren't greedy. You're a good man, Damon." As soon as she said the last, her expression changed, and she withdrew her hand.

"I am a good man. I learned from the worst how not to be a bad one. I wish you trusted me about that, Ruby."

She resumed eating, not acknowledging him. Damon let it go. Eventually she had to start believing him. And if not, he had to find a way to let her go.

WITH RUBY ENGROSSED in a remote-learning nursing course and Maya falling asleep on the couch, Damon went downstairs to work. He closed tonight. He was relieved Ruby and Maya would be right upstairs and he could keep a lookout for Santiago and his men.

He started his shift and worked for a few hours before Carl approached the bar.

"How does a bartender attract a woman like Ruby? She had Kid Mercer. He had tons of money. What do you have to offer?"

More than you, Damon wanted to say. "Kid took her daughter from her."

"Only because she wanted to leave him. He was teaching her a lesson. He would have taken her back once she came to reason."

Reason. Damon wanted to give this man a reason to go to the dentist.

"She's with me now," Damon said.

Carl laughed deep and sinisterly. "I doubt that."

Did this derelict honestly think he could win Ruby's heart just because she had been with Kid? Or did he think Ruby was available because he could sense the friction between her and Damon? None of these men knew Ruby, not beyond her name and her relationship with Kid. They only associated her with a drug-and-arms dealer.

Just then Ruby appeared before the bar. Damon became mesmerized by her. Such a dark beauty. She had changed into a sexy black sleeveless dress Damon wished she hadn't chosen to wear. What was she doing? Was she trying to make him lose his restraint?

She sat on a stool.

"You didn't tell me you were coming down here," he said.

Her glowing gaze was faked, but only he would know that. "I wanted to surprise you."

"You succeeded." Damon glanced at Carl, who observed their exchange in between licentious glances at Ruby's upper body.

Reaching for him, Ruby put her hand on Damon's. "I also wanted to apologize for arguing with you."

Damon fell completely out of his role. "You did?"

"Yes. I know you're dealing with a lot right now, and I haven't been much help. I want to change that." She glanced at Carl, who looked rapt. "If we find Kid's weapons, we stand to gain a lot, but it's more than that to me. You're more to me than that."

Wow. She was really pouring on the syrup.

"Okay. That's great, baby. I'm so glad you came down here to tell me that." He felt like nudging her or something. If she overacted, they'd be blown.

"You were ready to leave him earlier," Carl said.

She sent him a warning cat look. "We made up."

"Did you?" Carl brushed her long, thick dark hair back from her shoulder. "You don't strike me as the settling kind."

"Settling?"

"He's a bartender."

"And what are you?"

"I'm a businessman. I make a lot of money. I'm important."

Damon saw the flicker in Ruby's eyes. She did not like that response. Likely it reminded her of Kid. He waited for her explosion and whatever followed.

"What makes you think Damon can't make a lot

of money?" she asked. "Damon is twice the man Kid was. You'd do well to recognize that." She tossed her head in the direction where Santiago sat, seeing, along with Damon, that he was watching their every move. "So would your boss."

Damon observed how Carl looked from her to Santiago.

"Ruby is off-limits to you," Damon said. "Or you can kiss your weapons goodbye."

Carl turned to him and leaned forward. "The weapons are ours. If you don't deliver, you have no future." He looked at Ruby. "But she might…with me."

Damon concentrated all his effort so as not to reach across and slam this putrid punk's head down onto the bar and knock him out. "Ruby is my girlfriend. Respect that or pay the price." He meant every word of that.

"Ooh, the man has some nerve," Carl said. "I saw that the other morning."

Although Carl acted bravely, Damon could see only Santiago's presence gave him power.

"It's time for you to go away," Ruby said. "I'm with Damon. No one else."

After looking at her several seconds, Carl gave a slight bow and walked away. He sat at Santiago's table and began talking to the group of men.

Damon couldn't wait to put him behind bars.

Unexpectedly, Ruby leaned forward and took hold of the collar of his shirt, pulling him toward her. Then she planted what felt like a heartfelt and passionate kiss on his mouth.

She knew Kid's men were watching. She did this on

purpose. While he felt the full impact of her affection, it wasn't affection to her. It was a show. He didn't like that. He didn't like it at all.

RUBY HEARD DAMON enter the apartment and lifted her head. She had fallen asleep on the couch, unable to fall sleep earlier. She was too bothered by having to play her role as his girlfriend.

She sat up as he approached.

"I didn't mean to wake you," he said.

"That's all right. I need to go to bed." She pushed the blanket off her and stood, facing him.

"Why did you do it?" he asked.

Hearing an edge in his tone, she said, "For Maya. Don't make the mistake of thinking I did it for you. I don't do fake relationships."

"Do me a favor and don't fake it anymore," he said.

She stepped back, surprised by the amount of emotion he exhibited. Had he felt it was real?

"I had to, Damon. They expect us to stay together. They think you can make me lead you to their weapons. If we aren't together, or they have a reason to believe we are drifting apart, then that puts us all in danger. I won't do that to Maya. She's been through enough."

"Yes. I've known that all along, Ruby. But that doesn't mean you need to make a spectacle. Only show me your affections when you really feel it."

Again, the amount of emotion took her aback. But he had been the one to deceive her, not the other way around.

"Oh, the way you showed me when I had no idea

who you really were?" His betrayal still hurt. She could not deny that.

"That isn't fair."

"No? Why not?" She'd love to hear this.

"I didn't know you. I only knew what I'd read about you. Nothing could have prepared me for meeting you in person."

That was good. Really good. Ruby found herself fighting the urge to believe him 100 percent.

"Nothing could have prepared me for falling for you," he said.

Her defenses deflated, although she remained cautious. She would always have to remain cautious with him. If not for herself, then for Maya. She could not forget Maya. Her daughter came first.

"I'm sure it was exciting for you to fall for someone who didn't know who you were. You played a role. You fell for me. It was excitement and nothing more."

"No." He sounded emphatic. "It was more."

"What are you saying, Damon, that you fell in love with me? What, exactly, do you mean by 'falling for' me?"

She watched him swallow and stare into her eyes. His uncertainty was palpable, which only served to hurt her more.

"I fell for you, Ruby. I can't explain the depth of it. All I can say is you put me under a spell. I had no control over my feelings. I fell for you. I can't say it's love at this point, but I can say it swept me off my feet. This mysterious attraction I have for you. Everything about you. You're beautiful. You're principled, and you're a great mom."

Okay, that disarmed her. Was he being honest, or did he intend to make her stop playing a role? She'd be more believable not pretending.

"I'm here until this is over and Maya is safe," she said.

He held her gaze for several seconds. "All right, then."

With that, he turned and walked to the hall toward his bedroom. She saw him pause at Maya's bedroom, checking on her before going to his room.

His concern touched her, reached beyond her barriers as many things about him did. She had to stay strong. She had to protect Maya.

Chapter Twelve

Maya didn't know that Ruby and Damon were taking her to Kid's club and a house he had owned before he met Ruby. Maya would most certainly recognize the club, and she might reveal a memory of seeing arms. Damon and Ruby might have missed some secret room.

Damon stopped across the street, looking around to make sure they weren't spotted. He had kept a careful vigil all the way here, ensuring their secrecy.

Ruby turned to see her daughter in the back seat, busy on her tablet with a game. She flapped her hand and said, "Maya?"

Maya stopped what she was doing and looked at her mother.

"Do you see that building?"

Maya turned toward where Ruby pointed. Then she looked at Ruby.

Yes. It's where Daddy did all of his bad stuff.

"Were the guns here, Maya?" Ruby asked.

No. Maya looked out the window and then back at her mother. *I don't want to go there. I want to leave.*

"All right, sweetheart. We're going to a tiny town. It's sort of like an outdoor museum."

A tiny town? Like dollhouses?

Yes.

Cool!

Ruby sat forward. "Let's take her by Kid's second house and then Tiny Town."

"Roger that."

Worried over Maya's aversion to Kid's club, Ruby rode in silence. Maya had made great progress in her therapy sessions, but reintroducing her to places that might have a negative impact on her could set her back. Ruby doubted Maya had any memory of Kid's second house, and going to Tiny Town would hopefully negate any bad memories that might creep up.

Ruby hated putting her daughter through this, but her main goal was to expunge Kid and his gang of thugs out of their lives forever. She looked over at Damon, undeniably grateful for his help and his affinity for Maya.

Damon caught her look as he stopped in front of Kid's house. He put his hand over hers.

"It's going to be all right," he said. "No matter what."

Meaning whether he and Ruby ended up together in a real relationship.

Warmth and love circled her soul.

Maya put her hand over theirs, and Ruby saw her big smile.

Family, she signed.

Ruby choked up and withdrew her hand. She signed, *Maya, do you remember this house?*

Maya looked and then shook her head.

"Let's go," Ruby said to Damon, disturbed and wanting more than anything for Maya to be able to live a normal life, away from all of this danger and these bad people.

DAMON UNDERSTOOD RUBY'S DISCONTENT. Taking Maya to Tiny Town had been a great success. Maya had loved all the miniature buildings and the train. Even better, none of Santiago's men had tailed them.

Now he took them both to see his brothers and Nicole. He wouldn't have risked it if they had been followed. He was long overdue a family visit, and he sensed Ruby desperately needed to get a good dose of loving relatives. Maya, too.

Nicole had planned a barbecue at her house. She lived in a suburb of Bartlett. Damon had always loved her house. An old redbrick Victorian she'd taken from his uncle during the divorce. The wood floors creaked in places, and some of the rooms were small like they would have been way back when. The living areas had obviously been renovated and redesigned. The main room was spacious and full of coziness. And of course the kitchen did not remotely reflect the age of the house. Clean, bright and with top-of-the-line appliances, antiques sprinkled throughout to create an air of history.

The huge back patio was all light stone with a fire

pit and seating both in the middle and under a metal gazebo. The yard was full of flowering plants and trees.

Maya took in the bright colors of the flowers, her tiny hand in Ruby's. They came in the grand entrance. This was familiar to Damon, but Ruby and Maya paused to take in the artistic mix of old and modern.

Something smelled great in the kitchen. Damon heard Nicole—his mother in every sense of the word—and Vita. Aaron, Nash and Uncle Rick sat in front of the television with a baseball game on.

All three glanced back and greeted them with a chorus of welcome. "Hey!"

"There he is!"

"Look who decided to show up!"

"Aaron, Nash, you remember Ruby," Damon said, hushing both brothers. They clearly weren't certain of the state of their relationship.

"Uncle Rick, this is Ruby, my girlfriend," Damon said.

Rick stood. He was in shape and had no shortage of personality and social fearlessness.

He came over to Ruby with such verve she took a step back.

"Nash and Aaron have told me about you," he said. "I'm so glad you see Damon for the good man he is."

Ruby looked at him unappreciatively.

Damon raised his hands. "I didn't tell them anything."

"January did," Nash said with a devilish grin. "She thinks another wedding is on the way."

"Come, come." Rick cupped Ruby's elbow and

took her closer to Nash and Aaron. "You haven't had a proper introduction to Damon's brothers."

Ruby resisted slightly, with another glance at Damon, as though she were being taken to a lion's den.

Damon smiled. "They don't bite."

"Aaron here used to box and now runs some successful gyms. We are all very proud of him. Nash here is an architect. Very artistic. Equally proud we are of him."

"Yes, I did hear a little about his brothers." She looked at Damon. "Before I knew he was an undercover DEA agent."

Rick patted her shoulder gently. "Forgive him for that. I meant it when I said he was a good man."

"In case you haven't noticed, our uncle is vivacious and friendly. His favorite pastime is spending time with family at gatherings exactly like this," Aaron said.

"I grew up in a big family," Rick said. "It stuck."

Ruby smiled, white teeth flashing and eyes twinkling. "That's enviable."

"Ruby has family in Wisconsin, and her mother lives here with her," Damon said.

"Ah, a Wisconsin girl," Rick said. "Fun *and* humble."

Ruby laughed again. "Not so much anymore."

Damon caught her gaze and hoped she knew not to talk about Kid here.

"You men seem more equipped to watch sports," she said. "I'm going to go see if I can help with the food."

"I'll introduce you and Maya," Damon said, and then to the others, "I'll be right back."

RUBY FOLLOWED DAMON into the kitchen, Maya's hand in hers. She entered into a glamorous cooking environment, bright and clean and uncluttered, splashed with color only an artist could pull off. Two women turned from the kitchen counter, their talking pausing as they faced the new arrivals.

"Mom." Damon went to a gently aging blue-eyed beauty wearing her dark blond hair up in sophisticated fashion. He hugged her with genuine love, and Ruby saw his mother's face over his shoulder, eyes closed with matching emotion.

Damon leaned back and turned to look at Ruby. "This is Ruby Duarte and her daughter Maya. Ruby, Nicole Colton." Nothing but proud devotion exuded from him.

She fell into hopeless attraction in this moment. Notwithstanding the obvious love, Damon said *Mom* so naturally Ruby was convinced he loved her as though she were his biological mother.

"Hello," Ruby said.

"Welcome, Ruby." She looked down at Maya. "Welcome, Maya."

Maya signed, *Hello.* Her daughter's face showed innocent fascination that bolstered Ruby's first impression of Nicole. The woman was full of heart.

Damon stepped back to include the other woman in the kitchen. "Never to diminish this woman's importance in my life, this is Vita Yates, Rick's wife and my aunt." Damon beamed.

Vita smiled at being announced as his aunt. Her light brown bob framed her lovely face. She was slightly heavier than Nicole but not at all less genuine. Damon had told her about his quite extended family. Ruby was touched that he had received and still received so much love. This truly felt like a family. She didn't know what to do with how she felt, so bright and tingly inside.

"Would Maya like a cartoon? I see she has her drawing book," Nicole said. "Can she understand what's being said on TV?"

"I turn on closed captioning. She gets enough to enjoy it. Plus, I think she likes the actions and the colors more than anything." Ruby began to feel as though she fit right in. Maya, too.

"Amazing child, for sure," Vita said. "She's so young…and yet seems so advanced."

"I suppose she had to learn early. And I have to agree." Ruby looked down at Maya and signed as she spoke. "She is very amazing." Ruby ran her hand from the top of Maya's head down the back of her hair, feeling full of abounding love.

Maya's eyes softened with innocent love. Ruby thought her heart would burst. She asked her if she'd like to watch television. Being surrounded by a crowd of adults, she eagerly nodded.

Laughing, she and Ruby followed Nicole into a den off the living room and kitchen. It had pretty French doors and windows on the far wall and another wall made of a built-in bookshelf. Cozy and colorful seating surrounded the television above a gas fireplace. Nicole turned on the TV.

Maya took the remote and began surfing to her favorite channel.

I'll be in the kitchen, Ruby signed.

Maya nodded.

Ruby followed Nicole back into the kitchen and saw two other women had joined them.

"I wondered if you came with Aaron," Damon said. "Ruby, this is Fee. She's with Aaron now."

"Hi." Fee smiled, a striking blonde with a thin build.

Good looks abounded in the Colton line. "Hello."

"And this is my cousin Lila. We were all close growing up," Damon said.

"Hi," Lila said cheerily, her green eyes smiling and dark hair up in a twist. "Damon is like a brother to me, so you better not hurt him."

She said it with friendly teasing, but Ruby had a sense she probably meant it.

"Lila manages an art gallery in North Center," Damon said, clearly proud of her.

"I work with art, but I am the furthest thing from an artist," she said.

"You must know a lot about art," Ruby said.

"She does," Damon said.

"Damon is biased," Lila said. "But I do love it, yes."

Ruby smiled. "Everyone should be so lucky as to do what they love."

"That's Mom, too," Damon said. "She runs a catering business, so this barbecue is going to be delicious." He leaned over and planted a kiss on Ruby's cheek before withdrawing. "I'll leave you in these capable hands."

"I don't mean to be rude, but I'm going to join them in front of the TV," Lila said.

"We have enough help in here," Nicole said.

Ruby could only stare after Damon as he led his cousin into the living room. He had kissed her as though it had been a natural reflex, not rehearsed at all.

"Well, well, well," Nicole cooed. "It looks like Damon found himself a new girl."

"I wouldn't say that." Ruby didn't know how to describe her relationship to him.

"How did you meet him?" Vita asked.

Fee stirred the potato salad that Nicole and Vita must have just finished. There was a green salad in the making as well and a pan of baked beans that would go into the oven.

"Um…he came into the coffee shop where I work, and then…kept coming," she said.

"So you've been dating him?"

"We dated, yes."

Nicole looked confused. "Dated?"

"Um…we…sort of…live together."

Nicole's mouth dropped open, and she took Ruby into an exuberant hug.

Vita took hold of her next. "Welcome to the family!"

Whoa. That was a bit much for Ruby. She felt stiff all over. When Vita moved back, Ruby caught Fee looking at her with what she could only call understanding.

"You got a good man, Ruby. Just like I did, thanks to these fine women right here." Fee smiled.

"Yes," Vita said. "About getting a good man, that

is. All of us in this room know what it's like to be with one that isn't."

"That's an understatement," Fee said, widening her eyes cynically.

Ruby suddenly was full of questions, but she didn't want to pry. "I know you, Nicole, were married to Damon's father. He doesn't seem fond of him."

"Not many are fond of his brother, Axel, either," Vita said. "I was married to him. He was awful. Selfish. Mean."

"But then she met Rick," Nicole said. "Those two are inseparable. It's a wonder to see."

"I was married to a man I found out later was a drug dealer," Ruby said, leaving out the part where he kept Maya from her. "I thought I'd never escape him."

Fee appeared beside her. "I had a similar experience. My husband was abusive. I had to move and change my name...until I met Aaron. Now everything is fabulous. I never dreamed I'd be this happy. So don't give up on Damon. I know you probably have a hard time trusting men, but don't let go of a good one to save yourself agony in case it doesn't work out. Even if it doesn't, you'll be better than you were when you were with your previous partner."

Ruby looked from her to Vita to Nicole and back to Fee. She was among kindred spirits.

The doorbell rang, and seconds later Ruby heard Damon say, "What are you doing here?"

She turned to look over the island at two men who had entered, alarmed by the tone of the newcomer.

"Why are Erik and Axel here?" Vita asked.

Ruby turned to them. These men were Damon's father and uncle? She looked back at them. One wore a scowl, and the other seemed more aloof.

"I'm sure it has something to do with their mother," Nicole said. "And this can't be good, if so."

"Why are you boys mingling with those traitorous Coltons?" Axel demanded.

Apparently they had discovered their kids had gone to a party to meet their cousins. And oh, what a party it had been. Glamourous and fun at first, but for Ruby it had a bad aftertaste now. For the Colton cousins, it had been the beginning of a family alliance.

Damon and Nash stood at the door, and Rick remained on the couch, looking on. Aaron joined them, standing beside Nash. The three of them looked like brothers. Ruby didn't miss the body language along with the physical resemblances. They were close.

"Which one is Damon's father?" she asked Nicole quietly.

"The one who is grayer," she said.

Ruby saw they both had green eyes. They looked like brothers and not twins. Maybe it was Erik's grayer hair. Maybe it was his sterner look, but he looked older than Axel. Axel appeared less stressed out—and not as angry as Erik. In fact, Ruby wouldn't be surprised if his brother had dragged him here.

"Axel is probably here because Erik made him come," Vita said, sounding derisive.

Ruby said nothing, just marveled over their similar line of thought.

"How could you?" Erik asked, bitterness dripping from his tone and looking from Damon to Nash.

"How could we what?" Nash asked, more like a challenge.

"Betray your own father."

Damon scoffed. "You're no *father*."

Erik subtly flinched, his head drawing back. Clearly he hadn't expected his son to say something so hurtful. *Could a man like Erik Colton be hurt by anyone?* Ruby wondered.

She saw how Aaron observed the exchange, eyes hardening as Erik pretended he had been a real father to his half brothers.

"One party with those…those…impostors, and now you insult me like that?" Erik said, incensed.

"What you're doing is wrong," Damon said. "Those people are nice and full of integrity."

Damon turned his back and walked into the living room. Erik followed, marching to get in front of Damon. Nash stayed near the entry, seeming reluctant to engage anymore.

Axel glanced at Nash and then went to stand before the television, near the couch where Rick still sat. He was more interested in that than his brother's ranting.

Nash looked toward his father and brother, regarding Erik in distain.

"What we're doing is taking what belongs to us." Erik pointed his finger at Damon.

"Everything those Coltons have doesn't belong to you," Nash said.

He and Aaron walked closer to Erik and Damon.

"Grandmother started this," Aaron said. "You're only doing her bidding. All of this—" he swept his hand up and down Erik's body, indicating his demeanor and storming temper "—is to please *her*."

"My mother is *right*. She deserved better from our father. She's only stepping up to defend us…and you, you ungrateful kids."

Damon shook his head, looking exasperated. "When are you going to wake up and realize she's been controlling you your entire life? You've been programmed to do whatever she wants, no matter how condemnable."

Erik stared at him, Aaron and Nash looking on, and Rick and Axel turning their heads to see Erik's reaction.

For a moment, Erik seemed stunned by the truth of what Damon said. But in a second, he reverted to his cantankerous self.

"You're all ganging up on me…and Axel."

Nash looked at Axel. "Uncle Axel?" he queried. "Are you in agreement with our dad?"

Aaron put his hands in his front pockets.

Axel looked from him to Aaron and then Damon, pausing there awhile before turning to his brother. "Yes."

So, he was under the grandmother's spell as well.

Ruby saw how neither Damon, Nash or Aaron were shocked by this declaration.

Some fathers didn't realize the impact they had on their families. Erik struck her as a man whose self-interests overruled any care or love he had for anyone around him. As long as people behaved according to his script, they were welcomed into his good graces. Disagree or go against his way of seeing things, and that made you an outcast, or at least subject to his wrath and contempt. Ruby had a friend from high school who grew up like that. She had watched the poor thing struggle to rise above damaging insecurities that wouldn't have been there had her father actually loved her for who she was and accepted her views regardless of how different they were from his.

Erik glanced around, satisfied that his brother had capitulated. "Where's Lila and Myles? Were they at that party, too?"

"Yes," Vita said.

Ruby became aware of her and Nicole on each side of her. Fee had taken a seat at the table, her feet up with ankles crossed on the adjacent chair, clearly entertained, albeit with cynical vibes.

"Yes, they were at the party," Damon said.

"What were you doing there? Turning your backs on your own family?" Erik asked.

"We wanted to meet them," Nash said.

"They're good people," Damon said. "You should talk Carin out of her lawsuit. It isn't right to do that to people who don't deserve it."

"Axel and I deserve an inheritance. Dean Colton was our father, too. What part of that isn't right to you?"

"You don't deserve the amount you're going for," Aaron said. "You weren't part of his life. You were part of Carin's. Stop her, Dad. Before it's too late."

Ruby could see there would be no reasoning with him. She almost pitied him. How terrible it would be to live a life full of wanting and blame. Greed. Erik, as a product of his mother, depended on the handouts from others to feel important, superior even. Maybe he even deluded himself into believing he was envied.

"I'm not stopping anything." Erik looked at his sons one by one with disdain. "What a disappointment you turned out to be. You should be fighting for your family."

"Our cousins are our family," Aaron said.

Nicole stepped forward, going into the living room. "All right. Enough!" Her commanding tone spoke of all the turmoil she had suffered being married to a man like this. "It's time for you to leave. No one invited you here today, and you aren't welcome."

Erik leveled her a hard look. "These are my kids, too."

"Leave before we call the police," Vita said.

Rick stood when his wife said that, ready to protect her if necessary. He had been watching the exchange quietly up until then.

Axel glanced from his attention on the television to Vita. He surely must have been listening. Ruby didn't know what to think of him. He must agree with his brother, but for some reason he wasn't as aggressive. Maybe he wanted the inheritance but wasn't as confrontational as his twin. Maybe he preferred to leave the fighting to Erik. He just went along for the ride.

Axel walked to him. "Let's go."

Erik looked at him and then cast a belligerent gaze at each person in the room.

When Erik didn't move, Axel said, "Vita *will* call the cops."

"Now you talk?" Erik spat. "You never have my back."

"I figured you'd handle it," Axel said.

Erik glanced back at Vita, who put her hand on her hip and cocked her head, cell phone in her other hand, ready to call 911.

Erik muttered something Ruby couldn't hear, and he and his brother left.

Nicole shut and locked the door.

She faced the room. "Never a dull moment in a Colton house."

Everyone laughed.

Damon came over to Ruby and put his hands on her upper arms. "Sorry about that."

"Don't be. You told me he wasn't the congenial type."

He smiled softly, and she fell into the twinkling affection of his eyes.

"How are things going in there?" He gestured with his head toward the kitchen, where Vita and Nicole had returned. But Nicole watched them closely.

"Really great. I love your mom. Fee and I have a lot in common when it comes to men."

"Oh, yeah? What does that mean for me?"

"Maybe something good." She smiled in a way that felt flirty.

He chuckled, and before she could prepare herself, he leaned down and kissed her, not deeply, just a gentle peck.

Tingling everywhere, Ruby stepped back and turned

to walk to the kitchen, seeing Nicole smiling her approval. Ruby took up a knife and started helping to prepare the salad, glancing up at Damon every so often. How did he make her feel so loved? And why was it so difficult for her to accept it?

Chapter Thirteen

Damon drove Ruby and Maya by two more places where Kid might have hidden weapons. They struck out again. Maya didn't show any sign of recognition. They even got out of the car and walked to give the child time to absorb sights, hoping something would trigger her memory.

The rest of the barbecue had gone smoothly—more than that. Damon could see Ruby warming to his family, and he loved it. He was afraid to believe she was also warming to him. She looked at him several times in a way that suggested her affinity to belonging to this—and him. But he was not one to make decisions based on instincts, good or bad. He followed them but didn't make life-altering changes just because they felt so damned good.

Now he had Ruby and Maya tucked safely away in his secure apartment, and he could go down to the bar to work. He crouched before Maya and told her he had to go to work and for her to mind her mother and have sweet dreams when she went to bed. Her eyes had taken on an innocent love, and she'd thrown her arms around his neck and kissed his cheek.

Damon was so touched he had kissed her cheek as well and said, "You are a precious little girl." He wanted to say *my precious little girl.*

It was true: Maya had found her way into his heart the moment he'd met her. Although he had known she was deaf, he hadn't been prepared for how smart she was for a five-year-old or how endearing. Then her personality had dug into him. Brave. Confident. Innocent. Even after living with the likes of Kid Mercer, she had overcome. Maybe it was her young age, but Damon preferred to think it was her strength that had gotten her through. Now she was like any other child her age. Except more special, as far as he was concerned.

Maya trotted off to the kitchen table, where she had her favorite coloring book.

When he stood up, he met Ruby's furious eyes. She wiggled her crooked finger for him to come out into the entryway, outside the door of the apartment.

"What the *hell* are you doing?" she hissed, hands on hips, mama bear wakened.

Damon took in her stance a bit longer and relented to honesty. "I love that kid, Ruby. I didn't plan on that. I didn't expect it. I've told you this before."

"My daughter is different. You can't mislead her!"

He raised his palms with two stop gestures and then lowered them to his sides. "I know. I am not misleading her. I truly adore her. More than that. She's…" He searched for the right words. "Special." No, that wasn't enough. "She's amazing…" No, that wasn't enough, either. "Ruby, she completely caught me off guard. I can't explain why she is so special to me. Maybe it's that she's deaf and doesn't let it get to her. Maybe it's how she likes me. I can't tell you. All I know…is I feel a powerful connection to her." He met her now-stunned look. "What that means for you and me, I don't care. I just hope I can keep being in her life. No matter how you feel about me."

Ruby continued to stare at him. And then she suddenly burst into tears and ran off into her bedroom, slamming the door.

Well, at least Maya wouldn't hear that.

Downcast and hoping he could pull off acting like a criminal bartender, Damon went downstairs and started his closing shift. It was early, so not many were filling the space, just the regulars who occupied barstools and likely sought to numb their pain.

He didn't take lightly Ruby's reaction to his and Maya's deepening bond. He was just as concerned about her as Ruby was. But Ruby would not believe that. Not yet. Frustration made him wipe the bar counter harder and more often than necessary.

The Foxhole owner eyed him every once in a while.

Damon checked himself. Ruby and Maya had to go on his cerebral shelf for a while.

An hour or so went by when Ruby appeared in front of him. She utterly surprised him until he rationalized she had waited for Maya to go to sleep and then had come down here to support his investigation. All premeditated, with the sole intent to protect her daughter. Or so she thought.

Damon would use this to his complete advantage—and not for his investigation. For her.

"Can I get you something to drink?" he asked.

"Ginger ale on the rocks."

Damon went to get her the requested drink, being sure to add an umbrella as a silent message. Flashy, just like their role-playing.

He put the glass before her.

"Thanks…lover."

He did not misinterpret her tone, although her expression revealed attraction. He wondered if at least that was real.

"Feeling restless tonight?" he asked.

"You stay away from Maya," she said in a low, growling voice. Mama bear again. She sipped through her straw with a hot look in her eyes. In the entire bar, no one but he would notice the extreme venom. She kept her face sexy, but her words and tone held completely different meaning. She didn't have four-inch, spiky-sharp teeth, but she sure could bite like she did.

Going to another customer, Damon was glad for the break so he could digest this extreme in Ruby. She'd do anything to protect her daughter. He got that. But her defenses spoke more from insecurity, threat. And Damon was a huge threat right now. To her and her alone. Her lack of trust was so deep he didn't think he'd ever be able to breach the barrier.

After a while he saw her glass of ginger ale was empty. "Another?" he asked.

"I think I'll have a beer. I can't leave too much of a teetotaling impression."

He brought her a light lager. "On the house." He glanced around, checking for signs of the gang.

Her eyes narrowed. Daggers flew at him. Ruby leaned back. "I know what you're doing."

"Tending bar?"

"You're playing your role. Showing Kid's gang members you're one of them," she said in a calm voice. She raised her hand casually, as though in conversation and not in anger.

"None of Kid's gang is here," he informed her.

"You stay away from Maya," she said, then took the beer and drank several swallows.

"No. I like her. A lot," he said.

Angrily, Ruby put the bottle onto the bar. She said nothing.

Just then, Damon saw Carl and the whole gang file into the pub.

He turned to Ruby. "Time for you to go upstairs."

She looked toward the door and saw what must be a souring reminder of all the pain Kid had caused her. Then she looked at him. "No. I think I'll have another drink, Mr. Jones." She finished her beer and handed him the bottle.

This was so out of character for her. It was worry over Maya and her attachment to Damon that fueled her anger. She was apprehensive about what this would lead to, and she must think it would lead to nothing, to him and her parting ways.

Oh, man. "No. Go upstairs."

"I'm a paying customer. You don't have to put it on the house. Give me another."

"Ruby…"

"One more. Now. Or this all ends now."

Meaning she'd blow his cover? Damon knew for sure she'd never do that. She was just mad that her daughter liked him.

"Okay." Damon got another bottle of beer. Putting it on the bar in front of her, he leaned forward. "After this, you go upstairs."

Ruby, with her elbows on the counter, leaned toward him like a drunken girlfriend, smiling sloppily and said, "Kiss me."

"We don't have to do that," he said.

"Do it."

At her commanding tone, he did.

He put his hand behind her head and brought her to him, kissing her firmly, unmistakably passionate. He did not have to fake it, and by the time the long kiss ended, he was certain she knew it.

He looked into her eyes, penetrating, telling her ruthlessly that she was treading on thin ice. He was the expert here, and there was no room for personal emotion.

Ruby leaned back on her stool and drank from the bottle.

He chuckled because Ruby rarely drank anything. "Will you be all right with Maya?"

"Yes. I'll have tea when I go back up. And a movie. I'm not going to be able to sleep."

"One thing I know for sure you are, Ruby, is a good mom."

Ruby nodded her thanks and took another swig.

Damon had to conceal his amusement before tending to other patrons. He kept an eye on Ruby, who remained seated, watching him. She'd go upstairs soon, but she must want to stay a bit to be around him.

Damon did not rely on his instincts when it came to women, but he would make sure nothing happened to her tonight. She would have a very mild buzz, enough to relax her and put her to sleep in pillowy slumber, but when he saw Carl approach, he went into kill mode.

He had to serve several customers and bar orders before he could go over to her and Carl.

"Carl was just telling me how beautiful I am and that he'd like to take me to dinner," Ruby said.

That was cheap. He turned to Carl. "Oh. That's charming. What did you say?"

"I said no." Ruby sounded like she'd deliberately slurred her words. "I need another beer."

Seeing her eyes, he knew what she meant. She played her role.

Damon got her another. She took a tiny sip and put the bottle down. She wasn't going to drink it all. She'd definitely had enough. She was probably feeling what she'd already had in a big way. Judging by her smile, he would say she was feeling pretty good right now.

Having to address his other customers again—the bar was filling up now—he left Ruby with Carl. He kept a close eye on her.

He could tell Carl was talking sweet gangster nothings to her and she was playing along, talking with him and smiling genuinely, or so it seemed. More like the beer had relaxed her enough to act.

He refreshed all his patrons and filled orders throughout the bar and then returned to Ruby and her ignorant suitor. The man clearly didn't know what he was dealing with. Tipsy or not, Ruby had unshakable principles.

"You are an amazing woman, Ruby," Carl said as Damon stopped at the bar.

"Yes, she most certainly is," Damon said. "She captured my heart the first time I ordered coffee."

Carl only then noticed him, or pretended to. He looked at him with displeasure.

"Santiago asked me to deliver you another message. You are taking too long to find what belongs to him. It's time to speed your progress along."

"We're working as fast as we can," Damon said.

"If Ruby knew where the stash was, you would have found it by now. The two of you appear to be close. Even…trusting. We've been watching you. So tell me… why have you not found it yet?"

"Ruby didn't know about the weapons, as I've told you. We're searching for them," Damon said. "We have some ideas on where Kid might have put them and are eliminating them one by one."

"Need I remind you that Santiago will be patient for only so much longer?"

"No. That message is loud and clear."

Ruby sighed like a satisfied cat. "I'm going up to the apartment." She stood from the stool with a gooey smile at Damon. "See you soon, darling."

"Can't wait," Damon answered, loving it.

RUBY STAYED UP with a book and a cup of tea. She had calmed down since going to confront Damon about his closeness with Maya. She was extremely worried about her daughter's well-being, but now that she'd had time to think, she realized she couldn't predict the future. Maya liked him, and he was a good influence on her. If they ended up parting ways, she'd be sad for a while, but she would bounce back. On the other hand, if Ruby and Damon ended up staying together, they'd continue as a family unit. Ruby admitted she feared that, and for good reason, but she couldn't live beneath that fear for the rest of her life.

She could, however, be discerning in her choice of men. Right now, it wouldn't be prudent to trust Damon completely.

Hearing someone coming up the stairs, she put her book down and twisted to see the door. The lock turned, and Damon appeared when he opened the door.

"Oh. You're still up," he said.

"Yes. I couldn't sleep." She held up her book.

He walked to the couch and sat. He seemed weighed down by something.

"Is everything all right?" she asked.

"I had a talk with Santiago again."

Ruby braced herself for more deadly threats over how long it was taking for her and Damon to track down the weapons.

"I asked him about your relationship with Kid," he said.

Why had he done that? He had trust issues the same as her. With both of them falling for each other, their hearts were on a chopping block with the knife getting ready to slam down.

"You did?" she asked.

"He told me one of Kid's men said Kid told you to leave because you had two affairs while you were with him."

Ruby scoffed. "And you believed him?"

"I didn't know what to believe," he said.

Imagining Damon having such a conversation with the likes of Santiago, Ruby came to two conclusions. "Okay, first of all, I didn't have any affairs, and secondly, Kid kept me from my daughter. Do you really think I wanted that?"

"Of course not, but he could have forced you to leave because of the affairs," Damon said.

"That would make sense if I had actually had affairs. Damon, I understand everything about fragile trust, but you're going to have to trust me on this one," she said.

He blinked, and she knew she had made headway.

"Besides, Santiago is probably trying to put a rift between us so that you'd be more likely to put pressure on me to find his weapons," Ruby said. "He wants you with me, but if you care too much about me, he loses control over you."

Damon blinked again.

Ruby scooted closer and put her hand on his cheek. "If I'd been in your shoes and someone told me something like that about you, I'd have reacted the same way."

Damon's eyes immediately softened, and he put his hand over hers. "You're right about Santiago. He had to be lying."

Feeling a deeper connection begin to grow between them, she knew this was an important moment for them. They both didn't trust easily, but he had just trusted her.

Acting on impulse, without thinking, she lowered her hand and leaned closer, kissing him. He moved his hand to the back of her head, and she rested hers on his chest. This felt so good, she kept on kissing him. She let her doubts go.

She couldn't stop this. It felt too right, too strong.

His arm slipped around her back and drew her against him. She put her other hand behind his head and sank her fingers into his soft hair. Their breathing intensified. Her heart raced, and her entire body heated and tingled with love. She wanted him. So bad.

As she continued to bestow him with heartfelt kisses, no tongue involved, she sensed his waning restraint. Endless minutes passed before he took over. She loved how he did that. The man in him took charge of this sexual encounter. Seducer. Lover. Protector of the weak and innocent. Gentle soul.

She allowed him to be in charge for this spectacular kiss, but now she was ready for more. Withdrawing, she supported herself with her hands on his shoulders and straddled him.

"No, no," he murmured. "It's my turn." He held her and effortlessly placed her onto her back on the couch.

With her beneath him and his sexy gaze penetrating hers, Ruby gave in to pure desire.

"And this isn't going to be quick," he said.

"Good," she said breathlessly.

He kissed her much as she had him: soft, tender and

full of love. Ruby tried to resist the powerful tide, but it was too strong. A tsunami of sensation. How he could do that with just a kiss she could not process.

Lying on the edge of the couch with his leg over both of hers, he ran his hand from her cheek down her neck and over her shoulder, before landing on her breast. He caressed a bit there and then progressed down to her waist, hip and then thigh. He just ran his hands along her body.

She raised her hands above her head and let him do as he pleased. After several moments of pleasuring, he kissed her, soft and slow as was the theme of this intimacy, it seemed.

Needing more, Ruby removed the *Drink Wisconsinbly* T-shirt she had on, seeing Damon's grin as she did so. He unclasped the front-fastening racerback bra, and her breasts sprang free.

She loved the way he took in the spectacle, taking his time, reveling. Then he unbuttoned his shirt and removed it. Letting him take the lead on this foreplay, Ruby kept her hands above her head. She watched him get up and strip them down. It was as though he understood she'd wait for him.

She would.

Naked, Damon returned to the couch, knees on either side of her. She watched him take in her pose, breathing long and slow and in passion. He moved so gracefully, powerfully.

Then he was on her, on top of her, flesh pressed to flesh. He had his elbows on each side of her. It felt so inexplicitly erotic. She would never be the kind to like being bound, but the surrender of giving him free access to her body numbed her mind to feel only ecstasy. It was *pure* ecstasy. For this night, she could give absolute trust. She realized just then, it was his trust that made her do this, to let go this way.

Ruby lifted her leg and draped it on the back of the couch, giving him room to lie between her legs. She felt his hardness against the place that craved him, but he didn't rush. He kissed her reverently. She matched it, effortlessly she realized. They danced in love.

Unable to resist any longer, Ruby brought her hands to his skin. She touched his shoulders, his biceps, the sides of his powerful torso, down to his rear and back up again, resting on his firm, smooth, muscular back.

Damon lifted his head, and she met his eyes. Beautiful, manly eyes so full of passion.

He positioned his erection at her opening and began pressing in. She was so wet it didn't take much effort. He slid right in.

Ruby dug the back of her head into the couch and spread her knees wider.

"Damon." His name came unbidden from her.

"Yes," he answered gruffly.

He began sliding in and drawing out just a bit, angling to brush her clitoris every other stroke. It was enough to bring her to a state of utter mindlessness. Nothing else existed but him and what he made her feel. She came too quickly.

But he came with her. As Ruby's world melted back down to reality, the thought dawned on her that no other man would ever match her like this one.

Chapter Fourteen

Watching Ruby spread peanut butter and jelly over a toasted muffin with mechanical movements, Damon recognized her mood. Ever since waking with her—yes, they slept in his bed—she sometimes had a dreamy look and less frequently a troubled one. Right now she appeared entranced, absorbed in thought. He hoped those thoughts were in the clouds and full of future imaginations. His certainly were.

After last night, he'd officially thrown in the towel. Ruby was what he wanted and needed in his life. And not just her. Maya, too. He feared what Ruby could do to him if she ran from her own insecurities and sought safer, loveless ground. But he was filled with a new and invigorating certainty he could no longer deny.

He kept this to himself. Ruby would not be able to handle such a declaration right now. He had to end this case and then concentrate on convincing her this was meant to be. Him. Her. Maya. A family. A real one. His heart soared just thinking about it.

A tug on his shirt brought his attention down to an adorable dark-haired five-year-old.

You're burning the eggs.

Damon looked at the pan of eggs he'd been working on and was startled to see he was, indeed, burning the eggs. Ruby's mechanical spreading of peanut butter came back and slapped him. They were both in some sort of trance.

Damon removed the eggs from the burner. Ruby had stopped moving her knife and looked at him, then the pan, then at Maya.

"Maya is an observant soul." Damon made sure she could see his lips but also signed.

She beamed a big smile and climbed up onto an island stool.

He washed out the pan and started over with fresh eggs, ever aware of Maya.

Ruby prepared a bowl of cubed cantaloupe, eyeing Damon and Maya, whose eyes were all for him. Ruby clearly did not like that.

Damon pretended not to notice. He finished the eggs and put together Maya's plate. Then he prepared his and Ruby's, ever aware of Ruby so close to him, their arms or shoulders brushing every once in a while.

Ruby sat on one side of Maya and he on the other at the island. This was all impromptu.

Maya was well into her meal by the time he and Ruby dug in. Damon noticed her glance at him often. She did that a lot. Watched. Being deaf, she must have amazing abilities to read people from only their body language.

After a time, breakfast approached an end as hunger waned. Ruby put her fork down and sipped some orange juice. She leaned back against the stool and watched her daughter for a time. Damon would never get tired of that, the vision of a mother like Ruby just watching her daughter.

"I had a thought today," Ruby said.

Maya had stopped eating and now drew in her notebook.

This seemed important to Ruby. She had clearly waited for Maya to be fed and preoccupied to bring this up. Plus, her demeanor was completely different. Whatever she had to say would carry big weight.

"Kid had another house in Chicago," she said. "Maybe he brought Maya there…without me."

Ruby stood and took her plate to the sink, beginning to clean up.

Seeing her distress, Damon went to her. He stood behind her and put his hand on her shoulder. "None of this is your fault, Ruby. This is Kid's doing. He made some bad choices in life, for whatever reason. You were sucked into his vortex. Deceitful vortex."

"That doesn't make it any easier," she said.

"I know. I'm going to be your champion, Ruby. I will expunge that man from your mind, and I will be the man you deserve," Damon said, meaning every word.

She faced him and met his eyes. "You mean that? You're being honest?"

"Yes."

He watched her struggle to believe that. He suppressed a grin. She had been that way since he'd first met her: reluctant, guarded. He had never had to work this hard for a woman's affection before, and he discovered he not only loved it, but he also had tremendous respect for Ruby. Her penchant for surety would also secure his. Except…he was already sure. He'd stop at nothing to win her trust.

He kissed the tip of her nose. "We'll go by there tomorrow, then we'll take Maya to the zoo. If she gets any negative vibes, that should take care of her."

Ruby turned, putting her hand over his on her shoulder. "You're an amazing man, Damon Colton."

He breathed a chuckle. "I'm just catching the bad guys."

"I just hope I'm enough for you."

"You are, Ruby. The only question is…am I enough for you?"

DAMON'S WORDS KEPT running through Ruby's mind as they drove toward Kid's old house. *Am I enough for you?*

She knew exactly what he meant. He didn't mean to question whether he, personally, was enough for her. He was. He meant was he enough for her to trust?

Damon pulled up to the house where Kid had stayed on occasion. He parked across the street.

"Maya." Ruby reached into the back seat and waved to get her attention.

Maya looked up from her coloring book.

Ruby signed, *Have you seen this house before?* Ruby pointed.

Looking out the window, Maya nodded.

Did you see any guns in there?

Maya shook her head, and Ruby let out a disappointed breath. She glanced at Damon. “I can’t think of any other places where Kid would have taken her.”

His expression became as grim as she felt.

“What now?” Ruby asked. Santiago would surely come after them. He’d want them dead if they came up empty-handed.

Then from the back seat, Maya poked Ruby’s shoulder.

She looked back and saw Maya stretch her arm out and point to the house next to the one Kid had owned.

A surge of hope ran through Ruby. The house appeared as though it had been left unmaintained for quite some time. Years. It was in poor condition. This was an older subdivision, and the houses much smaller than the one she and Kid had lived in. But Kid had found the charm irresistible and purchased a house here.

Damon took out his phone and called someone. “Yeah. Colton here. I think we found them.”

He must be talking to his boss or some other member of his undercover team. He gave the address and said it was an abandoned house. At some point he must have informed them that Maya had drawn pictures.

“I’ll wait to hear from you,” Damon said.

Then he turned to Ruby. “They’re going to find out what happened to the owner or their family. If the owner intentionally left with no plans to return or the family just doesn’t care, I can go in without a warrant.”

Ruby sat with him in silence while they waited. Who knew how long it would take?

"How many people are working your case with you?" she asked.

"Quite a few. There's administratives, other agents, special-forces types. Not all of them know the details of my cover, for obvious reasons, but they are all ready for a raid. I report to the agent in charge."

They were all waiting for an end to this investigation. Just like her. Except Ruby wasn't law enforcement, and her stake in this was personal.

"This reminds me of my grandmother's house. In a way." He took in the other houses, many like the one his estranged and dead grandfather had bought for her.

"How so?" Ruby asked.

"It was a Federal-style mansion built in the 1800s."

"These aren't mansions," Ruby said. "That's probably why Kid didn't come here much. He had fantasies of riches he'd never be able to possess."

Damon could see that. People who gambled their lives on drugs and violence usually wound up dead or in prison. Not many made it as far as El Chapo.

He rested his head back, content to wait for his team to dig up information on the abandoned house and to spend the time with Ruby.

"What's your grandmother's house like?" Ruby asked.

He rolled his head to see her. She had leaned back as he had. He smiled gently. They were two peas in a pod.

Rolling his head straight again, he said, "Old. Too big for her to manage." He took a mental tour through the home. "Even the furniture is old. Most of it belonged to the previous owner."

"Sounds nice to me," she said.

"Grandmother can't afford the upkeep on a place like that. Most of it is boarded up. She needs money to fix it up. That's one reason she's going for the aorta to get our cousins' money."

Ruby turned her head to look out the passenger window. He could see she was in thought.

"It's kind of sad your grandmother is that way," she finally said, turning back to look out the windshield. She sighed slowly, relaxed. "There is so much more to life… Family… Love."

That made him sigh the same way. "Yeah."

Their moment was rudely interrupted by his phone going off. He answered. It was his team.

"What does the exterior look like?" the agent asked.

"Basement windows are boarded up. Weeds everywhere. Paint chipping. Second-story windows are also boarded."

"We couldn't get a hold of the owner. Go in and see what's inside. If it appears abandoned, do the search. Call if you need backup."

"Roger." Damon lowered his phone and looked at her. "I'm going in. You wait here with Maya."

Ruby readily agreed. Maya was now absorbed in her book. She was a voracious reader. Watching Damon disappear around the back of the house, she tried to stave off a wave of worry. What if someone was in that house?

DAMON PEERED INTO several windows and saw the house wasn't furnished and was in grave disrepair. When he opened the single screen door, it fell off its rusting hinges. Leaning it against the house, he tried the doorknob. It didn't budge. The handle looked new, probably the only new thing on the property in decades. To Damon, this was a good sign. Kid would have thought to secure his stash.

Seeing the kitchen window was cracked, he used a rock to break the glass. Clearing the shards, he crawled through. Dirt and broken cabinets greeted him. It smelled moldy. He walked through the rooms, looking out the front window to check on Ruby and Maya. Ruby looked toward the house, and Maya entertained herself in the back seat.

He checked every closet and searched for secret doors. The second level was empty and filthy like the first. Damon hadn't expected to find much up here. He headed down to the main level and went to the basement stairs. The door was padlocked. A sure sign something valuable was down there. Damon left it untouched. The weapons had to be here.

He returned to the car, on the way telling his team to move in. He didn't want to risk being here longer than necessary, lest he alert Santiago and blow his cover.

Time to go to the zoo.

MAYA SAT NEXT to the giant giraffe Damon had bought for her yesterday. Morning now, Ruby prepared cheesy scrambled eggs, toast and fruit for breakfast. Damon sat at the table working on his laptop. He'd been on the phone for hours last night. The DEA had found Kid's stash of weapons and ammo in the basement of the abandoned house.

Ruby shied at believing her nightmare would finally be over. Even in death, Kid could still haunt her.

She brought plates to the table, then went to get Maya's attention. She left her morning cartoon, awkwardly and adorably carrying the giraffe. She put the stuffed animal on the chair beside her.

Ruby took the seat adjacent. Having placed a plate next to Damon's computer, she waited for him to pry himself away from work and notice.

He grinned. "Sorry."

She felt his excitement. It matched her own.

They began eating, Maya taking intermissions to have a signing conversation with Giraffe.

Ruby enjoyed the peaceful moments while they shared a meal as a family. She was ever curious to know what resulted from all his work so far today.

"So…what are you going to do with Santiago and the guns?" she asked.

Maya was busy eating and carrying on with her giraffe.

"I'm going to use the weapons to coerce him into a deal. I'll demand money for them. It'll be a sting. If he goes for it, we'll arrange to meet at the abandoned house, make the deal and carry out the raid."

Ruby worried at that. "But Santiago thinks he's in charge of you. You're like…his boy."

Damon chuckled. "I am not his boy. I have the weapons. He doesn't know where they are. All he expected from me was to find them. He didn't anticipate I'd use them against him. I made sure of that. His greed and power-hungry ego will be his downfall."

That had been his plan all along. Make Santiago believe he was acting to protect Ruby and Maya, that his main goal was to be accepted into the criminal organization, to make money. He had done that. Santiago had no idea who he was dealing with. More than an undercover agent, Damon was no man's man.

Chapter Fifteen

Although Damon didn't like taking Ruby with him to meet Santiago, for the sake of the investigation her appearance would be best. After all, Santiago believed she was the one who had led him to the weapons and ammo. They had dropped Maya off at January and Sean's home. Damon would take Ruby there before he and his task force met Santiago at the vacant house. Santiago wouldn't want to wait.

Damon spotted Santiago sitting at his claimed table with Carl and Orlando, two of his most dangerous men.

He pulled a chair out for Ruby and she sat, looking sexy in a white summer dress. He sat beside her.

"I assume there is a reason for this urgent meeting," Santiago said. "Why not just tell me over the phone?"

"We found the guns and ammo," Damon said.

Santiago's eyes moved to Ruby. "You finally gave in and told him?"

"I didn't know where they were. I only knew where Kid would have gone. It was a process of elimination," she said.

Now Santiago looked pleased. "Very good. Very

good. Where are they? We need to arrange shipment to one of my warehouses."

Damon remained calm, meeting Santiago's eyes intently. "It's not going to be that simple, Santiago."

Santiago's brow rose. "Oh?"

Carl and Orlando glanced at each other, then watched Santiago for signs of whatever order he might decide to pass on to them. Damon always marveled over the psychology that drove criminals like them. They were pawns. They took orders. They lived in threat of being killed. And for what? He doubted even they knew the truth of that. They grew up in volatile homes with little or no love. They learned crime and lived crime.

"We want a finder's fee," Damon said to Santiago.

"You want money." He said it flatly, glaring at Ruby as though blaming her for this.

"Those guns and ammo don't belong to you. Not yet. They belonged to Kid Mercer. The way I see it, whoever find them gets them. Now, I'm a generous man. I can be reasonable. I think ten percent of their value should do it."

"You've got balls demanding that," Santiago said. "I took over in Kid's place. Anything that belonged to him now belongs to me."

"That's why I called it a finder's fee. You've been on me to give them to you, now I can, but you have to pay for all my effort."

Santiago half stood and pounded his hand on the table. "How dare you?"

Ruby flinched and stood, backing away from the table. Orlando drew his gun.

"You will give me every one of those guns and the ammunition. I want them tonight. If you don't bring them to me, I'll have you killed." He looked at Orlando, who nodded once.

Damon stood and took Ruby's hand to reassure her. He was accustomed to dealing with characters like this; she wasn't.

"You don't seem to understand," Damon said. "I have your weapons. I know where they are. If you want them, you'll pay me my finder's fee."

"Your finder's fee." Santiago looked at Ruby.

"Ruby has nothing to do with this deal. This is my deal." Damon leaned over the table, his palms supporting him, bringing his face inches from Santiago's. "Give me the address for your warehouse. I'll bring the guns and ammo. When you pay me ten percent of their value, I'll give them to you."

Santiago met his eyes hard for a while before cynicism took over. "You surprise me, Mr. Jones. I had you pegged for another follower. But here I discover you are more than that."

"I am much more than that. I can make you a lot of money if you give me a chance."

"I thought that's what I did when I gave you the opportunity to find and hand over my weapons."

"Which I have done. I found your weapons. Now I expect to be paid for that service," Damon said.

After a moment, Santiago's expression changed

from dangerous to grinning evilly. "I like your style, Mr. Jones. I always have."

"Santiago," Orlando said in a warning tone.

Santiago lifted his palm to silence him. "No. I'll give you this deal. Ten percent." He turned to Carl. "Get everyone ready." Then he faced Damon. "The alley behind Kid's nightclub. Midnight tonight."

That would be difficult to orchestrate with his team. "I'll be there."

RUBY WAS EXTREMELY WORRIED. Damon dropped her off at January and Sean's, kissed her quickly and said he'd call when it was over. Now her imagination ran wild. She had no illusion as to the kind of men he was up against. Kid had been ruthless in his doling out punishments when his men didn't rise to his ridiculous expectations. Santiago was every bit the tyrant Kid had been.

Sitting on the back patio with January drinking iced tea, Ruby was glad Maya wanted to color. She was too distracted by her thoughts.

"He knows what he's doing, Ruby," January said.

Ruby looked at her, realizing her worry was transparent. "I know. It's just… I was with Kid long enough to know what they're capable of."

"Damon is a DEA agent. He's in law enforcement, like Sean. They are good at what they do. You just have to trust him."

"Huh. Trust." Now there was a word.

January laughed lightly. "It's always hard going into a new relationship. You never know which way it's going to go."

Ruby appreciated her candor. "Yes, and both Damon and I have been through rough past relationships. His role-playing while he was undercover didn't help. I admit I'm overly cautious and maybe a little paranoid, but I can't help it. It's just…ingrained in me based on experience." Horrible experience.

"You'll be fine. Once all the turmoil is over, it'll just be you and him."

That would be nice. Ruby wasn't sure it was that simple, though. "Maya has grown close to him."

"That's great! She needs an influence like Damon in her life. He's a hero, not a criminal. I think he'd make an awesome dad. I mean, I can't say I know him well yet, but he seems like an honorable man."

"He is," Ruby had to say. It was the truth. "Every time I meet someone new, I try to tell myself not to have any expectations, but I want to. I want to believe I can have a life with someone like Damon, but I'm so afraid to let go."

"Everyone is. Just give it time. It'll all work out in the end."

Ruby liked January's optimism, but she had already gone through the trials with Sean. They were a solid couple now. Ruby could not say that about her and Damon.

"I can tell you love him," January said.

Did she love Damon? Thinking about the man in that context, she got all warm and tingly inside.

"And I saw the way he looked at you at the party. He's a goner. He's fallen for you hard."

Ruby laughed, full of joy, unbidden and without

prior thought. Natural. She caught her breath. No. Damon had the power to break her heart like no other. And Maya's.

She turned her gaze away from January and found herself looking out at trees and flowers. It didn't soothe her. Damon might very well not survive what he was about to attempt. He had told her before he dropped her off that it would be best if she came with him to make the deal. She was an integral part of the investigation. But Ruby had thought only of Maya and resisted. Damon, being the man he was, hadn't pushed her.

"Ruby?" January said.

Ruby sprang up. "I have to go. Will you watch Maya?"

"What are you doing?" January stood.

Sean had gone out to get dinner, so he wouldn't get in her way. "I have to go to him."

"No, Ruby. It's too dangerous."

"January, please. I know Kid and his gang. They'll be suspicious if I'm not there. I *have* to go. Now."

January met her eyes, and Ruby saw her understanding. She related to what it was like to be with men who weren't afraid of confronting bad people. She had a protective nature like Ruby.

"Okay," she said. "Maya is safe here."

Ruby threw her arms around her and breathed a thank-you.

"Just come back alive, all right?"

"I will. Nothing will keep me from my daughter."

As she hurried from the house, Ruby wondered if this situation might be the one to keep her from her daughter—if she didn't survive the night.

But she could not stand by and do nothing. Damon was in law enforcement, but Ruby knew way more than him about the evil that surrounded Kid.

STANDING IN THE back of a conference room, Damon listened to his boss lay out the strategy of the raid. They'd already gone through the drill, but this was a refresher and also a pep talk, a strength-booster. They had the element of surprise. Santiago had no clue what was coming. The task force had the advantage, but they could not underestimate the enemy.

"One more time," Brian McNatt said. Special agent in charge of the Chicago Field Division of the US Drug Enforcement Administration, he had a commanding presence. "Somebody tell me the plan."

The DEA had partnered with federal, state and local law-enforcement agencies to bring down Kid Mercer's reign of terror.

"We loaded the weapons into a truck and are ready to meet Santiago at the nightclub," Damon said. "We'll have snipers in position and a team surrounding the alley, some inside buildings, some out of sight outside. There are more agents in vehicles who will sweep in once the exchange of money happens."

"And you're certain Santiago and his men aren't aware of your identity?" the agent asked.

"I'm certain." Thanks to Ruby for helping him with that. Kid's gang of thugs would not expect the DEA descending on them. Damon would relish every moment, even as dangerous as this move would be.

"What about Duarte? Why isn't she here?" Brian asked.

Damon ground his teeth, He needed her with him to make this go smoothly. He hadn't forced her, though. He had gotten her into this mess. He didn't want to put her through any more stress.

"She's somewhere safe," he said.

"You didn't tell her to be here?"

"No, sir."

Brian studied him a while. "I understand. You have to be extra careful without her. She was Kid's girlfriend, the mother of his child. She's the reason we found the weapons."

"I'm aware of that."

The room was silent as the gravity of the situation sank in.

"All right." Brian checked the time. "Let's get this done."

Before anyone could move, the sound of running feet and the door to the big conference room bursting open stopped everyone. Damon turned to look and saw Ruby, breathing fast in her rush to get there.

Damon's heart swelled with love. She had come to help him.

He stood as she walked hurriedly to him and threw her arms around him. Conscious of the crowd of burly agents surrounding them, he held her through the brief hug.

Then she leaned back. "I had to come here. You need me. You all do."

He grinned. Not caring who saw, he kissed her. Cat calls erupted along with clapping.

"My brave woman," he said when the kiss ended.

"Let's go crush Kid's gang."

Yeah, and then start a new life together. Damon didn't say that now, but he felt sure of the course ahead of him. He just had to convince her she had the same one. With him.

RUBY AND DAMON arrived at the meeting place. She saw Santiago with his entourage of armed men. Carl, Orlando and Sonny flanked him, each carrying mean-looking automatic weapons. Her heart raced. This could go so bad in such a short amount of time. She looked over at Damon.

He winked at her.

She smiled. He was totally in his element. A flood of trust and love suffused her. She had never felt anything like it before.

He would get them through this.

She got out of the car and walked with him toward Santiago.

"Where are my guns?" Santiago asked.

"Parked not far from here," Damon answered.

"You have someone else involved? Who is with them now?" he demanded.

"No one. Ruby is going to go get the truck and bring it here as soon as I know you have my money," he said, calm as could be.

He amazed her. She could tell he wasn't playing any role right now. He was Damon Colton, not Damon Jones. Santiago wouldn't know that, though. That was when Ruby realized Damon had not really been faking it the whole time. For the most part, his confident personality drove his character as a bartender looking to make some illegal cash.

"I need to see the guns before I give you the cash," Santiago said.

Orlando stepped forward, holding his weapon aimed at the ground—for now.

"Show me the cash, and then we'll bring the guns," Damon said, clearly not afraid. His entire demeanor was daunting. Ruby marveled over that. He was such a man.

She saw Santiago take note of that. Damon would not back down. If he wanted his guns, he'd do as Damon asked.

Santiago turned to Carl and gave a nod. Carl, the obedient dog he was, went to a black SUV with dark-tinted windows. At the back, he withdrew a duffel bag. Returning to the group, he dropped it on the ground, then unzipped the top, jerking the opening wide to reveal an impressive pile of money.

Damon stepped forward and crouched, examining the bundles, fanning a few of them to make sure they were not counterfeit. Appearing satisfied, he stood and looked at Ruby. This was her cue to go get the truck.

She went to the car and drove the two blocks to where the agents had left the truck full of weapons. She saw an agent sitting on a bus-stop bench. She only knew he was an agent because Damon had told her he'd be there. His presence gave her some reassurance.

There were more agents surrounding the drop site, but she didn't see them. They were experts at covert operations. She began to feel empowered, part of something big and dangerous, with the law on her side.

Driving slowly, she turned into the alley behind the club. The group of men waited and watched her approach. Damon and his commander told her to wait in the truck.

Damon led Santiago and his men to the back of the truck, where he opened the door to show them the contents. Carl carried the bag of money.

Ruby could see a little of what transpired back there in the outside rearview mirror. She could hear Santiago's pleased voice.

"Good work, Damon. I think you'll fit right in," he said.

Damon moved to shake Santiago's hand, and she could now see his back. Carl handed him the bag of money. As soon as that happened, chaos erupted.

DEA agents poured out of buildings and into the open from every angle, guns aimed. They came from the back door of the nightclub, from around corners of buildings and into the alley. Ruby saw a sniper on the roof of a four-story building behind the club.

In the outside mirror of the truck, Ruby watched Santiago and his men glance around in shock. Then Santiago turned to Damon. "You son of a bitch."

To her horror, he took out a gun and fired. Damon flew backward and landed on the ground.

A sniper's shot hit Santiago in the head. His body collapsed to the ground.

Santiago's men began firing at agents.

Gunshots rang out. Worried sick about Damon,

Ruby ducked down in the truck as the volley of shots continued for endless seconds.

Then the shots quieted, and all Ruby heard were agents yelling for Santiago's men to drop their weapons. She sat up and looked around. Agents passed the truck and ordered Santiago's men on the ground with their hands up.

As soon as she knew it was safe, Ruby got out of the truck and ran to Damon, kneeling by his side. He grimaced in pain and held his shoulder.

"Let me see."

He moved his hand, full of blood. More blood drained from the wound.

"Oh." Urgency overtook Ruby. The shot was too high to have damaged any organs, but he was bleeding badly.

She ripped his shirt to expose the wound and checked for an exit. There was one. There was no bullet left in his body.

A man with a DEA Agent jacket on knelt beside her. "I'm a paramedic."

Ruby gave him room but stayed near Damon. He dug into his backpack and produced a bandage.

Ruby took it from him and applied pressure while the paramedic secured it with tape, tightly to stop the bleeding.

"You a nurse?" the paramedic asked.

"I will be, as soon as I finish school," she said.

"She's a nurse," Damon said. "And I'm her first patient." Damon grinned and all but stopped Ruby's heart. How could he smile at a time like this? A moment later, she had her answer. This was Damon Colton. DEA agent. Brave. Handsome. But most of all, a hero.

Ruby looked down at Damon, meeting his eyes, secure with the sense that he was going to be all right.

"You're so beautiful," he said.

"You're just saying that because you've lost too much blood."

He chuckled, then winced.

Ruby kept pressure on his wound. "Sorry. A nurse shouldn't joke at a time like this."

"I'll get an ambulance," the paramedic said. He stood and rushed off.

Looking from his departure to Damon again, she touched his cheek, and they shared warmth in the intangible feelings they had for each other. Ruby appreciated his ability to rise above the pain he must be in.

Hearing someone approach, she assumed it was the paramedic, but instead it was a six-foot man with close-cropped medium-brown hair and beard. His green eyes with a grayish tint were serious. Ruby recognized him through her association with Sean. He was Harry Cartwright, a detective with the Chicago PD.

"Is he all right?"

"He's going to be," Ruby said. "The shot went through his shoulder."

The ambulance arrived, and Ruby stood.

Damon winced in pain as he was moved onto a gurney.

Ruby put her hand on his chest. "I'll follow you to the hospital." Leaning over, she kissed him briefly.

His expression smoothed, a fleeting alleviation of pain that put a grin on his mouth.

Always a gentleman, maybe a ladies' man. He had a pure soul. She squeezed his hand before he was rolled away, seeing him meet her gaze until she couldn't see him anymore. "Seems I have some catching up to do," Harry said.

Ruby turned to him, wondering at first what he meant and then catching on. He could tell she and Damon had more going on than the Mercer investigation. With a beard that only just covered his skin around his mouth and chin, his eyes held the somber resolve of a devoted detective. She saw the same in Damon. She checked his ring finger and found it bare of jewelry. She found it odd—or maybe unfortunate—that he hadn't found a woman to share his life with. But then…neither had she. People had reasons for not diving into relationships.

"You know Damon?" she asked.

He nodded. "I work in Narcotics. Yes, I know him, and I was part of this task force."

"Working in the background?" Not having to lie…

"Yes. I suppose you can say that. Damon had to be undercover, as I'm sure you can understand."

She did. Damon could not reveal his identity. Doing so would have put his life at risk. Even Ruby had to admit he had done what he had to do with her. They hadn't known each other. He couldn't trust her as a stranger. As hurt as she was by his betrayal, she did understand. But she still had to get past the hurt. Emotions didn't come with conditions. They were felt, and humans had to come to terms with them. In some way.

Harry eyed her speculatively. "Or maybe you don't."

Ruby bowed her head, self-conscious at her transparency. Then she met Harry's eyes. "I met Damon as a bartender. I didn't know he was a DEA agent."

Harry took some time before he replied. He seemed to assess her and her connection to Damon.

"I've been on the periphery of this investigation. Working behind the scenes, as it were. But from what little I've seen of the two of you, I'd have to say Damon's cover ID doesn't matter all that much."

His insight both speared her with fright for the state of her heart and hope for a fairy-tale future. "You seem like a nice man, Mr. Cartwright."

"Harry."

"Harry. Thank you for telling me what you did." She meant it. He had eased her mind over what had tormented her and continued to do so. She wasn't sure if she could overcome all she'd been through because of Damon and his investigation. Granted, he had saved her from the aftermath of Kid, but he wasn't the man she'd met that first time he bought coffee.

"Damon is a very lucky man," Harry said.

Lucky? How?

"You got away from a very dangerous man," Harry said, as though reading her thoughts. Maybe he had. Maybe he had picked up on something in her eyes.

"You got your daughter back, and you helped us take down the rest of Kid's organization," Harry said.

He made her feel important, as though she had played a key role in the investigation. Maybe she had.

Yes, she had. Without her, Santiago and his men would not have been stopped. She would have been haunted the rest of her life.

"I..." She didn't know what to say. *Thank you* seemed inadequate.

No problem...

"Hey, just living my life and trying to protect my daughter..."

Looking for love...

Harry chuckled. "I can see why Damon is so captivated by you."

"Oh... I..." He was making her so uncomfortable.

Harry chuckled again. "Sorry. I just want to thank you. A lot of people worked very hard bringing Kid's organization down, and it couldn't have been done without you."

"Oh..." She knew that to be true, but she didn't know how to respond. She didn't feel instrumental. She felt like more of a victim.

"I... I need to get to the hospital."

"I have a car for you. Come with me."

As she followed Harry, she contemplated his insight, whether he had planned to provide it or not. He'd told the truth, that's all, and she struggled with what that meant for her and Maya's future. Kid was permanently gone from their lives. None of his followers would pose a threat to her and Maya anymore. To be released from that felt...surreal. She had lived in fear for so many years, to finally be free of that—of Kid—

felt so abrupt. But she was free. Maybe she just needed some time to adjust.

Damon.

Now that his investigation was over, what would he do? With the absence of excitement, would he still want her? How would their relationship change?

Ruby dreamed of having a family: mom, dad and daughter. A playset in the backyard. A barbecue. A home full of homeyness. Was that possible with a federal agent?

She didn't want any excitement beyond school activities and community participation. Neighborhood friends. Would Damon be happy with that?

Damon was more like Ruby and reluctant to form casual relationships. More and more she had to face the fact that they might be meant for each other. She was still too afraid to let go, at least not completely. She'd been burned before. She would not be burned again.

Chapter Sixteen

Ruby paced the waiting area at the hospital. She bit her thumbnail. She folded her arms. Damon's team was busy processing the arrests of Kid's men and the death of Santiago. She was alone. She had decided not to call January yet. She didn't want to alarm Maya.

Finally, a doctor approached.

"Ruby Duarte?"

"Yes." Her heart raced with apprehension. Nothing mattered more than Damon right now.

"Damon is going to be all right."

Ruby took a few deep breaths, closing her eyes.

"We did surgery on the wound, and he should have a full recovery," the doctor said.

She tipped her head back. "Oh. That's wonderful to hear."

The doctor smiled, flashing not teeth but fondness. "He's demanding to see you. He's been quite the uncooperative patient ever since he woke from anesthesia."

She breathed a laugh. "That sounds like Damon." Damon needed to be in control, fighting for justice.

"Come with me." The doctor wore a slight grin as

he led her to the elevators. They rode up a few seconds before the doctor said, "Congratulations, by the way."

She looked at him. "Pardon me?"

"Damon said you two are getting married."

Married? Why had he said that to the doctor?

"What kind of drugs did you give him?" she asked.

The doctor chuckled. "The kind to make some people honest. Although, his confession did seem genuine, like he'd say it without being in pain and on meds."

Ruby was speechless. Damon had professed marriage to strangers. Had he lost his mind? No. Drugs. That had to be it. Or was it…?

"I don't normally reveal things like that to those who aren't my patients, but he told me about you and how he feared you'd never trust him."

When she turned shocked eyes to him, he said, "That's all I can say. He told me a lot more, but I risk my medical license telling you what I have already. I did so because I believe it's worth it."

Numbly, Ruby nodded. "I understand, and…thank you." The doctor had clearly seen something special in Damon and his feelings for Ruby. Why else would he go out of his way to make her understand?

He extended his arm.

Ruby realized they were at the door of Damon's room.

She entered and heard the doctor close the door, no doubt for privacy. She admired his discretion as much as his compassionate and interactive insight. He must have seen something in Damon that made him subtly intervene.

She stepped slowly toward Damon's hospital bed. He was slightly inclined, and his arm was in a sling.

Hearing her, he turned his head.

Ruby stopped. Even sleepy and wounded he was still so gorgeous and strong.

"The nurse taking care of me is completely inferior to you," he said.

She laughed, so glad he was all right. She went to the side of the bed, sitting on the edge and putting her hand on the side of his face.

"Did you meet Doc?" he asked.

"Yes."

"I think he is on my side."

"I think you have painkillers running through your veins. You told him too much."

She moved her hand to his chest, patting him a few gentle times.

"I told him the truth."

"Drugs cloud minds. Stop."

He put his hand over hers on his chest, the one that didn't have an IV in it. "Not when it comes to love, Ruby."

"You confided in a stranger," she said. But inside, her soul rejoiced. Dare she believe?

Damon sighed, tiredly. "I did."

His confession only dug deeper into her heart. He would be a permanent resident there if she wasn't careful. "I should let you get some sleep. I just wanted to make sure you were going to be okay."

"Are you trying to run away again, Ruby? Because if you are, you don't have to," he said.

Okay, he was being way too candid. "I should go." She started to get up, but he grasped her hand.

"Don't go," he said. "Stay with me."

"In the hospital?"

"No, forever."

"Damon..." She felt so flustered. Did he mean this? "Why?"

"Because you love me, too."

Unable to refute that, Ruby said nothing. And she was rescued when more visitors arrived.

January and Sean brought flowers and hugs. Damon's brothers visited for a bit. His cousins came as well.

Ruby was about to tell them all to go away and let him sleep, but Damon's spirits were so high she refrained. He loved family so much. It touched her heart in a way she had never experienced before.

A few minutes later, Damon's family began saying goodbye and filing out of the room. Next, in walked Damon's commander, Brian McNatt, a big man with dark brown hair and eyes that had seen too much. Damon had a busy room.

"Damon." Brian walked over to the bed. "How are you feeling?"

"They've got me comfortable. Keeping me overnight for observation."

"Good. You got lucky. It could have gone another way," he said.

Ruby was all too aware of that. If Santiago's aim had been better, she might be dealing with never seeing Damon again. The thought of losing him filled her with an awful feeling.

"Did you get all of Santiago's men?" Damon asked.

Not all of them had been present at the raid.

"We're rounding them up." Brian looked at Ruby. "If you need a safe place to stay, I can arrange that for you."

"She's going to stay with me," Damon said, then looked at her. "At my real home."

The way he said that warmed her through and through. What he hadn't said but she knew he meant for her to understand was he wanted her to know more about him, Damon Colton.

"All right," Brian said. "My main reason for coming here today is to commend you on a job well done. We couldn't have taken down Mercer's gang without you." He looked at Ruby. "You, too. The DEA thanks you both."

You're welcome didn't seem appropriate to Ruby, so she said nothing.

"Just doing my job," Damon said.

"I'll leave you two. Get some rest." Brian left.

Unfortunately, Damon would not be able to get rest. His next visitor was Harry.

"They said you were in Recovery," Harry said. He walked to the bed and took Damon's hand in a manly grasp. "How are you?"

"I'm fine."

"Hey, you did great back there. I wanted to personally tell you that, friend."

"Thanks. It's good to see you. Are you still with Narcotics?"

"Yeah."

"Maybe we could work together on a case sometime," Damon said.

"I'd be honored, but that won't happen. I've been promoted to head of Homicide."

"Really? That's great. Congratulations, man," Damon said.

Ruby listened to them talk about work. After about twenty minutes, Harry bade farewell and left.

"I heard he dated Carly Colton and he's a bit of a womanizer," Ruby said.

"He lost his wife and child to a murderer," Damon said. "He's got some issues from it."

That was terrible, but still, any woman who fell for him might lose her heart. Maybe that was Ruby talking from her own experiences, though.

"Better watch Lila. The last thing another Colton woman needs is to fall for him too much."

Damon chuckled. "Ruby, come here."

She did, and he took her hand and drew her closer. She leaned over as he put his hand behind her head and kissed her, long and slow. When he finally released her she was breathless and hot.

"You're lucky you're in this hospital bed," she said.

"More like unlucky," he said.

BY EVENING THE next day, Ruby drove Damon to his house. He gave her directions on the way. In a modern neighborhood, he had an average house that was clean and well maintained. Inside the entry, he saw her look around. The six-by-six-foot tiled entry branched off to the living room on the left, family room on the right, and an L-shaped stairway led to the upper level. He wasn't much of a decorator, so furniture and the modern architecture did the work for him.

She wandered through all the rooms on the first level, then went upstairs. He had three bedrooms up there. Plenty for the three of them. He tried not to hope too much.

Moments later she reappeared.

"The basement is partially finished," he said. "I want to make another master bedroom and a family room down there."

"It's nice, Damon."

She seemed guarded again, as she always was when something struck her as genuine—when it came to him. Hope grew too strong, and she resisted.

"We should get you settled in." She put down her overnight bag.

"I can sit on the couch." His shoulder hurt, but he wasn't an invalid. "Let's order delivery."

"I can make dinner," she said.

"We've been through enough, don't you think? Let's relax tonight."

She smiled slightly. "Pizza and wings?"

"Loaded?" he asked. "A Supreme with everything on it?"

"Yes. Screw the calorie counting worries tonight. I'm starving."

"No anchovies, though."

"Yuck. No. Meat and lots of peppers, onions and mushrooms."

"Extra cheese and tomatoes."

Ruby took out her cell phone. "A man after my heart."

They liked the same kind of pizza. What more of a sign did they need to be convinced they belonged together?

Damon wasn't under any illusions, however. Ruby wasn't ready to give herself to him completely. He fully expected her to tell him they should take things slow. He had known that about her shortly after meeting her. Wasn't that one of the reasons why he had taken so long to take her out on a date?

He had to respect her for that. After his bout with a deceitful woman, he could take all the time necessary to secure a healthy relationship with Ruby. But that didn't mean he wouldn't try to convince her to live with him.

She ordered their meal and then looked around as though uncertain what to do next.

"There's some chilled wine in the refrigerator," he said.

"Do you want a glass?"

"My pain medication is enough. You should have one, though," he said.

"Is it that obvious that I don't know what to do with myself?" she asked with a smile.

"Yes, Ruby. I've told you before that you're transparent. Get some wine, and come here and sit with me."

She looked at him a moment as though contemplating what sitting close to him would lead to. Sipping some wine.

He chuckled. "There's no way I'll be able to make love. You're safe."

She laughed lightly. "You seem to know me so well."

"I do."

Seeming a little bashful or uncertain, she went to rummage up a wineglass. While she proceeded to uncork the wine and pour herself a moderate helping, he found an old family movie, something calming. Then she came over to the couch and sat beside him on his uninjured side.

Hiding a grimace, he put his arm across the back of the couch, and she snuggled in, curling up her legs.

He remained with her like that a while, not really paying attention to the television. He suspected she wasn't, either. This was the first time they were both truly free of Kid Mercer's bad influence. He wanted to begin getting Ruby thinking about their future.

"Now that our lives are back to normal, we can start fresh," he said, waiting to see how she'd react.

"Normal," she murmured and took another sip. "I can't remember what that is anymore."

Disenchantment had a way of doing that to a person. The bliss of innocence faded with life experiences. He used to have that attitude.

"I couldn't, either, before I met you," he said. "Meeting you has given me a whole new outlook."

She tipped her head to look at him.

He could see she was trying to gauge whether to believe him or not. "Don't worry." He rubbed her arm.

"I know you need some time. But I would like you to stay here with me. You and Maya."

She rested her head on his shoulder. "I'm not sure about that, Damon."

"I know. All I'm asking is you give me a chance to earn your trust. The investigation is over. You have me to yourself now."

"Until your next investigation?" she said.

"You won't be involved in that. You'll be safe."

After a while she sighed. "My lease is up at my house at the end of this month."

Damon felt that was a stroke of luck for him. "Then, it's decided. You, Maya and your mother—if she wants to—can come and live here."

Ruby moved to sit up, putting her glass on the coffee table. Then she angled herself to face him, clasping her hands on her lap.

He knew what she was going to say before she spoke.

"I'm not quite ready for that. With all that's happened, being reunited with Maya so recently, and surviving the aftermath of Kid. And…you… I…"

Damon reached to put his hand over hers. "It's all right, Ruby. I have a suggestion."

She met his eyes, listening and interested.

"Nicole came to see me when you went down to the cafeteria before I was released. She asked about us, and I told her everything. She offered for you to come and stay with her. You, Maya and your mother. She has plenty of room, and she'd love the company.

Apparently you made quite an impression on her." His mother had told him if Ruby needed space after all she'd been through that she should stay with her. She wanted to help Damon keep her in his life.

A soft smile emerged on Ruby's beautiful face. She was more than physically beautiful. She had an inner glow, a purity about her. More than ever Damon wanted her in his life.

"And we can date?" she asked.

"You'll see me every day, sweetheart. We just won't be sleeping together. The DEA is going to give me a lot of time off."

He sensed her weighing her options. His no-pressure approach appeared to be working. He grew encouraged.

"Nicole said she would help watch Maya while you went to school. She's excited about having a child in her life. She's a really great mother figure."

Again, he sensed Ruby contemplating all he said.

"You won't have to work anymore until you graduate," he said.

She turned to look at him again.

"Just say yes, Ruby," he said.

With a big smile, she said, "Yes."

The ring of his cell phone interrupted. He winced as he moved to get it from his back pocket. Seeing it was Erik, he wasn't surprised the man had ruined a good moment with Ruby.

"Dad?"

"Hello, son. I heard what happened and wanted to call and see how you were doing."

Erik never showed signs of concern toward him. This was highly unusual.

"I'm recovering fine."

"Good. Good." He cleared his throat. "I also wanted to apologize for barging in on you at the barbecue."

Erik Colton…*apologizing?*

"That was a little dramatic. Are you sure you want to pursue that lawsuit?" Damon asked, wondering if the question would incite Erik's notorious temper.

Erik sighed. "It wasn't my decision to dispute the will."

"No, it was Grandmother's. That doesn't mean you and Axel have to support it," Damon said.

"It's too late to back down now. Can you just go along with it?"

So, that was the real reason Erik had called. Maybe he had genuinely wanted to make sure his son was all right, but he'd used the opportunity to his advantage.

"Why can't you stand up to her? You and Axel both."

"It's not about standing up to her, son. She does have a valid point that my brother and I deserve to at least be recognized as part of Dad's family."

"You'll destroy our cousins' lives if you win the lawsuit," Damon said.

Erik didn't respond. "I don't want to destroy anyone's life, Damon, but Mother has a right to claim what belongs to us. And like I said, Axel and I can't back off now."

Then, there was nothing else he had to say to his father. "I get it. Thanks for calling."

"I wish you could understand," Erik said.

"I do." More than he could possibly comprehend, having been molded from childhood by Carin.

"I'll check in on you in a few days," Erik said.

And Damon gladly ended the call.

Chapter Seventeen

Ruby stayed with Damon until Brian told them all of Kid's criminal associates were now in jail awaiting trial. Damon made it easy for her to agree to live with Nicole for a while. She had spoken with her mother, who had decided to live with Ruby's sister. She missed Wisconsin and promised to come visit often. Ruby had been saddened by the news. She had grown accustomed to having her mother around all the time, but she understood. There were things she missed about Wisconsin, too.

Come to think of it, her mother had likely come to stay with her because of all she'd been through. In their last conversation, she told Ruby how happy she was for her, meaning that she had found Damon. Her mother felt all right about leaving her, returning to her hometown.

She turned from the lovely view of manicured landscaping to find Nicole approaching.

"Maya loves her room," Nicole said.

Nicole had told her she had redecorated one of the

bedrooms, one right next to where Ruby would stay. And one of her help had taken Maya there.

"You shouldn't have done that. You're spoiling her."

"Not that much." Nicole took her hand. "You haven't seen it yet. Come with me."

Ruby began to feel that familiar defense swell. "I'll tuck my own daughter into bed." She had spent too many years without hugs and *I love you*s. People needed affection. Kids needed that even more. In dysfunctional environments, kids didn't get enough hugs and *I love you*s. Ruby would not tolerate anyone out of line with that.

"Oh." Nicole stopped. "Ruby, I meant no harm. Just come and see."

Ruby went with her, feeling a strange sense of trust, despite the fact that she didn't really know the woman Damon called Mom.

At the door of Maya's room, Nicole stepped aside so Ruby could see inside.

Soft lights and color took Ruby's breath away. Stars rotated on the ceiling. Flowing, silky drapes covered tall windows, and there was a canopy bed befitting Cinderella.

But what truly captured her was Maya in front of a lighted dollhouse. A huge one. She was immersed in a fairy-tale, dreamlike state.

"Ni—"

"Nope," Nicole cut her off in a soft tone. "Let her."

Let her...

Ruby's entire being shifted and tingled with newfound love.

"You deserve this," Nicole said. "You deserve it like Damon and Nash deserved a real home."

Her words hit her on impact. Ruby turned before Maya could see her and went into her room, sitting on the bed and breaking down into a torrent of tears. It was as though all the trauma she'd endured flowed out of her now that the threat had vanished. An emotional release. Like a war veteran, only they were so fortunate to find their way to any kind of release.

Ruby felt like a war veteran.

Surrounded by people who offered love and support, she breached a wall that had protected her for years. It fell. It crumbled. What was left was new hope for a happy future. With Damon. With his brothers and Nicole and aunts and cousins. Everyone. With her family.

Family.

Nicole sat beside her, careful not to infringe on her space.

Ruby cried harder and turned to bury herself against Nicole, soaking up the comfort freely offered.

Maya tugged hard on her shirt.

The urgency brought Ruby's immediate attention. Nicole moved away.

Ruby crouched to her daughter and took her into her arms. Leaning back she signed, *Mommy's fine, baby. We're with family now.*

Maya smiled and relaxed, signing, *Where is my new dad?*

He's not your new dad yet, Maya.

Yes, he is.

Do you know what weddings are?

Maya's perplexed look gave her the answer.

You've seen them in your cartoons. It's when a man and a woman, meaning me and Damon, get married. We dress up nice and pledge our love for each other. That's a wedding.

Maya's adorably innocent, young eyes met hers as she digested that.

If that happens with me and Damon, then he will be your new dad, Ruby signed.

After continuing to think over what Ruby said, Maya signed, *Then, you have to have a wedding with him.*

Ruby smiled, bursting with love, and pecked a kiss on the tip of her tiny, soft nose.

"That's a lovely thought, Maya." She signed as well.

For the first time since before she'd met Kid, Ruby felt safe pondering a future with a man.

DAMON PLANNED A few dates with Ruby and some time at home with Maya. Today it was Picnic Day. He took them to a park with a playground. He'd been taking it slow with her for over a week now.

Maya occupied herself on the slide while Ruby and Damon set up a picnic table with their lunch.

"I could get used to this," Damon said. "Outings with my family."

With his smile, she lowered her gaze and finished fixing Maya a peanut butter and jelly sandwich. She added some cheddar flavored chips to a plate and then waved to her daughter, catching her attention.

Maya came to the table and sat before her plate, digging in.

Ruby made Damon and herself turkey sandwiches and dished out potato salad and coleslaw. He popped open three sodas, giving one to Maya.

Handing him a plate, Ruby began eating, looking at Maya and then out across the park.

"Do you trust me yet?" Damon kept asking her that, mostly teasing, but today he was serious.

She turned to him. "A little bit more every day."

Her soft tone told him she had given him an honest answer. "I can't ask for more than that. But it's time I told you something."

He put his hand over hers on the table. He wanted her to pay close attention.

She waited, but he saw that she had stiffened almost imperceptibly. She expected him to reveal something else he hadn't told her.

"I'm not going anywhere, Ruby," he said.

She angled her head slightly in misunderstanding.

"I'm going to keep coming around as often as possible—with your permission, of course. And I don't care how long it takes for you to be completely and totally comfortable with me and trust me when I say I love you."

Her mouth dropped open a bit, and her eyes became acutely alert.

"Yes. I love you, Ruby. I'm certain of it. No matter what happens, no matter what you ultimately decide, I won't have any regrets. I love you like no other woman, so if you won't have me, I'll let you go with the hopes that you will find happiness with someone else. No regrets."

Now she appeared stunned into silence.

"You can take as long as you need to feel safe with me. For your heart to feel safe in my hands and my love. I'll wait as long as it takes. The important thing for you to know is I'm not going anywhere. I won't give up on you. Not ever. Until you tell me you want me to go and I believe you."

It was the most heartfelt confession he had ever made to anyone. He was risking everything with her right now. But she was worth it. She was a hundred times the woman his fiancée had been.

After several moments, tears brimmed in Ruby's eyes. "You have no idea what that means to me."

"No, I don't, and I'd like for you to tell me."

She put her other hand over his. "Damon, my heart screams out that you are trustworthy despite all the deception." She lowered her head as she gathered her thoughts and chose words. "But in my mind… I…have trouble. All that I've been through."

"I know, Ruby. That's why you have all the time you need. I want you. I want to marry you and be a father to Maya. I want us to be a family. For real."

A tear slipped down her cheek. "Damon, I want that, too."

Joy swelled within him. They were going to be all right. She was going to be his wife…someday.

He caught Maya staring at them. She had likely read most of what they said.

She looked at him and signed, *My new daddy.*

* * * * *